WE HOLD

THESE

TRUTHS

D0071651

WE HOLD THESE TRUTHS

DAVID S. MITCHELL

PROJECT Z BOOKS
A DIVISION OF PROJECT Z LLC
DISTRICT OF COLUMBIA

PROJECT Z BOOKS and colophon are trademarks of Project Z LLC.

ISBN 978-0-692-72013-4
ebook ISBN 978-0-692-72017-2

Set in Minion Pro

10 9 8 7 6 5 4 3 2

First Edition

For Grandpa, who abhorred a task unfinished,
the District of Columbia, my first love,
and the great state of North Carolina,
where the sky is darkest just before the light

Change will not come if we wait for some other person or if we wait for some other time. We are the ones we've been waiting for. We are the change that we seek. We are the hope of those boys who have so little, who've been told that they cannot have what they dream, that they cannot be what they imagine. Yes, they can.

—Barack Obama, February 5, 2008

Was so elated,
We celebrated like Obama waited until his last day in office to tell the
  nation brothers is getting their reparations, hey—
A man can dream, can't he?
No disrespect in terms of change, I haven't seen any.

—J. Cole,
Late Night with David Letterman, December 10, 2014

WE HOLD THESE TRUTHS

CHAPTER ONE

THE PLAN for our last Friday night in law school had been set in stone for at least a month by the time we reached the weekend before graduation Monday: Middlesex nightclub for the bimonthly YoYo 90s hip-hop party. The whole gang had agreed to meet there at ten o'clock. Just a few minutes after showering and dressing—at around nine o'clock—there were knocks at the door.

"Come in!" I yelled over the music.

"What up, what up?" Darden said.

"What's good, D?" I said. "Thought I was meeting you at the club later."

"Change in plans," Darden said, walking past me and into the kitchen. "I'm ready to get the night going. Mind if I join you for a drink or two?"

"Of course not."

He pulled two highball glasses from the cabinet. "Since this is our last night out, it just feels right doing the preparty where we always did it—right here. Now we just need Simmons. Have you heard from him? He needs to be here."

"Nope," I said. "Everyone's scrambling with family coming into town. I'd be shocked if anyone made it to Middlesex by ten."

Darden poured the first round of the night—a vodka soda for him and bourbon on the rocks for me—as Aaliyah's "Back and Forth" filled the air with hazy memories of summers long gone.

After raising our glasses skyward, we each took a sip. "I can't believe how fast these three years went by," Darden said. "We arrived in our midtwenties . . . now we're damn near thirty."

I chuckled. "Crazy, right?" My phone buzzed loudly on the kitchen countertop.

"Uncle Tom!" I answered. "What's good?"

"New School!" he said. "Look . . . I just checked in at the hotel across the street from your building. Your mother got a block of rooms for the family."

"You wanna swing by for a taste?"

"My man!" he said. "I'll be over in a minute."

"Do you have the address?" I said to the dial tone. It was unquestionably the shortest phone call I'd ever had with Uncle Tom. You could read the entire Old Testament in the time it usually took to coax him off the line.

"Is he coming through?" Darden said, settling into the couch.

I took a seat at my desk. "Looks like it."

He grinned. "Uncle Tom is out of control."

"When did you meet him? Was it summer of '07?"

"Summer of 2008. He was living in Brooklyn at the time. Best summer on record."

"Basically," I said. "Everybody was in New York that summer."

"Except Bristol, right?" he said. "Wasn't she working at some nonprofit in DC?"

"That's right. Good thing she wasn't there."

Darden furrowed his brow. "Why's that?" he asked.

"I was a mess."

He shook his head. "*Was* a mess? Brotha, your past is your present. But you're right. You never would've heard the end of it from Bristol."

"I'm not that bad now . . . am I?"

His eyes twinkled. "Do you remember Memorial Day weekend?"

"What am I, hard of remembering?" I said. "Of course I remember that weekend! That was the weekend of that crazy party in Manhattan. Bliss, right?"

He chuckled. "Man, stop pretending you don't remember the name of that party. Every able-bodied black Ivy League student or recent grad in the tristate was in the building for that one."

"My man!" Uncle Tom said. His six-foot-six frame was a shade thinner than when I'd seen him over Christmas. We shook hands and hugged.

"I didn't even know you were coming to graduation," I said. "Was the door unlocked?"

"You never know when I'm gonna make an appearance nephew . . . that's how I move."

I slapped his abdomen twice. "Looks like you've been *moving* a lot since Christmas. You been jogging?"

Uncle Tom smiled broadly before retreating to the kitchen. "Gotta keep it tight, my fair-complexioned nephew."

"You've met Darden," I said.

"What's up, Unc?" Darden said.

"Good to see you again, son," Uncle Tom said, glancing up briefly while pouring a cognac. "Put some Old School on, Al," he said. Uncle Tom returned to the living room and took a sip while easing himself down onto the end of the couch. "So . . . what do you think about Obama's election?"

Darden turned toward him from the other end of the couch. "One for our team."

"And you know how I feel about it," I said, returning to my desk chair. "Skeptical, but hopeful."

"Where's your boy from New York? Givens, right?"

"Simmons," I said.

"Simmons!" he exclaimed. "You know I'm terrible with names."

"You and the rest of the family," I added.

"Simmons is usually pretty . . . ah . . . levelheaded about politics," Uncle Tom said, "even though he's a damned Republican."

"He's meeting us out later," I said.

Darden turned back toward Uncle Tom. "What are *your* thoughts on the election?"

"It's bullshit," Uncle Tom said without an ounce of emotion.

Darden spit out most of the sip he'd just taken. "Excuse me?" he said.

"I believe he said, 'It's bullshit,'" I said.

"What about Obama's election is BS?" Darden said, now sitting erect on the edge of the couch.

"I have the benefit of having lived twice as long as you boys, so I know a raw deal when I see one. See, I lived through that stuff you boys read about in your history books."

"What, specifically, are you saying is bull?" Darden asked.

"I thought I told you to put on some of that Old School, Al," Uncle Tom said. "Put Marvin on." I pulled up my Marvin Gaye playlist and clicked on the first song of Uncle Tom's favorite album, *What's Going On*. I was immediately transported to the backseat of Uncle Tom's black 7 Series almost twenty years earlier. He'd played this album over and over again while Billy and I absorbed the sounds and words. At the time we were blissfully ignorant of their meaning though we sang each word without error.

"That's my *jam* right there, boy!" Uncle Tom exclaimed. "You *know* that."

"Great album," Darden said.

"Ahhhhh come on, Darden!" Uncle Tom said. "You don't know nothin' about this music. See, if you did, you'd understand why Obama's election isn't worth a damn." I couldn't help but laugh. Although I hadn't seen this particular Uncle Tom movie before, I knew the genre.

"Let me break it down for you, Darden, and you too, Al," he said after joining Marvin in that line about judgment and long hair. "You see, I'm not a scholar like you guys," he started, gradually leaning forward as he always did when preparing to hold court. "I didn't go to Harvard or Yale. But I've lived, see. They don't teach you the stuff I've lived through. Oh . . . they claim to, but they don't."

"Go on," I said.

"You see, they've got you so-called elite black men all dressed up—shiny patent leather shoes, crisp white shirt, designer tuck—only problem is, you're not *really* invited to the banquet. Sure . . . they sent you the invitation, and you RSVP'd and everything, but it's kinda hard to walk around with a two-ton piece of steel tied to your foot."

"The hell is a *tuck*?" Darden said.

I grinned. "Tuxedo," I said. "Settle in, my friend."

"See, you guys bet on the market, but I bet on experience. You guys are about to become doctors of the law. But I've got a PhD you can't get from any university."

"And what, precisely, is this *experience* you're betting on, doc?" I said.

"Here's the reality," he continued. "Obama's election won't change a damn thing, and that's because he wasn't elected to change a damn thing. White folks voted for Obama to show the world that we've moved past all the shit white folks did to black folks. And why would white folks want that? I'll tell you why: Who wants to walk around feeling guilty all the damned time?"

"Okay," Darden said. "But you'd agree that black folks had to vote for Obama in record numbers for him to get elected."

"That's right, *counselor*," Uncle Tom said, taking another sip. "And we'll get there . . . we'll talk about our people too. But first you need to understand the framework. See, there's levels to this, son . . . levels."

"Frame it, Unc!" I said.

"See, these so-called progressives that got Obama elected . . . and I'm talking about blacks and whites here . . . most of them really only care about the *demonstration* of progress. Follow me on this. See, I'm about to drop straight science on you Crimson kids."

"Oh, I'm listening," Darden said, leaning in.

"If you understand that fact . . . if you understand that most folks aren't serious about progress, you'll begin to understand why it's rational for so many of your black brothas in these streets to reject traditional paths to success. See, no one really wants to give them a chance. And then there's you guys. They're using you. It all looks good on paper, but what happens when the excess jobs go away . . . the ones they don't mind givin' you when the market is booming? Well, the music stopped in August, didn't it? With all your promise and all your debt, do you really think you guys are better off than the dope boy on the street? Maybe your jobs will still be around when you graduate, but what about next year? Or the year after that? This is the stuff you boys need to be thinkin' about."

Darden turned toward me, wide-eyed. "He's serious, isn't he?"

"Quite," I replied.

"They're just out here demonstratin'," Uncle Tom said. "That's all. There's nothing real behind it. No substance."

"Preach!" I said.

"The drug game may be more risky than the path you've taken," Uncle Tom continued, "but the path you've taken deprives you of the economic freedom to do the things you really want to do. Once you take on all this debt to get the Ivy League stamp of approval, you're just as much a slave to the system as the dope boys are to the drug game. You can't get out just as surely as they can't get out."

"Wait, wait," I said. "You're going down another road now. Let's hear more about this demonstration project point you raised a minute ago."

"I said 'demonstration of progress'—but I like that more," he said. "'Demonstration project'—you don't mind if I use that, do you?"

"Not at all," I said. "You inspired it. The least I can do is let you use it—with attribution, of course." Darden chuckled.

"So we have this demonstration project being perpetrated by so-called progressives," Uncle Tom resumed. "What I've learned in my years on this earth is that a major part of the strategy of oppression, and its maintenance, is the creation of exceptions that contradict the ah . . . status quo. See, I have to use terms your brilliant minds can comprehend."

"For the love of God," I said. At that, a devious smile crept across Uncle Tom's face. I knew it well.

"See, in order for the oppressed to accept their oppressed state, the oppressors must concoct examples—follow me, now—where a lucky few periodically rise above their circumstances, thereby creating the false hope among the remaining oppressed that the same is possible for them."

"I agree with that narrow point," Darden said. "But I'm still not sure how this relates to Obama's election. Are you saying that Obama's election was part of some ongoing conspiracy by the oppressing class—and I assume you mean certain racist whites—to keep blacks from revolting against this oppressing class?"

"That's part of it," he replied. "The other part is that most Americans, and I mean across the races, don't really give a damn about progress."

"Wow," I said.

"Let me break it down for you smart guys," he continued. "See, throughout this country's history, we've been all about showing our commitment to this or that ideology. But when it comes down to taking meaningful steps to change the underlying substance, to making real progress, we only do it when it makes political or economic sense, or when we're otherwise required to do so. See, we don't really care about the thing we claim to commit to . . . the commitment is to the commitment itself."

Darden turned his attention to the courtyard below. "A commitment to commit," he said.

"Exactly, Harlan!" Uncle Tom exclaimed. "We take steps to change the underlying problem only when there is some other, usually personal gain to be had. You were a history major, Al. You should be able to come up with examples of this stuff."

"Sure . . . I can . . . just give me a minute."

"No time for that, nephew. You boys have partying to do tonight, I'm sure."

Darden smiled. "This guy," he said.

"Let's take the Declaration of Independence, for instance," Uncle Tom said.

"You're going straight for the jugular, aren't you?" I said.

"Isn't that what they taught you in law school?" Uncle Tom replied.

"I suppose so," I said.

"'We hold these truths to be self-evident,'" Uncle Tom said. "What does that even mean?"

"It means that they believed certain truths to be so basic to the . . . the human condition that they need not be explained," Darden said.

"Classic rookie mistake," Uncle Tom said. "Don't worry—you aren't the first to take the bait. These were smart guys, after all."

"Enlighten us, please," I said.

"See, the key word in that phrase is *hold*," Uncle Tom said. "What does it mean to hold something?"

"It means to believe in the thing being held," I said.

"Aha!" Uncle Tom said, slapping the coffee table. "Does it really?"

"Does it not?" Darden asked.

"Critical thinking is so important," Uncle Tom said. "They start teaching it on the first day of kindergarten, but there's a twist. You've been conditioned to think critically only in certain circumstances."

"They've made fools of us, Darden," I said.

Uncle Tom leaned in slowly toward me. "Yes . . . they have. Let me simplify things a taste for you scholars." Uncle Tom pushed off from the couch and walked to the refrigerator. After removing a can of beer, he returned to the courtroom. "You see me holding this beer, right? It's in my hand, and I'm supporting all of its weight."

"Assuming what I'm seeing is consistent with reality, then yes," Darden said.

"Good, Darden," Uncle Tom said. "See, now you're using your head for something other than a hatrack."

I chuckled. "It's been awhile since I've heard that one, Uncle Tom," I said. "You're really enjoying this, aren't you?"

He grinned. "I love schooling scholars who think they've taken every class that matters. Anyway, we've established that I am in fact holding this can, assuming that I'm not deceiving you through some ah . . . artifice."

"Good one," I said.

"Thank you," Uncle Tom said. "And Al said that to hold something means to believe in the thing being held. But can't it also mean that I'm physically holding it, and nothing more—that I'm literally just holding it?"

"Well, you are literally just holding it," Darden said. "It's a can, not a belief."

"That's right. I'm just holding this can of beer. I have no beliefs about this can of beer beyond the expectation that this can contains beer."

I let out a deep breath. "Are you going somewhere with this?" I asked.

"They've also taught you the art of impatience, which prevents you from learning the true nature of things. To wit: how they've convinced you that this Declaration of Independence represented the wholesale commitment of its drafters to the substantive ideals contained in it. That holding a beer is the same as drinking a beer. Who cares that I'm holding a beer?"

"We hold this beer to be self-evident," Darden said.

"Yes, that's it!" Uncle Tom said. "Until I drink this beer, it's nothing more than a beer I'm holding. Until I drink this beer, it's a beer that I can do any number of things with. I might pour it out, I could toss it in the trash . . . I have unlimited options."

"Would you not agree," I said, "that given the context in which the term *hold* was used, and the way the founding generation spoke and wrote generally, they intended to convey in the Declaration of Independence that they actually *believed* what they were saying?"

Darden raised his eyebrows. "Who are you, Scalia? I never thought I'd hear you using original intent doctrine to make a point. I'm noting both the time and date for the record."

"Who wrote the Declaration of Independence?" Uncle Tom asked.

"Thomas Jefferson was the principal author, I believe," I said.

"He was a lawyer, right?" Uncle Tom continued.

"Yes," I said. "How did you know that?"

"I've read some things."

"Well I'm impressed," I said.

Uncle Tom shook his head. "You would be. See, these are the kinds of things they condition you to be impressed with. Anyway, so you agree that a lawyer wrote the document—you lawyers, kings and queens of double-talk. TJ was a brilliant man, an avid reader, inventor, and lots of other shit. Wouldn't he have known that the term *hold* has multiple meanings?"

"I don't know the full etymology of the word," I said, "but yes, I'm pretty sure he knew that the term *hold* could be taken in the more literal sense you're suggesting he intended."

"Very well," Uncle Tom said, beginning to pace back and forth. "So you'd agree, counselor to be, that it's possible that the Declaration of Independence was really nothing more than a declaration of a commitment to commit to certain truths, rather than an ah . . . espousal of the truths set forth therein?"

"Who are you, and what have you done with my Uncle Tom?" I said.

"Darden, would you agree?" Uncle Tom said.

"I agree that Jefferson would have been aware of the existence of multiple usages of the term," Darden replied. "Anything beyond that is a stretch."

"But it's possible, right?" Uncle Tom said.

Darden frowned. "I suppose anything is—"

"And you, nephew?" Uncle Tom asked, swiveling his head sharply toward me.

"I . . . I ah . . . I guess so," I mumbled.

"I'm sorry, counselor to be, but the court reporter may have had some trouble hearing your response," Uncle Tom said, his eyes twinkling. "Again please."

"Yes!" I said.

Uncle Tom plopped back onto the couch. "Very well."

Darden nodded with tightened lips. "He's good."

"Very droll, gentlemen," I said.

Uncle Tom narrowed his eyes. "What the hell does *droll* mean?"

"It means my undergraduate degree may not have been a total waste after all."

"Why is that?" Uncle Tom said. "Because you can show off for people who didn't go to fancy schools? You boys go ahead and hold on tightly to your Declarations of Independence, and your Emancipation Proclamations, and all the other demonstration projects your teachers have spoon-fed you."

I grinned broadly. "I need a beer."

"Here you go," Uncle Tom said, flipping me the can he'd been holding. "I'm done holding it. Now what'll you do with it? You have options. What did Jefferson and Washington and Adams and all the rest of those dead white guys do with the beer they were holding?" And then Uncle Tom finished his lesson: "'We hold these truths to be self-evident, that all men are created equal, that they are endowed by their creator with certain unalienable rights, that among these are life, liberty and the pursuit of happiness. Prudence, indeed, will dictate that governments long established should not be changed for light and transient causes; and accordingly all experience hath shown, that mankind are more disposed to suffer, while evils are sufferable, than to right themselves by abolishing the forms to which they are accustomed.'"

"Game, set, and match," Darden said, sharing a high five with Uncle Tom.

"I don't have to tell you about the purple elephant—or should I say black elephant—hiding among those words," Uncle Tom said.

"No, you don't," I said.

"I can't make this stuff up," Uncle Tom said. "Couldn't Jefferson just as easily have said, 'we *believe* in these *self-evident truths*'?"

"I suppose he could've," I said, "but that's how they spoke back—"

"But he didn't, and you know why. This wasn't an oversight. This was artifice. This was a skilled lawyer making the best argument possible in light of the facts. This was an American demonstration project aimed at convincing British oppressors, and posterity, that the colonists were committed to certain basic rights—not that they were committed to ensuring all of mankind enjoyed them." Uncle Tom rejoined Marvin just in time for the second verse of "Flyin' High." It was one of those moments when life and art meet at precisely the right time and place, so Darden and I did what one ought to do in such moments: watch, listen, give thanks, and say nothing. His voice and story, like Marvin's, were at once angelic and tragic.

I held my tongue until an appropriate amount of time had passed. "Marvin tried to tell us too, huh? By the way, it's 'and accordingly all experience hath *shewn*.'"

"What did I say?" Uncle Tom said.

"You said 'shown,'" I replied. Darden shook his head.

"I suppose that discredits my entire argument?" Uncle Tom said.

"We lawyers rely on ridiculous technicalities," I said. "Sometimes it's the only way we can win."

"I couldn't have put it better myself," Uncle Tom said. "So what do you boys have planned tonight?"

"We're going to a nineties party," Darden said. "You should come."

"Noooo, no, no," Uncle Tom said. "I wouldn't last five minutes. I'm gonna head back to the hotel and sleep this one off. Got me drunk in here. Hey, you're not upset are you, Al?"

"No," I said. "It seems to me that the New School still has a lot to learn from the Old."

"You've learned all you need from the Old School. The challenge for you now is to take the best of the Old and the New, and make them work together. But never stop questioning the things you think you know for certain. When you stop doing that . . . well, you might as well pack it in. And make sure you question the good things just as much as the bad things, because it's the bad disguised as good that's most dangerous. Take it from me, nephew . . . your good looks will only get you so far in this world. Keep your eyes open." Uncle Tom walked to the refrigerator, removed another can of beer, and broke the seal. He took a long swig. "For balance," he said. "Night, boys. Oh . . . one more thing. Earlier, Harlan suggested that the conspiring, oppressing class is made up of white racists. He was right, but they're not alone. Let that marinate. Congratulations on your achievement. I'm proud of you both. I really mean that."

"Thanks," we said in near unison as he closed the door behind him. And then we heard the final pair of lines from the last song on the album. With Uncle Tom's departure, they seemed to emerge from the background.

When the song was safely concluded, I turned to Darden and

smiled. "That was my last beer."

"I've never really been a huge beer fan," Darden said.

"*Harlan*, let's get outta here," I said. "There's a party with our names on it."

CHAPTER TWO

You'd never know it looking at me, but I'm pretty insecure. My father's absence likely has a lot to do with that, but I've never had my head shrunk, so I suppose I can't blame him conclusively. When I was twelve, I stumbled across a shoebox of photos that had been neatly tucked away in a hallway closet. These are my memories of him. I inherited his high cheekbones, triangular head shape, cleft chin, and curly dark-brown hair. I spent many days of my first twenty-eight years wondering how different things could have been had he chosen to stick around.

At six feet two inches, I'm taller than most men, and in high school, the girls called me Pretty Brown Eyes—but those things can only do so much for a man's insides. My mother is a strong, hardworking woman who provided me with all the things she thought I needed as a growing boy. Foremost among those was her unflinching love, and so I was rich. But there's a limit to what a mother can do for her son. As an only child, I learned to deal with a lot of things on my own: fears, flaws, failures, and even successes, to a degree. My friends would probably tell you that I've got it all figured out, and that I'm one of the most polished, charismatic, and well-adjusted people they know. And I'm happy about that. I've worked hard to give them that impression. But in truth, the effort I've expended in building that emblem has come at a huge price.

For a long time, I never got to know me. I didn't take time to figure out what I stand for, and what things I truly believe in. And so, while friends, acquaintances, and even strangers marveled at the image I projected onto the world, I often watched them with envy, wishing I had the tools and fortitude to figure myself out, and then actually be me.

In spite of these challenges, and maybe—at least in part—because of them, I still figured out how to excel at life on paper. I'd also been the beneficiary of what you might call a ridiculous lucky streak—ridiculous with respect to both the extent of the luck and the duration of the streak. But being of sound mind, I also knew that this semicharmed ride would have to end someday. So I tried to live each day with a controlled recklessness that permitted me to extract enormous fun from life while still functioning at a frighteningly high level. One close friend put it this way: "It's like you're sprinting in a one hundred-yard dash where the loser will be condemned to death, and while everyone else is focused on getting to the finish line, you're trying to determine the precise color of the sky, studying the shapes of the clouds, measuring the temperature, figuring the barometric pressure, lavishing in the scent of roses two hundred yards behind you—and all this while running near the head of the pack." What he doesn't know is that I'm afraid I won't make it to the finish line.

I should also say something else about my first twenty-eight years: I was a case study in contradictions. I was continuously skeptical of conventional thinking on most subjects, yet a victim of the intense pressure to conform that frequently frames pubescence and even adulthood. I was forward-looking and prudent, yet shortsighted and impractical—careful and not careful. These extremes coexisted in relative peace because of my unique ability to compartmentalize: school and career in the bucket marked "take care," social interaction and women in the bucket marked "care less." I eventually learned that while compartmentalization is an excellent aid in holding one's professional course through tumultuous personal affairs, it is only an aid, and as one's professional pursuits and personal entanglements increase in complexity, the once impenetrable Chinese wall that neatly separated the two can be easily scaled by skilled invaders.

*****

WHILE SITTING in my bar exam review course on a late June morning in 2009, I received an e-mail memorandum from the presiding partner of Sullivan & Katz, the law firm I was slated to join in September of that year. The memorandum offered members of that year's incoming class of associates the option to either start in the fall, as scheduled, or defer their start date for a year in exchange for half of one year's salary—in one lump sum and with no strings attached. When I informed family friend and recently declared US Senate candidate Ron Johnson of this unforeseen turn of events, he commenced the full-court press. "You absolutely have to come down here and be a part of my team!" he exclaimed on hearing the news. Since seeing me during the Inaugural festivities back in January, Ron had called periodically during my final semester to "check in." He ended each phone call with a renewed and slightly more refined version of his January request that I join his still nonexistent campaign staff promptly after graduation.

By Friday, July 31, 2009, with the horrors of the New York State Bar Exam just two days behind me, I'd recovered sufficiently both physically and emotionally to focus on the business of planning the next year of my life. I very badly wanted to join Ron's campaign, and my motivations for doing so owed mostly to my stout academic and intellectual curiosity around, on the one hand, the recent election of that guy from Hawaii and, on the other, the American history that would follow. I knew Ron's would be among the first campaigns to test a major thesis arising from the presidential election of 2008 regarding black candidates seeking important elected offices, a thesis I'd repeatedly seen articulated in scores of articles since November 4 of that year: that Barack Obama's election would change the way Americans across ethnic and racial lines view the viability—and desirability—of black candidates. But there were other questions that the success or failure of candidates like Ron Johnson would begin to answer. Could Democratic America's captivation with Obama extend to anything or anyone beyond Obama himself? Had Americans actually bought into the progress and increased access to opportunity represented by his candidacy? And, finally, would African Americans stay engaged and return to the polls in 2010—the same folks who turned out in record-shattering numbers in 2008 to vote for Obama at a rate of ninety-five out of every one hundred?

Admittedly, I had another more selfish interest in Ron's candidacy: it would be a once-in-a-lifetime opportunity to hold a senior position in a US Senate campaign as a twentysomething. Most appealing of all was the specter of exerting influence over Ron's candidacy and, perhaps, the outcome of a race that was sure to be kinetic, challenging, and—who knows?—maybe even historic.

I had a reputation among friends and family for extreme impulsivity. This characteristic had served me quite well in life, for the most part, and on the rare occasions when bad decisions led me down the wrong road, I'd always managed to shift course before irreversibly harming myself. Even I knew this decision was too significant to leave to impulse.

I reached out to Larry Jackson, my former Harvard Law School professor, a leading scholar on the intersection of politics and race, and a trusted advisor. Professor Jackson happened to be in DC for a conference that week, so I asked him to meet for a drink downtown at the Jefferson Room. I'd spent that summer at home in DC studying for the bar exam along with Darden Leslie, one of my closest friends from law school and a native of northern Virginia. We didn't put a hard stop on happy hours and clubbing until after July 4, the traditional date around which recent law grads preparing to sit for the New York State Bar Exam in late July experience their first official "freak-out" of the summer. From what I hear—as well as my own experience—this lapse in mental toughness generally falls somewhere on the relatively short continuum between intense anxiety and total psychotic meltdown. While my friends suffered through, and quickly recovered from, the standard July 4 hellfire of self-doubt, I successfully repressed the fear to which they bravely succumbed only to suffer my own, lengthier psychotic interlude on July 15, a mere week outside of the exam— and to my knowledge, the July freak-out, like Father Time, remains undefeated.

I stepped into the Jefferson Room at around nine thirty that evening and found Professor Jackson sitting in a brown, Victorian-dimpled leather chair next to a window fronting a wet Sixteenth Street. One of those quick afternoon summertime monsoons had just passed in and out of the city, leaving more than a few broken limbs in its wake. The moments immediately following these storms were amazing. The typically thick summertime air would break a little as a barely perceptible cool breeze scurried through the downtown grid. The low-profile table in front of Professor Jackson's chair was hewn from a heavy oak and finished with a deep, dark cherry-red shellac. The room was thick with the pungent, inviting aroma of scotch and cognac, and the burn of oily cigar tobacco.

A slender white gentleman sat across from him. The professor's companion wore a perfectly tailored navy blue suit, and the buttonhole on his left lapel bore the pin most members of Congress don when appearing publicly in an official capacity. The stranger's posture was almost awkwardly perfect, and he held his head such that his chin bottom pointed at the professor rather than the floor. His dusty blonde hair was parted across the left side of his head.

The professor's attire met the baseline requirements for a man of his age, sterling reputation, and line of work: matching jacket and slacks, properly pressed white shirt, and a serviceable, muted striped tie. I wore black skinny jeans, a navy blue sport coat along with a custom-tailored white shirt and dark olive knit tie I'd splurged on after graduation in June, and a favorite pair of black patent leather loafers, sans socks. I stood awhile longer just beyond the threshold, watching as they began striking matches. With countenances of utter contentment, they commenced the special ritual of preparing their cigars for drawing.

"Carpenter!" Professor Jackson exclaimed as I approached the pair.

"Professor," I responded. Professor Jackson rose slowly from his chair to shake my hand. The bespoke, Carolina blue bow-tied gentleman remained seated, but he did reach for my hand.

"Al Carpenter, meet Congressman Darling—Congressman, Al Carpenter."

The Congressman glanced at me briefly. "A pleasure, young man," he said in an inviting, molasses-laden, western North Carolina drawl. He was at least ten years younger than Professor Jackson—a sixty-two-year-old who'd been raised in Camden, New Jersey.

"All mine," I replied, taking the vacant seat next to the Congressman.

"How'd the bar exam go?" Professor Jackson said, plopping back into his chair. He sat with his arms resting on the chair's arms, his cigar clutched between his lips and protruding out the right corner of his mouth.

"I think it went well. Hopefully well enough to pass the thing."

"I know you're happy to have that hell behind you, son," said the Congressman. "Seems like only yesterday I was doin' that myself."

"I'm sure you did fine, just fine," Professor Jackson said. "So tell me, Carpenter—what can I do for you?"

"Well, Professor . . . I'm considering going to North Carolina to work for Ron Johnson."

Professor Jackson chuckled. "You know, I ran into Ron about a month ago down in Charlotte. He mentioned that he'd gotten into that Senate race. I'll tell you like I told him: I think it's important for young black candidates to throw their hats into the ring, but I also don't think he can get out of the primary."

"Why not?" I said.

Professor Jackson leaned in slowly toward me. "There's a formula for getting elected to statewide office in North Carolina: Scots-Irish lineage, good ol' boy money, and black votes. That formula doesn't include black candidates."

"Not even if Ron mobilizes the blacks and progressives who came together for Obama?" I said.

"Those folks aren't coming out for this election," Professor

Jackson said, leaning back. "It's an off-year cycle, and frankly, Ron Johnson ain't no Barack Obama. Ron's never held elected office. He's a corporate lawyer, not a politician."

"Ron's been crunching some numbers," I said. "Historically in North Carolina, thirty percent of primary election voters are African American. If he's able to excite that community and get, say, eighty-five percent of that voting bloc, he'd be well over halfway to the forty percent he needs to win the primary outright."

"That's assumin' a lot," Darling said. "Even if he gets eighty-five percent of the black vote, where would he get the other fifteen he needs for forty?"

"Progressives and the nonprofit community," I said. "His personal story appeals to them, and in terms of policy, in areas like education, clean tech, and affordable housing, he'll be the most progressive candidate in the field."

"You make a mighty compellin' case, son, but this ain't a court of law," Darling said. "And you're talkin' about a state that's never elected a black senator or governor. There's a reason for that, and it's not because qualified candidates haven't tried. You may not be old enough to remember Helms versus Gantt back in 1990, but that got right nasty."

"I've heard stories," I said.

"'There's no joy in Mudville tonight,'" Professor Jackson said. "That's what Helms said the night he beat Gantt."

"That was almost twenty years ago!" I exclaimed.

"There's really no mistakin' the meanin' there," Darling said. "I'm not sayin' race is as much of an issue now, but it's still there, and white politicians are using it to their advantage—they've just gotten much better at hidin' it."

"And then there's the matter of the DSCC," Professor Jackson said. "You've got to factor those jokers into the mix."

"The DSCC?" I said.

"The Democratic Senatorial Campaign Committee," Professor Jackson said. "You always want those folks in your corner to drive fundraising. Without their backing, Ron would have a devil of a time convincing big donors to take his candidacy seriously—rank-and-file voters too. I suppose there's an outside chance the DSCC will stay out of this one—and that would be best for Ron since they're not likely to back him—but that seems unlikely since Republicans are liable to throw the kitchen sink at this race to make sure Senator Rodney keeps his seat."

"The DSCC doesn't take risks when it gets involved in US Senate races," Darling said. "Backing a black political neophyte with no name recognition in a Southern state—well, I just don't see it happenin'."

"With all due respect, Congressman," I said, "lots of people thought Barack Obama didn't have a chance in hell against Clinton, a proven fundraiser with one hundred percent name recognition."

"Ron better be banking on building some sort of a mass movement," Professor Jackson said. "Because that's exactly what it's going to take."

"Look, I know there must be a million reasons why he shouldn't run, and why he'll probably lose," I began. "But—I do think there's a willingness right now among Democrats, even Southern Democrats, to look at qualified black candidates a little differently than before. If we stop now, we risk sending a dangerous message to Americans of all races."

Darling cocked his right eyebrow. "Which is?" he asked.

"That Obama's election was just a blip on the radar—something that cannot, and perhaps even should not, be repeated," I explained. "The true value of Obama's election—and we can unlock it right now—is the potential it has to drive momentum for progress going forward. We have to make the case that Obama isn't the only smart, charismatic, idealistic, nonwhite politician out there capable of building broad coalitions."

Professor Jackson studied me carefully before turning toward Congressman Darling. "I don't know," he said, letting out a deep breath. "Whatta you think, Branford?"

"The kid is dreaming," Darling said. "That's what kids do. That's what we did at his age. Hell, that's part of why we have a black president today."

"What does it take these days to run a statewide US Senate race, Branford?" Professor Jackson asked. "A mill?"

"Minimally, and that just gets you outta the primary," Darling said. "There's no money out there. The economy is—well, this is the kind of race where a big name could pop up and bulldoze his way through the primary."

A waitress approached. "Can I get you anything?" she said.

"A million bucks if you can spare it," I said. The Two Wise Men smirked in mild amusement.

She grinned. "I'm sorry, sir, but we're in the business of making money, not giving it away."

"Who said anything about givin' it away?" Darling said. "There's a price tag for everything under the sun."

"I'd settle for a good bourbon," I said. "But if you change your mind about that million, please let me know. It would make someone

I know very happy."

"Will do," she said before sliding off to the pair of patrons next door.

"They don't build 'em like that anymore, son," Darling said.

"Sure they do, sir," I replied. "Perhaps just not in your district."

"He's got a point there, Branford," Professor Jackson said. "I've been to your district. It's slim pickins."

"You're right," Darling said. "That's probably why my wife gets so cranky when I'm up here in Washington."

"Or maybe she just misses you," I said. Professor Jackson and Congressman Darling looked at each other for a few seconds before bursting into laughter.

"Good one, Carpenter," Darling said.

"Any rumblings about what the DSCC will do this cycle, Branford?" Professor Jackson said.

"Word is they've been encouragin' the lieutenant governor to run," Darling replied.

"Ray Pruitt?" I asked.

"That's right, son," Darling said.

"No way Ray gets in," I said. "It's no secret he wants to run for governor in 2012."

"I see you've been keepin' tabs on state politics," Darling said. "What's your connection to North Carolina?"

"His grandparents on his mom's side live in Nash County," Professor Jackson said.

"That's right," I said. "Spent a fair amount of time down there as a kid during summer breaks."

"How's your granddad, by the way?" Professor Jackson said. "He's quite a character. Took the time at graduation to thank me for giving you such a hard time in law school. Is he still serving up that good ol' tough love?"

"You know it," I replied. "I hear his voice in my head at least once a day. Some people call that voice their conscience. I call it Grandpa."

Darling turned to me. "Do you fish, son?"

"Abbbsolutely," I said.

"We oughtta get out on my boat sometime when we're both down there," Darling said.

"I'd love to," I replied.

"Perhaps I'll join you," Professor Jackson said.

"Who says you're invited, Professor?" Darling said, winking.

"I know where the bodies are buried, Carpenter," Professor Jackson said, winking back at Darling. "So I don't really worry much about getting invitations from Branford here. They always find their way into my mailbox."

Darling shook his head. "How do you like that, Carpenter? With friends like this one . . ."

"So you think the primary field is wide open, Branford?" Professor Jackson asked.

"I don't see any of the big names gettin' in this year," Darling replied. "It's gonna be mighty difficult to unseat a Republican incumbent in a midterm election with a Democrat sittin' in the White House. And Rodney's got millions in the bank ready to pummel the poor soul who comes outta the Democratic primary."

"So there *is* a chance for an unknown like Ron to win the primary," I said.

"He's still gotta raise a whole helluva lot of money," Darling said. "No money, no DSCC, no GOTV, no victory. It's a long shot, son, but he *could* squeak past in the primary."

"That's all I need to hear," I said.

"Progress in race and politics happens incrementally," Darling said. "You know that. Without candidate Jesse Jackson, there would be no President Barack Obama. Folks have to gradually get used to the idea of black political leadership."

"I'll tell you the issue he's gonna have in the black community," Professor Jackson began. "Many may see him as stepping up out of turn. Things are done a certain way in politics. There's an order to things. You work your way up. There are blacks down in Carolina who've been doing that, and they may work against what Ron's trying to do."

"If he raises enough money and gets on TV, that won't be an issue," Darling said. "But as I said, money may not be out there this cycle."

"He's going to need something big to drive fundraising," I said. "I'm not sure messaging alone will do that. People have been messaged to death about change and progress. I mean, we'll have to run the Obama playbook to an extent, but we're gonna need something else. We'll figure it out along the way."

"Sounds like you've made your decision, son," Darling said.

"I guess I have," I said.

Professor Jackson took a hearty sip from his lowball glass. "I'll do what I can to help. And if you twist Branford's arm far enough, you might even get an endorsement out of him." Congressman Darling smiled uneasily before swiftly downing the last of his drink.

"It'll be good experience for you, win or lose," Professor Jackson said. "I really don't see any downside for you." With that, he rose slowly to his feet. The congressman and I quickly followed suit. I was almost floored by Darling's height. He was at least six-foot-six.

"Gentlemen," Professor Jackson said, reaching to shake the congressman's hand, then mine. "I have a 6:00 a.m. flight back to Boston tomorrow. What do you have planned for the remainder of the evening, Carpenter?"

"I'm about to meet up with Darden."

"Give Mr. Leslie my best," Professor Jackson said.

"I will, and thanks again for meeting me," I said. "Congressman— great meeting you. And thanks for your insight."

"Best of luck to you, son," he said. "I'll see you down in North Carolina." Before exiting into the hotel lobby, Jackson and Darling stopped to chat with three important-looking, heavyset men standing near the entrance.

The waitress returned with my bourbon a few minutes later. "What happened to your friends?" she said.

"I had more pressing matters so I asked them to leave."

She chuckled. "I bet," she said.

"Can I have the bill?"

"It's on me," she said. "Consider this an in-kind campaign contribution."

"Thank you very much, but how do you know about the campaign? And just how does this contribute to it?"

"I overheard some of your conversation. Consider this a contribution to your sanity."

"Thanks," I said. "Ever been to North Carolina?"

"A few years ago I went down to Charlotte for a wedding. It wasn't at all what I expected."

"What did you expect?"

"Dirt roads . . . heavy drawls . . . you know, the country."

"You know, Charlotte is the banking capital of the South," I said.

She shrugged. "Yeah, but it's still the South."

"True."

"Well, good luck!" she said. As she walked away, I took a sip. Then I turned my seat so that it faced the window. I spent the next hour watching cars travel up and down Sixteenth Street. The light from the lamps lining the thoroughfare sparkled on contact with the layer of water covering the asphalt and the final cadence of raindrops from the passing storm.

*****

I STEPPED INTO THE DARK night a minute or two after eleven o'clock. Fifteen minutes earlier, I'd received a text from Darden saying he was on his way downtown. I scrolled to Darden's cell number while walking southward down Sixteenth Street. The White House stood bright and majestic in the distance.

"Coming up Fourteenth Street now," Darden said. "I just hit downtown. How was your meeting with Professor Jackson?"

"I think I convinced myself to go to North Carolina."

"You say you want to run someday. You might as well go see what it's like."

"True."

"Plus it'll be a great way for us to test your thesis that things will be easier for qualified black candidates after Obama."

"That's your thesis!" I said.

"By the way . . . I got a job at the D triple-C."

"The D triple—oh, the Democratic *Congressional* Campaign Committee? I didn't know what the DSCC was until a few minutes ago. Congratulations, although I wish you had applied to the DSCC. What about your job at Williams & Rinehart?"

"I got deferred a year."

"That's becoming a trend. Foley & Rogers did the same to Simmons a few days ago."

"Too bad I won't be any help to you and Ron at the D triple-C."

"You'll be running in the same circles as DSCC folks."

"I guess. Anyway, congrats on your decision. We have to celebrate hard tonight."

"Most definitely."

I continued down Sixteenth Street, passing the University Club on the left before crossing L Street. Instead of turning left onto K Street, I remained on Sixteenth and walked through Lafayette Park until I stood before the black fence encircling the front lawn of the White House. I couldn't remember the last time I'd been there at night. It was breathtaking. For a moment I recalled traveling on Pennsylvania Avenue as a child, before the stretch fronting the White House was permanently cut off to motor traffic.

Then I heard my Uncle Tom: *Until I drink this beer, it's nothing more than a beer I'm holding.* After a few more moments, I turned eastward and walked briskly down Pennsylvania Avenue. I knew Darden couldn't be too far from the club.

CHAPTER THREE

ELECTION DAY
TUESDAY, NOVEMBER 4, 2008

As we entered the eleventh month of 2008, once again Americans prepared to jump wittingly into a sea of their own carefully curated delusion. I followed the polls pretty closely during the latter weeks of that year's presidential election. By October, most of them signaled that an Obama victory was all but certain. I wasn't convinced. My undergraduate courses in American history were a constant reminder that the election of a black president in America could never be certain. Frankly, the fact that we were talking about Obama having a real shot at winning was fairly supernatural.

It was almost noon on Election Day when I finally made my way out of class and headed toward Massachusetts Avenue. The plan was to go home, eat a quick lunch, then immediately start catching up on two weeks of ignored Trusts and Estates reading.

While I walked, I thought about what might happen if Obama didn't win, or worse, if some lunatic took him out. I'd heard stories from my grandparents about the riots in Los Angeles and DC in the wake of Dr. King's murder. My Uncle Tom had also talked many times about black folks' reaction to the assassination of John F. Kennedy, a man many of them saw as a serious advocate for civil rights. *What will happen to our "postracial America" then?*

As I turned to cross the street, I spotted Darden bouncing toward me. At our law school, each incoming class is divided into smaller sections of students who take their core, first-year courses together. Darden and I were grouped in the same section and hit it off instantly.

We had all the same interests: the Redskins, R&B and soul, and pretty women from Prince George's County, Maryland. He stood at about five feet ten inches, kept his haircut low, and never wore facial hair. People often remarked that he looked like a brown-skinned version of a youthful Andrew Young, which was ironic since they'd both graduated from Howard University. Darden and I—and our best friend, Simmons—were each twenty-four years old when we met in September 2006, but Darden still looked nineteen. Being the mildest-mannered member of the triumvirate, Darden often found himself in the crosshairs of my frequent squabbles with Simmons. Darden was probably the smartest of the group too, although you'd never know it from spending time with us—and though he'd never admit it.

"Sup, Al?"

"Not much," I said. "Heading home to knock out some reading."

"You wanna get lunch?"

I should've gone home, but politicking with Darden was plainly preferable to sitting at my desk trying to wrap my brain around the intricacies of the rule against perpetuities. "Yeah, I'm down," I said. "The usual?"

"Unless you have a better idea."

"CC it is." With that, we began the short walk up that familiar, aesthetically unexceptional stretch of Massachusetts Avenue.

"You gonna watch the election returns at Simmons's apartment?" he asked. I held the door open as we entered the always unreasonably dark foyer of Cambridge Commons.

"That's the plan," I said. "What time are you gettin' over there?"

"Around eight. A decent number of states should have numbers by then."

"Good deal." Once inside, the hostess led us to one of the booths. CC was packed that day with its typical, surprisingly soluble mixture of locals and law students. After she left us to study the menus, I turned to Darden, who sat across from me. "Word on the street is you and Roxi are back on again," I said. "I thought two people had to break up before they could get back together."

"People don't know what they're talking about," he said. "Me and Roxi are the same as always."

"And?"

Darden looked down at the table. "And—I'm just not ready to commit."

"You know, these women are getting to be at that age," I said. "Plus there's so few of us black men . . . you've got the police locking us up left and right. You can't really blame them for trying to dig their heels in."

"True," Darden said.

"The key to this whole *relationship* thing is managing expectations," I said. "You have to be inconsistent but considerate. If your behavior becomes too regular, you create all these expectations."

"That's exactly how I've been approaching things with Roxi, but it's an impossible balancing act. I'm just gonna end it . . . this week."

"And Bush is gonna end the war in Iraq this week too. Get outta here with that!"

"I'm serious," he said. "It's for the best."

"I don't doubt it's for the best—I do doubt you'll go through with it. Much, much easier said than done."

"Ten bucks says I'll do it," he offered.

"Easiest ten I'll ever make."

When the waitress came a few moments later, we ordered lunch, which we wolfed down at the speed that characterized most of our law school activities. As we finished, I asked, "Who do you think Obama would put on the Supreme Court? John Paul is old as hell. He can't hold out much longer."

"He's probably just holding out for a Democrat to get back in office," Darden said. "I actually think Obama should put another woman on the Court, a black woman, but I don't see him doing it."

"Kagan's gotta be on the short list," I said.

"True, but she's got a great gig here," Darden opined. "Students love her, and she's got the faculty on a string, but you've gotta think the Supreme Court is her end game."

"Plus I hear she's pretty tight with Barack."

"Well, Barack's gotta win first," he said. "But I think it's in the bag."

"You never know," I said.

"You're right. It's not guaranteed, but he's created a movement. He's killing McCain's fundraising with five- and ten-dollar online contributions. That's unheard of. Hell, I'm broke and I contributed."

"How much?" I asked.

"One hundred."

"Jesus."

He shook his head. "Right? Like I have a hundred dollars to throw around. I may not be able to cover tuition next semester, but hell, I'll figure that out when the time comes. I've got that Obama hope in me."

"Wow," I said, chuckling. "You're *all* the way in."

"Damn right. Just think about what it would mean for him to win."

"I think the bigger question is what his election would mean going forward," I said. "Do you think it would change how whites perceive black candidates?"

"His election completely changes the game," Darden replied. "Strong black candidates will have a much easier time gaining traction with white voters than they do now."

"No way," I said, shaking my head. "A huge part of this Obama fever comes from his story. He's as close to perfect as you can get—president of the *Law Review*, graduated magna cum laude, blah blah blah. Most white voters just see him as an anomaly, a purple squirrel. If he gets elected, and that's still a big if, most people will think this type of moment can never—and maybe *should* never—be repeated with other black candidates, no matter how strong they are."

"I see your point," he said. "I mean, it's hella pessimistic, but I see it. Sounds like something my grandfather would say."

"Mine too," I said.

"He's eighty . . . what's your excuse?"

I chuckled. "Simple. This is America."

"That's right, America, the so-called land of opportunity," he said.

"Problem is the dust under the rug is reaching capacity. But most folks just wanna keep on sweeping."

"Okay, Malcolm X," he said.

I couldn't help but crack a smile. "Let's pay the bill and get outta here," I said.

"I just wish we could've voted like regular people this morning," Darden said.

"I hear you," I said. "Sending in absentee ballots weeks before isn't really the story we want to tell our grandkids."

While walking back down Massachusetts Avenue, we discussed plans for Friday night as we had countless times before. We decided that we'd go out but didn't settle on a location. I told Darden I'd call Simmons to see if he had any leads—Simmons always had something going on. When we reached the corner of Everett Street and Massachusetts Avenue, Darden turned left and began walking toward his apartment while I headed in the opposite direction. "How about that Barack Obama?" he shouted.

"We'll see!" I said, glancing back toward him. "We'll see."

At that time, I was unconvinced that an Obama victory would do much to alleviate America's race-based ailments in the short term, and highly skeptical about its capacity to move the needle over the long term. In a paper I wrote that semester in a class taught by Professor Jackson—it was called Barack Obama and the Presidential Election of 2008—I argued that the most marginalized, at-risk young people would pay little or no attention to an Obama victory because their day-to-day reality, and that of their parents, is almost entirely unaffected by presidential politics, and because an Obama victory would do little to change the outlook of the role models from whom such young people take their cues.

This wildly popular class brought together a cross-section of viewpoints and backgrounds: run-of-the-mill Republicans and Democrats, black and Hispanic Republicans, gay and lesbian conservatives, libertarians and nihilists—and no single group had the market cornered on idiocy.

"Perhaps," I asserted during the penultimate class before Election Day, "Obama is all those things: terrorist, communist, antichrist, and a racist. That's not a totally radical conclusion to draw if one also buys the claim that Obama is the Manchurian Candidate whose every word and action is manipulated by some clandestine corporate entity. The former assertions are no more ridiculous than the latter."

"What if he is the Manchurian Candidate?" Darden posited from his seat near the back of the amphitheater-style classroom. A near-deafening silence replaced the synchronized sounds of students shifting their attention away from me and toward Darden.

Professor Jackson narrowed his eyes. "Are you suggesting that he is, Mr. Leslie?"

"I challenge anyone in this room to make a succinct argument supporting the premise that he isn't," Darden responded. Within five seconds, the latest line of the now hour-long Google chat conversation with my classmate, close friend, and neighbor Bristol Davis popped up: *Get your boy.*

"Mr. Carpenter," Professor Jackson said. "Care to respond?"

I grinned. "I suppose that's not the most ridiculous assertion I've heard," I said. "That might explain why Obama's doing so well."

There was a ten-second silence before Darden spoke. "How else would you explain what's going on here?" he said. "Postracialism?"

"Let's bookmark this for next week," Professor Jackson said, robbing me of the rare opportunity to debate Darden before a captive audience. As the other students closed their laptops and gathered their belongings, I said good-bye to Bristol, ascended the stairs, and crossed over to Darden.

"The Manchurian Candidate, brotha?" I said.

Darden flashed me the smirk of a boy who'd just been caught stealing from the cookie jar. "You brought it up," he said.

"I was tired of listening to folks dance around the things they really wanted to say—so I said it for them."

"Figured as much," he replied. "I thought that by jumping in, we might really get something going. We haven't gone back and forth in a while—what, since 1-L year in Torts?"

"I won that exchange, by the way," I said.

"You're developing an extremely selective memory—or is this the historian in you trying to rewrite history?"

"Let's go eat, man," I said. "We'll worry about history next week."

*****

I ACTUALLY got a pretty good amount of studying done that afternoon, though the rule against perpetuities still eluded me as dinnertime approached. After scarfing down some nearly inedible meatloaf, I walked to Simmons's apartment to watch election returns. The voices emanating from Simmons's apartment were audible well before I'd reached the third-floor landing. Just before knocking I abruptly caught myself, remembering that Simmons was probably the only living person from New York City who kept their home unlocked. The pungent, enticing scent of buffalo wings welcomed me as I crossed the threshold. With the exception of Bristol, who'd spent the day knocking on doors for Obama in her native North Carolina, the whole gang was present—Darden, Simmons, and Jennifer. The remaining guests were friends of Simmons whom I knew only in passing. Their boisterous conversations overpowered the tiny living room, drowning out the election coverage in the background. Half of the group sat on two tan couches while the late arrivals, like myself, milled around behind them. In total, there were about fifteen of us.

While catching up with Simmons, I noticed for the first time in the two-year period I'd known him that he was just a hair shorter than me, though at least fifteen pounds more slight. We had something else in common too. The complexities surrounding, on the one hand, our mercurial day-to-day conduct and, on the other, our firm though unspoken policy against opening up to others, made us impossible to characterize definitively.

Simmons Esposito, a self-proclaimed "mutt" of mixed African-American, Italian, and Dominican heritage, was like the protagonist of a well-scripted drama: too complex to exist in real life but still entirely believable. You often found yourself wanting to pinch him to see if he'd respond. He consistently wowed classmates and professors alike with his crackerjack intelligence, unparalleled command of the King's English, and silky baritone while simultaneously refusing to shed the core sensibilities he'd picked up from the Bronx neighborhood where he'd spent his formative years. He was also the consummate gentleman—at least when ladies were watching. The occasional yarn from "back home"—and a heavier New York City accent—might sneak forth here and there on nights when spirits got the better of him, but these transparent moments of reflection were rare. In sober moments, Simmons could occasionally be heard saying, "I came from the hood to the big house in Cambridge," but that was typically the extent of his autobiographical musings. At his core, he was a guy's guy—boisterous and sufficiently crude among the fellas. But he could flip the switch in a heartbeat.

Before I could pour my first drink, Darden had convinced me to make what, in hindsight, were two really stupid bets. I bet him sixty dollars Obama would lose in Virginia and one hundred dollars Obama wouldn't win three hundred electoral votes, even though a credible study I'd seen that week predicted he'd easily pass that mark.

The entire room went silent when the TV anchor announced that a McCain victory was mathematically impossible. Even Darden, who for weeks was certain Obama would win, wore a face of total shock. For as long as I breathe air and retain control of my mental faculties, I will never forget the moment the presidential election of 2008 was called for Barack Obama. And I suppose no one else will either. To describe that moment as surreal would be rather like noting the color of the White House—totally unnecessary and unequivocally accurate. While standing in a room alongside some of my closest friends, I felt physically absent. In that moment, it was as if I was looking down on myself from above, seemingly unaffected by this titanic moment but acutely aware of its life-altering impact on everyone else. I struggled to seize the emotion they experienced so effortlessly but could only do so vicariously through them.

The silence in the room became deafening as the president-elect walked across the stage at Chicago's Grant Park. At first the group—mostly African American—could only gaze at him, wide-eyed. Jennifer sat statuesque on the edge of the couch, plainly stunned by the words running across the bottom of the screen: BARACK OBAMA ELECTED PRESIDENT. She mouthed them silently. Meanwhile, Darden leaned back against the wall opposite the television—his eyes closed and his hands secured firmly behind his head—as if he lay on the sands of some exotic beach that, having just tendered the final monthly payment, he now owned free and clear. And the perpetually restless Simmons, who'd spent most of the evening engaged in his customary game of How Close Can I Toss the Tennis Ball to the Ceiling without Permitting the Two to Touch?, decided a timeout was in order. After a few moments, I scanned the room again. All eyes were glued to the television. The flock awaited confirmation from its savior. And then he took center stage.

"If there is anyone out there who still doubts that America is a place where all things are possible, who still wonders if the dream of our founders is alive in our time, who still questions the power of our democracy, tonight is your answer," President-elect Obama said. For more than fifteen minutes, they all watched him unblinkingly. "And where we are met with cynicism and doubt," Obama continued, "and those who tell us that we can't, we will respond with that timeless creed that sums up the spirit of a people: 'yes we can.'"

Eventually I murmured, "I'll be damned . . . he won."

Darden turned to me and said, "Will you be paying in cash or check?" And then at once the group, friends and strangers, began to embrace one another. Our embraces communicated what words could not: the generations of blood and tears that layered the path leading to this day; the anger and shame borne by generations of mothers and fathers, slaves and freedmen; and the pride of the grandparents, great-aunts, and great-uncles who lived long enough to see Senator Obama but only long enough to dream of President Obama.

Then there was an awkward moment. While everyone else giddily weighed options for celebrating that evening, I found myself trapped in a decidedly noncelebratory mood. I stood, tied my scarf around my neck, and stepped toward the door.

"Where you going?" Darden asked.

"I'm tired," I replied. "I'm just gonna go home and crash."

Darden scrunched his face. "Go home and crash? Are you crazy? Boston is guaranteed to be stupid tonight!"

"He's lost his mind," Simmons said. "Too much Trusts and Estates reading would be my guess. Somebody make this guy another drink."

"I'm just not up to it," I said. "Let me know where you end up. Maybe I'll catch up with you guys later." I walked out the door as Darden and Simmons made new arguments against my departure. But I didn't stop.

A cool breeze whipped autumn's debris around me as I exited the building. The sound of leaves scampering across the sidewalk engineered a perfect counterpoint to the report of air blowing through the trees. As I began the ten-minute walk back to my building, I noticed I'd received some twenty-one-odd text messages in as many minutes. My mother asked where I was, Bristol wondered where we were heading to party, and my cousin Billy declared, *We did it. We got into 1600 Penn Ave cuzzo!*

Billy's text gave me pause. I couldn't help but smile at the realization that this great symbol of power and prestige, which for centuries has been the exclusive domain of white men, would soon be called home by a black man, his black wife, and their two beautiful black children. I stopped dead in my tracks and shouted, "Dammit, we did it!"

"*Excuse you*, young man!" The voice belonged to a white woman who, unbeknownst to me, had been trailing close behind with her two small children.

"Oh, sorry," I said, somewhat disingenuously.

"I guess you think you can say and do anything now?"

"What do you mean?" I said, knowing full well what she was getting at.

"I told my husband this would happen if that damned Obama won this election!"

"What would happen?"

"I suppose you think you've got a shot now?" she said, wagging her finger at my chest.

I chuckled. "Ma'am, you'll be happy to know I have no chance of becoming president. I didn't even make it onto the *Harvard Law Review*."

"Where are you from?" she demanded.

I puffed out my chest just a taste. "The District of Columbia."

She sneered. "Were you around when that Marion Barry was mayor?"

"Abbbsolutely," I said. "My mother served in the second and third Barry administrations. She's got some pretty good stories too. Apparently, he's a genius. He'd just kinda stroll into meetings with literally no briefing and fully grasp the complexities of the issues raised within seconds of hearing them. He's brilliant."

"*Brilliant*?" she scoffed. "He was a total embarrassment! The capital of the free world had a cokehead for a mayor, followed by an adulterer as president."

"Well, Barry easily won reelection after embarrassing us so much, and Clinton could win reelection whenever he wanted, if it were constitutional. And I don't know why you're so upset about Barack. It's not like he's the *first* black president. We got that done back in '92!"

She stood still, her face twisted in rage. Meanwhile, her young son and daughter looked on, giggling nervously. She grabbed them by their wrists and walked briskly past. The children looked back at me, oblivious to the racial undertones coloring the back-and-forth they'd just witnessed—at least, I hoped so. I wondered what conclusions their little brains had drawn from that exchange, and whether they'd grow up to see people like me the way their mother did: as part of the problem and not the solution. Then a stunning realization hit me: if Obama won a second term, as teenagers, those two children probably wouldn't be able to recall a time when there wasn't a black president.

*****

I DIDN'T CALL DARDEN that night, but he informed me by text at 12:30 a.m. that the party was *right* and that some of Boston's finest ladies were *out looking for their Barack*. Being a red-blooded male, I was tempted for a time, but the idea of sitting in my 8:30 a.m. class the next morning on virtually no sleep wasn't too appealing in that moment.

I showered, poured a bourbon I didn't really want, and plopped on the couch. I tried to totally space out, but my mind wasn't done mulling over the history that was made earlier that evening. I wondered at the raging sea of popular opinion across America that night, the tidal waves of joyous tears mixed with fear and anger, and undercurrents of skepticism and uncertainty. I longed to know just how many Americans out there were enraged by the election of our first black president solely because of his race. More than anything else, though, I wanted to know whether Obama's heterogeneous army of supporters would now go to work to effect the systemic changes it so overwhelmingly demanded that evening.

Surely there were others who shared my skepticism about the capacity of this moment to effect meaningful, lasting change in American social and political institutions in the years ahead. I stared down into the dark-blue courtyard below. While my friends partied, I pondered the fate of a nation. *What's next?* I thought. *What will we do now?*

CHAPTER FOUR

TUESDAY, JANUARY 20, 2009

IT TOOK US NEARLY FORTY-FIVE MINUTES to get to the Inaugural Ball at the Main Post Office. On any other day it's a fifteen-minute trip from my house, door to door. But this was Inauguration weekend, which meant that all the most convenient routes to any place a significant number of people might want to travel were shut down. It's as if a handful of Federal agents sat down with a map of Washington, DC, and said, "Alright, let's make driving downtown as annoying as possible so people will take the Metro instead." That plan probably deterred thousands of people from driving, but my guess is that the vast majority of black folks who ventured into the city that night did so in their cars, heat blasting.

Those Federal agents had clearly never been around black folks when the temperature dips below thirty-two or, alternatively, did not factor black people into their calculus. It was a chilly twenty-seven degrees when we left the house that evening, which meant that there was about as much of a chance that my mother, aunt, and uncle were going to take the Metro as there was that John McCain and Barack Obama would share a beer the next afternoon in the Oval Office to celebrate the latter's housewarming.

While working our way around the maze of shutdown streets surrounding Union Station, my mother spotted Ron and Casey Johnson walking toward the front steps of the Main Post Office. Ron had been my Uncle Malcolm's closest friend since their fraternity days at Duke. Casey, also a Duke grad, was Ron's beautiful, effervescent wife.

My Aunt Kelly rolled the window down just enough to fit her arm outside. A stream of frigid air immediately poured into the car. "Casey . . . Ronny!" she shouted, waving frantically. "Over here!" They turned without interrupting their ascent up the stairs. Casey's eyes seemed to widen as we came into focus. After pointing us out to Ron, they both quickly descended the steps toward our heater on wheels. In heels, Casey stood at her husband's height of six feet flat.

"Where in hell did you guys park?" Uncle Malcolm said, uncharacteristically dispensing with his usual pleasantries.

"In that lot over there," Ron said, pointing at Union Station's enormous parking deck. My mother, Aunt Kelly, and Casey wasted no time delving into that "Oh my god, you look so great, you've lost so much weight!" chatter that, through force of habit and on the recommendation of trusted male elders, I've come to almost completely tune out.

"Why don't you ladies go inside while we park," Uncle Malcolm said. "No need for all of us to freeze." While my mother, Aunt Kelly, and Casey sped up the stairs wrapped in a blanket of black evening wear, Ron hopped into the car and we headed toward the parking deck.

"Well how in hell did you get into that parking deck?" Uncle Malcolm asked, massaging his perfectly manicured salt-and-pepper beard. "They've got it blocked off."

"Yeah—one entrance is blocked off," Ron responded. "You have to circle all the way around to get to the one that's open." I was shocked that Ron still had so little gray hair, despite being the same age as my decidedly graying uncle.

"Circle?" Uncle Malcolm said incredulously. "What circle? Every street within a stone's throw of that parking deck is shut down. I asked one of the eighty police officers surrounding the place if the deck was open. You'd think one, just one, might disclose the fairly critical information that the deck is in fact open on the other side."

Ron looked back at me from the front passenger seat, smirking. "Well, Malcolm, most days you've got the touch, and on some days, I've got your touch," he said.

"So how's business down in North Carolina, Ron?" Uncle Malcolm said, pulling into a parking space.

"Good, Malcolm, good." Ron turned to me again. "And how's school coming along? You're in your last semester, right?"

"That's right," I said. "All's well. Just trying to stay motivated."

Ron laughed. "If memory serves me correctly, that's a pretty tall order."

"You got that right," I said. "Every day is a new struggle to make myself open a book and read. Law school really shouldn't last more than two years."

"Well maybe you should go over to the dean's office when you get back—tell her to quit stalling and confer your degree a semester early," Ron said.

"And cancel the boatload of loans I took out for next semester," I added.

"That too," Ron said. My uncle took a phone call as we walked down North Capital Street. I could barely feel my fingers.

"So what's new with you?" I said. "Still plugging away at the firm?"

"Yeah, I'm still there, but thinking about something else."

"What's that?"

"There's a US Senate seat up next year. I'm considering a run."

"Wow, that's great Ron. Really exciting." *Negro, please*, I thought. "That's a major move," I continued. "You think you can win?"

"I think this is an election where someone with a compelling personal story and a clear vision for progress can be successful—even in North Carolina." Ron locked eyes with mine. "Al, you should come down and be a part of this. It would be a great opportunity to see a Senate race at ground zero . . . you know, figure out if this is something you want to do down the road."

"That would be great, but I've got a job lined up already after graduation."

"I'm gonna need young, talented folks on my team if this is gonna happen," he continued.

"It's just that—"

"Give it some thought Al. No rush. Offer's on the table."

Uncle Malcolm was still on the phone. "How about we inaugurate Obama before we start talking about North Carolina?" he chimed in, walking a few feet ahead.

"Hey man, we've got to stay ahead of the game," Ron said. "This is the time to make sure the progress we voted for last year sticks."

"True," I said.

"Keep me posted, and I'll let you know how things are going on my end."

"Will do."

"In the meantime, maybe you can help me recruit a talented young woman to join the campaign as press secretary," Ron said. "Someone with a strong voice and superior confidence—someone who's not going to back down from opinionated, know-it-all men like you and me." He chuckled. "Know anyone like that?"

Do I know anyone like that? I thought. He'd just described Bristol Davis. "Let me think on that," I said.

"Bring me back a few Cubans and we'll call it even," Uncle Malcolm said, wrapping up his call.

"That's your uncle . . . always cutting a deal," Ron said. "What's fun is when you find yourself an unexpected beneficiary of one of them."

I smiled. "The sweet life," I said.

Several wretchedly frigid minutes later, we stepped into the grand foyer of the Main Post Office. It was a Beaux-Arts style hall, one I'd been in many times before, but that night I marveled at the extraordinarily high, engraved ceilings anew. The white marble floors were surpassed in beauty only by the women, who were exquisitely appointed and paired with clean-cut, tuxedoed partners. Their conversations converged into a symphony of anticipation and excitement. At seemingly every turn, there was a stranger greeting me with a warm smile, a "Hello, how are you?" or a "So nice to meet you!" This party had all the pomp and circumstance one would expect to find at a haute Washington soiree without the gaping void of personality and substance that typically spoils Washington gatherings.

Within minutes, Uncle Malcolm had introduced me to two chief executives, twice that number of general counsels, and still more vice presidents. After catching up with a young lady with whom I'd attended elementary school, I turned around and found a group of men I didn't know descending on Uncle Malcolm and Ron like a swarm of bees. Before I could protest, one of them thrust a camera into my hands—yes, an actual camera. "Hey, you mind?" he said. "We're fraternity brothers from back in the day."

"*Way* back in the day!" Uncle Malcolm quipped, to much laughter from his Omega brothers. Each of them contorted their arms into the appropriate character of the Greek alphabet. Their eyes revealed a world in which time had temporarily reversed and an empty hope that if they left the building and came back in, just maybe a frat party with all their Delta sweethearts might welcome them.

Not yet freed from my temporary service to the nation of Omega, I snapped a second picture with the boys—this time with their wives. The men mustered wide, vapid smiles for this final shot. Then I quickly scanned the room. Unfortunately for me, there were only a handful of twentysomethings present, and only a handful of those were eligible members of the fairer sex. I resigned myself to an unremarkable evening of social drinking and networking.

When he was done reminiscing with the boys, my uncle introduced me to his good friend, Brenda Jazmin, the newly minted general counsel of a prestigious Fortune 500. Now this was the kind of woman you wanted in the boardroom—late forties and still a total knockout. She wore a black, form-hugging evening gown—I know it was Oscar de la Renta because she told me—and her ears sagged under the weight of ridiculously large diamond earrings. Her left ring finger bore the indention of a wedding band.

Uncle Malcolm and Ron hugged her with the kind of restrained excitement a married man is expected to display when greeting the female acquaintances of his primeval past. It's as if right before two people marry they sit down separately, review the annals of their past sexual lives, and redact all the details the rules of marriage require them to pretend to forget.

"Brenda Jazmin, meet my nephew, Al Carpenter. He's about to become one of your fellow IILS alums and is starting at Sullivan & Katz in the fall."

"Pleasure to meet you, Ms. Jazmin," I said.

"Mr. Carpenter . . . if I hear you say '*Ms.* Jazmin' again, I'll take offense—unless we make acquaintance again along with my mother."

"Understood," I said, smiling. "You'll find you only have to tell me once."

"I like that in a man," she said, cocking her head sideways. Then she lowered her voice slightly. "If you were twenty years older, I might have married you and suffered through three divorces instead of two."

I continued to smile politely. *God is good.* The older I get, the more I appreciate meeting women like this. They've been through so much drama and heartache that they draw cathartic relief from putting their most sensitive personal business on Front Street. Younger women still battling the pain of soured relationships often exude far less confidence and, consequently, can be far stingier with personal details.

"If I were a little older I'd run off with you tonight," I said, eager to see just how far she might run with it.

The two women flanking Brenda had turned away as my uncle introduced me to Brenda. "And who might you be, young man?" one of them asked.

"If I were twenty years older, this woman's husband," I said, now gazing at Brenda. "But I assume that's not the information you're after. My apologies. My name is Al Carpenter, and that's my uncle Malcolm.

"Malcolm's your uncle?" she asked.

"That's what my aunt Kelly keeps telling me."

"Charmed," she said.

I wanted to ask her if she would kindly lose herself. But instead I said, "The pleasure is all mine, of course."

The second of the initially uninterested women now looked unblinkingly at Ron while he did his best to distract his wife in conversation. Grinning slightly, Casey positioned the tip of her right forefinger between her partially opened rouge lips.

"Well, black people—how about a drink?" Brenda said, eyeing the members of the circle that had formed roughly around her.

"Yes, let's," Casey said, stepping toward Brenda and leaving the predator to its prey. "Brenda, right? My name's Casey. I'm Ron's wife."

"Oh yes, Casey!" Brenda boomed, fixing her face to match the hubbub in her voice. "I've heard so much about you over the years, Casey. It's so nice to *finally* meet you." I smiled and laughed out loud despite my best effort at keeping my amusement to myself. *Life is funny*, I thought. No matter how successful or wealthy people become, no matter how old they grow, they remain essentially driven by the same needs and moved by the same concerns: money, power, and sex, but rarely in that order.

"What's so funny, nephew?" Uncle Malcolm whispered.

I leaned in. "It's funny how little things change between men and women, even as they grow older and more financially stable."

He turned back to Brenda and the others. "We'll catch up with you guys at the bar," he said, nudging me away from the group toward a bar on the opposite side of the room. "Keen observation," he said. "You'll just get better and better at ignoring the things that, if you paid too much attention to them, would screw you."

"I don't think I'll ever get there."

"I know the feeling," he said. "But the time will come when you'll be able to do it with some ease, mostly because you'll start tuning certain things and people out. Soon you'll only see the portions of people you can view with safety."

"That sounds horrible."

"If you find yourself enjoying it, you're doing something wrong."

"So the goal, if I hear you correctly, is to avoid fun."

"Correct," he said. "You'll still have golf, the occasional night out with the boys—and I use the term *occasional* in the 'good luck finding an oasis in the middle of the desert' sense of the word."

"And this is for the rest of my life?"

"Until the bitter end."

"And what if I don't acquire that skill?"

"You will."

"But what if I don't?"

He looked deeply into my eyes after ordering two scotches. Then he took a sip while sliding a second glass of the peaty, brown liquid toward me. "Then God save you," he said, without a drop of humor. "But dammit—enjoy the ride before you get there. That's an order."

"Yes, sir," I said, saluting smartly. "One more thing."

"What's that?" he said.

"Why do men get married?"

"It's a rite of passage, like First Communion. When it's time, you do it."

"And is that why you got married?"

"Yes . . . and no."

"I've always assumed that women get married when they find 'the one,' and men marry when it's time. But the older I get, the more confused I am about when exactly that time is."

"I think your assumptions are dead on. As for the time piece, the best I can tell you is that one day, you'll find yourself going through the motions of bachelorhood, and you'll ask yourself, 'What the hell am I doing?' When you have your 'What the hell am I doing?' moment, you'll know, and that's when it's time to choose."

"Interesting," I said. "Not exactly how it plays out in the movies."

"Not at all."

"So why do so many women believe in all that Hollywood *When Harry Met Sally* foolishness?"

"Two reasons," he said. "First, because we raise them to believe in it. Second, because women are almost completely delusional."

"Completely delusional," I said. "Yeah, I'm seeing signs of that already."

"One important caveat to add, though."

"What's that?"

"They're only delusional because men make them that way. If we stopped doing crazy shit, they'd probably be in a much better place. How about we go back and check on your aunt and mother?"

We pushed off from the bar and back toward the other side of that colossal hall. "You barely touched your drink," I said.

"You're right. And that brings me to tonight's final lesson on this matter."

"What's that?" I asked.

He took his second—and last—sip of scotch before placing the glass on a tray carried by one of the passing wait staff. Oh, how his eyes twinkled. "Marriage is not the cure to promiscuity, but alcohol surely is the gateway to adultery."

I laughed. He wrapped his arm around my shoulder as we walked. "It's a cold world out there, son," he continued. "At some point, when you finally settle down, you'll have to ask yourself one question just about every day of your married life: Is it more important to be right—or to be happy? And if you haven't already, you'll soon find it's all a game. A game not of checkers, but of chess."

I turned his words over in my head for a few seconds. "Did you read *Candide* in high school?" I asked.

"I believe so."

"Remember Dr. Pangloss and his ridiculous optimism?"

He smiled into the crowd ahead while swiping his nose with his thumb. "'We live in the best of all possible worlds!'" he said.

"That's it. I'm beginning to feel like Candide."

"Yes—life does breed disillusionment. You can't avoid it. I'm sure you also read *Hamlet*?"

"I did."

"You know my favorite quote?" he said.

"Which one?"

"'Get thee to a nunnery: why wouldst thou be a breeder of sinners?'"

"Love that quote," I said. "But over time, when I consider the strong likelihood that my sins against women will likely be punished with a litter of adolescent-male bait, the more I identify with what follows that quote." I looked up and found myself back in the company of Brenda and the rest.

"Well, go ahead," Uncle Malcolm stammered. "You were about to recite a quote from Mr. Shakespeare."

Trusting in his judgment and social IQ, I stepped into the abyss. "'I am myself indifferent honest; but yet I could accuse me of such things that it were better my mother had not borne me: I am very proud, revengeful, ambitious, with more offences at my beck than I have thoughts to put them in, imagination to give them shape, or time to act them in. What should such fellows as I do crawling between earth and heaven? We are arrant knaves, all; believe none of us. Go thy ways to a nunnery.'"

Brenda started the applause, and it spread with the contagion of a late-night yawn. "There's no better education than the one you get by living life," Uncle Malcolm announced.

Brenda winked at Uncle Malcolm before turning back to me. "You'll find that's the hardest one to finish," she offered. "Makes law school look like a walk in the park."

This tony group of African-American emperors and empresses returned to their several conversations as I sought to privately conclude my discussion with Uncle Malcolm. "Humans spend most of their lives chasing something that's impossible to attain," I said.

"We have the necessary mental equipment, but we lack the physical capacity. It's like flying."

He tapped me twice on my back. "Mercifully, it all ends sooner or later," he said.

I noticed Ron just off to our left. The mixture of relief and fatigue on his face indicated that Casey had completely squelched the earlier manhunt. His countenance was reminiscent of that night during freshman year in college when, after thirty minutes of self-coaxing, I successfully pulled the trigger and freed myself of the four shots of Bacardi 151 I'd consumed over a one-hour period, completely ignorant of what "151" meant.

Meanwhile, Brenda was once again revving her engine. "Where'd you boys wander off to?" she said, handing Uncle Malcolm a scotch while casually cupping her body into his. Then she looked up and into his eyes. "Where on earth could you find better company?"

Uncle Malcolm took a step to his right before downing the entire drink in four seconds flat. "That's the trouble with women these days," he said, immediately commanding the eyes of everyone within earshot. "You give them an inch, and they take—"

"Liberated man!" Casey interrupted. "It's a wonder we ever got the vote—and he's one of the good ones!" The circle exhaled in amusement as Brenda brought her eyes back to Uncle Malcolm's.

"It seems I forgot to impart one last lesson onto my nephew." The crowd again waited with bated breath. "Never volunteer information," he said. "We men aren't smart enough to successfully lie our way out of the trouble we'll inevitably get ourselves into." A sonic boom of laughter ricocheted off the walls, and it seemed the entire hall narrowed its gaze toward this coterie of thirty or so folks in the corner. Uncle Malcolm leaned in. "That wasn't funny," he whispered. "What's wrong with these people?"

A woman almost twenty feet away noticed our group. After squinting for a moment, she turned to a gray-bearded man standing next to her and loudly whispered, "Harry, who is that? He looks familiar." The marble floors had betrayed her anonymity.

"Looks like Malcolm St. John, out of Atlanta," he replied. The man raised his arm and began waving at Uncle Malcolm. "You oughtta run in 2016, Malcolm," he shouted.

"I don't think so Harry," Uncle Malcolm replied, chuckling. "I'm just an ordinary businessman. I'll leave that racket to you lawyers."

Aunt Kelly, now standing next to her husband, looked at him, tapped his abdomen once, and said, "Good answer."

I turned away and looked out across the sea of brown faces. This was a proud people, tempest tossed, but still standing. About a half hour after our arrival, a handsome, very presidential-looking Barack Obama glided across the stage, accompanied by his beautiful wife. His cool, casual gate gushed of the level-headedness about which folks in his inner circle so often opined. But she seemed just a touch cooler.

I guess I could never fully appreciate what this moment meant to the elder black folks in that hall as I hadn't lived through the nightmares this celebration surely conjured in their hearts and minds.

Then I saw my fourteen-year-old iteration standing on the rooftop patio of a prominent law firm on an icy January afternoon in 1997. He watched carefully as William Jefferson Clinton strode across the intersection of Fifteenth Street and Pennsylvania Avenue. That boy stood engrossed in Clinton's disarming smile. Almost two years later in November 1998, he was standing before a podium at the Hilton. He addressed the Washington press corps and their blinding, red-hot lights just moments after his boss, Anthony A. Williams, was elected Washington, DC's fifth mayor. "I'd like to thank you all for making me the youngest mayor in American history," I said. The crowd laughed for a good twenty seconds. "Change has come to our city this evening," I continued, "and a new day full of hope and promise."

Awestruck, I watched the Obamas dance to "Sign, Sealed, Delivered." Ron and Casey, standing a few feet away, turned toward each other. He held her hand tightly and kissed her forehead before whispering in her ear. Casey smiled as she looked into his eyes for several long moments. When she finally closed them, a single tear came streaming down her cheek.

Then a loud voice reverberated throughout the hall: "Ladies and gentlemen, the president and first lady of the United States of America." How sweet it was to hear those words in reference to that man and that woman. In that crevice of time, I was content merely to stand among all those black folks, bearing witness to that mellifluous, impossible-sounding dream come true.

CHAPTER FIVE

SATURDAY, AUGUST 22, 2009

NINTH STREET WAS ABSOLUTELY PACKED that night, so I drove in circles for a while before locating a parking space on a side street three blocks away from the bar where we'd planned to meet. Though I'd been to Durham several times before that night, those trips were now beyond my mind's reach—with two exceptions. I'd come four years earlier in 2005 to visit a girlfriend from back home who was a sophomore at Duke University at the time, but I didn't leave campus during that visit. Before that, during the summer before my junior year of high school, I spent three weeks at Duke's Fuqua School of Business participating in a program for academically promising, racially diverse students handpicked from around the country. I can't say I remember much from those three weeks beyond some of the details of my nonacademic pursuits and the ubiquitous news coverage of John F. Kennedy Jr.'s tragic death during the program's final week.

This was my first time in Durham as a bona fide, bill-paying adult. It was also my first time hanging out on Ninth Street, the only bar district in the Trinity Heights section of Durham where Bristol grew up. A purely cosmetic assessment of the establishments lining this recently reasphalted, two-lane drag revealed a clash of the quaint and the urban, and the burgeoning tension between the neighborhood's not-so-distant provincial past and the cresting tidal wave of bustling, forward-thinking youths and their insatiable hunger for the trappings of modernity. I'd been instructed to meet her at a bar near the northern end of this odd little strip.

After parking, I phoned to see if she'd already arrived and to get the name of the bar again.

"Hey, are you there?" I asked.

"Yeah, I just pulled up," Bristol said. "I'm parked right in front of the bar." Her voice carried a twang I'd only previously heard during the two or three days after her return to Cambridge from Thanksgiving and Christmas breaks.

"Great," I said. "I just parked, and I'm walking down Ninth Street now."

"Where? I don't see you."

"I'm wearing a reddish-orange T-shirt and blue sneakers."

"How was your drive from Rock City?" she asked.

"Much shorter than I remember it being," I said. "Before I left, my grandmother asked about a thousand questions . . . 'Where are you going? Who are you meeting?'"

"Ah—perpetual childhood," Bristol said, her voice pregnant with reminiscence. "I think our families may be cut from a similar cloth."

"An anal-retentive obsession with the whereabouts of relatives—children and adults alike—strikes me as a trait endemic to black families, especially in the South."

"I see you now," she said. Soon after pressing the End button on my late-model silver BlackBerry, I spotted her some thirty feet away. I hadn't seen Bristol since graduation in June, and we hadn't spent this much time apart since I first laid eyes on her in September 2006. And then she came into focus ahead of me on the sidewalk. Bristol Davis was five feet six inches tall. She had ebullient green eyes; an unforgettably smooth, almond-brown complexion; curly chestnut-brown hair, and a smile to end all female smiling. My stomach was twisted into a million knots, and my heart pounded comfortably beneath my rib cage to the rhythm of her choosing. *What's wrong with me?*

"Bristol Davis, right?" I stopped dramatically a few feet in front of her to take in the grand view. I studied her carefully, snapping a thousand photographs in my mind with the adolescently foolish hope that I'd never forget a single detail of this, our not-so-first encounter.

"In the flesh," she said. I accepted her outstretched arms with what I believed was a cool eagerness. She ran her hand through my hair while looking up at me. "Letting that curly hair of yours grow out again, I see."

"More laziness than anything," I said. "I kinda let myself go this summer while studying for the bar."

"Please—don't remind me of that craziness."

Her scent was new yet insanely familiar. Seconds later, I found myself still embracing her amid the inviting rays of the cascading sun and the unseasonable breeze of that late-August evening.

"You know, people will think we're in love," I said.

"I really don't care what people think," she said. "You know that Al. I do what I want." The hug ended but our eyes remained locked for several more moments, each one a little sweeter than the one before.

I turned around to investigate the building behind us in a thinly veiled effort to gather myself at least a little. "Is this the place?" I asked. The exterior was fairly unexceptional and in desperate need of a few fresh coats of paint.

She sighed. "This is it. We don't have to stay here, but I figured it would be a decent place to start."

As soon as we entered the bar, Bristol was recognized by three women sitting near the entrance. They eyed her with the combination of exuberance and failed surreptitiousness one would expect from a group of sweet sixteens walking past a minor pop star.

"Oh damn," she whispered. "It's my best friend's arch nemesis from high school."

"Hey there Bristol!" said one of the teenyboppers.

"Hey Monica—ladies—how are you?" Bristol said, flashing that murderous smile again.

Monica turned toward me. "Doing well, and sooooo freakin' happy the week's over," she said, her vapid smile easily overpowered by her inquisitive, crow-footed eyes. "But *who* do we have *here*?" I quickly surmised that this jejune young woman must have been their high school's resident Joan Rivers.

"This is my good friend from law school, Al Carpenter."

"Good evening, ladies," I said with a warm smile and a rainbow wave.

"Hello," the three said in near unison.

"Well just in case we don't run into you later, you guys have a great night!" Bristol said, furtively nudging me away from the table. We both waved our good-byes before commencing evasive maneuvers through the dense crowd and toward the bar.

"Friends of yours?" I asked, smirking.

"Hardly."

"You sure put on a great performance."

Bristol flashed that smile once more. "My mother always told me, 'you get more bees with honey than with vinegar.'"

"Here I am trying to avoid bees all my life, and you're actively trying to attract them," I said. "Maybe that's what I've been doing wrong."

"Al, it's a figure of speech."

"You don't say?" I replied. "I've always attracted women possessed of that most dangerous characteristic of the bee."

"Al, you keep getting stung because you can't settle on just one. You need to calm down with all that." Bristol pulled out two stools from a prime location near the middle of the bar.

"I'm not so good at the whole monogamy thing," I said.

She gasped. "You don't say?"

A grinning bartender galloped toward us. "Do my eyes deceive me, or has the great Bristol Davis come home?" he said.

"I don't know about great, Bobby, but yes, I'm home—for now."

"Welcome home, kid," Bobby said, hugging Bristol over the bar top. "Hope you stay awhile."

"Thanks, Bobby. Bobby, meet Al, a close friend from law school."

"Great to meet you, Bobby."

He smiled broadly while shaking my hand. "Same here, pal." He placed two square, unusually thick paper coasters on the wooden bar top.

I turned to Bristol. "What'll it be?"

"Whatever," she said. "You choose."

"Alright," I said. "Bobby, can we get two bourbons with a splash of ginger, please?"

Bobby raised his eyebrows. "I think this is the first time I've poured her something other than a prosecco or champagne."

I shook my head. "Who are you, and what have you done with Bristol Davis?" I said.

"Al, I don't know what you're talking about." She began staring into my eyes again. I had that familiar, almost spiritual sensation that accompanies meeting an attractive woman with whom there's an instant connection. There's an almost erotic feeling of newness and infinite possibility unique to moments like those. I wanted to press the fast-forward button, but I also wanted to take the time to get to know her this time around and uncover—in due course, moment by moment—all the things that made her tick. And looking back now, I think I actually wanted her to know me too.

We made short work of the first round. As I returned from the restroom, the second was being delivered. "Thirsty?" I asked.

"Stop it," she said. "I just wanted a fresh drink to be waiting for you when you got back." *Who is this woman?*

I figured I'd get the run-of-the-mill first-date questions out of the way as expeditiously as we'd dispensed with that first round of bourbon. I decided to open with the question single women universally love to be asked. "Why don't you have a boyfriend, Bristol?"

She placed her elbow on the bar and slid her chin into her palm. "I thought I'd go to law school and find a sea of eligible men . . . maybe even graduate with a new last name."

"So what happened?"

"Maybe there's something in the water up there in Boston, but you Northern men are on something else entirely. Dating men down here during high school and after college did nothing to prepare me for your kind."

"My kind?" I said. "What in the world does—you know what, let's not even discuss it."

"From time to time in law school, you mentioned a girlfriend you had before we got to Harvard. What happened there?"

"She was great," I said. "And ready to get super serious. I just wasn't there yet."

She raised her brow. "What do you mean by 'super serious'?"

"She started asking all the wrong questions," I said. "You know, like, 'So, what neighborhood will we live in?' and 'When should I start looking for a job in New York?' There's no coming back from questions like those if a guy isn't ready to move forward. That's why I give all my female friends in so-called serious relationships the same advice."

"And what, dare I ask, might that be?" she asked.

"Before you jump off the Brooklyn Bridge, you really ought to give the bungee cable the ol' once-over."

"Must you always speak in metaphors?" she said, smirking and shaking her head. I shrugged.

"So you broke up with her?" she continued.

"Yes. I've been technically single since we started law school."

Bristol turned her gaze down into her glass. "'Technically single,'" she said. "Gotta love your species. When you guys are trying to get a girl, you'll throw everything at her but the kitchen sink. But when it comes time to talk relationships, you all turn into lawyers."

I grinned. "What can I say? We're the best."

"And the worst. So why is that?"

"Why is what?"

"Why have you been 'technically single' since we started law school?"

"You know—I just got tired of cheating on girlfriends," I admitted. "I think I just decided at some point that it was no longer socially acceptable behavior. When a male's twenty-one, I think society can deal with it and is pretty much expected to kind of just avert its collective eye away from his dalliances. At twenty-seven, though, what was, 'Oh, he's just getting it out of his system' becomes, 'He's a bad guy.'"

"Think you're ready for a serious relationship now?"

"I want to be. I think if the right woman came along, I'd get there."

She turned her eyes back down to her drink. "So . . . ah . . . what did you want to talk about?" she said. "What's the big emergency?"

"I have a proposition for you," I said, straightening on my stool.

She began shaking her head vigorously. "Nope. See, that's my cue to leave. I know that look, Al. That look convinced me to take an accounting class with you two years ago. No sir. Fool me once—"

"Seriously, Bristol."

"I'm *being* serious, black man."

"I promise this idea is much better than that accounting thing."

She snickered. "That's your argument for why I should listen to whatever's percolating in that head of yours? Please."

"Bristol!"

"Okay, okay. I'll listen, but that's it."

I let out a deep breath. "What are your thoughts on joining Ron's campaign?"

She gave me her patented side-eye before releasing a deep breath of her own. "Al . . . you know I love you, and I'm all about progress in race and politics, and any friend of yours is a friend of mine—but hell no."

"Won't you at least think—"

"Al . . . no. He cannot win."

"I can't believe I'm hearing this from you," I said. "Bristol Davis, right? The same woman who told me some guy named Barack Hussein Obama was going to be president before I even knew who the guy was."

"Al, you just spent some summers in North Carolina. I grew up here. Politics is different down here. This race thing is a different beast once you cross into Dixie. Some of the things I heard come out of folks' mouths when I came down to knock doors on election night . . . just a few blocks away from here, a middle-aged white woman opened the door. Before I could even say 'hello,' she said, 'Don't worry, I'm votin' for the nigra' and slammed the door in my face. No sir, he can't do it, Al. I respect you for coming down here to fight the good fight, but I can't join you."

"You know, I told Ron you'd say that."

"Say what?"

"Yep. I told him I thought you might be jaded by what's happened since Obama's election . . . Obama's racist detractors and—"

"That's not true!"

"Isn't it?"

"He's not Barack Obama. He's Ron Johnson. And I'm not jaded. I just know that Obama's victory in North Carolina wasn't exactly a bellwether for postracialism."

I reached into my pocket to retrieve my money clip, pulled two Jacksons out, and placed them on the bar top.

"Oh, so you're walking out because I won't join? What does he want me to do, anyway?"

I turned back toward her, grinning. "Press secretary." The half-second twinkle in her eye was unmistakable. "Thought you might have an interest in putting that master's degree in journalism to use."

She sighed. "I'd be working under you, wouldn't I?"

"A minor detail."

"That's not sweetening the deal, let me tell you," she said, cracking a half smile.

"Look," I said. "I know from many conversations with you, and from your actions last year, that you care about what we do with this opportunity in this cycle. I think we should both take some concrete action to keep things moving forward. Joining Ron's camp doesn't necessarily have to be that concrete action for you. But—"

"I'll do it," she said, staring into the rows of liquor behind the bar.

"What?"

"I said I'll do it." Her eyes widened as she turned to look at me. "Aston & Wheeler deferred my start date for a year, so I've been looking for jobs anyway. This is an exciting opportunity . . . but I've got a few conditions."

I snickered. "Here comes the drama. Now that's the Bristol I know!"

"Al, I'm serious."

"Okay. Let's hear it."

"We cannot let our personal relationship—wherever that's headed—interfere with work. And our friendship has to survive all this."

"Done. What else?"

"You may be the boss on the job, but don't forget who's the boss at the end of the workday."

"You drive a hard bargain, Ms. Davis. I didn't expect anything less." I cleared my throat. "But I should warn you—the pay isn't great."

"Al, I'm not new to politics. This'll be my third campaign. I know how the money flows."

"I'm just saying."

A smile crept forth. "So when do I start?"

"Does Monday morning work?"

"Okay. I need to make a hair appointment for tomorrow, get my nails done today—sorry to cut this short, but I need to leave right now if I'm gonna be ready by then." She slid the two twenty-dollar bills toward me with her index finger. "And I've got the check."

"I asked for the meeting," I said. "It's on me."

"Meeting, huh?"

As the concluding bars of Glenn Lewis's "Don't You Forget It" registered with my brain, I suddenly realized that nearly every song played since we'd arrived was a classic R&B or neo-soul track from our preteen and teenage years. "It's a shame no one's here," I said. "The music is fire!"

"What do you mean no one is here?" she said, scrunching her brow. "This place is packed!"

"I mean no one who really appreciates this music—who appreciates what's happening here."

"Life is like that, isn't it? You rarely get to see all the elements come together at once."

"And on the rare occasions when you are so lucky, it all gets blasted to pieces."

"Wait a minute!" she exclaimed. "Are they playing Erykah? No they didn't just play 'Green Eyes'!" Bristol joined Queen Badu just in time for the second refrain of those indelible opening lyrics.

"Well how about that," I said. "They're playing 'Green Eyes' for you, Green Eyes."

"Only difference is my eyes aren't green with envy," she shot back.

"Perhaps not right now, but I'm sure at some point in the last, oh, say ten years, your eyes turned green with envy for some ex-boyfriend's new friend."

"Yeah, and I'll bet that somewhere in Cambridge, Boston, New York, and the District of Columbia, there are at least a handful of women whose eyes would instantly turn green if they knew you had eyes for these eyes."

"So, based on my knowledge of this song—and I know it well—you're saying there are at least a handful of women *in love* with me at this very moment."

"Correct," she replied resolutely, turning her eyes sharply away from mine.

"Let me ask you something," I said. "Something I've never asked anyone else."

"Shoot," she said.

"What are your thoughts on the last movement of this song?" I asked.

She closed her eyes and released a deep breath. "My God—the way that piano comes in is chilling," she said. "Alone and staggering but determined to carry out its mission. And then come those lush horns with that rich bass—they cradle those inconsolable piano chords."

Then she reopened her eyes.

"The way I see it, those chords represent a woman walking toward a cliff, and just as she's about to jump, here come the horns and bass. They gently snatch her up and say, 'It's not your time. You've got everything to live for. You just can't see past the pain right now.' It's one of the most heartbreakingly beautiful five minutes of music I've ever heard—and such agonizingly real lyrics. I mean, she's already in the throes of depression because he's asked her to leave, and in the middle of that emptiness, she realizes she's too deep in love to leave."

"So you don't think she leaves him?" I said.

"Well, we don't know for sure. But I think the last two lines suggest she doesn't."

"Even though she acknowledges that things between them can never be the same?"

"That's the thing about love," she said. "True love, at least."

"What's that?"

"You don't make the decision to stay or leave because of some cost-benefit analysis," she said. "Sometimes, no matter how much someone has hurt you, you just stay."

"In the hope that things will turn out alright in the end?"

"Not really," she said. "I mean, of course you hope things will work out, but that hope isn't the thing that makes you stay."

"Then why?"

"Because your life depends on it," she said, looking up and into my eyes. "Because he's become a part of your soul." Before I knew it, she was halfway to the door. I raced to catch up with her.

"So—where are you off to?" I asked, holding the door as we walked out. Outside the street was consumed by darkness. We stood facing each other in the middle of the sidewalk. The slight breeze seemed to swirl around us rather than between us, an impenetrable nexus that resisted intrusion from the outside world. There we stood alone in the universe—the untouchables—at once protected and incapacitated by some previously unfelt feeling that must have been unknowable to all others.

She placed her hands on my shoulders, rose to her toes, and kissed my cheek softly. "I'll see you Monday," she said. "Send me the details. I mean paperwork—whatever."

"Of course."

"One more thing," she said, looking down and swiping at her skintight light-blue jeans.

"What?"

"I don't know what's happening . . . I mean, what could be happening here. But I just ask that if we do get involved, and later on you decide you want to go another direction, please tell me before you move on."

"Of course."

"Al, I'm serious. I can't take any more heartbreak—and I know you."

"Bristol Davis—I promise to take good care of it."

She searched my eyes carefully. "I trust you," she said, gently palming my cheek. "I'm not exactly sure why, but I do."

"I won't let you down."

She turned abruptly and began walking up Ninth Street. "You and I are going to win this thing," she said without turning back.

"We can't lose." I pulled out my phone and texted Ron: *Bristol's in.*

CHAPTER SIX

I OFFICIALLY BEGAN my tenure on the Ron Johnson campaign in Durham on August 24, just two days after convincing Bristol to join the team. In an unofficial capacity, I'd been by the office several times already and spent a handful of hours talking shop with Ron and Carmichael. After Bristol and I had settled into our first-floor offices—the campaign was temporarily renting a newly refurbished two-story white house near downtown Durham on the cheap—Ron, Carmichael, Bristol, and I gathered in Ron's second-floor office. It was 9:18 a.m.

With his legs crossed and propped up on a beautiful Southern live oak desk, Ron smiled brilliantly as he gazed at his numerically slight campaign staff. "Carmichael," Ron said, "I'd like you to meet our secret weapon in this campaign, Bristol Davis. I can't say I've come across a person more resourceful than Bristol in my entire lifetime. At least, that's what I'm led to believe based on Al's recommendation. Apologies, Al, but sounds like she may have you beat by a hair." Ron snickered.

"None necessary," I said. "The truth is the truth. She's also pretty persuasive. Bristol and her team won two moot court competitions back in law school. Be careful around her, both of you. In the blink of an eye, she can convince an orthodox Jew that Christmas is one of the High Holidays." We all laughed, including Bristol.

"But seriously," I said, "on a lean campaign like ours, we need as many brilliant, charismatic women as possible. Fortunately, we have two. And let me tell you, the two of them are worth at least ten of

Jane's staffers."

"Thanks, Al," Bristol said. "Ron, I'm dying to meet Casey. Is she coming in today?"

"She should be in shortly," Ron said, sitting up. "She had to drop the kids off at school. Bristol, I know I hired you to serve as press secretary, but I think we'd be doing you and this campaign a great disservice if we didn't get you out on the campaign trail too."

"I'm willing to help however I can," she said.

"Ms. Davis, I'm sure you're every bit the talent they say you are," Carmichael said, "but honestly, I'm just happy to have one more person around to dilute the foolishness constantly spewing from Carpenter's trap. Great to have you on." Carmichael gently collected Bristol's right hand and kissed it.

Bristol covered her mouth with her free hand. "It's a pleasure to meet you, Carmichael," she said. "And please, call me Bristol. Al, hope you're taking notes. This is how a Southern gentleman conducts himself." Ron winked in my direction.

Carmichael was a junior staffer hired to handle a variety of tasks, from political outreach to management of day-to-day administrative matters and, on occasion, collecting lunch orders. He also served as Ron's driver, a task he executed largely without complaint despite his degree in history from the University of North Carolina at Chapel Hill. He was a lanky, six-foot-six, twenty-four-year-old white kid from Raleigh with a surprising facility for engaging black folks—especially black women. A week after meeting Carmichael, the two of us hit a downtown Durham pub after I stopped by the office for a quick chat with Ron. Carmichael ordered the first round, promptly pushed back from the bar, and walked to the other side where three beautiful black women were sipping pink cocktails. He brought them back within forty-five seconds. After he'd introduced them to me, I leaned toward him and said, "What in hell did you say to them?" He grinned, placed his hand on my shoulder, and said, "Game recognize game."

At twelve thirty, Ron and I left for lunch. Carmichael had departed just ten minutes earlier for a doctor's appointment. Though we encouraged the ladies to join us, Casey had insisted that she and Bristol have lunch together in Raleigh without us. The dynamic duo had spent much of the morning discussing the Carolina Panthers' prospects for the upcoming season. As they left, Casey said she thought Ron and I, both ardent Redskins fans, might quickly run thin on patience during a long lunch.

*****

"We've got to make sure the progressives are with us," Ron said as we followed the hostess to our table at a popular new Durham restaurant called Mezcal. The clanking of dishes and silverware and the raucous chorus of voices was almost deafening. "That was key to Obama's election."

"Progressives *are* critical," I said, "but having them won't mean a damned thing if we don't get blacks to the polls."

"Right, right, right—if we can mobilize a supermajority of blacks, all the rest becomes somewhat academic—at least for the primary."

"We can pull that off," I said. "I mean, it won't be easy, but it's doable."

"Don't underestimate Jane Woodall's support in the black community," Ron said. "We'll have to hustle for those votes. If we can't convince them I'm viable, and quickly, they won't even think about voting for me. That's why we have to make sure we're making solid inroads with progressives."

"We don't have the manpower or time to go after both groups aggressively. I think the strategy should be to *appear* equally focused on both while spending most of our resources on black votes. If we can snag an endorsement from a major progressive organization, who knows? Others just might fall right in line. That kind of endorsement could also move individual white progressives. Before long, the illusion of a groundswell becomes real."

"I like that a lot," he said, grinning. "The 'fake it 'til you make it' approach to insurgent politics."

"And with your corporate law background," I continued, "you already have strong connections with a decent number of folks in clean tech and biotech. Now you've just gotta take off your lawyer's hat and turn on the charm."

"Speaking of which," Ron said, "there's a new start-up out of Raleigh that's working on wind and solar technology. They're called NCSEP—North Carolina Sustainable Energy Partners. I met their CEO—young guy named Jim Randolph—during a clean tech convention I attended with a client a few months back in San Fran. Supersmart guy; seems to have a better head for politics than most career electeds I know. Anyway, this company's counting on pending federal legislation that, if it goes into effect, will require traditional energy concerns to substantially reduce their carbon footprint over time. It's called the American Clean Energy and Environmental Protection Act of 2009, but everyone just calls it the carbon bill."

"I've heard of it—imposes a system of cap and trade," I said. "But didn't that legislation already go into effect?"

"Obama already signed it into law, but the caps it imposes on carbon emissions phase in over time. The first caps phase in on July first, 2011. NCSEP and other clean tech companies are worried that Republicans could gain enough seats in the Senate next November to kill the law before it takes effect, so they're desperate for Democrats to reach a filibuster-proof majority this cycle."

"What about the House?" I asked.

"They're convinced the GOP will easily reclaim a significant majority in the House this cycle," he replied.

"I don't follow," I began. "The only way to kill a prior act of Congress—without the courts, at least—is for Congress to pass another piece of legislation that the president signs into law or that two-thirds of Congress pass over the president's veto."

"That's true."

"The GOP won't gain a two-thirds majority in both the Senate and House this cycle," I asserted.

"Probably not," he replied, clearly amused by my failure to locate the loophole he had in mind. "Go ahead and toss your thinking cap on for this one, Carp. I mentioned the filibuster for a reason."

"Aha!" I said. "Republicans in the Senate could use the filibuster to keep other items on the president's agenda from ever going to a vote, and they can leverage that power to force Obama into signing a bill that eviscerates the carbon bill."

"Right—or one that waters it down to a point where it has no real teeth," Ron added. "They've got an uphill battle in front of them, and not just because of resistance they're expecting from the GOP. Many Democrats—including Jane and Bill—won't go anywhere near NCSEP because so many voters think the carbon bill will increase their already sky-high energy costs. I see this as an opportunity for us. We'll make the argument that in the long run, consumers will actually incur greater costs if we don't take action now to reduce our carbon footprint through sustainable, clean energy alternatives."

"Great angle," I said. "Burning the ozone layer today will lead to increased taxes for consumers over time. Federal, state, and local governments will have to spend billions to counteract the environmental damage carbon is causing—not to mention the human costs associated with increased natural disasters."

"It's just patently unfair to kick the can down the road and burden future generations when we can do something right now." Ron leaned forward. "As your first official campaign assignment, I want you to call Jim when we get back to the office. Let's get on his calendar ASAP.

I should warn you: Even though they need us as much, if not more, than we need them, getting a meeting might be tough. I think Jim still believes he can convince Jane or Bill to get on board with the carbon bill, so you'll have to be creative. If you get him on the phone, give him the hard sell immediately. Tell him that if they endorse, we'll give prominence to clean tech and alternative energy on the stump and on our website. And let him know that when I'm elected, I'll not only vote against any attempts to kill the carbon bill, I'll also be a dependable champion of NCSEP, clean tech, and alternative energy."

"Sounds like a plan," I said. "But there's one minor problem."

"What's that?"

"We're still polling pretty far behind Jane," I said. "Hell, we're behind Bill, and he hasn't even officially declared his candidacy. And it's only August. Jim won't be in any rush to endorse us. He'll at least wait to see if Bill gets in."

"Neither Jane or Bill is going to ally with NCSEP."

"I get that, but why would NCSEP endorse a candidate that's polling so far behind? Why wouldn't they just wait and see if we make progress over the next few months?"

Ron smiled. "Good questions all," he said. "But you're missing the point. "We need them *now*, so you have to come up with an argument that sells them on why they need us now too."

"That's a *really* tall order, Ron. I don't even think LBJ could've pulled off something like this—at least not legally."

"That's why I have you," Ron said. "You'll get Jim on the phone and make the best argument you can for why they absolutely have to endorse us right now. Reach through the phone and smack him if you have to."

I let out a deep breath. "Alright."

"Think about all they stand to gain from endorsing us," Ron began. "You don't think they'd benefit from having a candidate for statewide office traveling around, county to county, making an impassioned case for clean tech and referring to them by name? It's free publicity. And they've got bills. If this legislation doesn't stand, they're finished."

"That *is* pretty compelling," I admitted.

"Once we get these guys on board, other progressives will follow. The bottom line is we need NCSEP. Now let's go get them."

"Understood."

"But to be clear, our primary focus is making sure that when the votes are all counted, we walk away with a supermajority of black votes. So you, Carmichael, Bristol—and the rest of our staff, once we've got one—will need to spend several hours a day calling black pastors in Winston-Salem, Raleigh, Durham, Fayetteville, Wilmington, and Charlotte. And I need to be speaking in somebody's church every Sunday."

"Got it."

"I'm working on getting us a staff, but for now, it's just the five of us: me, you, Bristol, Carmichael, and Casey."

"I like our chances."

"We're always going to be a smaller campaign than the others, but what we lack in size we'll make up in smarts. We have to be strategic and focused in everything we do." Ron leaned in and tented his fingers. "The Obama campaign was notable for many reasons, but nothing was more impressive than its discipline. They didn't allow themselves to be distracted from their plan. If they received a debate invitation, they assessed whether attending that particular debate furthered their campaign goals. If it didn't, they turned it down. Their entire campaign was built on maintaining this amazing discipline, and it was critical to their ultimate success—particularly in the early days when they didn't have a lot of resources. This election will turn on how well we focus on executing *our* campaign."

"Understood."

"And one more thing."

"What's that?"

He grinned. "Let's have some fun. We're both making sacrifices to do this. We might as well enjoy the ride. You ready?"

"I wouldn't have come down here if I wasn't ready," I said.

"If we don't give Obama the tools he needs in the House and Senate to pass and preserve progressive legislation in areas like environmental reform, fair and affordable housing, immigration, unemployment insurance, and health care, his election becomes a mere blip on the radar. We have to articulate for folks that electing Obama was just the beginning of the social and political revolution we seek. We can't just sit back now and say, 'look at this great thing we did' and slip back into business as usual. I think articulating that concept in a truly compelling way may end up being our biggest challenge."

"You mean explaining why these midterm elections are more important than the 2008 presidential election?" I asked.

"Exactly."

We studied the menus for several moments. "So, have you thought about who you're gonna hire as campaign manager?" I asked.

"You're it—at least for the time being. You're smart, resourceful, and perhaps most important, extremely affordable."

"Yes, I suppose a salary of zero dollars is quite attractive."

"I'm pretty resourceful too," he said with a wink. "We'll learn as we go. I'll be learning how to be a candidate for statewide office, and you'll be learning how to manage a statewide political campaign. It's going to be challenging, but I've got a lot of confidence in us. This is where those law degrees of ours start paying dividends. Law school taught us how to think through novel, seemingly insurmountable problems. We'll have no shortage of those."

A black woman approached the table, wheezing heavily. "I'm so sorry for the wait, gentlemen," she said. "Welcome to Mezcal."

Ron's eyes widened. "No problem at all," he said. "How are you today?"

"Busy. One of the other girls called in sick, so we're shorthanded," she said. "I'm terribly sorry."

"No worries," I said. "Why don't you have a sit-down and join us for lunch, and we'll call it even. What do you say?"

She smiled, exposing deep dimples. "Well if that isn't the best idea I've heard all week!" she said. "But sadly, I'm gonna have to decline."

"All work and no play . . ." I said.

"You sound like my ex-husband. He used to say that. He didn't work nearly enough and spent way too much time playin'. I can play and end up on the street like him, or I can work and pay my bills."

"Well, when Ron here is elected to the US Senate, he's gonna make sure you've got unemployment insurance, so go ahead and sit. As long as you vote for Ron, you'll be just fine."

"Ron Johnson," he said while reaching to shake her hand.

Her eyes darted frantically around the restaurant. "Claudette Morris," she said. "You're running for the ah—Senate, did he say?"

"Yes, ma'am, I am."

"Well let me go and get ya'll some water," she said. "When I get back, maybe you can tell me what the Senate is." With that, she scurried toward the kitchen.

I shook my head. "You know, when you said this was going to be challenging, I thought you meant we had to work hard to get folks to appreciate the importance of electing good Democrats."

"Looks like you have your work cut out for you."

"Your waters, guys," Claudette said, now totally out of breath.

"Those waters just didn't come fast enough," Ron said. "I'm never comin' here again."

"I'm afraid that makes two of us," I said.

"Now you boys better quit teasing me," she said, smiling ear to ear. "Now about this Senate you were talking about. What exactly is that? Is it anything like the House of Representions?"

I eyed Ron for a split second. "I'll tell you what," I said. "When this election's over, I'll take you to Washington and show you where the Senate meets. All you've gotta do is vote for Ron and tell your friends to do the same."

"You've got my vote!" she said.

"Beautiful," Ron said.

"Can I have the fish tacos?"

"And may I please have the steak tacos?" Ron said.

"I'll put those orders in for you right now, and I'm gonna tell all my friends here at the restaurant to vote for you too," she said.

"Will Al here have to take all your friends to Washington too?" Ron asked.

"Of course he will!" she said before taking off again toward the kitchen.

When she was out of earshot, Ron said, "Keep it up. And remember—you're *never* off the clock. In that sense, this job's a lot like being a corporate lawyer, so this'll be good practice for you. Just keep getting us votes. I don't care how you do it—just don't break the law." We both laughed heartily.

"And while I'm logging all these hours of practice, what will you be doing?"

"Begging strangers for money eight hours a day," he said.

I furrowed my brow. "Strangers? Don't you mean friends and colleagues?"

"Yup—but that status changes once they realize why I'm calling. Wanna trade?"

"Abbbsolutely not."

CHAPTER SEVEN

THE SUN was well into its downward crawl when the team pulled up to the cobblestone entrance of the famous Grove Park Inn.

"Alright," Ron said. "That didn't take so long." Carmichael looked at me through the rearview mirror and rolled his eyes from the driver's seat. It had taken us over four hours to travel from Durham to Asheville.

"Women and their feet clearly weren't on the architect's mind when he was designing this place," Casey noted.

"Welcome to the Grove Park Inn," the freckle-faced valet said warmly. "Can I get you guys anything?"

"Yeah, an asphalt walkway for starters," Bristol muttered.

"I'm sorry, ma'am," the valet said.

"No, *I'm* sorry," Bristol said. "I guess I'm just a smidge irritable from that long drive."

"Can I offer you this voucher for a free massage?" he asked.

"Why thank you . . . Larry," she said after locating his name tag. "How kind of you."

"Don't mention it," he beamed.

As we entered the hotel, we immediately saw a huge white Jane Woodall sign sitting on a perfectly located tripod. "Not bad, Jane," I said.

"We should've done something like this," Ron muttered.

"With what money?" I replied.

Ron shook his head and walked to the concierge's desk while Bristol and I took a turn around the airy, inviting lobby. If I had my druthers, we would have continued wandering the grounds for another hour or more. The scent of fresh apple cider sweetened a cauldron already delicious from balsam firs and sugar maples. There wasn't a sad face in the house. Sensing my wanderlust, Bristol shot me a side-eye and nudged me along. We were looking for one of those large, back-in-the-day paper cutters. The printing service we'd hired to produce our handbills totally botched the cutting job—again. To the untrained eye, crooked handbills might seem to be little more than a nuisance; but when you're running an insurgent campaign with limited resources, appearance is everything.

After a minute or so, we found a door bearing a black-and-white sign that read "Employees Only"—so we walked right in.

As soon as we stepped into the office, a rotund white woman approached us. "Now ya'll can't come in here!" she growled. "Didn't cha see the sign? I swear, if one more person comes through that door, I'm gonna lose it!"

"I'm so sorry, ma'am," Bristol said. "My name is Bristol, and this is Al. I'm just looking for a pen. Could I trouble you for one? I guess we just missed the sign."

"Oh, is that all, darlin'?" the woman said. "Jonathan!" she screamed at a disheveled man hunched over a desk in the far corner. "Get these nice folks a writin' pen, then kindly escort them back into the lobby. You *can* handle that simple task, can't cha?"

"Ye . . . ye . . . yes'm," he stuttered, bolting up awkwardly from his desk and banging his knee.

She turned to us. "Ya'll here for the Vance-Aycock dinner?"

"That's right," I said.

"Well enjoy," she said. "I'm hopin' to sneak a peek at that Bill Billingsworth fella. I hear he's just the cutest thing you ever did see. He's gonna be our next United States senator, ya know?"

Bristol smiled. "Yes, Bill's a real doll."

The woman nodded, then hurried off into an adjoining room. We walked over to Jonathan, who must've been about thirty-five years old. There was nothing exceptional about him beyond the fact that his spine seemed to bend at a sixty-degree angle four inches below the base of his neck.

"Hello, Jonathan. How are you?" Bristol said. "My name is Bristol."

"I'm, I'm doing just fine to . . . to . . . today," he said, nervously organizing what little there was on his desk. "And ya . . . you, ma'am?"

"Just fine, Jonathan, thank you for asking, sweetheart. Jonathan, can I ask you a really big favor?"

"Sure."

"We need to cut these handbills so that all the sides are even." She removed a handbill from my grasp and showed it to him. "Do you have a paper cutter we can use?"

"Well, Br . . . Bristol, we do have a paper cutter, but I'm . . . we're not allowed to let guests use it."

"Well, could you do it for me just this once?" she said. "We really don't have time to go *all the way back down the mountain* and find a store that can do it. It would mean *soooo much* to me." She unleashed that smile again.

Jonathan grinned shyly. "Well, as I say, ma'am, it's for workers' use only . . . but you *are* in a jam. I guess it . . . it couldn't hurt this once."

"Thanks, Jonathan," she said. "You're such a sweetheart!"

Jonathan went to work repairing the large stack of handbills while Bristol looked on. "Do you need any help?" she asked.

"No thanks," he replied. "Please allow me."

As Jonathan worked, Bristol asked about his hometown, what he did for fun, and whether he planned to attend the dinner. Then she began chatting about Ron's campaign. The transition was seamless. After spinning off a few fun facts about Ron, she brought her argument for Ron's candidacy to summation: "I honestly don't see how you could vote for anyone else, Jonathan. Ron's clearly your guy!"

"He's got my vote!" he said. "Here are your flyers, all fixed now."

"Thank you, Jonathan," I said. "This was a huge help."

"No problem. I'm just glad I could help."

"Take care of yourself, Jonathan," Bristol said, giving him a hug.

"Bye, Bristol," he said, peering awkwardly back at her.

As we reentered the lobby, I leaned over to whisper, "Was all that *really* necessary, Ms. Davis? I mean, that was really thick."

"What can I say?" she said. "When there's a job to do, I get it done."

"You most certainly do."

Her eyes narrowed. "There's nothing wrong with being nice to people," she said.

"Not at all. All I'm saying is that when you bamboozle folks, ten times out of ten, someone's gonna turn around and bamboozle you."

"Again with the karma, huh?"

"'Again with the karma, huh?'" I mocked.

"What I did back there wasn't bamboozling, and you know it." She shook her head. "Casey was right."

"About what?" I said.

"About politics. My first day on the job, she shared one of her favorite quotes: 'If you want something said, ask a man. If you want something done, ask a woman.'"

Mercifully my phone vibrated before I could piece together a response to that irrefutable truism. It was a text from Carmichael: *We're setting up shop in room 531.*

"Who's that?" Bristol said.

"Just another groupie texting me her room number," I said. "You want it?"

"Stop playing."

"Oooooooooooh—do I sense a hint of jealously, Bristol Davis?"

"You're such an ass," she said, unable to fight off a smile.

"It was just Carmichael. He says we're in room 531."

"Oh, nice!" she said. "By the way, where are the volunteers who were supposed to meet us here?"

"They all bailed."

She frowned. "I hope that doesn't become a trend."

"You and me both," I said. "Let's go up to the room."

We headed across the lobby toward the northwest wing of the hotel, cutting past the jam-packed bar before pausing at one of the expansive, towering windows cut periodically into the stone-walled hallway leading to the elevators. Outside, the plush dark-green grass cascading down majestic Sunset Mountain twinkled in the glow of the fading twilight, while the red-and-orange speckled Blue Ridge Mountain chain rolled up and down into the deep-purple sky as far as my eyes could see. We stopped in front of one of the windows. When I turned to Bristol, I found a countenance pregnant with a complete and interminable solace that, in that moment, I believed could at once cradle and console the whole world.

"It's so pretty," she observed.

"Not bad," I said, returning my eyes to the divine scene before us. "If perfection's your thing."

"I know it's your thing, you perfectionist."

"Pot calling the kettle—"

"Oh shut up," she said, grinning.

"I'm not a perfectionist," I said. "I'd just like to have perfect control over everything that matters to me—at all times."

"Modest wants. I like that in a man." I raised my eyebrow.

"This hotel—this place—it's almost perfect," she said. Then she shot me a wry smile. "All it needs is some color."

I chuckled. "We're here, aren't we?"

"I mean in addition to the color we brought with us."

"Oh, I saw a few," I said. "One carried Ron's bags to the elevator bay, and the other one—well, he was serving apple cider in the lobby."

"So that makes six of us. Getting to critical mass now."

"And they allowed Senator Barack Obama on the premises to speak at last year's dinner."

"Just a month before a presidential election at an annual Democratic Party event," she said. "This place must've been packed to the brim."

"Yeah," I said. "He came and left through the kitchen."

"You're a trip, Al," she said. "You know they do that for security reasons."

"Can't you just let a good joke stand?"

As we turned toward the elevators, a swarm of reporters came toward us. They were circling an attractive bow-tied gentleman who looked to be around fifty and very well off, judging from the cut and quality of his dark-blue suit.

"Look, it's Congressman Darling," Bristol said. "For the life of me I can't understand why voters let such an obvious blue dog Democrat get away with calling himself a progressive."

"He's certainly one of a kind."

"Look at the reporters! They're like puppies the way they're following him around."

"Well, he's a big deal 'round these parts, as they say. His district's right next door."

Bristol grimaced. "Look at those female reporters hanging all over him, especially that Jessica Parker. He's not *that* good looking."

"What's your issue with Jessica Parker?" As the mob crept slowly toward us, I observed Darling looking intently in my direction.

Bristol grabbed my arm firmly. "Your friend Bristol Davis from law school wouldn't have shared this with you, but I guess things are different now. Jessica and I both grew up in Durham. She's three years younger. When I was a senior in high school, there was this guy. Jessica—"

"Excuse me!" Darling shouted above the noise, waving away the reporters. "Could we have just one moment, ladies and gentlemen? Mighty obliged." The dispirited group parted just enough to let Darling stroll through. "Y'all work for Ron Johnson, don't ya?" he said, peering at the campaign button on my lapel.

"Yes sir, we do," I said.

"You tell Ron his old pal . . . tell him Congressman Darling says hello."

"Congressman, Ron is here," I said. "If you'd like, I can arrange a meeting for—"

"Now you just go ahead and give him the message if ya don't mind, son."

"Will do, Congressman," I said.

"Nice handbills," he said. He winked and shook my hand, which I didn't recall offering. Within mere seconds, he'd been sucked back into the hive. Revived, the small army pressed on.

We stepped into the elevator. "That was strange," Bristol said.

"I know. What was that all about? 'His old pal'?"

"Did you know they were friends?" she said.

"Friends? I didn't know they'd ever met."

"Why hasn't Ron gotten an endorsement from his *old pal*?" Bristol drawled.

"My guess is politics. He's a conservative Democrat who occasionally votes with the more centrist members of the House caucus. He gives lip service to progressive causes from time to time, but if he actually endorsed a progressive, his constituency would eat him alive."

"I don't know," she said. "His district has grown increasingly progressive over the last few cycles. There's been an influx of out-of-state college students and young professionals, and they've been voting. I think he keeps getting elected more on the strength of his personality than because of his politics. There are progressives out there who've noticed the demographic shift but refuse to run against him because they don't think they have a snowball's chance in hell."

"And they don't."

"Maybe not now, but that's gonna change soon if he's not careful."

"Who knew you were an expert on western North Carolina politics?"

She smiled and cocked her head. "I have eyes and ears—I just choose not to use my mouth as often as everyone else in this racket."

"I see."

We stepped out of the elevator and into the hallway, Bristol leading the way.

"To be clear," she continued, "getting Darling's endorsement will still be a challenge. But I think it'll be less an issue of politics than of race."

"You mean racism."

"No," she said, stopping in the middle of the hallway. "Racism requires hatred on account of race. I don't think people hate Ron because he's black. I mean, some clearly do. But mostly, I think it's just that some of the older folks around here aren't used to seeing black folks runnin' something other than food to and from a kitchen."

"Aren't you the one who just said things are changing out here?"

"Yes, they are changing," she said. "But there are still plenty of hardline conservatives around."

"So it's mostly fear, not hate. Interesting point."

"It's a fear of what might lie ahead," she said. "Obama's election is still fresh in their minds, after all."

"True. But I'm more concerned about the massive elephant in the room: Why didn't Ron tell us he and Darling are friends? He's constantly talking about the importance of endorsements. Getting one from Darling would be a long shot, but if it happened, it would increase our visibility across the state exponentially."

"Maybe he thinks it's more than a long shot."

"Our entire campaign is more than a long shot," I said. "Ron's always telling me to think outside the box, to come up with creative solutions to our problems. Even if there is some roadblock to getting Darling's endorsement, why would we treat that problem any differently? It just doesn't add up."

"Well, we're not going to figure it out by standing here. Let's keep going."

The door to room 531 was slightly ajar when we arrived. Inside, a miniature waterfall cascaded down the wall next to the door. The room was large—so large I couldn't locate a bed before walking some fifteen steps in and around the corner.

"What is this, the honeymoon suite?" I said.

"Al!" Bristol shouted from the other side of the sliding door. "Come look at the view from the balcony!"

I walked outside and found Carmichael staring at the western horizon. "Am I crazy, or didn't I just hear Bristol call me from out here?" I said.

"Both," Carmichael said, not bothering to turn around. "She's on the other side, around the corner."

"There's another side," I said. "Of course. Why wouldn't there be another side?"

"This view is pretty amazing," Carmichael said. He gripped the steel railing with both hands while cautiously stretching his lanky frame toward the sky in the same way I imagine he'd leaned into the personal space of some freckle-faced Wake County brunette a decade earlier for what he hoped would be his first kiss.

"Around the corner, you say?"

"That's right, Einstein," Carmichael said. It's rarely discussed—undoubtedly because of our obsession with half-full glasses—but I've often noticed that beauty doesn't always trigger happy memories. It can just as easily remind us of the things and people for which we've longed and loved, and the reciprocity we waited for in vain.

"This isn't a balcony," I said, turning the corner. "This thing is larger than my law school apartment."

I recognized Bristol's new scent before my eyes were able to confirm her presence. Then she appeared, leaning against the railing, her hands cupping her chin. She stared off into that spectacular place in the rapidly darkening distance where the tree line of the Pisgah National Forest met the blushing northern sky.

"So this is western North Carolina," I said. "Did you get out here much as a kid?"

"Daddy took me and my little brother camping out here a couple times," she said, still taking in the view.

"What about Mom?"

She laughed. "Yeah, right. You couldn't pay her to come out here. Those were good times, though." When she turned around, I felt her gaze through my eyes and straight into my soul. In that moment, I realized I'd loved her for years—and that I'd nearly fallen again six weeks back, on Ninth Street.

"Let's get a move on," I said. "This is a hospitality suite. It has to be ready for guests soon."

"Where are Ron and Casey staying?"

"In the next room over," I said.

"And Carmichael?"

"He's staying at a lodge down the road. Said he wanted to spend some quality time alone with the bears and wolves—you know, his extended family. Apparently, he spent some time here too, back in the day."

Without a word, she pushed past me and back toward the sliding door.

"Hey, where are you going?" I shouted.

"We have to get this suite looking hospitable," she called back. "This place isn't going to prepare itself. Let's get to work!"

"Yessir!" I said. A middle finger peeked around the corner and quickly disappeared. "Flattery will get you nowhere," I said, reentering the suite.

"What time does this dinner start?" Carmichael asked, sliding the door shut behind him.

"Eight o'clock," I said.

"Shouldn't we head down to the ballroom and get our campaign lit on the chairs?" Carmichael said.

"Good call," I said. "It's probably gonna take more than one of us to get that done quickly."

"It's 7:15, so let's all go now," Bristol said. "We can finish setting up in here during dinner. But first I need to change into flats. I won't be any good to anyone in these heels."

With a few hundred handbills in tow, we made our way to the ballroom. On arrival, we stumbled on a truly macabre scene: Two dozen or so Jane and Bill staffers were milling outside the ballroom entrance, chatting with dinner guests during what appeared to be a predinner cocktail party. Most of the staffers, who wore attractive T-shirts advertising their respective principals, looked to be in their early twenties. A steady procession of freshly suited and booted dinner guests began to make their way into the rectangular room while tuxedoed waitstaff moved swiftly between caucuses, offering a bounty of succulent hors d'oeuvres and shimmering bubbly. Makeshift bars adorned with white linen cloth flanked both ends of the room.

"I need a drink," I said. "What about you guys?"

"Absolutely," Carmichael said.

"God yes," Bristol said.

"Three bourbons, please," I said, turning to the empty bar next to us.

"Do you have a brand preference?" the bartender asked.

"Yes—whatever's closest," I said.

"I can't believe Bill brought so many people," Bristol said. "He's not even officially in the race."

Carmichael turned to me. "Did you know this was happening?"

"That can't be a serious question," I said.

"So once again, the party's screwed us," Carmichael said.

I nodded. "I called a few weeks back to get the ground rules for tonight. They said no formal campaigning would be permitted outside the ballroom."

"And you believed them?" Carmichael said, slamming his lowball glass on the bar. "This is one of the biggest social gatherings of state Democrats all year . . . prime time for campaigning. That's the only reason we're here!"

"Enough!" I said. "The guy told me it's a rule."

Carmichael looked at me incredulously. "A rule? Who ever heard of campaigning rules? There are no rules in campaigning. Look up the term *campaigning* in the dictionary. It'll say 'the execution of actions and procedures in the absence of rules.'"

"Look, I'll deal with our friend at the party later," I said. "For now, we've got to make up for lost time."

"We should hand out some of this literature and try to talk to people," Bristol said.

"Good idea," I said. "You guys mingle. I'm gonna see about getting the rest of these handbills into the ballroom." I grabbed most of the handbills in the box and made a beeline for the ballroom doors.

"Excuse me, but you can't go in there," said one of the waitstaff. If I'd been blind, I might've mistaken him for Congressman Darling himself.

"Pardon me," I said, "but I was told the campaigns would have access to the ballroom before dinner to stick literature on the chairs."

"That's correct, sir, but the deadline for that is an hour before the dinner. As you can see, dinner starts in less than forty-five minutes. Didn't you folks get the notice?"

"No, we didn't."

"Well, I'm sorry, but I can't let ya in."

Somehow I successfully scuttled the urge to knock him clear into Catawba County. Then another hotel employee exiting the ballroom held the door open just long enough for me to steal a look inside. To my chagrin, I saw an even worse nightmare than the one we'd encountered a few moments before: tables and chairs plastered with Jane and Bill's faces, along with candidates running in other statewide and local races.

"Couldn't you make an exception just this once?" I asked. "Surely you can understand how critical it is that we get our information in there with the other candidates' materials. It's only fair."

"I'm sorry, but there's nothin' I can do at this time," he said.

Just then, a young woman wearing a Jane Woodall T-shirt slid out the ballroom door and past us carrying campaign literature. She smiled at the waiter. "Thanks for letting me in a little late," she whispered. "I went as fast as I could!"

I waited a few moments until she was out of earshot. "I guess the same rules don't apply to everyone, do they, *brotha*?" I said.

"I *beg* your pardon, sir," he said, straightening to his full height. "I'm gonna have to ask you to step away from these doors and me, or I'll be forced to call security."

After taking a deep breath, I said, "Please excuse me," dredging forth the best tight-lipped smile I could muster. Only one person could save us now.

I weaved in and out of several caucuses of Democratic Party faithful, which now filled the room to near capacity. When I found Bristol, I nudged her away from the quintet she'd been entertaining with as much civility as I could summon. "The screwings are ongoing," I whispered in her ear. "We've got to get in there."

"How do you—"

"Look!" I said, pointing toward the kitchen.

"Right!" she said. "The kitchen connects to the ballroom."

"Go work your magic. You're our last chance."

She sauntered to the wall, extracting more elegance from blue jeans and flats than I'd previously thought humanly possible, collected the box of handbills, and hastened toward the kitchen door. As she arrived, a waiter exited the kitchen. She smiled, leaned toward him, and began speaking. Within a few seconds, they'd both disappeared behind the door.

Carmichael came up to me. "Did you get into the ballroom?"

"Why did only half of those ladies get our literature?" I said.

"They all got lit," he replied. "The three facing you must've dropped theirs on seeing that monstrosity you call a face. Under the circumstances, three outta six ain't half bad."

I stood silently, assessing the quality of young Carmichael's barb. "You know, that wasn't half bad."

"Thank you. You didn't get into the ballroom, did you?"

"No, but I think Bristol just did."

"Beautiful," he said. "Why didn't they let *you* in?"

"Why did my grandparents sit at the back of buses in the fifties?"

"Wasn't it a black guy standing guard?"

"Yep."

"And you and your robust lexicon still couldn't talk your way in?"

"Not a chance," I said. "I'm beginning to see why so many people couldn't understand why I took this job. We can't even catch a break with our own people. Little things like not having our stuff in those chairs matter. It all adds up and just ratifies folks' initial belief that our campaign isn't legit."

"Don't look now," Carmichael said, "but we've got two fine thangs strollin' this way at ten o'clock."

"Carmichael, we don't have time to play games with—"

"Pardon me, gentlemen," one of the aforementioned fine thangs said. "And good evening to both of you."

"Good evening," I said. "This is Brett Carmichael, and I'm Al Carpenter."

"An absolute pleasure to meet you both," she said. "I'm J. C. Lockhart, and this is one of my very best friends, Mary-Jane Fenway." They were both average height and in their early twenties. J. C. appeared to be a natural blonde and wore heavy makeup. Her irises were so blue that I initially had difficulty making sustained eye contact. Mary-Jane, a brunette with light-brown eyes, was far more attractive than J. C. Unlike her partner, she wore just a touch of eye shadow.

"The pleasure is all mine," I said, shaking their hands.

"Pleasure to meet you both," Carmichael said.

"So, you guys work for Ron Johnson," J. C. said.

"Unless you know something we don't, I believe we still do," I said.

"Oh, I know you, Al Carpenter," J. C. said. "Your title and reputation precede you. The only question is, who's your boss?"

My reputation? I've only been in the state for six weeks. Who is this woman? "Ron," I replied.

"So he *hasn't* hired a campaign manager yet," J. C. said.

"We're sharing those duties among several staff members," I said. "And who might you represent?"

"We represent ourselves," Mary-Jane chimed in.

"Ah, independent contractors," I said. "Nothing wrong with that. Make your own decisions, no one deducting taxes from your paychecks. It's just about the best gig going, if you ask me."

"And rare at these kinds of events," Carmichael said.

"That's certainly true," Mary-Jane said.

"But you'll be voting in the primary next May, right?" I said. "Tell me—who do ya fancy in the US Senate race?"

"I've known Jane Woodall since I was a little girl," J. C. said. "My mom was an advisor when Jane first ran for attorney general nine years ago. Jane's done so much for me since then. I mean, my first job out of college was in the attorney general's office! How many people can say that? I just don't see how I couldn't vote for her." J. C. reached out and ran a finger across the campaign button on my lapel. "But maybe you'll convince me to change my mind."

Carmichael cleared his throat loudly. "And you, Mary-Jane?"

"I'm not sure. It's too early to tell, but I've heard the college students are tripping all over each other trying to land jobs on Bill's still nonexistent campaign. They think he's their ticket to Washington—as if anyone would actually want to live there."

"You have a bone to pick with Washington?" I said.

"There's nothing wrong with Washington," Mary-Jane said, "if you enjoy watching paint dry. Because that's what Capitol Hill cocktail parties are like."

"Next time you're in DC, let me know," I said. "I think you've been hangin' out with the wrong crowd."

"Maybe. Anyway, I don't know much about Ron. Everyone knows Jane, but I'm not nearly as beholden to her as some people around here." At this she gave J. C. a pointed look. "Meanwhile, Bill's making all the candidate stops like he's actually declared."

"If I were getting the reception he's been getting, I'd probably do the same thing," J. C. said.

I did my best to keep a tight smile plastered on my face. "Well, if they keep at it, I'm sure the party will eventually convince him to run," I said.

"One thing Bill doesn't need is convincing," J. C. said. "He's just holding out for the DSCC's support so he can time his filing with the news that he's got their backing."

"Must be nice to have all that attention," Carmichael said.

"Well, ladies, you'll have to excuse us," I said. "We really ought to mingle. You know—get the good word out about Ron."

"Of course, of course," J. C. said.

"We'll be receiving folks in our hospitality suite directly after dinner," I continued. "Stop by, and bring friends."

"Maybe we will," J. C. said, gently squeezing my arm. "Mary-Jane, I'm absolutely parched, aren't you? Cocktail?"

"I hear the bartender at the other end pours a decent bourbon, but don't quote me," I said.

"Thanks for the tip," Mary-Jane said.

"Ladies," Carmichael and I said in concert. We watched, and didn't blink, as J. C. and Mary-Jane strolled toward the bar.

"What was that?" I said. "They can't be out of Raleigh. I haven't seen them at any of the political events around town."

"Me neither," Carmichael said. "But I think you've got fans."

"Ron told me to be creative and resourceful in getting votes. He also said I might have to take one for the team here and there."

"They hardly qualify as taking one for the team," Carmichael said. "Especially that Mary-Jane. I'll take that one for the team. I can't let you shoulder the entire burden of this campaign. I've got to make sacrifices too. You know the rules." He slapped my shoulder twice.

"This guy," I said. "Now he wants to talk about rules."

Carmichael and I spent the balance of the time before dinner shaking hands and plugging Ron. These were mostly party folks, so many of them had already made up their minds about supporting Jane or Bill. In their estimation, either would provide just the right amount of progressivism: not too much. At 7:55 p.m., Ron left the private reception for candidates and party officials, joining us for some last-minute predinner mingling.

Ron was no stranger to these party folks. He'd worked closely with the party over the preceding two decades, and during the last few election cycles he'd become an indispensable partner in fundraising and candidate recruitment. When Ron expressed an interest in taking on a more significant role in those capacities back in 2004, the party welcomed him with open arms. But in his present capacity as a US Senate candidate, most party people saw Ron as a liability. These folks were at once furious about and perturbed by Ron's decision to step outside the box in which he'd so obediently remained for all these years, furious because he had no business running for Senate and perturbed that such an intelligent man didn't understand why a black man running for Senate in North Carolina was an exercise in futility. His candidacy was widely perceived among party faithful as a disease that would divide the party's base, paralyze its messaging, and ultimately guarantee Senator Rodney's reelection in November.

No one was more disappointed with Ron's decision to run than the party's recently installed chairman, Preston Roberts. Preston's famously sunny disposition instantly vanished whenever their paths crossed. If you didn't know their history, you'd have thought Ron had stolen his girlfriend in some messy eighth-grade affair.

Four cycles back, when Preston challenged the insanely popular one-term incumbent Branford Darling, he'd asked for Ron's support. During the three months preceding Preston's decision to run, he and Ron had worked together developing a strategy to defeat vulnerable Republican congressmen throughout the state. They'd built a strong rapport during those three months, and it was for that reason that Ron traveled three hours to deliver the news that he couldn't support Preston's campaign that year. Preston immediately kicked Ron out of his house—at ten o'clock at night. Ron practically begged Preston to hear him out, but Preston wasn't interested in explanations. Since then, Preston had held the stinging memory of Ron's betrayal with both hands. He was polite to Ron at social gatherings, but he could never totally disguise his simmering hatred.

Eventually Carmichael and I returned to the hospitality suite, where Bristol was putting the final touches on the room.

"Wow, this place looks amazing," Carmichael said. "And great job getting into the ballroom."

"What can I say?" she said. "I like a challenge. That's why I went to law school."

"Does this woman have any flaws?" Carmichael said.

"Not that I know of," I said. "Listen, I'm gonna head back downstairs and see where they are in the program."

"Roger that," Carmichael said. "Keep us posted."

"Will do," I replied. "Carmichael—don't do anything I wouldn't do."

"So you're essentially taking nothing off the table," he said.

"You two are in serious need of counseling," Bristol said. "Let me know if you want to go down that road—I know a guy."

Downstairs, as I approached the ballroom door, I immediately recognized Preston's droning voice. "Just last year," he said, "a young senator named Barack Obama addressed us in this very room. He spoke of a new nation, one in which both the government and the governed put aside the divisive politics of the past, opting instead for a politics of inclusiveness. Senator Obama taught us that the only impossible achievements are the ones we refuse to strive for. He taught us to set aside the pessimistic dogmas so many of us clung to out of habit—and out of irrational fear—rather than out of reasoned ideology. And together, we did what once seemed impossible. We elected our nation's first black president. And we elected this fine American not because he was black, but because he inspired us to come together once again in the service of our nation—because he reminded us that the only way to move forward successfully is to do so together. Together, we delivered the state of North Carolina—and with it, the presidential election of 2008—for the causes of inclusiveness and change!"

As the crowd erupted in a standing ovation, I leaned against the wall in the back of the room, my arms crossed. *This guy.*

"It gives me great pleasure," Preston continued, "to introduce the three Democrats we have running for the United States Senate this year—Democrats who will carry the torch of change into the general election in the fall and send Senator Rodney back home to Winston-Salem, where he belongs."

I turned to the elderly gentleman standing next to me. "I thought there were only two Democratic candidates for Senate," I said.

"No, there's three," he said. "Jane, Bill, and that new kid, Ron somethin' or other."

"It's Ron *Johnson*," I said, "And he's not new. In fact, he's been a huge help to the party over the last twenty years. He's helped them raise a ton of cash."

"I had no idea," he replied. "I don't know much about this Bill Billingsworth character either, but I like what I've seen."

"What about him impresses you?"

"Can't really put my finger on it, son," he said. "I guess I haven't really seen much ta speak on."

"I don't think he's even filed as a candidate."

"I don't know about all the formalities, but I assume he's filed since the chairman just called him a candidate. He oughtta know."

"I'm pretty sure he hasn't," I said. "At least, not as of this morning."

"Well I'll be a monkey's uncle!" he exclaimed. "If that isn't a sweetheart deal fer ya, I don't know what is. He gets recognized as a candidate at all the events and gets to speak too—and he isn't even a candidate. That must burn Jane and that Johnson boy darn near to a crisp."

"I imagine it does," I muttered.

Just then, Casey approached us and tapped me on the shoulder. "Hey there!" she whispered.

"Hey," I said. "Ron's at that table near the middle of the room. See it?"

"They couldn't put him any closer?"

I smiled. "Count your blessings. If certain folks had their way, he'd be in the back washing dishes."

"I know that's right," she said.

I turned back to my new friend. "Sorry, sir. I didn't catch your name."

"Sanford, Arnold Sanford," he said.

"Sanford, Sanford . . . any relation to former Senator Sanford?"

"He was my older brother," he replied.

"Nice to meet you, Mr. Sanford!" I said. "I'm Al Carpenter, and this is Casey Johnson, Ron Johnson's wife."

His eyes widened. "Well I'll be!" Arnold bowed deeply from the waist, holding it for several long moments before struggling back to standing. "So nice to meet cha, m'dam."

Casey grinned. "You're too kind, Mr. Sanford. You know, my husband really would appreciate your support. We'd love to have you onboard!"

"Count me in!" he said. "I'll do whatever's required."

I winked at Casey and smiled. "Casey, why don't you get to the table before Ron walks up to the dais."

"Okay. I'll see you in the hospitality suite when this is over?"

"Absolutely."

Casey headed for the table, taking the most circuitous route possible and stopping to greet every person she knew, thought she knew, or was determined to sway to Ron's side. If she'd been the candidate, Jane and Bill wouldn't have had a prayer.

"What's the room number for that there hospitality suite Missus Johnson mentioned?" Arnold said.

"Five thirty-one," I said. "You plannin' on stoppin' by?"

"Was Dick Nixon paranoid?" he said. "Of course I plan on stoppin' by." Arnold shook my hand firmly before walking nimbly to his seat near the front of the room. I couldn't help but chuckle as I watched the surprisingly spry Arnold Sanford park next to Jane Woodall. I half expected him to replace his orthopedic sneakers with a pair of hard-soled wing tips and peel off his mask to reveal the elastic skin of a twenty-one-year-old staffer.

*****

LATER THAT EVENING, Ron dragged himself into the suite and slumped into a chair. "Speech was flat tonight, wasn't it?" he said.

"Just a bit, but I think it went over alright," I said. "You'll get another bite at the apple as people circulate. Besides, it's way more important for people to get a good impression talking to you one on one. There's not much anyone can do in a three-minute speech."

Casey, who'd arrived just a few minutes before Ron, rushed over to tender a hug and kiss as soon as Ron walked in. "I think Al's right, but you need to have a speech at the ready. You give enough of these things now that you should be able to nail it every time." As she spoke, Bristol joined us.

"You're right," Ron said. "I need a five-minute version of my longer speech."

"We'll get on that early next week," I said.

"You guys were able to get the handbills into the ballroom," Ron said. "Did you have any trouble?"

Bristol winked. "Of course we had trouble," she said. "But nothing we couldn't handle." At that, she and Casey shared a crisp high five.

"She just won't be denied," I said.

"That's what we need more of in this campaign," Ron said. "Say, were you guys able to spread the word about the suite?"

"Yep," I said. "And the three of us handed out lit before the dinner."

"Beautiful, beautiful, beautiful," Ron said. "What do we have to snack on? I barely ate at dinner."

"Let me show you," Bristol said, leading us to the refreshments she'd set up on the counter.

I leaned in toward Carmichael. "Jesus," I whispered. "You think you bought enough hooch?" I counted fifteen bottles of wine and four cases of beer.

"Gotta give the people what they're after," Carmichael said. "My sources tell me that the suite with the most alcohol gets the most foot traffic. You may not know this, old man, but with the advent of the Internet and smartphones, folks will know what we're working with in real time."

Ron gulped half a glass of white wine—red is vino non grata for candidates on the trail—and scarfed down a handful of cheese and crackers before the party faithful began trickling in. I was pouring myself some wine when a middle-aged white woman and her twentysomething clone walked in.

"Welcome," I said to the younger clone. I turned to her companion. "And this must be your much younger sister."

The elder woman smiled and said, "This is my daughter! You must be running for office, young man."

"No, ma'am," I said.

"Well, you ought to," she said. "I'd vote for you too, provided that you started with something small and appropriate. I'm just as tired as I can be of folks jumpin' in out of turn."

"I'm afraid I haven't acquired the stomach for this business quite yet," I said with a false smile. "Will you ladies have a refreshment—an hors d'oeuvre or a drink perhaps?"

"Sure," the mother replied. "Do you have red wine?"

"Abbbsolutely," I said.

As I poured two cups, Bristol joined the circle. "Good evening, ladies," she said, reaching to shake their hands. "I'm Bristol. Welcome." As I attempted to distribute the wine, Bristol deftly blocked the transfer by stepping between us.

"How old are you, darlin'?" Bristol asked the younger clone.

"Twenty," she said. "My birthday's on Monday."

"Oh, a Libra!" Bristol exclaimed. "Happy birthday!"

"Thanks!" she replied.

"My mom's a Libra too," Bristol said. "Prettiest woman I've ever seen, except for your mother here. Can't wait to call her in the morning and report that I found her long-lost twin."

The clones both grinned ear to ear. I placed one cup on the counter and handed the other to Bristol's long-lost aunt.

"Thank you," the mother said. "Bristol, you're such a lovely young lady!"

"Why thank you!" she exclaimed.

"This is my daughter, Cassie, and my name is Elizabeth."

"Well, Elizabeth and Cassie, please make yourselves at home, and be sure to meet Ron, our next senator!" Bristol said. "He's right over there."

"We will, and thanks for being so hospitable," Elizabeth said.

"Of course!" Bristol said. Before I could get another word in, Elizabeth and Cassie were gone. I prodded Bristol out onto the terrace.

"Why did you do that?" I said. "She turns twenty-one in two days."

"You just graduated from law school," Bristol said. "Is that what you'd tell the judge when you're arraigned for distribution of alcohol to a minor?"

"Oh, so now you wanna do everything by the book?" I said. "What about Jonathan?"

"Are you still on that?" she said. "Please."

"Look, all these folks wanna do is have a good time. The mother was fine with it!"

"You were only interested in flirting," she said. "I guess I interrupted the show."

"You're jealous of Elizabeth?" I said.

"No, of course not," she said. "It's just that we have to be responsible. If Cassie fell and broke her ankle, or worse, do you think your charm would save us from Elizabeth's lawsuit? Do you think the district attorney wouldn't catch wind of this and file charges? And let's not even get started with the negative publicity for the campaign."

"You're right," I said. "You did the right thing. And now we've lost two votes."

"Are you kidding?" she said. "If anything, we just picked up two."

"In case you haven't noticed," I said, "Ron is black, and we're in North Carolina. We've got to take a chance here and there. We're gonna have to convert more than a few party folks if we're gonna get through the primary. You did it by the book. But we're not going to win doing things by the book." I tried, and failed, to explain to myself how anything she'd done in the preceding minutes had actually hurt our campaign, or how anything I'd said made even a hint of sense.

"Alexander Christopher Carpenter, I think the lack of REM sleep is finally getting to you," she said. "Either you've gone completely mad or, even more troubling, you're somehow jealous of how well I handled that situation, or upset that I stole your thunder."

I stood there for several seconds, grasping at straws for a crushing comeback, but I couldn't summon a response that wouldn't leave me looking weak or vulnerable. So I turned and walked back into the suite.

Upon returning to the safety of the other side of the glass, I joined a lively repartee between Ron, a local candidate for judge, and two elderly female voters. A few moments after Ron introduced me to the circle, J. C. and Mary-Jane sauntered into the suite. Raleigh newshound Jessica Parker entered just seconds later, and I knew it before I turned to confirm it. They stole the show for an entire ten seconds, a political eternity. These were the moments I lived for on the campaign trail—the clash of politics, both personal and professional.

Jessica tendered her recognition of my existence by pointing in my direction, as usual, and I accepted with a quick nod. I'd met Jessica Parker in Raleigh on the Wednesday after Bristol and I formally joined the campaign, while sitting down to dinner at a sports bar on Glenwood Avenue. Jessica had approached the table to introduce herself to Ron and say hello to Carmichael. It turned out that Jessica and Carmichael had attended grade school together and grew up in the same section of Raleigh. Just after Jessica's twelfth birthday, her family moved to Durham. Since the night we'd met, I'd run into Jessica on a handful of occasions, both in Raleigh and at political events around the state. On two of those occasions, in Charlotte and Wilmington, we'd kept the party going after the formal events were done. After several drinks at the bar (she called them "nightcaps"), we'd retired to her hotel room and debated art, politics, and life into the wee hours of the morning.

The first thing you noticed about Jessica, after the pretty face and deep dimples, was her presence. She commanded a room like few people I've come across in life—she was on a level with Uncle Malcolm. Jessica was also well above average height for a woman. When I stood to shake her hand, I didn't have to look down.

As she walked away, Ron eyed me and snickered. "You sure you haven't met her before?" he said.

"Of course. Why?"

"That fine sista was watching you like you stole something."

"And how would you know that?" I asked. Ron grinned.

"Let's stay focused here," Carmichael said. "She's a reporter with Channel 7, and we need more earned media. But my mom says she's supporting Bill."

"How does your mom know that?" Ron asked.

"Our moms play bridge one night a week."

"Well, looks like this Parker character isn't gonna be terribly valuable for us," I said.

"Maybe you can turn her," Carmichael said. "Look, I don't know any other reporters in this state, and we need all the earned media we can get."

"What are you suggesting, Carmichael?" I said.

"I'm suggesting you get to work," Carmichael said, winking.

I remained with the two candidates and the golden girls until the conversation sufficiently sputtered out, as the rules required. Then I made my way over to Jessica, who was standing alone with a beer.

"Imagine finding you here," she said.

"Were you looking for me, Ms. Parker?"

"I got tired of watching you chase me all over the state, so I figured I'd give a dog a bone." As she spoke, she removed her right hand from the pocket of her form-hugging black pants, gently snaked her fingertips clockwise from the back of my neck to the front, paused there for a few seconds, then abruptly returned her hand to her pocket.

I snickered. "Being a dog has its benefits, I see."

"Short-lived, but yes—I suppose there are perks attributable to all forms of life." She swiveled her neck toward Bristol. "Why don't you just allow yourself to love her?"

"You should mind your business," I retorted.

"I'm just trying to help a brotha out," she said. "I'm not what you need—I'm just what you want at the moment. Don't you get tired of women like me? You've been after our kind for years, Carpenter. I'll ruin you. The others may not have, but I will."

"Thanks for the warning. So, what're you doing in Asheville anyway? Did Channel 7 run out of reporters and call in the B team?"

"I'm not working tonight, Mr. Carpenter, unlike you. I'm mingling."

"You're always working, Parker. We're the same, you and I. Always working an angle."

"We're not the same, Carpenter," she said. "As much as it pains me to say so, you're a good person. Why you're fighting yourself so hard, I don't know. That grandfather of yours taught you right from wrong, how to be a good man. I can tell from the way you talk about him. Way, *waaaaaaaay* deep down, you care about people other than yourself. Me on the other hand? I don't give a damn about anyone but me."

"Never thought it'd be you telling me I'm not such a bad guy." Out of the corner of my eye, I spotted J. C. and Mary-Jane keeping close tabs on me and Jessica from across the room. "So, were you at the dinner?"

"I was. Sat at Ron's table, actually."

"Is that a fact? Sorry you couldn't sit closer to the front with your boy Bill. The fact that you're supporting him is one of the worst-kept secrets in the state. Be careful. Your black card might soon be in danger."

"My *boy* Bill? You mean the next United States senator from North Carolina?"

"I don't know, Parker. It's awful tough to win an election when your name isn't on the ballot. But then again, if anyone can pull it off, it's your boy B Squared."

Jessica rolled her eyes. "Will you come off that filing nonsense? I'm so tired of hearing about it."

"Probably as tired as I am of talking about it. Why not just get him to go ahead and file? Voters are gonna start wondering why he's making all the campaign stops when he isn't really a candidate. And you can count on my people to bring it to their attention."

"He's still exploring the possibility."

"You mean exploring the possibility of getting the DSCC's blessing."

She snickered. "That too."

"Well someone should tell Preston to stop calling him a candidate. It's probably against party rules—and it stinks."

"Well, Mr. Carpenter, you certainly have given this issue some serious thought," she said. "How have you been occupying yourself when you're not obsessing over whether or not Bill's going to file?"

"Oh, you know me—work harder than everyone, play harder than everyone."

"So I've been hearing," she said. "J. C. tells me you're the toast of Raleigh."

"That's odd since I only met her earlier today," I said.

"Raleigh's a small town, at least among political folks. And she knows everyone. I assume you've been making the rounds at after-work and political events in Raleigh, and being your social self."

"Seems like a nice girl."

"Seems—you hit the nail on the head."

"This sounds personal, Parker. I want details."

"She makes it her business to know everything about everyone in politics. She's been that way since I met her a few years back. She's a regular at important functions in Raleigh and around the state. I'm pretty sure she's stalking you. Anyway, we've been good frenemies almost since the day we met. She dated the guy I'm seeing now right before he and I got together. She loves it."

"Really?" I said.

"It's like she thinks I've got her sloppy seconds."

"Well, don't you?"

"Perhaps, to the untrained eye, but I'm smarter than that."

"Why did they break up?" I asked.

"Oh, she broke up with Robert because he wasn't doing enough for her career. She still flirts with him incessantly."

"Aha."

"She imagines she's a politician," Jessica continued. "She's dating some quasi-political type now just because she thinks he can help her climb the ladder faster. I think she really believes she'll be governor of North Carolina one day. And she's only twenty-two!"

"You're only twenty-four, and you think you're the next Diane Sawyer."

Jessica snorted. "All I know is that as long as I'm in the news business, she won't be governor."

"Looks like you plan on wielding a lot of power from your fiefdom at Channel 7."

"What can I say? Everyone's got a television."

"Well cheers to you, Jessica Parker," I said, raising my cup. "May all your enemies' dreams fail miserably."

"Here, here," she said, sipping her beer. "Oh look—here come the govnah and her lieutenant now."

"Jessica darling!" J. C. said. "Now what have I told you about talking to strange men?"

"The same thing I told you about talking to taken men," Jessica replied.

"Now, now ladies," Mary-Jane said. "There's a gentleman here. Let's try to show at least a modicum of gentility."

"Modicum?" J. C. said. "How long have you been waiting to slip that into a conversation?"

Mary-Jane rolled her eyes and turned toward me. "So, Al," she said. "Convince me in one sentence why I should vote for Ron."

Hearing his name, Ron came strolling toward us. "Now I'd like to think you're over here campaigning, Al, but I know better," he said, flashing a grin. "How's everyone doing?"

"I just asked Mr. Carpenter here to explain in one sentence why I should support you."

"I should run this drill with all my staffers. I'm sorry, I don't believe we've met Ms.—"

"Fenway. Mary-Jane Fenway."

"Great meeting you, Mary-Jane. I hope Ms. Parker and Ms. Lockhart here haven't fooled you into believing that we don't have a chance in this race."

"Fortunately for you, I'm not easily fooled," Mary-Jane replied. "I'm an independent contractor, and I'm still deciding."

"Well, Al, go ahead," Ron said. "Let's see if they taught you how to think on your feet at HLS." The girls laughed nervously.

"One sentence," I said. "It's time to turn the page."

"*It's time to turn the page*?" Ron exclaimed. "Is that all I get? One measly page?"

"Ron, do you have any idea how hard it is to get folks to turn pages?" J. C. asked.

"Thanks, J. C.," I said. "Plus, the pitch shouldn't be too narrow. It oughtta make folks think. This election isn't just about Ron Johnson. It's about seizing the progress made possible in 2008."

"Brilliant save, Carpenter," Jessica said. "But that was more than one sentence."

"Thanks, Parker," I said.

"So, Parker, you still riding on Bill's bandwagon?" Ron asked. "If so, hold on tight to the sides, because there's no bottom."

"I'd expect that from Carpenter," Jessica said. "He's not always as intelligent as he looks. But I expected more from you."

"I just hoped you'd see the light by now," Ron said. "We've got a chance to continue what we started. We all voted for change in 2008, and Obama's election was an important first step. The question now is whether we'll implement the *substance* of what we demanded. That's what this election is all about. We have to give the president the votes he needs in the Senate to move forward with legislation that grants education and job opportunities to more folks—and legislation that preserves the environment for generations to come."

"You know I don't take sides publicly, Ron," Jessica responded. "I'm a reporter, not a pundit." I chuckled.

"It's not about taking sides," Ron continued. "It's about doing what's right and supporting the candidate who will work with the president to expand access to opportunity as widely as possible. Isn't that what we Democrats are all about? Isn't that what 2008 was all about?"

"I wouldn't put it quite like that, but . . . yes, that's it . . . roughly," Jessica said.

"Tough crowd," Mary-Jane said.

"Then I challenge you to cast your vote for the candidate who gives us the best shot at continuing what we started," Ron said. "Nothing more, nothing less. If you think that candidate is Bill, assuming he becomes a candidate, then you should vote for Bill. That's the whole point of this primary."

"Now that was compelling," Mary-Jane said.

"Don't worry, Parker, you still have time," I said. "We'll keep the light on for you, but not for much longer."

"And you, J. C.?" Ron asked.

"You know I have to support Jane," she replied. "Nothing personal."

"Of course not," Ron said. "I just want to make sure you end up on the right side of history. I respect loyalty when there's a basis for it, but you can't let loyalty get in the way of voting your conscience. In your case, I get it. As for Parker . . . well, that's a different story."

"You never know," Jessica said. "Maybe I'll come around."

"I look forward to it," Ron said. "Well . . . I hate to run ladies, but I've gotta shake some more hands and kiss some more babies if we're gonna win this thing. Thanks for coming by, have a good time, and watch out for this guy. There's a reason I've got him on my team." Ron slapped me on the back and whispered, "Work the room."

By ten o'clock the suite was packed, but we hadn't achieved the foot traffic I'd hoped for. A quick glance at the bar revealed a significant decimation of what initially seemed an inexhaustible supply of vino and brew.

Suddenly, the rigor of the day caught up to me, and an incontestable lethargy began to settle in. I sat in a plush armchair near the television and put my feet up on an ottoman. I'd probably had more drinks than I should've that night, but not enough to show. In contrast, the woman sitting in the armchair next to me was toasted. Through the evening, she'd transitioned from coherent, charismatic party activist to blitzed stand-up comedian. Her head now rolled to face me. "Hey, let me ask you a question. What's your guy dooooing anyway running for Senate?"

"What do you mean . . . Susan, wasn't it?"

"That's right! I'm Susan," she said with a lopsided grin. "Anyway, he doesn't have a chance!"

"Yeah, so you've been saying," I said. "I heard you loud and clear the first ten times."

"Well good, because I—I just don't see whyyyyyyy he's doing this. He's not following the rules. You convince me whyyyyyyy he should be doing . . . this." She tilted forward and came dangerously close to dropping her head on the coffee table in front of us. Casey caught a glimpse of this near tragedy and temporarily lost track of the conversation she and Ron were having with a couple of thirtysomethings I hadn't met.

"I saw those girls flirtin' with you," my unbalanced, honest friend continued. "If I was twenty years younger, you wouldn't look twice at them."

"Is that a fact?" I said.

"It most certainly is a fact!" she continued, unsuccessfully straightening in her chair. She leaned toward me in an attempt to make some secret disclosure in my ear, but her internal volume controls malfunctioned badly. Carmichael excused himself from a discussion with J. C. and Mary-Jane and scurried across the room to the couch directly across from my buddy and me. He watched us intently.

"I was a knockout back then!" Susan continued. She raised her hands dramatically into the air before attempting to raise herself from her chair.

"Please, let me help you," I said, rising to my feet. Carmichael did the same.

"No!" she exclaimed. "I'm not drunk. I don't need your help. You tell your guy to give it up. It's not worth the *effort*. No one's buying what he's selling."

I gritted my teeth. "Let me walk you to your room," I said. "You're in no shape to—"

"North Carolina isn't ready for all that!" she stammered. "Why would you people want to divide Democrats? He can't get enough votes to beat Jane or Bill anyway."

"Bill's not a candidate," I snapped.

"Oh yes he is. Everybody knows Jane . . . and Bill, he's ginnin' up a lot of excitement." She tried to stand but fell to the ground like a sack of potatoes. She now had the floor in all senses, and although her audience had seemed quite captivated by her sober first act earlier in the evening, they appeared strangely unaffected by this messy little curtain call.

Bristol came rushing over. "Are you alright?"

"Am I alright?" Susan asked. "Why wouldn't I be? That's the problem with you so-called *progressives*. Running around saying we've got all these problems. Take a seat. Things are fine."

"You've got to get her out of here before she hurts herself," Bristol whispered to me.

"Please, let us give you a hand," I said as Carmichael and I reached to raise her off the floor.

"Leave me alone!" she said, offering no resistance as Carmichael and I lifted her back onto the chair.

J. C. darted toward Susan from across the room. "I'll take her to her room," she said.

"Does she do this often?" I asked quietly.

"Often enough," she whispered back. "I'll bet half the people here have seen it before."

"Do you need help getting her to her room?"

"I've gotten strong from practice," she replied. "I can manage."

"Call me," Susan mumbled as she and J. C. made their way toward the door. Just as they crossed the threshold, Susan turned around. "Democrats!" she shouted. "Have a grrrreeaaaaat night! Cheers to Jane! Cheers to progress!" J. C. tugged on Susan's arm, and with painstaking slowness they disappeared behind the door.

"Good old Susan," Jessica said. "She always knows how to make an exit. Only problem is she ruins it for the rest of us. Who can compete with that?"

Hearty laughter quaked the suite. And then, with the life of the party gone, the remaining guests swiftly but gracefully began to leave. Within five minutes, I stood in the ruins of the party with the rest of Team Johnson.

CHAPTER EIGHT

"WELL, THAT WAS A LOT OF FUN," Ron said, executing a deep stretch and yawn. "I think we really made a dent tonight, notwithstanding that little episode."

"Apparently she does that on a somewhat regular basis," I said.

"Never mind that," Ron said. "I think our campaign became real for people tonight."

"Who was that woman?" Casey asked.

"Who, Susan?" I said. "I just met her tonight. Big party activist. I hear she was a major Obama supporter. Straight shooter too. At least you know where she stands. That's more than I can say about most of these folks."

"I spoke with her for a while too, maybe an hour ago . . . before she went south," Ron said. "She asked some really insightful questions. Told me she thought I couldn't win so she couldn't support me, but she also said she'll be watching to see if we show her something."

Carmichael snorted. "That's party speak for 'go jump off a ledge somewhere,'" he whispered to me.

"That's the same argument we heard folks using before Iowa last year to explain why they were supporting Hillary instead of Barack," Casey said.

"All we can do is stay the course," Ron said. "I think North Carolina is ready—we just have to keep reminding folks that change requires sustained action."

"Things will start getting interesting now," I said. "That's for sure."

"We all did good work today," Ron said. "But the game ball goes to Bristol for her ingenuity and good old-fashioned stick-to-itiveness. Great job getting our literature inside that ballroom."

Bristol winked at Casey as we applauded. "Thanks guys," she

said. "But it was a team effort. Couldn't have done it without Al and Carmichael."

"We should all get some rest," Casey said. "Long trip back east tomorrow."

"Why don't you and Ron head back to your room?" I said. "We'll take it from here."

"Good deal," Ron said. "See you guys in the morning."

"You too, Carmichael," I said.

"Sure you don't need me to stick around?" Carmichael said.

"Absolutely," I said. "We need you fresh tomorrow."

"Alright," Carmichael said. "I'll check in with you in the morning."

After seeing the three of them out, Bristol whisked past me toward the bathroom.

"What's wrong with you?" I said.

"Let's just finish cleaning up and go to bed," she said. "There's no point discussing it."

"You're obviously upset," I said. "Why not discuss it now? I promised in August that I'd take care of our friendship, but you've got to work with me here. Let's talk."

"With most people, discussing problems actually helps," she said. "With you, I actually feel worse afterward because you always find a way to flip the script. This isn't law school, Al. School's out." She stormed off into the bathroom and slammed the door.

I stood motionless awhile before venturing onto the terrace, jacketless, to enjoy a few final moments of that crisp October night. While looking at the moonlit mountain range, I imagined I was alone out there, unable to find my way back. Perceiving the sound of an unyielding northerly wind rushing through the thousands of trees below, I felt a sharp pang of anxiety. I was afraid of what the night might bring. Would I make it out alive? Might I freeze to death in the frigid air on that exposed, rugged mountain surface? Surely hundreds before me had survived cold nights in these very mountains, but that gave me little comfort. Oh well. *There's no turning back now* I thought. I was already in the thick of it. I had to be strategic to survive. I would have to seek some cavern cut in the side of a mountain, set a trap to catch a hapless animal seeking nourishment of its own, and start a fire. I'd seen it done before on those nature shows. I needed a rock, a few dry branches, and some dead foliage. I could do it. I'd just have to think outside the box. *What I wouldn't give to be back in law school just one more Friday night.* Then I wandered back to a time just eleven months earlier—the Friday after Obama's election.

By FRIDAY, NOVEMBER 7, 2008, the initial excitement surrounding Tuesday's election had receded somewhat as we settled back into our daily routines. During my law school years, I made a point of spending as many Fridays as possible engaging in activities unrelated to law school and requiring little to no brain power. As a rule, I didn't step on campus after Thursday except to attend classes or meetings.

On most Fridays of 3-L year, after having lunch with Bristol, I hopped in the car and drove into Boston. A critical mass of Boston's high-end 'shoppes' and boutiques are located on Newbury Street, the main vein of the ritzy Back Bay area. Newbury Street is to Back Bay and Boston what M Street is to Georgetown and Washington, DC—a playground where the attractive (and not-so-attractive) old money scions come to see and, most important, be seen. Newbury Street was also my escape from dreary Cambridge and the rigors of the law.

I awakened that Friday morning longing for an escape to Newbury Street. I texted Darden around eleven o'clock to see if he wanted to join me. I dressed quickly, and as I opened my apartment door, I found Bristol standing there, her knocking hand at the ready. Her appearance was consistent with her typical Friday morning look: most of her hair pulled back into a frizzy ponytail, glasses situated halfway down her nose until periodically pushed back closer to her face, and those loose-fitting Carolina blue cotton sweatpants hanging precariously just below her waist. It would've been a terrible look for most women. Bristol and I had grown close during that last year of school, but crossing the line was never on the table. It would be too convenient—and too risky. Plus, I had a firm policy against dating anyone enrolled at the law school.

"Where are you going?" she said. "Aren't we having lunch?"

"Can't today. Going straight to Newbury."

"Newbury Comics? Again? Don't you have enough records already?"

"I'm not going to Newbury Comics."

"You promised you'd take me to the grocery store today."

"I should be back in a couple of hours."

"Okay. You going with Darden and Simmons?"

"With Darden," I said. "I haven't spoken to Simmons in a few days. Which reminds me . . . I need to call him."

"What's poppin' tonight?"

"Not sure, but I'm probably goin' out with Darden. Hopefully Simmons'll reappear within the next few hours."

"That dude may be in New York this weekend. You know he stays taking that bus to the City."

"True," I said. "I'll try him in a few minutes."

"Okay. Call me when you're on the way back."

"Will do." I took the elevator down to the garage and hopped into my black 3 Series. When I was a few blocks from Darden's usual pickup spot on Everett Street, I texted him. As I pulled up to the curb, my phone vibrated on the bucket seat next to me. Simmons was back online.

"Simmons—my man," I said. Darden climbed into the passenger seat.

"Carp, what's good, son?" Simmons said.

"I called to see what's up for tonight, and to see if you wanted to roll to Newbury with me and Darden right now."

"No plans for tonight, and sure, I'll roll. I need to check out Ralph anyway."

"Is that Simmons?" Darden asked.

I nodded. "Simmons, you at your place?" I said.

"Yeah, where are you?"

"I just scooped Darden. I'll swing by your place now."

"Bet," Simmons said.

"Yeah!" I said with that quick, sharp delivery I usually employed in terminating conversations with only these two friends. Simmons lived three blocks away from Darden. On the way, Darden and I spotted the twenty-two-year-old Puerto Rican 1-L who had been all the rage on campus since she arrived in August.

"It just doesn't make any sense," I said. We both stared as she walked down the sidewalk.

"It's enough to make you wanna give the whole game up," Darden said. "Go get your girl, Al."

"You're crazy," I said. "A girl like that, at HLS? Too much attention, brotha. You know how highly I value my privacy when it comes to women 'cause you're the same way."

"Privacy?" Darden said, smiling. "I would want the whole world to know."

"No you wouldn't."

He laughed. "Yeah, you're right."

We pulled up to Simmons's apartment building and found him standing on the corner, his arms engaged in their usual exercise of rigid gesticulation as he spoke into the earpiece attached to his iPhone. While climbing in, he shook Darden's hand in the manner known in African-American circles as "giving dap" and rapped my right shoulder twice. "Gentlemen," he bellowed. "Pray tell, what *are* we getting into tonight?"

"Nothing but trouble," I said. "We haven't been out in a minute, so we've gotta make up for the arrearage."

"*Arrearage?*" Simmons said. "This guy . . . talkin' about an arrearage. Somebody get me a thesaurus. Why can't you just say 'lost time' or use some other phrase that's at least remotely decipherable by the rest of humanity?"

"*Decipherable?*" I said. "Get outta here!"

Darden snorted. "It *has* been awhile," he said. "And I know that because I haven't had a headache like this since the last time I was with you two idiots."

Simmons snickered. "True, true."

"It's supposed be a nice night," Darden said. "Sixty degrees. And there's a party tonight at Tryst."

"Great venue," I said. "Who's doing this one?"

"This promoter guy I know e-mailed me about it. Should be right. Good mix of people too."

"Sounds like a plan," Simmons said. "Pregame at your place, Al, as per usual?"

"Obviously," I replied.

While heading down Massachusetts Avenue, Simmons filled us in on the previous night's first date.

"What about Natasha?" Darden asked.

"Yeah . . . I don't know about her," Simmons said. "I'm getting a little restless." During the third course of their dinner, Natasha's best friend had spotted Simmons on the other side of the restaurant with a girl who wasn't Natasha. The next morning, Natasha e-mailed Simmons the iPhone-captured picture her best friend took of him and his latest prospect.

"Busted!" Darden said. "Technology: it giveth—"

"And it taketh away," I said. "Damage control?"

"I called Natasha immediately," Simmons said. "She was furious. I came clean. Told her it was a random chick and that I'd only gone on the date because I've been having doubts about our situation."

"Not bad," Darden said.

"And truthful," I added. "You can't lie to women in these situations. They may hate you in the short term, but you'll have their respect."

"What happened next?" Darden said.

"I apologized, and she said, 'You've got some serious making up to do.'"

"So how is it that you're able to hang out with us tonight?" Darden said.

I had been admiring a red Porsche traveling in the lane to our right, but after hearing Darden's question, I immediately turned my focus to the rearview mirror. Simmons leaned back, turned toward the window, released a deep breath, and smiled. "That's gonna take some politics," he said.

The Porsche peeled off ahead of us and out of sight. As we made our way down Storrow Drive, my eyes scanned the Charles River on the left. It had been frozen for the last two weeks, but several large cracks were now visible on the surface. Warm rays of sun beamed into my face through the sunroof, and cars intermittently reflected sunlight into my eyes as they moved in and out of the lane in front of me. I reached into the glove compartment and retrieved my shades, still focused on the compromised ice. All the windows were cracked except for mine, which I'd rolled down completely. The mixture of cool air and hot sun was like the feeling of slowly submerging oneself into an outdoor hot tub on a late December night.

We spent a few hours browsing on Newbury Street, bouncing in and out of our usual go-to retailers. Against my better judgment, I bought a beautiful pair of brown snakeskin loafers from Cole Haan. After only a few minutes in that establishment, Simmons decided to move on to the Ralph Lauren store before visiting some of the shoppes on the other end of Newbury Street. By the time Darden and I arrived at the Ralph Lauren store, Simmons had already come and gone. We'd come to this location so many times that Darden and I were on a first-name basis with several of the sales clerks. After twenty minutes of perusing—record speed for us in that place—I tried and failed to open the door.

Darden grinned. "Maybe you should stop skimpin' on the gym, bro," he said. When I finally got the door slightly ajar, it swung open violently, and a mighty wind gust hit my face like ten icy buckets of water—buckets included. As Darden and I struggled against the headwind tunneling down Newbury Street, we spotted Simmons walking toward us.

"Any luck with Ralph?" Simmons said.

"No, but there was a discount section at Cole Haan," Darden said. "Thirty percent off. Al found and bought the only shoes worth grabbing."

"What did you get?" Simmons asked me.

"Brown loafers."

"More loafers, son?" Simmons exclaimed. "How was the price?"

"A little aggressive. But at thirty percent off, I took the bait."

"You only live once, and they can't send the debt with you when you die," Simmons said.

"That's what I keep telling myself," I said.

"Mind if we head back?" Darden said, running his hand over his head. "I need a haircut."

"Ditto that," Simmons said.

"Yeah, let's go," I said. "I'm well over my budget for the next two months as it is."

The sky had grayed substantially in the time since we arrived downtown. It was one of those familiar Boston afternoons. A hefty, sustained sequence of gusts slowed our pace as we battled our way toward the car.

"It's cold as hell!" Darden said.

"It's November," I said. "It's supposed to be cold. Besides, it can't be less than fifty-five degrees out here." In truth, it was probably more like thirty-five. I enjoyed giving Simmons and Darden a hard time about their thin skin. Because the temperature was a balmy fifty-one degrees when we left Cambridge, Darden and Simmons opted to leave their heavier winter gear in the closet. In my four years at Yale, I grew to love cold weather and became accustomed to temperatures maxing out near forty in November. Fifty-one degrees in November just seemed wrong to me—like the natural order of things was off.

As we approached the car, I noticed a familiar face that sent a deep chill through my body. We locked eyes, and as nearness confirmed her identity, I flashed that smirk with which I'd typically welcomed her during freshman year whenever she visited my dorm room for one of our late afternoon study sessions.

"Well, well, well . . . who *do* we have here?" I said. My stomach slammed against the pavement. "Angie Rodriguez." Up until about a year before that encounter, I'd believed we would marry, although we hadn't had any significant relationship since our freshman year of college.

"How are you?" she asked, hugging me tightly. She smelled exactly the same. In that moment, we were eighteen once more, and I saw her again for the first time standing on the beautiful white granite steps fronting Beineke Plaza, her nearly jet-black curly hair in that familiar unwieldy ponytail and her bronzed skin absorbing the late summer sun's rays. I suspect that a man is blessed with only one such moment in life if he's lucky. There was a time when the sun didn't rise and set without at least one thought of her.

"I'm doing well," I said. "Are you in Boston now?"

"Just visiting a friend who's in business school here. I would have told you if I was moving to Boston!"

"Right, of course," I said. "How's *he* doing?" She snapped her eyes toward the traffic in the street.

I snorted. "Have you come to your senses yet?" I said.

She turned her eyes back to mine. "I suppose I haven't," she said, a smile creeping forth. Darden laughed under his breath.

"How long are you in town?" I said.

"Just tonight." Simmons cleared his throat loudly, having finally reached his threshold for passive observation.

"I'm sorry," I started. Standing next to Angie was an attractive, shorter woman. She looked at me like I'd broken into her house, stolen her grandmother's diamond earrings, and gotten away with it. The combination of her foul attitudinal disposition and the three-to-two gender ratio finally proved too much. Angie and I made slapdash introductions before agreeing with our eyes to bring this fortuitous meeting to an awkwardly speedy but necessary conclusion.

"We've ah . . . gotta run," Angie said, looking down at her bare right forearm.

"You gonna be out tonight?" I asked.

"Yeah," she said. "Call me tonight. Same number."

"Aye aye," I said. I kissed her cheek in the manner that someone with intimate knowledge of a person might, dangerously close to her incandescent pink lips. She trembled slightly at my touch before raising her hands to my chest and pushing slightly.

"Nice to meet you . . . ah . . . Darden, Simmons," Angie said without turning to look at either of them.

"Angela," Darden and Simmons said in near chorus. I watched my partners in crime watch her walk away as I unlocked the car, which was only a few feet away.

"How about that haircut, *gentlemen*?" I said.

"Yeah . . . the haaaaaaaair—cut," Darden said, still following Angie with his eyes.

"Details, counselor," Simmons said as he opened the right rear door.

"Angie freakin' Rodriguez," I said, slamming my head against the headrest.

"Clearly the one that got away," Darden said, clicking his seatbelt for dramatic effect before singing the opening line of the Jackson 5 classic, "Never Can Say Goodbye." Simmons and I both broke into laughter.

"That's the one," I said.

"Engaged too," Darden said.

"Right again," I said. "You're two for two."

"Engaged, mon frère, but not married," Simmons said. "She's bad. You gotta make one last attempt."

I snickered. "You're crazy."

"Son . . . she told you to call her *tonight*," Simmons continued. "An engaged woman who runs into an old college flame and asks him to call her *tonight* isn't looking to meet up later to play Scrabble—not the board game, anyway."

"Maybe what she's after is a friendly game of tiddledywinks," Darden added.

"Do you even know what tiddledywinks is?" Simmons said.

"It's not far off from the version of Scrabble you're suggesting Angela has in mind," Darden replied.

"You guys are idiots," I said.

"Whatever helps you sleep at night," Simmons said.

I took Massachusetts Avenue all the way back to Cambridge. It wasn't the most direct route, but I relished the hustle and bustle of Central Square, and Massachusetts Avenue runs right through it. This small section of town felt more like Washington, DC or Queens than Cambridge. After two hours in the barbershop, I took Simmons and Darden home. Before heading back to my place, I stopped by Newbury Comics in Harvard Square to peruse their latest shipment of vinyl. After purchasing a Miles Davis Quintet album I'd been trying to find for several weeks, I rushed back to my apartment.

The first song, "Just Squeeze Me," opens with a few bright chords from pianist Red Garland, followed by an unassuming, almost shy Miles entry. Miles plays a simple melody but in that rich, warm manner and with the kind of meticulous care for each note that is so reminiscent of Coltrane's *Ballads*. Then Coltrane enters. He raises the bar with his searching yet confident response to Miles. Coltrane's delivery is both frenetic and controlled, exploring while remaining committed to the melody. *Angie Rodriguez.*

I settled farther into my black leather couch while looking out into the shadowy courtyard below. As I dozed, I was jolted by the recollection of my promise to take Bristol to the store. I hopped up, walked across the hall, and knocked on her door.

No answer.

After returning to my apartment, I phoned her.

"Yes, Al," she answered.

"I'm back. Where are you?"

"I got a ride to the store," she said dryly.

"Thanks for telling me."

"Don't pretend you're annoyed. Anyway, dinner tonight?"

"What time are you getting back?"

"Probably around six thirty," she said.

"Okay."

"I have a need for pizza from that new spot over in Central Square."

"I don't know about pizza. I'm on a diet."

"A diet? And how exactly did last night's burger fit in?" I snickered. "I'm starting today."

"Right. I'll see you soon."

"Okay. We can do pizza. But I'm starting this diet tomorrow."

"You feeling lucky today, counselor? Fifty bucks says you won't start a diet tomorrow, next week, or next month."

"I'm too smart to bet someone who knows me as well as you do."

"And getting smarter every day. See you later."

"Later."

*****

"AL!" Bristol yelled from the other side of the sliding door, yanking me violently back into reality.

"Yeah!" I shouted.

"Your cell is vibrating!"

"Thanks!" I yelled back. As I approached her and my phone, I looked down at my watch. It read 12:15 a.m.

She tossed the phone toward me. "Don't wait up," I said. "This might take a while. I'll clean up the rest of this mess." I kissed her forehead before returning to the terrace, this time wearing a jacket and toting the last remaining beer.

"What did the drunk Southern white woman say to the black deputy campaign manager after telling him his black boss should throw in the towel?" I asked.

"I don't know," Darden said. "What?"

"'Cheers to progress!'" I replied.

"What kind of a mess have you gotten yourself into down there?" Darden asked.

"I have no idea," I said. "I thought I knew what I was getting myself into with this campaign. It's the real deal down here."

"Mr. Carpenter," said a voice that didn't belong to Darden.

"Simmons?" I said.

"Did you forget our monthly conference call?" Simmons asked.

"Oh man," I said. "I totally forgot with all this craziness."

"Poor form, Carp," Simmons said. "Absolutely unforgivable. We're supposed to be your boys. Stop pretending to be so busy."

"Well, in the last few hours," I began, "I've been chewed out for trying to serve wine to a twenty-year, three-hundred-and-sixty-four-day-old minor with her mother's consent, Bristol and I are at each other's throats, I watched a middle-aged drunk woman almost embarrass our campaign into further oblivion. And oh yeah, did I mention that Ron Johnson is black, and that the party—the same folks who worked their rear ends off to elect Obama—is pissed that Ron is running?"

"Unreal," Darden said. "Have they forgotten Obama's race—and his race?"

"I think they'd like to forget both," I said. "These folks are more excited about a guy who couldn't be much further to the right of Obama politically and still remain in the Democratic Party."

"That Billingsworth character?" Simmons said.

"Well, he does look the part," Darden admitted.

"I'll bet they think Ron will divide the party and ruin Dems in the general election," Simmons said.

"That's right," I said.

"Those talking points aren't just being used against Ron," Simmons continued. "They're being used against black Dems in races across the country."

"Why is Ron being blamed for making this a three-way race?" I said. "That's what happens if Bill gets in."

"Remember Prof Jackson's equation," Darden said. "Last I checked, Ron isn't Scots-Irish."

"Neither was Obama," I said. "I told you guys months ago that Obama's election wasn't going to do jack for black candidates in state and local elections."

"That's not quite what you said, counselor," Simmons noted. "You said the jury was still out on the question. That's why you're down there. To infiltrate that jury. Giving up already?"

"I'm not giving up," I said. "Just frustrated. And don't even get me started on endorsements."

"Having a tough time with that too?" Darden asked.

"Yeah, and from folks you'd assume would be with us as a matter of policy, politics, and general principle."

Simmons laughed. "Gotta love the black tax. That's just one of many reasons I joined the Republican Party."

"I just knew certain folks would be with us, and not just black folks," I said. "Black electeds, the major black PACs, progressives—they're missing in action. And then you have the college kids. Aside from the handful playing inside baseball in established political orgs like the Young Dems, those cats have totally checked out too."

"Sounds like the Obama Coalition is MIA," Darden concluded. "Uncle Tom warned you about the status quo parading around in the cloak of progressivism."

"I still can't believe I missed that performance, son!" Simmons said. "Where was I?"

"Sky's the limit, really," I said. "Could've been Cassandra, Rachel, Robin, or maybe Julie, Katrina, Jamie, or perhaps—"

"Point taken, Carp," Simmons said.

"I just don't get it," I said. "I've been trying to get an endorsement from this up-and-coming clean energy outfit down here. I think I'd have an easier time walking on water."

"You find a way to do that, and I'll bet those endorsements will come pouring in," Simmons quipped.

"Doubt it," I said. "Not even that could convince these folks to rethink the conventional wisdom that black folks can't win statewide elections."

"Just national ones," Darden said.

"Wild and crazy stuff," I said. "It's like a teacher telling a student, 'Hey kid, great job on last night's homework assignment. Now stop doing your homework. Your parents never made it to college, and neither will you. It's not your fault. That's just the way it is.'"

"Wasn't it Darden who said Obama's election would change everything?" Simmons asked.

"Yes, but I didn't say Carp could just sweep into a Southern Senate race and get a black man elected without putting in serious work," Darden replied. "Obama's election showed folks what's possible. It didn't—it couldn't possibly—erase institutionalized attitudes and biases reinforced over centuries. We're talking about the South!"

"We're hearing caveats and qualifications from counsel that we weren't hearing back in Cambridge," Simmons said. "You're losing credibility."

"So what's your advice, Darden?" I asked. "You're part of the reason I'm in this mess."

"Do what you always do," Darden began. "Work smarter than everyone else. You can't win by just replicating the Obama model. You already knew that. So figure out how to win using the tools you have. Innovate."

"And stop complaining, Carp," Simmons said. "You're not that busy."

"So what's the latest with you guys?" I said. "Please tell me you're having an easier go of it than me."

"Working for Paterson is a struggle, son," Simmons said.

"I told you not to take that job," Darden said. "Only you, Simmons, would take a job with a governor affiliated with the political party diametrically opposed to your own."

"Politics . . . it's all smoke and mirrors," Simmons said. "And for ninety-nine percent of the population, the illusion has become real. It's all infrastructure maintained by a select few to acquire more power and more money. The bells and whistles we call political parties, party conventions, debates, and all the rest—it's all used to keep the masses from realizing how badly they're being bamboozled."

"Are you putting that econ background to work for the governor, or is this more of a political position?" I asked.

"You take no interest in my work, Carp," Simmons said. "We've discussed this at least a thousand times."

"Somebody get this guy a box of tissues and a bouquet of roses and ship them up to New York City," I said.

"You guys are idiots," Darden said.

"What about you, Darden?" Simmons asked. "How are things at the D-trip?"

"Making the world safe for democracy one congressional seat at a time," he replied.

"Well, unless there's any other pressing business on the agenda, I move that we end a little earlier than usual," Simmons said. "I'm beat."

"I've got just one thing," I said. "I need to pick Darden's brain about a certain Congressman Branford Darling."

"The infamous Branford Darling," Darden said, releasing a deep breath. "Looks like he may have a legitimate primary challenger for the first time since he won that seat. I'm guessing he hasn't found time to take you fishing yet."

"Don't they call him 'Congressman for Life' down there?" Simmons said.

"Infamous?" I said.

"Does he really have a serious primary challenger?" Simmons asked. "That's odd. He's easily the most popular Democratic congressman in the state of North Carolina—maybe in the entire Congress—and the fact that I know this says a lot because I know nothing about Democratic politics in that state."

"Darden, why'd you refer to Darling as 'infamous'?" I said.

"Can we please move on?" Darden said.

"I saw Darling today for the first time since that meeting with Prof Jackson," I said. "He acted like we never met."

"Did you actually speak with him?" Simmons asked.

"Briefly," I said. "He treated me like some random campaign staffer."

"Strange," Darden said.

"Now wait a minute, Carp," Simmons started. "Let me play a little devil's advocate here before you get all bent out of shape."

"Now there's a role you've always excelled in, and almost always on your own behalf," I said.

"He must meet a thousand people over the course of a single month," Simmons said, "and I'd wager ninety percent of them are better looking, more articulate, and more important than you."

"Maybe, but how many of them has he sat down with and had a drink?" Darden said.

"Well, that muddies the analysis a little," Simmons said. "What do you know about this guy, Darden? You're at the D-trip. Darling's up for reelection against a legit primary challenger, according to you. You must have *some* fresh intel on the guy."

"I haven't been directly involved in that race," Darden said.

"During our brief exchange," I said, "Darling asked me to tell Ron—his *old pal*—that he said hello."

"They're friends?" Simmons said.

"Why don't you just ask Ron about this?" Darden said.

"Wouldn't Darling have mentioned that he and Ron were old friends during that meeting in July?" Simmons said.

I snickered. "You would think so, right?"

"This smells bad," Simmons said.

"Darden, are you sure you don't have any info on this guy?" I said. "Doesn't the D-trip keep files on these people?"

Ten seconds passed without interruption. "Well, there is one thing," Darden finally said. "But it's not really relevant to you or Ron."

"What is it?" I asked.

"I got a random call about a week ago," Darden said.

"What?" I exclaimed. "You've been holding out?"

"I really shouldn't be telling you this," Darden said.

"Darden!" I said.

"This information has nothing to do with you, Ron, or this Senate race," Darden said.

"Then why'd you bring it up?" Simmons asked.

Darden released a deep breath. "You owe me for this one," he said.

"When Simmons is governor of New York, I'll convince him to appoint you chief of staff."

Simmons snickered. "Right. Because I'll be making all

appointments through Carpenter."

"So," Darden said, "I get this random call, and this guy tells me that Darling's first congressional campaign back in 2000 was financed by some big oil guy—a multibillionaire."

"Oh wow," Simmons said.

"Apparently this billionaire was a rabid Confederate and racist," Darden continued. "Drove around in a pickup truck with a bumper sticker that said, 'The South Shall Rise Again.'"

"There's no law against accepting money from a racist, rabid or otherwise," I said.

"Democratic voters in the Tenth District haven't historically been fierce advocates for racial equality, but they probably wouldn't stand quietly by while Darling took money from a known racist," Simmons said.

"I thought you knew nothing about North Carolina politics?" Darden asked.

"I dabble," Simmons replied. "Plus, Darling's opponents would've pounced on this information. The billionaire's contributions would've been disclosed in Darling's FEC reports."

"But those wouldn't have been all that damning," I said. "Individual donations are capped."

"I'm talking hundreds of thousands of dollars," Darden said. "More than what could have been legally disclosed in FEC reports. In exchange, Darling agreed to vote against any legislation that would benefit African Americans or women at the expense of white men. I did some research. It's hard to track because there aren't too many bills with titles like the Black Jobs Act or the Women's Jobs Act, but from what little digging I did, Darling's record in Congress supports the existence of such an agreement."

"But isn't it also possible that Darling just happened to vote conservatively in each instance you found?" I said. "He's conservative. Does a correlation really prove anything?"

"Wait a minute," Simmons said. "This doesn't make sense. Wouldn't someone have noticed that Darling's campaign was spending well beyond the amounts he was reporting?"

"Not necessarily," I said. "A few bucks here for refreshments at a rally, a few bucks there to buy off political operatives and grass tops. If carefully orchestrated, this stuff could easily fly under the radar. There's also the possibility that this money was being funneled legally into PACs."

"That's true," Simmons said, "but not likely as a practical matter. There's a cap on what individuals can contribute to a single PAC, and not enough PACs would've been playing in Darling's race for our billionaire friend to spread out that kind of cash. But if this *Citizens United* case goes the wrong way . . . well, then we're talking unlimited contributions to PACs and unlimited corporate spending in elections as long as there's no coordination with individual campaigns."

"You're right," I said. "He couldn't have stuffed all that money into PACs—at least not legally. But even if PACs were an option, cash sitting in PAC bank accounts wouldn't have helped Darling keep the lights on. He needed cash to fund day-to-day campaign operations."

"Look, I'm not sure how the donations were made," Darden said. "The guy just said they were off the books."

"If the donations were off the books, how does your source know about them?" Simmons asked.

"I asked that," Darden said. "The billionaire was the source's father."

"Was?" I asked.

"He died last year."

"Jesus," I said. "But what incentive does this guy have to rat out his dead father?"

"Maybe a clear conscience?" Simmons said.

"If that's what he's after, he would've just written an op-ed in the *New York Times*," I said. "I'm assuming you didn't get the billionaire's name?"

"He didn't give me a name, but he gave me enough," Darden said. "I figured it out."

"Putting that otherwise worthless law school degree to use, I see," Simmons said.

"He wanted you to figure it out," I reasoned. "This is nuts."

"The billionaire's name is Jim Randolph Sr.," Darden said. "He moved to Hickory, North Carolina, from Dallas about a year before Darling's first congressional bid in 2000."

"Wait a minute," I said, sweating heavily.

"What?" Darden asked.

"The CEO of NCSEP—that clean energy outfit I've been trying to convince to endorse Ron—his name is Jim Randolph Jr."

"Well now, boys—I think we've officially got ourselves a scandal," Simmons said.

"Were you *actually* going to keep this information from me?" I said.

"It really has nothing to do with Ron's campaign," Darden said.

"Are you kidding?" I said. "An endorsement from Darling could change the entire posture of our campaign overnight. It would send

Jane's camp into a tailspin. And maybe keep Bill out. He won't file unless the DSCC blesses him, and the DSCC won't if they don't think he's a lock to get out of this primary. Both Jane and Bill are counting on getting the moderate and conservative Democratic blocs in the state. Bill figures he'll get a critical mass of progressives because of his relative youth vis-à-vis Jane and because he assumes that progressives, like many others, won't waste their votes on a black man with no chance of winning. Darling is loved by conservatives, liked by moderates, and tolerated by many progressives."

"How's Darling been able to hold together such a broad coalition of voters who often disagree on the issues?" Simmons asked.

"Because he's been crazy strategic with his votes in Congress," I said. "He's been careful not to block key pieces of progressive legislation, moderates respect his independent streak in Congress, and conservatives love him because he consistently votes with them on the issues they see as totally nonnegotiable."

"A chameleon," Simmons said. "He's obviously got a brilliant political mind."

"Yep, and what little he lacks in political acumen he makes up in charisma," I said.

"And you think an endorsement from Darling will get you enough moderates and progressives to keep Bill from entering?" Simmons asked.

"It can't hurt," I said. "We need every vote we can scrounge up. Plus, my sense is that a good deal of Darling's support is based more on his charisma than his voting record. I really believe that for many voters, their perceived connection with him is more important than his substantive stance on issues. That's how he keeps it all together."

"He's like a white Barack Obama," Darden suggested.

"Because of his ability to bring together a broad coalition?" I asked.

"That too," Darden began, "but I was referring to the way Darling uses his personal appeal to avoid the pitfalls that would otherwise tear this coalition apart. Obama's base is black people. Short of calling for the return of slavery, they're gonna support him. There are obviously big historical reasons explaining why he gets such a major pass from blacks on so many issues—rightly or wrongly—but at the end of the day, he's gonna have their support. This gives him the ability to take stances that, if taken by white Democrats, would incur the career-ending wrath of the black community. And even in cases when Obama does piss black folks off, he's able to deploy charisma to calm their rage. The unflinching support Darling has among conservative Democrats in the Tenth District is no different. He's one of them—

conservative, Southern, and white. You'd think he was born in the Blue Ridge Mountains right along with them. He's even got their accent. As long as he stays true to core principles, these folks are gonna support him. And on the rare occasion when he has to step off the plantation briefly to appease moderates or progressives, he just serves up a healthy helping of that Darling charm, and all is forgotten."

"Well said, D," I said.

"Obama and Darling—same guy, different race," Simmons said. "How about that."

"As political animals, absolutely," Darden concluded.

"Well, Carp," Simmons said, "for many political reasons, I don't see Obama racing down to North Carolina to campaign for your boy. So how are you guys gonna get black folks onboard?"

"They've been just as hard to lock down as the other constituencies," I said. "From what I can tell so far, most of the new black voters Obama brought into play checked out after last November. As far as they're concerned, they've done their duty. Then there are the black folks who always vote, whether there's an Obama on the ballot or not. Most of them are already in Jane's back pocket."

"So what are you gonna do about that?" Simmons asked.

"I'll figure that out," I said. "I'll just work smarter than everyone else, right?"

"Sounds like you've got it all figured out," Darden said. "But there's one not-so-minor problem. This intel about Darling doesn't get you any closer to an endorsement . . . unless you plan on—"

"Lightly nudging the congressman," I said.

"I think you may also be able to nudge Jim Jr.," Simmons said. "Two endorsements for the price of one."

"I think it's pretty obvious that Jim Jr. wants to be nudged," I said. "The question is, why?"

"Be careful," Darden said. "This isn't one of our harebrained law school schemes to get Simmons out of some ridiculous lust triangle. This is major-league stuff. Darling could ruin you."

"I get it," I said.

"I need protection here," Darden said. "I need your word that you'll take precautions. This can never be traced back to me."

"Of course," I said.

"Obviously," Simmons said. "Dammit! I forgot to call Cass back."

"How is Cassandra?" Darden asked.

"She asked the wrong question last week," Simmons said.

"What was that?" Darden asked.

"'What's the password to your phone?'" Simmons said.

"At least she asked," I said. "You know they've got technology now where they can break in without the password."

"Who's 'they'?" Darden asked.

"Women," I replied. We all laughed heartily. "Gentlemen, it's been a pleasure, but I've got a six o'clock start tomorrow."

"It's only one o'clock now," Simmons said. "Al Carpenter is losing his edge—what else have you lost?"

"My patience," I said. "Let's do this again next month. Same time?"

"Let's try for a little earlier," Simmons said.

"You guys are the ones working around the clock," Darden said. "I'm nine to five."

"Let's try for nine o'clock," Simmons suggested.

"Good deal," I said. "This has been productive. Thanks for the info and analysis."

"What info?" Darden asked.

"Oh—right," I said. "Thanks for nothing."

"Later," Darden said.

"Before you guys go—I just did a quick search on Randolph Sr.," Simmons said. "Wife died ten years before he moved to North Carolina. Two children, Sean and Jim Jr. Also looks like they aren't exactly close. Sean wrote a nasty op-ed in the *Washington Post* a few months back about NCSEP. Sean isn't exactly a fan of sustainable energy."

"Or maybe he just hates his brother," Darden said.

"So the call could've come from Sean," I said.

"But in dragging their father's name through the mud, aren't they also hurting themselves?" Simmons asked. "They've still got his name."

"There's also the possibility that the story isn't true," I said. "Maybe there were no illegal contributions—and maybe Darling didn't cut a deal with Jim Sr."

"My gut says this is legit," Simmons said.

"Yeah, your gut," I said. "Is this, by chance, the same gut that once infamously advised you to take three different girls out on the same night? Yeah, that worked out well."

"Nevertheless," Simmons replied.

"Looks like your work is cut out for you, Carp," Darden said. "Night."

I sighed. "Looks that way. Good night."

"I still won," Simmons said, defending his actions in that debacle for what must've been the twentieth time. "That's what matters."

"Be patient—and careful—with Bristol, Carp," Darden said.

"There's more at stake there than whether you guys finally stop playing around and get together. She's also Jennifer's best friend."

"Why are you focusing on Jennifer?" Simmons said. "Bristol's your friend too. Darden, what's going on with—"

"Good night, boys," I said. "I've got it under control."

CHAPTER NINE

I AWOKE to the familiar cadence of Ron's stump speech. The trees lining Interstate 40 swayed gently in the breeze as reddish-brown and orange-yellow leaves set sail for unknown destinations. Bristol slept awkwardly to my right, her head nudged between the seatback and the window. I could hear Casey gently snoring in the backseat.

"What you should do is incorporate some of Bill's stump speech," I said.

"Oh yeah?" Ron said. "What parts?"

"I guess the sarcasm didn't quite shine through that time," I replied.

"Why don't you come up here and drive," Carmichael said. "I'll come back there and coach. You've been worthless the last two hours."

"I didn't know I'd slept that long," I said, stifling a yawn. "Well, Vance-Aycock is officially in the books."

"I really think that was a useful event," Ron said. "We made a good splash, and I think we looked much larger than we are."

"Perception is reality," Bristol said, roused from her slumber.

"On Monday we need to circle back to NCSEP," Ron said. "It would've been nice to have that endorsement to parade around all those party people."

"I'll try Jim again first thing tomorrow morning," I said.

"I heard Darling made an appearance yesterday," Carmichael said.

"I actually spoke with him briefly," I said. "Which reminds me . . . Ron, do you have a personal relationship with him?"

Ron pursed his lips and ran a hand through his hair. "Not really," he said at last. "At least not anymore."

"What happened?" Bristol asked.

Ron let out a deep breath. "We were best friends growing up in Winston-Salem. Folks don't really know about that."

"Yeah, no kidding," I said.

"Funny, right?" Ron said, smiling. "We were pretty close back in the day. He'd come over to play at my house and vice versa. And that was back when that sort of thing wasn't really done. In the thick of the movement."

"Your parents were pretty forward thinking, huh?" I said.

"I'd say our friendship developed in spite of our parents," Ron said. "We hit it off day one of first grade. I remember the first time I asked my mother if I could play at his house. My parents did a pretty good job of shielding me from the racism in Winston, so I didn't really have a sense of what it meant to be black versus white."

"That's pretty remarkable," I said. "To be—what, five or six years old?—in the sixties and blissfully ignorant of America's primary preoccupation."

"I guess that's right," Ron said. "At first my mother said I couldn't go. She reeled off a bunch of reasons why—it wasn't convenient to drive across town, she didn't know Branford's parents, she didn't feel comfortable with me being at a stranger's house, et cetera, et cetera. But as the saying goes, you can't stop the rain from falling. Before long, we were hangin' out every Friday night, sleepovers, the whole deal. He lived in the biggest house I'd ever seen."

"They were wealthy?" I asked.

"Very."

"Tobacco money?" Carmichael said.

"No idea. Neither of his parents worked. Anyway, they lost most of it in the crash of '87. Years down the line, we both went to Duke, same major. We partied together on weekends. We were inseparable."

"I'm assuming Uncle Malcolm was around for this too," I said.

"Around is a *major* understatement," Ron said, grinning. "Your uncle never saw a party he didn't like. I'd say the three of us were a lot like you, Darden, and Simmons, at least personality wise."

"Really?" I said.

Ron nodded. "Darden is like me—unassuming, almost gentle, but you sleep on us at your own risk. Then there's Malcolm. He was our Simmons—outgoing, gregarious, candid almost to a fault, and maybe even a little chip on the shoulder. It's their big hearts that save them both. Then there's Branford." He paused. "He was a good guy, but he's also the one you always had to watch out for if he wasn't on your team.

He was our resident consigliere. Nothing important ever got done without running it past him first."

"When was the last time you talked to him?" Carmichael said.

"It's probably been ten years since we sat down and had a real conversation—you know, talked about our kids, wives, and the like. I see him socially at events, but it's always just a 'hey there' or 'hiya, old pal.'"

"So what happened?" I asked. "How does a friendship that beat all those odds end up dead in the water?"

"Race—the thing that almost kept us from becoming friends in the first place. It finally caught up to him."

"What do you mean 'caught up to him'?" I said.

"Picture it. Junior year of college. Sociology class. Our professor's latest research focused on how closely linked humans are. Being the product of black and white parents, she had a particular interest in interracial connections. She paired us up for a family tree project. The assignment was to see if any of the pairs had a convergence somewhere in their respective trees. It counted for thirty percent of our final grade."

"Wait a minute," I said. "How large was this class? I don't see how this kind of assignment could work in a big lecture class, logistically I mean."

"Good observation," Ron said. "It was an eight-person seminar, and impossible to get into—the joke on campus was that you had a better chance of being struck by lightning. There was also a rigorous application process. Branford and I were determined to get into that seminar, and we vowed to do just that from the day we learned about it during the second week of freshman year. Of course we had to wait a short eternity for that day to come since it was only open to second-semester juniors."

"I'm having a little trouble connecting the dots here," I said. "Why would two presumably normal eighteen-year-olds be so hell-bent on getting into some random sociology seminar more than two years before they were even eligible?"

"Because the people who got into that seminar were minor celebrities because of it."

"Now *that* I can see," I replied. "That's plausible eighteen-year-old conduct. How was the class?"

"The class was pretty good," Ron said. "The professor was out of this world. Juanita Acheson . . . uhmm, uhmm, uhmm—she was something. An all-star, plain and simple. At the time she was just thirty years old, but she'd already published three major works in her field. One of them was already being called the most important sociological work in race and ethnicity in fifty years."

"And she was African American too," I said.

Ron chuckled. "Starting to get the picture now?"

"Oh, it's coming into focus quite nicely," I replied.

"Anyway, Branford and I spent something like nine hours pulling together our applications for this seminar. Acheson wanted to know where we grew up, where our parents were born and raised, and their parents too—not to mention all of their occupations and educational backgrounds. We probably spent another nine hours trying to figure out why she was after all that information in the first place. I should also tell you that basically everything about that seminar was kept secret. We signed a nondisclosure agreement as part of the application. We all agreed that if selected, we wouldn't repeat anything discussed during class sessions with anyone other than the folks in the seminar room, until her death."

"I've never heard of anything like this," I said.

"She died two years back—breast cancer."

"Oh my God," Bristol sighed.

"Went to the funeral, actually," Ron continued. "You'd have thought the pope died. That's how big she was. Jimmy Carter even showed up. They were both from Plains."

"Plains, Georgia," I said.

"That's the one," Ron said. "But Acheson didn't meet Carter until she made it big as an academic."

"That's rich," I said. "There are more people living on a New York City block than in all of Plains."

"That's enough from you, *Britannica*," Bristol said. "Tell us about the assignment, Ron."

"So Branford and I get into the class."

"And you were paired together," Bristol said.

"Yes, because we're from the same town," Ron said. He shook his head at the memory.

"That explains the ridiculous application," I said. "She needed to pair people from the same town to make the assignment effective."

"That's right," Ron said. "Professor Acheson not only arranged for the funding from the university but also got our other professors to agree to let us miss up to a week of classes so that we could go home to conduct research. Luckily Branford and I didn't have too far to travel. One afternoon we were combing through records at the Register of Deeds office in Forsyth County. We'd both gotten all the way back to our great-great-grandfathers when I found something. I forget what the document was, but it showed that his paternal great-great-great-grandparents had a child named Rutherford who was one of five children. My great-great-grandfather's name was Rutherford Johnson III."

"Rutherford's not the most common name, but there must've been a handful in Forsyth County back then," I said.

"True. But then Branford found another document. This one showed his paternal great-great-great-grandparents had only four children, and Rutherford wasn't on that list."

"So you two figured that Darling's folks concealed Rutherford's birth because he had a different mother?" Carmichael asked.

"Your great-great-great-grandmother," Bristol said.

"Yes, that was the conclusion we came to," Ron said. "It was like Branford had the wind knocked out of him."

"I don't understand," I said. "Why would he care that some guy way back in his family history had an affair?"

"Because they were probably slave owners," Bristol said. "The mother was probably a slave."

Ron nodded. "The irony," he continued, "was that Branford was president of some superleftist group on campus. A libertarian outfit, I think. I can't remember what it was called. He even led a rally to protest the school's attempt to name a library after a huge donor descended from a line of slave owners. Anyway, nothing was the same after that. We finished our report, turned it in, and got an A. But our friendship was over."

"Did you have to present your findings to the class?" I asked.

"No. Branford asked Acheson to excuse us given the nature of the information we found. It took some doing, but he convinced her. I'm not sure anyone else could've pulled that off."

"And now you two are running for office in the same state at the same time," Carmichael said. "How long can it be before some reporter makes the connection?"

"Yeah," I said. "Even assuming the press doesn't discover the family connection, won't someone at least ask why you guys aren't closer? A lot of people must remember you were best friends in college."

"I don't think it'll come up," Ron said. "Our friendship came and went long before social media and the twenty-four-hour news cycle. In fact, I'd ask that you guys keep this to yourselves. I have no interest in putting Branford in an awkward position during this election." We all nodded in assent.

"By the way," I said, "when I spoke to him yesterday, he asked me to tell his *old pal* he said hello."

Ron turned toward the window as if looking to the cascading leaves for a response.

"We need his endorsement," I said.

"Are you out of your mind, Carpenter?" Carmichael said. "His district is as blue dog as they come. He wouldn't dare."

"Historically, yes, they're pretty conservative. But word on the street is his district's become significantly more progressive with the influx of more liberal-leaning students and young professionals," I said, winking at Bristol. "If we get a big name like Darling, I think we'll pick up a significant number of progressive votes statewide because of the press it'll get. Hell, we might even pick up some of the moderates. At a minimum, it'll grab their attention. Then we can work from there."

"I don't know," Carmichael said. "I don't think even the great Lyndon Johnson could convince Darling to endorse Ron, and he got Southern Democrats to vote for the Civil Rights Act!"

"Stranger things have happened," Casey added, rising from her nap.

Ron shook his head. "I have to agree with Carmichael. I don't see what Branford stands to gain from endorsing. I do see what he stands to lose."

"We shouldn't underestimate the growing progressive element in the Tenth District," Bristol began. "And for the first time, he's got a competitive primary battle against a *female* progressive—Julia Remini. The fact that someone with that profile is willing to run speaks volumes, doesn't it? In the last poll I saw, she was at thirty-five percent to his fifty. Endorsing Ron would be a strong signal that he's serious about taking a more liberal stance on the issues that matter to women and progressives."

"But won't he alienate the more conservative voters?" Carmichael asked. "He needs them to win, right?"

"He needs conservatives," Bristol began, "but he also needs a critical mass of progressives. My guess is that most truly conservative Dems will vote for him, even with the endorsement, because they're absolutely not going to vote for a woman. And he'll pick off a critical mass of progressives by endorsing Ron, by far the most progressive US Senate candidate. It's a win-win for Darling and us."

"From where I'm sitting, it looks more like a win-win for us and a might-win for Darling," Carmichael said.

"I have to say, Bristol," Ron said, "I like your argument. The ultimate question is whether Branford and his staffers are willing to step outside of the old way of thinking. There's a reason North

Carolina has never elected a black senator."

"Maybe Obama's election has opened the door to new thinking," Casey said.

"He opened the door alright—problem is, no one's home," I said. "It's obviously your call, Ron, but I think it's doable."

Ron ran his hands through his hair again. "I don't think he'll do it," he said. "But I don't know that we have much of a choice in asking him. We're getting killed out here. I'll leave the logistics to you, Carp—but be careful. And I don't want him embarrassed."

"I'll go ahead and call his people," I said. "Like Casey said, 'stranger things have happened.'" I winked at Bristol, tapped the tip of her nose, and settled into the seat, hoping to catch a few more minutes of shut-eye before arriving in Raleigh.

I closed my eyes. "Tomorrow afternoon you've got that in-studio interview with WRAL," I said.

"What time?" Ron asked.

"Three thirty," Carmichael said.

"Impressive, Carmichael," I said. "Did you write it down on the back of your hand?"

Carmichael brandished a middle finger in the rearview mirror.

"Attaboy!" I said. "After that Lyndon Johnson comment, a strange feeling was beginning to well up inside me—respect, I think. Thanks for putting the universe back in order. And I'll tell you people something else: You guys are gonna stop flipping me off. I'll tell ya that right now."

"I do *not* feel like giving this speech today," Ron said. He had become adept at using his bubble to filter out the constant bickering between Carmichael and me. I'd concluded that he'd perfected this skill more out of necessity than a lack of interest.

"Hey, Bristol, why don't you give this speech for me? You did a bang-up job at that teachers' event a few weeks back when Casey and I had that conflict."

"You can't back out last minute," Bristol said.

"Sure I can," Ron said. "Just tell them I got food poisoning."

"I wouldn't joke about that," I said. "Roberts could've arranged for that."

"I just don't have any gas left in the tank after this weekend."

"Don't use the word *gas*," I said. "Clean energy, remember?"

"Right," Ron said.

"Better get some rest now," I said. "You go on in a few hours. You've gotta nail this speech. We need to eventually get the WC-CSP's endorsement."

"That's the black 501(c)(4) in Wake County, right?" Carmichael said.

"Yep," I said. "The Wake County Committee for Social Progress."

Ron turned to me. "You've been taking care of Keri Jameson, I assume?"

"I think so," I said.

"Well, let's not think so—let's know so," Ron said. "I know WC-CSP doesn't usually endorse until early April, but Keri has a long memory. Any contact with the other guy we know on the endorsement committee? What's his name—Raymond, isn't it?"

"I've called him a few times, but you know how that goes," I said.

"He's been giving you the old 'what've you done for me lately?' routine, has he?" Carmichael said.

"Oh, he's been giving you the shakedown as well, Carmichael?" Ron said.

"Raymond's tight with lots of ministers in Wake County," Carmichael replied. "He knows I can get to them much faster through him than through cold calls."

"I don't care how you get Ron into the pulpit and speaking in those churches on Sundays, but get him in there," I said.

"Understood," Carmichael said.

"We're headed to Carp's place so I can shower and change before WC-CSP, right?" Ron said.

"Yes," Carmichael said.

"Beautiful," Ron said. "Until then, I hereby declare it naptime."

"Just one more thing before you start counting sheep," I said. "If you and Darling are both from the same town, how is it that you don't share the same heavy drawl?"

"Let me put it to you this way," Ron said. "I don't know anyone from Winston-Salem with an accent like Branford's."

*****

As soon as we walked into my apartment, I nudged Bristol into my bedroom. "What's your schedule look like for the rest of the day?" I said.

"I have a decent amount of work I need to catch up on at the office. Why, what's up?"

"I need you to do a little digging on Darling. We need to know what we don't know."

"I'm sure there's a ton we don't know about him," she said. "But we don't have time to go on a wild goose chase."

"Well, let's start with that protest at Duke," I said. "One of the school papers would've covered it. I have a hunch there's some other reason Darling's kept his distance from Ron all this time."

"You don't think it's enough that Ron knows Darling's descended from slave owners? And that Ron's folks were probably his folks' slaves?"

"That's pretty screwed up, but how would ignoring Ron prevent that story from coming out? Plus, he knows Ron's too good a guy to bring that up and risk embarrassing him."

"I suppose."

"Well, let's dig a little deeper and see if we can figure out what he's *really* scared of."

Her eyes widened. "You're going to blackmail Darling? What happened to talking to his people?"

"Those guys are hacks. They can't think outside the box. They'll just keep running his campaigns the same old way until it stops working."

"So much for changing hearts and minds."

"We can still do that," I said. "But let's focus on changing the voters' hearts and minds instead of the consultants'."

"Fair enough," she said. "But what are you going to do? You can't just call headquarters and ask for him."

"I can and I will. I'll throw out just enough details to get him to meet with me. But first I need more information."

She sighed. "I'll head to the library now."

"Please give my regards to Professor Davis."

"I'll tell Mom you said hello." She gave my arm a quick squeeze and kissed my cheek before leaving me alone in the room.

"Where did Bristol run off to?" Carmichael said as I reentered the living room.

"The library, to dig up dirt on Darling," I said. "Where's Casey?"

"She took the car back to Chapel Hill—has to pick one of the kids up from piano lessons."

"Is Ron almost ready?"

"Well, I don't hear the shower running anymore, so I imagine he's getting close."

"Good," I said. "We've got to keep him in good spirits. I think he's fading a little. Part of that means getting a campaign manager so he spends less time worrying about logistics and more time perfecting his stump and raising money."

"I mention it from time to time, but he always says, 'I'll hire one tomorrow if you pay for it.'"

"Keep at it, please," I said. "You're with him more than anyone. If we're gonna win, we have to raise more money. That means getting him in the right mindset and freeing him up to make more money calls."

"Gotcha," he said. "I'll go check on the candidate."

"Wait a minute, Carmichael."

"What's up?"

I gripped his shoulder. "Thank you."

"For what?"

"For everything."

"You're welcome," he said, shaking my outstretched hand. "But you're still an ass."

"Carmichael—that's my job."

CHAPTER TEN

THE NEXT MORNING, I rose at six and got a full workout in at my apartment building's first-floor gym. I couldn't stop thinking about the events of the past few days. I was also becoming more than a little nervous about the path I was preparing to take. Darden was right—this was the big leagues. If I shot and missed, Darling would destroy me. I couldn't bet the whole campaign, my career, and Darling's on some anonymous campaign finance fraud story.

Although I wasn't prepared to bet the farm on it, there was a seemingly insignificant piece of evidence buttressing that caller's story: the fact that he called the D triple-C. Who would call them to blow the whistle on a corrupt politician? Ninety-nine percent of Americans couldn't tell you what the D triple-C is to save their lives. I didn't know until a few months back, and here I was running a US Senate campaign. But still, I couldn't use this information. The whole thing was just a little too convenient. Even though I'd decided not to use the fraud story, I was still desperately curious to know who had called it in. Was it Jim or his brother Sean? And why? Whoever called Darden was no amateur—and it seemed he'd done so with the specific intent of getting that information to me.

As I entered mile three of five on the treadmill, I began to experience significant discomfort in my stomach, much like the feeling you have as you walk into a final exam for which you know with absolute certainty you haven't adequately prepared. I pushed on despite this annoyance and finished all five miles. Then I sprinted to the bathroom next to the gym and promptly regurgitated all over the sink, toilet, and floor. Utterly exhausted and embarrassed, I approached the cleaning lady mopping the hardwood floors in the building's foyer, tucked a twenty into the front pocket of her smock, and said, "I'm really sorry about the bathroom."

I promptly started a pot of coffee after returning to my apartment. I scanned the seemingly unending queue of unread e-mail that had flooded my inbox overnight. The rising sun shone so brightly against the computer screen that I could no longer make out any characters, so I decided to join the sun out on the balcony for a bit, finish my coffee, and watch the cars intermittently scuttle up and down the otherwise quiet street below.

Within a few minutes, my phone began screaming for my attention. *Can't I have even this anymore?*

"Good morning, Ms. Davis," I said when I answered.

"Good morning, Alex. How was your coffee?"

"Near perfection. Did you find anything on Darling?"

"Where there's smoke—"

"There's some idiot who just tossed his cigarette," I said excitedly. "What did you find?"

"A news article from that library dedication."

"Yes!" I shouted, falling back against the brick wall.

"You were right. There's definitely something else he doesn't want the world to know. He was quoted in that article."

"Why is it that college kids can never keep their traps shut? What did he say?"

"And I quote, 'No one descended from folks who trafficked in human beings should have his or her name attached to anything meaningful, and that includes a library belonging to an institution whose students, faculty, and board adhere to the principles of equality and justice for all. Slave owners are among the most detestable animals this world has ever seen, and their progeny should be treated as such.'"

"Is that all?" I asked. "Where's the rest of it?"

"Are you kidding?"

"Of course! You just changed the course of a US Senate race! How long did this take to find?"

"Only a few hours," she said. "Editions of this newspaper weren't available electronically that far back, so I had to go to the microfilm. But it didn't end there."

"What do you mean?"

"The spool containing this article was misfiled."

"A cover-up," I said. "We're Carl Bernstein and Bob Woodward. Did you make copies?"

"What am I, an amateur?" she said. "Of course I made copies."

I felt a sudden pang of anxiety, then sadness. "If this gets out, it might ruin him."

"You're right," Bristol said. "You've got a lot of power right now. Use it wisely."

"So this is what real-world politics feels like. Big stakes now."

"I also found a picture of Branford and Ron. It's from a tailgate at a Duke-UNC football game their sophomore year. They really *were* good friends. It's oozing from the photo. Got it from the yearbook."

"Wow."

"Well, I think you have enough to get what you want from him," she said. "Be nice. Oh, have you seen today's paper yet?"

"Not yet."

"Darling's gonna be in Raleigh today meeting with the governor. Four o'clock."

"Interesting," I said. "Can you bring the copies to the office?"

"Obviously."

"Thanks for all this."

"Yeah, yeah, yeah. I thought about making you do the research when you asked yesterday. Then I realized you'd probably botch it, so I just did it myself."

"Occasionally someone else on this campaign has to get some glory. Besides, you've got the journalism degree, not me."

"Bye, Al."

*****

MY PHONE RANG as I made the familiar left turn onto Wade Avenue heading toward Durham.

"Morning!" Ron said.

"Good morning," I said. "You're online awful early today, and awfully chipper. It isn't even nine yet, is it?"

"It's 8:58. I woke up with endorsements on the brain."

"That's every morning for you."

"I guess that's right," he said. "Have you been able to get in touch with Jim yet?"

"Not yet, but I'm heading into the office now," I said.

"Why not just call now?" he said. "I think he gets in around seven most mornings. I want this off your plate before lunchtime so you can focus on the thousand other things that need to get done."

"I'll call as soon as we hang up."

"Thanks."

"See you later." After taking a third sip from my second cup of coffee, I dialed NCSEP.

"Good morning, North Carolina Sustainable Energy Partners. How may I direct your call?"

"Good morning. Can I have Jim Randolph, please?"

"I don't believe he's in yet, but I think Mrs. Craven is. May I ask who's calling?"

"Bill Billingsworth," I said. *Please let this work.*

"Oh! Good morning, Mr. Billingsworth. How are you?"

"I'm doin' . . . mighty good, darlin'. And how are you this mornin'?"

"Well, hearing from you has just made my day! Wait 'til I tell my sister who *I* spoke to this morning. My goodness! Well, good luck to you in the primary! Hold one moment, please."

Within seconds, Linda came on. "Good morning, Bill!" she said. "Did you have a change of heart about the carbon bill?"

"Good mornin', Linda! How are you?"

"Mr. Carpenter," she said, exhaling loudly. "Did you have your name changed?"

"Linda, darlin', I haven't, but I've been thinkin' we oughtta change yours. Mrs. Linda Carpenter. Has a nice ring to it, doesn't it? Here's what we'll do. I'll swing by your office, propose properly, then we'll head over to the courthouse. We'll be hitched before lunchtime."

"Mr. Carpenter, we've been over this. We cannot afford to endorse a candidate with no chance of winning. It's nothing personal." The last time I'd called, the week before, she'd been more blunt: "A black candidate has no chance of winning a US Senate race in North Carolina." She'd also asked that I keep that particular comment off the record.

"Mrs. Craven, I understand your position one hundred percent. But you know just as well as I do that NCSEP can't afford to have this carbon legislation gutted in the next Congress."

"I'm not sure I follow, Mr. Carpenter."

"I know you're waiting on Bill, or even Jane to get behind you guys on clean energy, but it's not gonna happen. You know it. I know it. My unborn children know it. It's just too politically risky for either of them. They're centrists, pure and simple. And try though he might to convince folks otherwise, Bill's stance on almost every issue is right in line with Jane's."

"Why is supporting the carbon bill any riskier politically for them than for Ron? Won't he lose the same supporters if you ally with us?"

"The difference is that Ron believes that reducing our carbon footprint isn't a matter of politics," I said. "It's just plainly the right thing to do for the environment and our children. We think it's important that NCSEP is able to move forward with its work, and we're prepared to lose some votes to make that happen."

"Well . . . I ah . . . had no idea Ron was so passionate about our work." That was a lie. I'd expressed the same sentiment the last time we spoke.

"Wouldn't it be nice for NCSEP if Ron mentioned your company and the importance of saving the carbon bill in every single stump speech he delivers between now and the primary?"

"And what about the time between the primary and the general?" she asked, newly curious.

"I thought you said Ron couldn't win the primary?"

"Hypothetically speaking, of course."

"Of course, Linda. When NCSEP endorses Ron, we become partners. That means we're partners before and after the primary. As a matter of principle, we want this legislation to survive just as much as you do, but we need an endorsement to justify spending more time talking about clean energy—and NCSEP."

"Everywhere he appears, every speech, and every debate—is that what you're offering?"

"Correct."

"Interesting. But this is risky for us. If Ron loses, our cause, our brand . . . it all takes a hit."

"First of all, he won't lose. Second, even if he were to lose, don't you think the benefits of having free publicity for seven months outweigh whatever collateral damage you may suffer should he lose? If he loses, there's a good chance NCSEP won't have the votes to save this legislation anyway. If history is any indication, Democrats will lose both the House and the Senate this cycle. Read any newspapers since Obama took office in January? The Republicans are determined to undermine him however and whenever they can. They're pushing a scorched earth policy, and they're not shy about it. Think about it, Linda. This is much more than an election. It's a battle for the soul of America. Are you really prepared to sit on the sideline and have no candidate so much as mention NCSEP? We're offering you free publicity on an almost daily basis. From where I'm sitting, you and Jim need us as much as we need you."

"How do you propose to win the primary?" she said. "Everyone knows Jane. You'd have to steal a lot of votes from her, and Bill, whenever he gets into the race."

"Did you know that thirty percent of the primary electorate is African American?" I said.

"I didn't."

"Most people don't, but when we win the primary, it won't matter that we did so with a majority of black votes. Ron will be the Democratic Party's nominee, and nothing else will matter."

"Perhaps."

"I might also add that I read the article in the *News & Observer* the other day about NCSEP. I read every single word of it. You guys are running low on cash. I also know that a good amount of Jim's fortune is tied up in assets he can't easily liquidate."

"What?" she spluttered. "That wasn't in the article! How'd you—I mean, you don't know—"

"You'll take my offer to Jim, won't you, Linda?"

"Of course. But no promises."

"Thank you very much, Linda."

"Good day, Mr. Carpenter."

"So I'm assuming the wedding isn't happening today?"

"You're pushing your luck, Mr. Carpenter."

"Have a great morning, Linda. I look forward to hearing from you."

*****

I PULLED UP TO THE OFFICE just as Ron and Carmichael were hopping out of the Tahoe. "There's nothing quite as unpleasant as seeing your face first thing in the morning," Carmichael said with a smile.

"What are you guys doing here so early?" I asked. "Shouldn't you be at that prayer breakfast in Greensboro?"

Ron shook his head. "We've got to be more strategic with my time. Nothing's more important right now than fundraising. I think Casey's already inside making calls, reaching out to key folks over at the North Carolina Association of Teachers."

"Awesome," I said. "I hear Jane's been going at them pretty hard."

Ron glanced up toward his office window on the second floor of the house. "I really hate begging for money," he said.

"Well, if it's any consolation," I said, "I'll be on the phone all morning begging too."

"Who's at the top of your list?" Ron said.

"Keri Jameson at WC-CSP and Jack Monroe at DC-OSP."

"Great," Ron said. "In the last six cycles, the candidate carrying WC-CSP's endorsement received no less than seventy-five percent of the black vote in five major counties."

"I know," I said. "Keri reminds me every time I see her."

"Wait a minute, did you say Jack Monroe?" Carmichael said. "He wouldn't be a short black guy from down east by any chance?"

"Yep," I said.

"He's a good guy," Carmichael said. "A little awkward but a nice guy nonetheless. I played some serious basketball with him back in the day. Haven't seen him in years."

"What the hell's 'serious basketball'?" I said. "You couldn't put a basketball through a hoop if your life depended on it. Besides, you're from Wake County, and he's from—what, Martin County? How did you end up balling with him?"

"His grandparents live in Wake County," Carmichael explained. "While you were spending summers in Nash County golfing and fishing, we were in Wake County ballin' down at the YMCA."

"I don't ever want to hear you say the word *ballin'* again, got that?" I said.

"Small world," Ron chimed in. "You're what, twenty-four, Carmichael?"

"Yup," he replied.

"I have a nephew from Wake County who also plays summer ball down at the Y, but he's a lot younger than you."

"Good old Jack Monroe," I said.

"What's his position over at DC-OSP?" Carmichael said.

"Well, there're two answers to that question," I said. "There's what the website says and there's what he actually gets paid to do."

Carmichael pulled up the Durham County Organization for Social Progress's website on his smartphone. His brow furrowed. "Director of Affordable Housing Policy," he read aloud. "Why do you need to talk to the guy in charge of affordable housing policy?"

Ron chuckled. "Because he gets paid to make sure DC-OSP endorses candidates who are going to win Democratic primaries," Ron said. "That Jack's a real climber. He doesn't take a single step unless he thinks it'll bring him closer to being a power player in North Carolina politics. Anyway, Al, what's the latest word on NCSEP?"

"I've got them in the pot," I said. "Now it's time to fill it with water."

"Good deal," Ron said.

"Again with the metaphors," Carmichael said.

I opened the back door of the house and held it open as Ron and Carmichael filed past the breakfast nook and into the kitchen. "It's my way of making sure you never have a clue what I'm talking about," I said.

Casey was leaning forward on the kitchen island, cell phone to her ear. "Morning, Casey," I whispered. She mouthed *good morning* as I passed by. Ron stopped to kiss her cheek before heading upstairs to start panhandling.

"Think you can manage ten thousand today?" I called after him.

"That's a little steep, no?" he said, abruptly pausing his ascent.

"Shoot for the stars and—"

"And if you miss, you'll end up far, far away from Foul Carpenter," Carmichael finished.

"Very good, Carmichael," I said. "I think you're finally ready for the second-grade curriculum."

Carmichael grinned. "That's all you've got for me?"

Ron snorted. "You two need help."

"Carmichael, why don't you pick up where you left off calling Democratic Party county chairs?" I said. "After lunch, you can get back to chasing down ministers."

"Sounds good," Carmichael said.

"And I'd like to get a plug for NCSEP, clean energy, and the carbon bill into Ron's stump," I said. "You can take a crack at drafting the new language."

"Sure, but why mention NCSEP specifically?" Carmichael asked.

"Because that's the deal we're cutting," I said. "And Ron, I don't want to see you again until you've raised at least five thousand."

"Aye aye, private," he said, continuing up the stairs at a moderate jog.

I turned into my office just under the stairwell, unpacked my laptop, and skimmed the call list I'd prepared the prior night. Keri topped the list, as I'd suspected. As I began dialing her number, another call came in. "NCSEP" popped up on the caller ID.

"Al Carpenter," I said.

"Morning, Al, Jim Randolph here."

"Jim," I said. "Getting an early start this morning?"

"This is actually a little late for me. I'm an early bird."

"Me too," I said. "Some habits never go away."

"Ain't that the truth?"

"Well, I'm hoping you're calling with good news."

"I am at that," he said. "I'd like to speak with you about formally endorsing Ron's campaign."

"Well, I'll tell you what, I wish every morning started like this."

"I take it this is good news?"

"Abbbsolutely," I said. "Ron will be thrilled."

"Linda will call you later to work out the details. I've gotta run to a meeting with some investors."

"Thanks, Jim. Looking forward to our partnership."

"Good-bye, Al."

I hung up and looked at my phone. *That was easy. A little too easy.* But I had too much on my mind to analyze the ins and outs behind the quick turnaround. I hopped up from my desk and returned to the den, where Carmichael sat rifling through a file folder at his window-side desk.

"Seen Bristol?"

"Not in yet," he said.

"What's Ron got scheduled for lunch?"

Carmichael consulted his notepad. "Nothing planned. We'll probably just shoot downtown and grab something quick."

"Good deal. I'm gonna have to run over to Nashville around twelve o'clock. Should be back by three thirty."

"Okay." I returned to my office, took a deep breath, and called Darling's campaign headquarters in Hickory.

"Darling for US Congress," a female voice answered.

"Can I have Congressman Darling, please?" I said.

"May I tell him who's calling?" she asked.

"Bill Billingsworth," I said. *Hey, it worked the first time.*

"Transferring you to the congressman, Mr. Billingsworth," she said cheerily. A brief silence, then "Mornin', Bill."

"Good morning, Congressman," I said. "But this isn't Bill Billingsworth—this is Al Carpenter."

"I'm sorry," he said. "But I don't believe I know anyone by that name."

"Sure you do," I said. "We ran into each other this past weekend in the lobby of the Grove Park. You asked me to say hello to Ron Johnson for you."

"Oh . . . right, right, right . . . Carpenter," he said. "Did ya give Ron my regards?"

"I did, Congressman." As Bristol and Casey tiptoed into my office, I quickly scribbled the words *Darling's on the phone* on my yellow legal pad and held it up. Bristol winked before following Casey back through the door.

"Oh, fine, fine," Darling said. "What can I do for ya, son?"

"Well, I tell ya, I hate to jam you up like this, but I really need to meet with you today—in person—over in Nashville."

"Well, I'd love to meet with ya, son, but I just don't know how I'd be able to swing that today."

"Aren't you gonna be in Raleigh today for a meeting with the governor?"

"Well . . . yes, but—"

"And that meeting isn't until four o'clock, so you'd have plenty of time."

"Well, son, my schedule's mighty tight today. I've got to stop over in Winston for an event and then hightail it over to Raleigh to see the governor. I just don't see how—"

"Let's meet at Pete's in Nashville," I interrupted. "You know the place?"

"Of course I know the place. Best small-town burger I ever did sink my teeth into. But I can't make it today, son. Maybe next time you'll give me a little more notice."

"Congressman, does the name Lovejoy Library mean anything to you?" I paused. "Why don't you just come on over to Nashville and have a burger with me?"

The line was silent save for the sound of a pen tapping an empty glass with metronomic precision. Finally, "Why the heck not? I haven't been over to Nashville in quite a spell."

"Now that's a time," I said. "Two o'clock then, Congressman?"

"Two o'clock."

"See you then."

"Good-bye."

I sat silent for a time, staring at a framed picture of Martin van Buren I'd hung on the back of the door. I spent several minutes a day looking at old Marty, hoping that something of his talent for king-making might rub off on me. When I was done with the eighth president of the United States, I spoke with Keri Jameson for thirty grueling minutes during which I must've thanked her ten times for allowing Ron to attend an informal gathering of top WC-CSP brass the day before. During the week preceding that gathering, Keri led us to believe that Ron would be addressing a "quasi-formal assembly" of folks at the home of the organization's vice-chairman. It wasn't until we arrived that we discovered the "quasi-formal assembly" was a barbecue in the backyard of some random member's house. Ron, Carmichael, and I were the only ones wearing suits. However, Ron was granted ten minutes to address the group and spent several more mingling with WC-CSP executive members one on one. So all things considered, thirty minutes on the phone with Keri and a future date with her glamorless niece was a small price to pay—we'd previously spent a lot more for a lot less.

That call with Keri was followed by a forty-five-minute tooth-puller with Jack Monroe. After agreeing to meet Jack for a drink sometime during the next few weeks to discuss Ron's vision for North Carolina—and the specifics of his plan to help improve the lives of

Durham's majority-black population—I grabbed my coat, walked briskly out of my office, and headed toward the back door. On my way, I found Ron and Casey chatting in the rear parlor.

"Whose arm are you speeding off to twist this afternoon?" Casey said.

"I have a meeting in Nash County," I said. "Is that the word on the street? That I'm relying on physical violence to make up for my lack of political experience?"

She laughed. "Not at all. You just have the look of a man on his way to twist another man's arm."

"Ron, did you already get to five thousand?"

"Not exactly. Took a break to spend some time with my wife, drill sergeant, sir."

"You should stop in to see your grandfather," Casey said.

"It's at the top of my list," I said.

"Give him our best," she said, reaching for the brown rectangular envelope resting beside her on the red velvet love seat. "Oh, and here's something from Bristol. She's on a long call with the *News & Observer* and asked me to give this to you." I released a deep breath.

"What is it?" Ron asked. "On second thought, I don't want to know."

"Ron raised three thousand dollars this morning," Casey said.

"I never thought there'd be anything less enjoyable than law school exams," Ron said.

"Play a trick on yourself," I said. "Pretend each call is . . . oh, I don't know. I know it sucks. But—"

"It's part of the game," he said.

"I'll see ya later," I said. The side door of the hundred-year-old house creaked loudly as I pulled it toward me.

"We've gotta get that fixed," Ron said.

"Are you kidding?" Casey said. "We can't even afford a can of WD-40."

"We'll splurge this once," Ron said. "By the way, Carp . . . how did your call with Keri go?"

"It went," I responded.

"What was the damage this time?" he asked.

"I have to take her niece to some black-tie thing in Raleigh next week," I said.

Casey and Ron laughed heartily at this news. "Well, it could've been worse," Ron said.

"You think so?" I said.

"At least you're not taking Keri out this time," Casey said. Keri

Jameson was a shorter-than-average woman—and just a touch overweight—with dark brown eyes, a fair complexion, and a short-cropped haircut. She was pretty, but time, the unrelenting stress accompanying the practice of small-town commercial litigation, and that nagging chip on her shoulder hadn't been very good to her. Her laugh lines and crow's-feet were far more advanced than one would expect of a forty-five-year-old black woman.

"Oh, I don't mind her all that much. She's an interesting character," I said. "Did you know she was prom queen?"

"I could see that," Ron said.

Casey's eyes widened. "Could you?"

"She shows signs of having been a situation in her youth," I said.

"A *situation*?" Casey said.

"Oh, that's what the kids are saying these days," Ron said. "It means 'something serious' or 'desirable.'"

Casey sat up straight, dumbfounded by Ron's familiarity with the latest in popular millennial urban speak.

"We do have two young children, you know," Ron said.

"I'm happy you remember," she shot back.

"And on that note, I'll leave you guys to it," I said.

"Knock 'em dead," Casey said.

"Give your grandfather our best," Ron added.

On my way out of Durham, I stopped by an office supply store to buy a ream of paper for the office printer. On my way there, I took a little detour down Ninth Street. As I drove past the raggedy bar where I'd convinced Bristol to join the campaign six weeks earlier, I drifted into the adjacent lane and narrowly avoided colliding with an oncoming vehicle.

*****

AS I PULLED INTO THE SMALL PARKING LOT that serviced my grandfather's dry cleaning business, the branch office of a local propane distributor, and a recently opened Chinese restaurant, my mind wandered back to the summer of 1998, the last full summer I'd spent with my grandparents in North Carolina. Before then, I'd always eagerly awaited the start of the summer and my return to my second home, my second set of parents in Rock City, and my annual summer job in next-door Nashville. After returning to DC that August, however, I never set foot inside that cleaners again—at least not as an employee.

The main problem was our inability to work together peaceably. My grandfather and I had always gotten along well outside the four walls of that dry cleaners, whether during our nightly feasts at the house with Grandma, while watching Tiger Woods's annual summertime demolition of his peers, or while doing chores in the yard. But once we stepped into that cleaners, we became different people, or more accurately, our quintessential selves. The recurring disputes stemmed from our mutual belief that we each knew all things about all things—delusions that made working together impossible.

As a younger man, I usually just accepted his way of doing things. He was the boss, after all. But with each passing year, my ego became a year more uncontrollable and my belief in the infallibility of my opinion a year more concrete. On one sweltering June afternoon in 1998, after a ridiculous argument about the proper technique for bagging clothes, I vowed never to work another day in that cleaners. In hindsight, I regret having lost my cool that day. I've since chalked it up to the heat. It certainly was the precipitating factor, but it was bound to happen. There was only room for one cook in that kitchen, and I knew as much from the experience of watching the brief apprenticeships of those whose indentured time had preceded my own. Between the ages of six and fourteen, I'd seen every other family member who'd ventured to work in that cleaners make precisely the same vow. At the end of each day, I think he liked being able to say he'd done it all himself—it gave him one more thing to complain about when he came home to Grandma.

I sat quietly in my car for a few more moments, watching through the propped-open doors as he laughed with a customer I knew by name. My grandfather's warm, inviting eyes sparkled in the early afternoon sun. People always talked about my grandfather as though he were their own father or grandfather. He was the kind of guy you wanted in your corner because no one ever uttered an unfriendly word about him.

As Mr. Hedgepeth exited the cleaners and walked toward his faded-blue pickup truck, he waved at me. "Is that you, Alex?" he said. "Well I'll be!"

I hurriedly removed myself from my car to shake his hand in a timely manner. He'd gained at least twenty pounds since I'd last seen him two years earlier. My mind darted back to an afternoon some fifteen years earlier when we closed up shop a little early to get a round of golf in at Crooked Branch Country Club in Rock City, a club that hadn't permitted blacks on the course, except caddies, for its entire seventy-year history before 1992, and only sparingly since then. Mr. Hedgepeth was a long-standing member like his father before him and had insisted that we join him for a round when he learned of my growing obsession with the game.

"Mr. Hedgepeth, sir," I said. "How are things?"

"Couldn't complain even if I wanted to," he said. "I swear . . . seems like just yesterday you were running around in that cleaners, driving your granddad stark crazy. Or was it the other way around?" We both laughed.

"It's a wonder he put up with me as long as he did," I said. "I spent more time out back hitting golf balls than indoors working."

"Who could blame ya?" he said. "Making a young boy work in the dead of summer!" He'd raised his voice to make sure Grandpa would hear. "How are things on the campaign trail?" he asked. "You and Ron givin' 'em hell over in Durham?"

"You know it," I said.

"Good, good. Heading to the course now. Got time for nine holes? I know you've got your clubs in the trunk."

"You know me well," I said. "Can't though. I've got a meeting in a bit. Rain check?"

"You betcha," he said, slapping my back. Then he slipped into his car, shut the door, and revved the engine.

"You hit 'em straight now," I shouted.

"You do the same," he said, winking.

"Come on in here, boy," Grandpa shouted, smiling ear to ear. "Leave that bum alone."

"Hey Grandpa," I said, slapped in the face by that all-too-familiar scent of perchloroethylene.

"Hey buddy," he said, reaching to shake my hand. It was always a shake with him, never a hug. I'd always chalked that up to his time in the navy and my general discomfort with physical displays of affection. Nevertheless, over the years, more than a handful of people had taken time to note that they'd never seen two people display more immense respect, pride, and love for one another than we did when we locked eyes and shook hands.

He still had the skin of a fifty-year-old though he was coming up on his eightieth birthday. His dark brown skin set against his curly mane, which had gone almost totally gray over the last few years, was stunning—and he'd recently taken to wearing a goatee. Grandpa was a committed husband and family man who never lost his penchant for respectable flirting. While leaning against the front counter, I chuckled as I recalled how women who were half his age often remarked, still, that he belonged in the movies.

"What brings you over this way, buddy?" he said. "Did Grandma make a lemon cake?"

"Just in the neighborhood . . . figured I'd check in on you."

"Since when did Raleigh and Nashville become the same neighborhood?"

"I've got a meeting," I said.

"In Nashville?"

"Yes, sir."

He narrowed his eyes. "You don't need any money, do you?" he asked with a wink.

"No, but I've never been one to turn down money when it's being given out."

"You got that right, boy! How's Ron doing?"

"Hopefully on the phone raising money."

"That's *what* he's doing. I asked *how* he's doing."

"He's doing okay, I guess."

"You guess!" he exclaimed. "What's to guess about? Don't you see him every day?"

"Pretty much . . . yes."

"Then you ought to know how he's doing."

"You're right."

"You tell ol' Ron I said hello, and to make sure he's working you hard. You don't look a bit tired."

"Oh, I'm plenty tired."

"Well, you don't look it."

"Well, I *am*."

"*I'll* be damned."

I let out a deep breath. "So, how's Grandma?"

"Oh, I don't know. She's at the house, no doubt, watching her stories."

"Please tell her I said hello."

"Will do. So . . . how's the campaign? Making any headway?"

"A little, day by day, you know?"

"Well, keep at it. Work hard while you're young."

"I will."

"Well . . . go on back to work. Keep making me proud."

"Okay, Grandpa."

"Say, when are you gonna bring that Bristol back by the house?"

"Ah . . . I don't know. Do you want me to invite her back for dinner?"

"Why haven't you already?"

"Well, you know, I . . . there's a lot going on with the campaign and she—"

He shook his head from side to side. "You're a piece of work, boy."

I smiled. "What?"

"You better go on and bring her by more often. Good Southern girl, that one. Grew up in Durham. Smart as a whip too. I haven't a damned clue as to why she's so darn crazy about you." He winked slowly.

"She's more than a catch. I know, Grandpa. I know."

"Do you?" he asked in a tone of genuine doubt. "Runnin' around with these others. She won't put up with it forever. She's reasonable, but she's not a machine."

"We're not together, Grandpa. We haven't defined our relationship or—"

"Stop being a lawyer all the damned time! That's not how this stuff works, boy."

I tendered a coy grin.

"You think you're invincible. That you have all the time in the world. That everything *has* to work out right for you—like it's preordained or something. What did I tell you about karma? I hope you haven't forgotten *everything* I taught you in this cleaners. Can't do what you want to do 'til you do what you need to do."

"I know I've got to do better."

"If you value your friendship with her, you'll either commit or let her go."

"I'll do better."

"Don't say you'll do better. Just do better. Let all the rest go."

"Easier said than done."

He sucked his teeth. "*I'll* be damned. Go on. Get on outta here. Get back to work."

"I'm gonna change," I reassured him. "I am. I promise. And I promise I won't let you down—no, I won't let *me* down."

"Work requires action and real commitment, not New Year's resolutions and clever excuses. Grandma said you're coming down next Sunday for dinner."

"That's the plan."

He reached to shake my hand. "Well, I'll expect to see you then—and with that Bristol in hand. You be good now."

"I will," I said. "Take care of yourself. And don't work too hard."

"Shoot. Hard work is why I'm still here."

"Nevertheless," I muttered, turning toward the entrance.

"What?"

"Nothing, Grandpa," I shouted back, stepping off the curb. As I backed out of the parking space, radio blaring, he walked out of the shop vigorously waving his arms.

"What's up?" I screamed over the music.

"Turn that jungle music down!" he shouted back. "You'll scare off the customers!"

"What customers?"

"Just turn that damned radio down," he said before turning back toward the open doors. I snickered.

"It just doesn't make any sense to play that mess so loudly," he continued as he reentered the shop. I laughed out loud as I recalled him repeatedly demanding that Uncle Tom's younger brother, Uncle Flip, turn his music down when he was my age and perpetually blasting 2Pac.

As I turned right onto Nashville's only major road, I estimated that I'd probably traveled up and down that street a thousand times in my lifetime. It refused to change. Nashville had successfully resisted the onslaught of the big-box store chains. While the rest of the world turned, hour by hour, day by day, this little town stood still, and perfectly charming.

I arrived at Pete's thirty minutes early. The parking lot was far more packed than I remembered it being this late into the lunch hour during my weekly lunch runs to Pete's over a decade ago with Grandpa. After parking and entering through the rear door, I walked past Darling's body man—he was clearly carrying—and found the beloved Tenth District representative sitting in the corner, impeccably bow-tied as always and reading a copy of the *News & Observer*. He'd already finished half his burger and was picking at the last few fries as I approached the table.

"Congressman," I said, reaching for his hand. "How are you?"

"Doing well," he replied, grasping my hand and meeting my eyes. "I hope you don't mind, son. I arrived a few minutes earlier than planned and was so dern hungry that I went right ahead and ordered." He gestured for me to have a seat. "Ordinarily I'd shoot the breeze with you a little, but I suspect we're both in no mood for that. What're you after?"

"Your endorsement, sir," I said.

"Endorsement?" he exclaimed. He tossed his newspaper onto the table next to his plate.

"That's right," I said. "And I think both camps will benefit mightily. You've got a tough primary—from what I read in the papers, Remini's not fading away like others have in the past. You can't count on conservatives and moderates to carry you this time."

Darling motioned toward his body man behind me. I turned and watched as he waved away the waitress who'd been walking toward our table. Then Darling smiled at me. "Julia's a tough cookie," he said. "She's got real spunk. I like that. I like her. But you and I both know it ain't gonna happen."

"You know, I told my people the same thing," I said, leaning in and lowering my volume. "I said, 'Darling's got a cult following. No way this young, *female* progressive is gonna take him out.' But then I got to thinking—dangerous pastime, I know, but I still do it from time to time. I thought to myself, nothing's forever, and no one wins forever. Time comes for everyone, even for you, Congressman. Now I don't wanna get into a thing with you. I've got far too much respect for you. So let's make this easy. Take your place in history, sir: Give us the endorsement and save your seat. A progressive is gonna win that primary. Let's make sure it's you."

His eyes narrowed as he chuckled. "I tell you what, son . . . you've got a pair on you. How dare you come in here and make demands of me?"

"I'm not demanding, sir. I'm asking you to do what's in your best interest."

"You are aware, aren't you, son, that I have the capacity to ruin you?"

"Fully, sir," I replied. "But with all due respect, I didn't come down here to lose."

"You'd sacrifice yourself to get Ron elected?"

"As Ron likes to say, 'change doesn't just come rolling in on the wheels of inevitability.'"

"Go on back to Durham, son. You're wastin' your time chuckin' Hail Marys in Nashville. I don't give a damn what you know about Lovejoy Library."

"Maybe you should look at this." I pulled the brown envelope from my breast pocket, removed the article, and slowly pushed it toward him. Darling gently lifted the page from the table before leaning back in his rickety wooden chair. After glancing at it for a few seconds, he shot me a menacing glare before placing the neatly folded article inside his breast pocket.

I leaned in. "You think that's something Remini might like to see?" I said.

He broke into a gentle laughter that gradually rose in volume until he was nearly doubled over. When he'd finally gathered himself, he said, "Blackmailing a member of the United States Congress. That's your intent?"

"I have no such intent, Congressman. I don't want anyone to see that article. I didn't want you to see it again either, but . . . you've left me with no real alternative."

He leaned toward me. "Is Ron in on this too?"

"Ron doesn't know anything about this," I replied. "He thinks the world of you, even though you've abandoned him."

Darling slumped back into his chair and looked toward the front of the restaurant. "I'm in no position to endorse now," he said. "As you're probably aware, there are complexities, both political and personal in nature, surroundin' an announcement like this. I'll need some time to work through this thing—you know, to soften the blow."

"I'll be reasonable. But this needs to happen quickly."

"January thirty-first is the earliest I could do it."

"That's not reasonable, Congressman," I said. "That's more than three months away. We need that endorsement now."

"What in Sam Hill do you think could happen between now and then that'll make my endorsement any less powerful?"

"Three weeks. I'll give you three weeks."

"Now you're the one being totally unreasonable, son. You've asked me—strike that, you're forcin' me to endorse a black candidate for the United States Senate. Now you're just gonna have to slow down a bit and give me time to prepare my people. Otherwise my more conservative constituents—heck, even some of the moderates—are gonna come over to Hickory and eat my lunch for me, and when they've had their fill of that, they'll take me out back to the shed and show me what it's like. I've got to make sure this doesn't look like I'm turning my back on them. I'm no good to you if I lose my base. You see, son, you need a strong, popular Branford Darling just as much as I do."

"But sir, Bill Billingsworth is about to—"

His cheeks reddened. "Why is everyone so damn worked up about Bill? He's nobody! The only chance in hell he has is if the DSCC blesses him, and they won't get involved in your race until March at the earliest, if at all."

"Seems you've got a crystal ball, Congressman," I said. "You give me that and I'll forget about what's in your breast pocket."

"I'm a five-term congressman, son. If it takes you longer than that to make the friends necessary to figure somethin' like that out, you're doing somethin' terribly wrong."

"If the DSCC does come out for Bill before January thirty-first, I can't guarantee Remini won't stumble on that article."

He scoffed. "No, I wouldn't imagine you could." He stood and offered his right hand.

I rose and gazed beyond his ocean-blue irises and into the depths of his bottomless pupils for evidence of deceit. "I'm not afraid to take this all the way," I said, shaking his hand firmly.

"Oh, I don't doubt it for a minute," he said. "The only question is whether you've got the stomach for the consequences."

As Darling gathered his overcoat and tucked his paper under his arm, a previously unknown terror enveloped me. He removed a pen and business card from his breast pocket and scribbled something on the blank side. "This is for you," he said. "Any further business between us—and I suspect there will be very little indeed—is to be conducted through our mutual friend, Jim Randolph. This is his personal cellular number. He tells me the two of you have some ongoing business. As of today, you have lost the right to call me or anyone else who is in any way affiliated with my campaign or congressional office. Do we understand each other, Mr. Carpenter?"

I nodded. "Is there anyone you aren't friends with?" I said.

He turned, walked toward the rear entrance, then stopped suddenly and swiveled to face me. "Is your house in order, Carpenter?"

"How do you mean, sir?"

He walked slowly back toward me until his face was a few inches from mine. His scent was a mixture of Old Spice and menthol. "If it was this easy for you to dig up this Lovejoy nonsense, how easy do you reckon it would be for me to uncover a few of the nasty little unmentionables you've got in your closet?"

I felt several heavy beads of sweat forming on my forehead. "Please give my regards to the governor," I said.

"Good day, Mr. Carpenter. And thanks for suggestin' this place. Still the best burger in the state." Before I knew it, Darling and his guy were gone. I jumped slightly at the sound of the rickety screen door slamming shut behind them.

The nearly incapacitating burger craving I'd brought with me into Pete's returned suddenly as I walked back to the table and took the same seat. After ordering my usual burger and chili cheese fries, firecrackers of nerves began exploding all over my body. It wasn't until then that I truly understood why professional ballplayers make so much money—I mean, the good ones. Any pitcher can throw a strike in practice.

The burger was amazing, better than ever, in fact. This was the only restaurant I knew of where the guy whose name is on the door also slaves over the grill in the back. I'll bet there was a time in the South not so long ago when folks like Pete were the rule rather than the exception—a time when an owner's pride in his product at least equaled his desire for the worldly things his skill might bring him.

On my way out, I ran into Pete. "Give my best to your granddad," he said. "And tell him to stop by more often."

"Will do," I said. "Say, Pete, don't you get tired of flipping burgers? I mean, wouldn't you rather be on the golf course or something?"

He snickered and slapped my shoulder twice while gazing into my eyes. "What I do makes folks happy," he said. "I know it 'cause I see it in their faces. They keep comin' back. I can't see that from the golf course or from the fishin' boat. Right here's all the fun I need."

CHAPTER ELEVEN

UNSURPRISINGLY, my flight out of LaGuardia back to Raleigh on Saturday, January 2, was delayed. A year earlier, I'd joked with another irritable passenger during the third hour of a four-hour-long delay at LaGuardia that instead of just posting the departure time after each flight, they really ought to add the phrase, "If you're lucky." My cousin Billy, who'd happily agreed to retrieve me from the airport at seven thirty that night, now reluctantly picked me up at ten thirty. In July 2009, while I studied for the bar exam, he'd moved from downtown Raleigh to an apartment complex in Cary conveniently located five minutes from the airport to "get away from the action." He'd succeeded in getting away from the action in Raleigh, but his close proximity to the airport meant his family and friends were keeping him and his late-model Acura more active than ever.

I plopped into the passenger seat. "How was New Year's Eve, cuzzo?" he said.

"Freezing cold," I said. "Did I miss anything down here?"

"Not a damned thing," he said. "I brought in the new year on Glenwood."

"Ahhh, Glenwood Ave," I said. "Nothing wrong with that."

"Anything interesting happen in New York?"

"Ran into Angie at a party just before midnight."

"Perfect time to run into an old flame. How's she doing?"

"She's good," I said. "Met the fiancé. I'm happy for her."

"No you're not."

I grinned. "You're right—I'm not."

"Come on, Al!" he exclaimed. "You can't BS me, man, I'm your cousin. Brotha from a different motha! I'll let you in on a little secret: if you want her, you can get her back."

"You're nuts. Where are you getting your intel?"

"It has nothing to do with her . . . just turn on that charm, cuzzo. We've both got it. It's in our genes."

"Yeah, well, it's becoming a liability," I said. "I think it comes from spending all that time with your dad growing up. Uncle Tom is a trip. Man . . . I remember he used to pull chicks like it was nothing."

Billy snickered. "Still does, quiet as it's kept."

"Grandpa told me a few months back that I should stick with Bristol and let the others go."

Billy began laughing hysterically. "Let the others go?" he said.

"You think I can't do it?" I said.

"We got a black president, so I suppose anything's possible."

"I think I can do it," I said. "I've just got to grow the hell up."

"What happened to all that talk about monogamy not being natural?"

"That's beside the point."

"Grandpa just wants to see us get married," he said. "He'll say anything at this point to make that happen."

"I think he really likes Bristol," I said. "I trust his judgment. Grandpa and Uncle Malcolm . . . I guess I got two fathers in place of the one I never got to know. Not a bad deal, all things considered."

"I hear you on that," Billy said. "So that's it? Bristol or bust? Closing up shop? Calling it a day? Hanging up the—"

"I'm not saying I'm proposing tomorrow. I'm just saying we—that means you too—need to start thinking about calming things down a bit. There's not a switch you can turn off just because you wake up one day and decide you're ready."

"Yeah, I'll think about it," he said. "But in the meantime, in between time—"

"You're stupid, you know that?"

He grabbed my shoulder with his right hand and began shaking me vigorously. "My man!" he said.

"Will you please pay attention to the road?"

"Look, I've been sittin' around the house waiting three hours to pick your narrow behind up. The way I see it, I've earned the right to shake you, slap you, or throw you out the car window if the good Lord should so move me."

We pulled onto my block at around eleven. I grabbed my duffle out of the backseat before returning to the passenger door. Billy had rolled the window down, as he always did before we parted ways.

"Appreciate the ride, cuzzo," I said, reaching through the window to shake his hand.

"Anytime." He sighed. "Look, I like Bristol. Had a good talk with her at Grandma and Grandpa's house awhile back at that dinner. She's cool people. And knows how to check you when need be too. I'll give it some thought about settling down and whatnot. I'm only twenty-six, but I guess it's not too early to start thinking about it."

"Good deal, brotha," I said. "Headed home?"

"Absolutely not. Got a little somethin' waiting for me across town. I'll get some good thinkin' done on the way there."

"I bet you will."

"Later, cuzzo." He peeled off around the corner.

The full extent of my exhaustion didn't set in until I stepped into the elevator of my building. On entering my apartment, I dropped my bag to the floor and washed my face at the kitchen sink before throwing myself onto my bed. After ten glorious seconds my phone rang. I picked it up without looking at the screen. "Hello?" I mumbled.

"Al!" Carmichael's voice boomed in my ear. "How was New Year's Eve in the Big Apple?"

"Carmichael," I groaned, "it's late and I'm tired, so make it quick."

"Fine, but only because I've resolved to cut you a little slack this year. I just dropped Ron off in Chapel Hill. I'm heading back to Raleigh now."

"How'd it go this weekend?"

"Productive, I'd say. We did community service yesterday morning just outside of Charlotte, then meetings with a few local electeds downtown. He also met with a few of the higher-ups at the Mecklenburg County Organization for Community Advancement."

"The MC-OCA," I said. "Nice. We really need to intensify our efforts with them and the other major black PACs."

"Yes," he said. "But you've been keeping pretty close tabs on WC-CSP and DC-OSP. So it's really just MC-OCA and CC-CSP we need to tighten up on."

"I've been chasing Keri and Jack pretty hard, but we need to have the endorsements of all those orgs in the bag, preferably by late March. So what else?"

"We spent this morning making the rounds with Reverend Peoples and Reverend Wilson and then met with a few local grass tops in the afternoon. Before we knew it, it was eight o'clock and we—I mean I— still had to make the three-hour drive back to Chapel Hill. I haven't had a full night's rest in six days."

"How's Ron doing?"

"He's good. I think he's starting to get a good handle on the stump speech. And he's been incorporating the NCSEP stuff well. Doesn't seem forced or anything."

"That's all good news."

"He mentioned the Darling endorsement today," Carmichael said. "He's still skeptical that Darling's gonna come through by the thirty-first."

"Darling gave me his word. I trust him."

"Why, because you shook on it? This is 2010, not 1910. Handshakes aren't worth a damn anymore. Not even down here."

"I'm shocked, Carmichael. You're a Southern boy. You've got to stand behind your culture."

"I've seen a lot over the last few months. I don't trust a man as far as I can see him."

"And what about women?"

"I thought you didn't have it tonight?"

I laughed. "Alright, what else ya got? Any other news?"

"Jane's at thirty-five percent, Bill's at fifteen—and we're at twelve."

"That's great!" I said. "We've pulled into a tie with Bill—a statistical tie, anyway."

"Yeah, but we're still well behind Jane, and the guy we're tied with hasn't even declared his candidacy yet."

"We'll catch up to Jane soon enough. Bill's not doing nearly as well as he thought he'd be doing by now. And most importantly, the DSCC's not going to get involved if we're polling so close to him. That would piss off too many black folks. They're not going to jeopardize the national party's standing with folks they absolutely need to get Obama reelected in 2012."

"We really need Darling's endorsement now," Carmichael said.

"Great insight, Captain Obvious," I said. "Now what about Remini?"

"She's basically flat at thirty-six percent. Darling's still at fifty."

"What?" I exclaimed. "Unbelievable. She hasn't gained any ground since early October!"

"And Darling hasn't lost any. What if he reneges on the endorsement?"

"Carmichael, I'm telling you, he won't back out! Now I'm done talking about it. Is there anything else?"

"A few things, but they can wait until tomorrow."

"Good deal."

"Good night. I hope a spider crawls into your mouth while you're sleeping."

*****

I WAS STARTLED AWAKE the next morning by a vibration at my waist. I turned the phone over and saw Ron's name on the screen. I answered it and muttered, "Hello."

"Al!" Ron said cheerily. "How's it going?"

"Alright," I replied, stifling a yawn. "I'm surprised you're awake. Carmichael told me you guys got back from Charlotte pretty late last night."

"Do you know what time it is?"

"No idea."

"Four in the afternoon." He chuckled. "I guess you had a pretty good time in New York?"

"No complaints," I said. "It was like the good old days from summer of '08. So what's up?"

"I just found out that the black PAC down in Fayetteville, the CC-CSP, is having their holiday party tonight."

"Holiday party?" I said. "It's January third."

"Don't you remember? They cancelled the original date because of that snowstorm."

"Oh right, last month's three-inch Snowmageddon."

"Look, I know you're tired, and so am I, but we need to be there. That's a group we really need to be working. And they've been known to endorse a little earlier than the other black PACs from time to time."

"How much earlier?"

"Sometimes as early as late February. That's not the norm, but maybe we can coax them into moving a little quicker this cycle. Cumberland County is obviously huge for us—big African-American population. We've got to stay visible down there. Jane's traveling on official state business so she won't be there, but Bill will almost certainly be there running the same tired plays."

"How's that?"

"It used to be that all a white candidate had to do to get black votes was show up at a few events—you know, just enough to show black folks he's comfortable around them. Now that legit black candidates are in the fold, that strategy's less effective, but only so long as black candidates are there to counter it."

"So you're saying I'm going to miss all the football today?"

He laughed. "You and me both. And we need to leave ASAP to get there by seven. Why don't you get Carmichael to take us?"

"I think he needs a day to himself," I said. "I'll drive you, Miss Daisy. I should be at your house by five."

"Good deal," he said. "Looking forward to chatting on the way down. See you in a bit."

"Yep."

"Oh Carp—maybe call Bristol and see if she wants to come."

"She doesn't get back from Vegas until tomorrow."

"That's right. How did you feel about her going to Vegas for New Year's?"

"Why should I care?"

He laughed. "Right. See you soon."

"See ya." I hung up and sighed. *Another Sunday shot to hell.*

*****

RON AND I SPENT about half of the trip to Fayetteville rehashing the story of how Bill Billingsworth had gotten in, out, back in, then back out of the 2008 US Senate primary.

"He said he got out of the race the first time," Ron recalled, "because he couldn't look voters square in the eyes and tell them why he should be their senator and what he would do when he got to Washington. Then, two weeks later, he decided to get back in the race because he realized, and I quote, 'We face challenges too great for me to sit on the sideline.'"

"Which is code for, 'None of the candidates the DSCC courted decided to run, and now I think I have a chance of winning.'"

"'Seventeen days ago, I didn't see a . . . pathway to . . . victory,'" Ron began, doing his best Bill Billingsworth. "'But now that I'll . . . probably have the DSCC's backing, I can see . . . a path.' All this guy does is talk about how he doesn't stand down from fights. But that's just what he did." Ron shook his head. "Thing is, he's not a bad guy. I just don't think he's right for the people. I also think the DSCC played him. I'm pretty sure they told him that if he got back in, they'd get behind him."

"I wish they'd keep their noses out of state primaries," I said. "Think they'll stay out of this one?"

"There's been some interesting DSCC back channeling recently. I got a call from the White House yesterday morning. They've definitely got an eye on our race, mostly because it went blue in '08. They're looking at it from every angle—at least the ones they want to see—and they're speaking to their people here in the state. They'll get behind whoever's got the best shot at replacing Joe Rodney, and there's no way they're going to conclude it's us."

"They're obviously of the opinion that what Obama did in North Carolina in '08 can't be replicated in 2010," I said.

"I think on some level, they don't want to put the work in to preserve and further expand the Obama Coalition here in North Carolina. And they've miscalculated too. They think they can throw their support behind a conservative Democrat who talks a pretty good progressive game and trick folks who voted for Obama into voting for the new guy. But voters aren't stupid."

"Maybe they don't think North Carolinians will send a truly progressive Democrat to Washington in an off-year election," I suggested. "Could be some merit to that."

"Only if you use the old paradigm," Ron said. "The old way of thinking presumes Democrats and Republicans are essentially fixed groups with very little movement in or out. But Obama changed all that. He won by energizing the party's base, converting a few conservatives here and there, *and* expanding the electorate. Judging from my conversation with the White House, I can tell you that they've missed the mark in calculating exactly what it's going to take to win in the fall. If African Americans and progressives aren't energized, no Democrat is going to defeat Rodney. The DSCC knows that, but they don't understand that picking a moderate or conservative won't get them there."

I nodded. "If they get involved," I said, "they'll back Bill thinking he'll squeak by on the strength of his military service and because he looks the part of a young, protestant Southern senator. Instead of working to preserve and expand the 2008 Obama Coalition, they've thrown their hands up and just assumed it can't be repeated this cycle. They're disregarding what voters *just* did. The reversionary power of the status quo is amazing, isn't it?"

Ron shook his head. "Exactly. Black folks could decide this race if they refused to be deprived of their power. Do you know how many people there are in North Carolina's General Baptist State Convention?"

"Somewhere in the neighborhood of seven hundred thousand, right?"

"No, it's eight hundred thousand!" Ron said. "And mostly black. Think about the kind of power they could wield! If just a fourth of those folks voted for us, we'd win easily."

"The vast majority of them just aren't engaged," I said. "That, or they're drinking the 'black candidates can't win' cocktail being served up all over the state."

Ron looked out the window, then straightened his shoulders. "All we can do is look folks in the eyes and make our case," he said. "But let's be clear on the messaging. We are not going to win by using race to divide and conquer. That's the old way. Our campaign is all about coming together, moving forward, and doing what's right. What's right is expanding opportunities to all people, what's right is creating more jobs, and what's right is using innovation as a means to sustain our environment and our economy."

"Save it for the stump," I said. "I don't need convincing."

"We're gonna get there Al, I promise you. We have to. This election is about so much more than whether a black guy wins. It's about beginning to turn the tide of injustice against everyone who's suffering. That was what drove Casey, the kids, and me to knock on doors all those cold Saturday mornings in 2008. The hope of delivering, more than two centuries later, on the original promise of America . . . ideals laid out in the Declaration of Independence and in the preamble to the Constitution."

We sat in silence for a few moments. "You know what?" I finally said. "To hell with your stump speech—except for the part about NCSEP. We've gotta keep that in. If you just speak from the heart like you just did, I think folks will start to listen."

"How's the preamble start?" he said. "'We the people of the United States, in order to form a more perfect union, establish justice . . .'"

"'Insure domestic tranquillity, provide for the common defense, promote the general welfare . . .'"

"'And secure the blessings of liberty to ourselves and our posterity, do ordain and establish this Constitution for the United States of America.' Al—that's what this whole thing is about. Keeping folks awake and waking up some more."

I turned to look at him, keeping one eye on the road. "You know, Ron, I came down here because this race interested me on an academic level. But that's changed. Watching you do this job, for no money, every day, even on days when I know you'd rather not—well, it's inspiring. And even if we don't get a single vote, I couldn't be prouder of you."

Ron was quiet for what felt like an eternity. At length, he found the words. "Tha—thank you, Al," he stammered. "Thanks for believing in me." Tears wound down his face. "You know, my father died ten minutes after they called it for Obama," he said, his voice cracking. "He hadn't spoken in three days, but right before he went, he said, 'Ronny—make your mark on this world. Finish the fight.'"

I let out a deep breath. "He's proud of the fight you're putting up," I said, willing my voice to remain steady. "And we're gonna keep fighting."

*****

WE PULLED INTO THE CHAMBER CLUB parking lot a few strokes after seven. The Chamber Club, built in 1870, was an austere two-story house. Rust stained the cracked white paint here and there, particularly around the crown of the structure where the iron roof met the aluminum siding.

As we walked toward the front entrance, Ron brought me up to speed. This social club, formerly a meetinghouse for Cumberland County's ranking businessmen and politicians, was not open to blacks or women until 1980, when it was discovered that the structure violated multiple county ordinances. Under pressure from an increasingly Democrat-dominated group of county commissioners, between 1980 and 2000 the club admitted roughly one black man and one white woman each year. It wasn't until 2001, when the one hundred-year-old son of the founding member died, that a significant number of minorities were admitted.

It was also in 2001 that the Chamber Club began opening its doors to the Cumberland County Committee for Social Progress. The mostly black members of the CC-CSP still thought it a big deal that they could annually congregate at what was once an all-white men's club.

When we made it inside, Ron immediately began working the room while I stood near the rear looking for familiar faces from the other two US Senate campaigns. About a hundred people milled around, most only half-listening to the program. Aside from the odd juxtaposition of Victorian furniture amid rows of foldout chairs, the room was notable only for its lack of nonblacks.

I scanned the crowd and was surprised to spot Keri Jameson standing in the corner, looking around expectantly. Over the months I'd spent courting her for the WC-CSP's endorsement, she'd asked me to do almost everything under the sun. Chief among my tasks was picking her up and driving her to various political and social gatherings around the state. *Wonder why she didn't ask for a ride tonight?* Before I could ask, Bill Billingsworth strolled in, smiling big and flanked by two familiar staffers and his omnipresent camera guy. Bill shook hands down the line until we stood face to face.

"Bill," I said, offering my hand.

He gave it a hearty shake. "Always good to see ya, Al."

"Didn't expect to see you here."

His eyes widened. "Are you kiddin'?" he said. "I wouldn't miss this for the world. These folks are my base."

I laughed in spite of myself. "And all this time Ron and I assumed these were our folks."

"Yet another miscalculation from you and Attorney Johnson," he said with a wink. "Say, I've got a bit of news you'll be ecstatic to hear."

"You're joining Greenpeace and shipping out tomorrow?"

He smiled broadly. "You wish. I'm filing tomorrow." Bill fired off another smug wink and continued down the line as my stomach dropped to the worn wooden floor planks.

"Ladies and gentlemen," a voice rang out. "We've now reached the part of our program where local and statewide candidates may make a few *brief* remarks." The voice belonged to the evening's emcee, Congressman Kelvin Lot. Lot, a Columbia Law School–educated black attorney, had been sent to Washington ten times in a row. His popularity in Fayetteville and throughout the Seventh District was such that he didn't have to do any formal campaigning that year.

Lot turned to Ron, who was standing next to the podium. "At this time, I'd like to introduce a good friend and a brilliant lawyer who also happens to be a candidate for US Senate—Attorney Ron Johnson." Ron had been a reliable arranger of fundraising dollars for the Congressman's reelection bids for a decade. I'd spoken with Lot on multiple occasions before that night about securing his endorsement. Lot's preference was to hold off until March or April, when, as he put it, "hopefully more people will be paying attention."

"Thank you, Congressman Lot," Ron said. "I'd just like to take a moment to recognize all the elected officials in attendance, as well as friends and colleagues gathered here today. You know, almost twenty years ago, I closed my first big community development transaction as a young lawyer. This deal was the result of a public-private partnership that resulted in the construction of affordable housing for disadvantaged but hardworking folks in Charlotte. It was because of Congressman Lot here that I had the opportunity to work on that matter. It's men like Congressman Lot—who take an interest in developing young talent, providing them with opportunities they never had—who have helped strengthen communities and level the playing field across this state. How about a round of applause for all the heroes—folks like you, Congressman—who have made reaching back and uplifting others their life's work." At that the crowd erupted into a standing ovation.

"I'm not going to take much more of your time tonight," Ron

continued. "There are a lot of candidates here, and I want to make sure they all have time to speak. But let me just say this: My name is Ron Johnson, and I'm running to be your United States senator to help continue the legacy of leaders like Congressman Lot. In Washington, I'll fight to make sure success stories like mine—a young black boy from the country who made it to Harvard Law School—are the rule and not the exception. I'm in this race to fight for laws that will ensure every young boy or girl with a dream can get the quality education they need to make it come true. I'm in this race to finish the job we started in 2008, and with each vote I cast as your senator, with each piece of legislation Barack Obama signs into law, we'll move this president's agenda forward and bring the change we all seek. Thank you, and I hope to have your vote on May fourth."

At the conclusion of Ron's remarks, Congressman Lot rose from his front-row seat and shook Ron's hand for the duration of the crowd's ten-second applause. Then the Congressman turned to the audience and said, "Will Bill Billingsworth please report to the front?"

Bill walked briskly from the rear of the room, waving and pointing indiscriminately. When he reached the podium, he squinted at the audience.

"Good evening . . . ladies and gentlemen," he began. "The name is ... Bill Billingsworth, and I'm running for . . . the US Senate." His jerky cadence, which he combined with Bill Clinton's patented bottom lip bite, came off as nightmarishly awkward, a robot's imitation of a politician. "I'm proud to have served my country in Afghanistan ... where, as an . . . army lawyer, I . . . argued the first ever case against ... corrupt contractors and received the Bronze Star . . . for my services. When I returned . . . from my tour of duty . . . I pinned that Bronze Star on my . . . two-year-old daughter . . . because even though she wasn't in Afghanistan . . . she served her country too." He paused to take in the sea of emotionless faces. "I got in this race because I . . . couldn't sit on the sidelines when we face such . . . grave challenges. Our families are literally struggling . . . to pay the bills each month. Our children deserve better schools . . . and our teachers . . . they deserve better pay. We've got a . . . whole range of challenges that we've gotta . . . meet head-on . . . I need your vote so that together . . . we can get North Carolinians back to work."

At the front of the room, Ron's face began to betray his impatience. A quick scan of the audience showed he wasn't alone. Congressman Lot rose abruptly and approached Bill. "Thank you, Mr. Billingsworth, for that," he said, very nearly hip-checking Bill away from the podium. Bill, clearly wounded, receded to the empty chair on the end of the front row.

"Well, that's interesting," said a familiar voice. I turned to find Jessica Parker standing just a few steps behind me. I hadn't noticed her arrival.

"What's interesting?"

"We've both heard Bill's stump a few times now," she said. "And we both know he wasn't done."

"Not even close," I said. "And yet, the program continues."

Jessica pulled a small pad and pen from the French designer carryall draped over her shoulder and began scribbling with her left hand.

"Wearing your reporter hat today I see."

"Not really."

"You undercover or something?"

"If you're asking if I'm here on assignment, the answer is no."

"I know you're a Billingsworth fan, but even the college groupies stayed home tonight. What gives?"

"If you must know, word on the street is that one of the junior anchors at the station is up for a promotion. They're looking to fill his seat with an in-house reporter."

"And you think you've got a shot?" I said. "I've gotta tell ya, Parker, that other reporter, that guy with the beard—"

"Whose name you don't even know."

"Yeah, well, he does better work," I continued. "I'm not saying he's more talented than you. His stuff's just more compelling."

"Well, Alex, I'd *like* to do a compelling story on this Senate race, but the candidates haven't been much help."

"Open your eyes, Parker. Everything you need for a good story is right in front of you. This isn't just some random US Senate primary. It's part of a battle for the soul of America. Maybe if you covered that story, viewers would start paying attention."

She snorted. "Don't kid yourself. This election's over. Bill's gonna file tomorrow, the DSCC will get behind him shortly thereafter, and all the fundraising Jane's counting on and Ron's scratching and clawing for will dry up."

"What is it with you people and the DSCC?" I said. "Why do you assume a handful of political hacks on Capitol Hill will do a better job picking North Carolina's representatives than the people who actually live here?"

"Last I checked they still hold elections in this state."

"Don't patronize me," I said. "You understand the power of the press as much as I do. How about reporting the news instead of finding facts to support the news you want the public to see?"

"Okay," she said. "You want me to report the news? Let's go. First question: Who's Ron's campaign manager?"

"We're still weighing options."

"Umm hmm," she said, nodding slowly. "And given the difficulty you've had raising money, just how do you plan on paying him or her?"

"We're actually thinking about hiring a dog and paying it in Kibbles 'n Bits. Maybe if that promotion at work doesn't pan out, you can interview for the position."

Jessica narrowed her eyes. "I wouldn't work on your train wreck campaign to save my life." She threw her notebook and pen back in her bag. "For his own good, Ron better not be anything like you, because if he is, he doesn't have a chance in hell." For the first time since meeting her, my words seemed to have pierced her notoriously thick skin.

I sighed. "I'm sorry, Jessica. That was below the belt, and I didn't mean it. It's just that . . . to hear you and your news buddies in Raleigh and Charlotte tell it, we don't even exist."

"Look, Al, we reporters do what our bosses tell us to do. You can't hold us responsible for the way your candidate is being covered. Blame the producers, don't blame the lowly reporters."

"So what's on the docket for tomorrow?" I said. "Any actual assignments or more rogue escapades?"

"Nothing earth shattering. A couple of things in Raleigh—Bill's announcement, of course—but that's it. Just another Monday on the beat."

"What are you doing when you get back to Raleigh tonight?" I asked.

"Probably straight to sleep . . . unless you've got any bright ideas."

"Just one."

"Well, I'm a reporter, Carpenter. I'll listen to anything."

"How about a drink?"

She snickered loudly. "One drink? Has Al Carpenter become a lightweight overnight? How about two?"

"You call me a lightweight then only raise the ante by one."

"By the time we get back to Raleigh, most places will be closed," she said.

"That's true. We could do my place."

She tendered a coy smile. "Your place? This is a momentous occasion. What, no more hotel bars?"

"Could do your place again."

"We've been there. I'm all about trying new things."

"Well, this is becoming an all-too-familiar sight," Ron said, smirking as he approached. "Al, what did I tell you about consorting with the enemy?"

"I wouldn't call it consorting so much as working to find a way to coexist peacefully," I said.

"We've still got a spot for you, Jessica," Ron said. "But I'm not sure how much longer we can hold out."

She widened her eyes. "Oh really?" she said. "Ron, your guy here has been giving me and my profession hell for allegedly not giving you a fair shake."

"Glad to hear he hasn't been totally wasting his time talking to you—unless you intend to stay the present course with Bill."

"I report the news," she snapped. "If you've got a gripe with the angle I take, you and Al can take it up with my bosses."

"They don't pay you to report the news," Ron said. "They pay you to make it."

She rolled her eyes. "I give up. Good evening, gentlemen," she said before stomping off.

Ron watched her for a moment, then turned to me. "That Parker's an attractive woman," he said.

"She certainly thinks so."

"So do you," he said. He narrowed his eyes. "Do you know what the intersection of business relationships and personal relationships is called?"

"A mistake?"

"No," he said. "Politics. You can have fun along the way, but don't forget that someone's always trying to leverage what happens at that intersection into a political advantage. For your own well-being, and the campaign's, you should assume that Parker—and whoever she's ultimately working for—is no exception."

"So you're saying I'm never off the clock."

"You knew that already," he said. "But I'm willing to exclude your time with Bristol from that general rule."

"Of course. She works for us."

"Precisely." Ron slapped my back, chuckling. "It's chess, not checkers." Ron surveyed the room and its dwindling crowd. "I think we've pressed enough flesh for tonight," he said. "Let's head home and get some rest."

"I heard a gem from Bill as he was making his rounds in there," I said. "Someone asked him if he thought he'd have a tough time raising money—you know, given his late entry into the race."

The intonation of Ron's chuckle indicated that while he couldn't possibly know the exact substance of Bill's response, he most certainly had it ballparked. "How did he respond?" he asked.

"He said he's not seriously worried, though he assumes fundraising will be dampened a bit since he's running against an African-American man and a woman."

Ron shook his head and grinned.

"You've gotta love this guy!" I said. "He's like the rich white kid interviewing for his first job out of college at an investment bank in Manhattan. The interviewer asks him, 'How's the interview process going?' and the kid says, 'I think it's going okay, except for one thing: I think I'm really being disadvantaged by all the blacks and women I'm up against.'"

It was pouring rain when we stepped outside. We walked briskly toward the car more out of a desire to get out of the rain quickly than a belief that walking fast would prevent our clothes from becoming completely drenched. Ron and I excitedly exchanged stories from that night for the first twenty-five minutes of the drive back up Highway 87. It was at the thirty-minute mark that I realized I'd been talking to myself during the previous five. An hour later, when the significant reduction in speed woke him from his nap, he sat up abruptly and said, "That really didn't take so long." Toward the end of my nearly forty-minute drive back to Raleigh, I called Carmichael.

"Sorry for giving you such a hard time last night," I said. "You must've been exhausted too. It's been so long since I've driven Ron home from an out-of-town event that I'd pretty much forgotten how solitary the experience can be."

"Any interest in becoming reacquainted with that experience on a more regular basis?"

"I called to apologize, not to tell you I'd lost my mind."

"Now that's the Al Carpenter I know. Thanks for calling."

"You got it, man."

CHAPTER TWELVE

It wasn't until the clock struck 11:59 p.m. on January 31, the deadline for Congressman Darling's endorsement, that I appreciated how thoroughly I'd been played. Over the more than three months since I'd cut the deal in Nashville, I'd spoken with Jim Randolph a grand total of five times. On each occasion he assured me that the congressman would keep his word. "A gentleman like Darling," Jim said, "holds nothing above his reputation." Though it became harder after each fruitless phone call, I'd managed to quell the panic building inside me. Now, as I stepped onto my balcony and gazed at the austere downtown Raleigh skyline, a wave of self-doubt threatened to rise up and crush me.

I briefly reentered the loft to fetch the box of Newports Billy left on my desk during last Saturday night's party before returning to my lonely outdoor perch to ponder my next move.

"'I'm not afraid to take this all the way,'" I muttered. Darling had no doubt laughed my words out of his mind the second he stepped out of Pete's. Then it suddenly hit me: *He never believed I had it in me because I never believed it myself.* I hadn't been prepared to out Darling because I'd assumed he would do whatever he had to do to keep that article under wraps. He'd read me perfectly and called my bluff. I wasn't willing to out him—and face whatever brand of retribution he and his minions might exact—until I believed Ron had no chance of winning this election otherwise.

I tossed the fourth cigarette butt of the night down onto the street below, went back inside and showered, and hit the sack just after one o'clock. In my final waking moments, I thought, *Time to up the ante.* Instead of fading into the sunset, I'd redouble my efforts to get the endorsement, and most important, I'd make Darling believe I was beginning to panic. As long as I seemed rational, he'd assume I wouldn't cross him. I rested comfortably that night, convinced I'd survive to fight another day.

*****

I HAD A PARTICULARLY ROUGH MORNING at the office the next day, which I spent calling the leadership of the various black PACs. As usual, Keri Jameson had asked me to do everything short of sitting on the toilet and taking a dump for her. So around eleven thirty, I decided to take a few laps around the block to clear my head. Before I reached the front door, the familiar melody of Ron and Bristol's laughter rang in my ears as they descended the stairs.

"Please tell me you're taking the rest of the morning off because you've already raised twenty grand today," I said.

Ron smiled. "Hey, who's the boss around here, anyway?"

"Depends on who you ask," I said. "If you ask me, it is, and always will be, Casey."

Ron laughed. "Your mother taught you well."

"So what are you guys yukking it up about?" I said. "I could use a good laugh. I've been on with the black PACs for the last fifty hours trying to set up another round of meetings."

"They won't meet with you?" Ron asked.

"They keep scheduling then cancelling last minute. I was supposed to meet with your boy Christian Tate, the executive director of the MC-OCA, last week in Raleigh. He was in town from Charlotte, which would've saved me a trip to the Queen City."

"Sounds perfect," Ron said.

"Yeah, until he cancelled thirty minutes before," I said. "Told me something came up. That was the third time he's cancelled in the last five weeks."

Ron sighed, then changed the subject. "Learn anything new this morning?"

"No, nothing," I said. "Jack Monroe keeps telling me he's still one hundred percent sure the DC-OSP will endorse us when it comes to a vote in early April."

"Keep the fire under his feet," Ron said. "Until we get that endorsement, he's Eddie Murphy and you're Arsenio Hall."

"Understood," I said, cringing. "So what were you guys laughing about?"

"Oh right, right," Ron said. "Speaking of the Queen City and

Christian Tate, Bristol was just telling me what happened down in Charlotte last night. I was so tired after my interview at DC-OSP that I went home and passed out."

"Oh yeah, the MC-OCA meet and greet."

"Meet and greet my butt," Bristol said, cutting her eyes playfully.

"Oh . . . this is gonna be good," I said. "My office?"

"Yeah, let's do that," Ron said.

"Where's Carmichael?" I said.

"Gave him the morning off."

I closed the door until the lock clicked into its slot. Ron sat in my chair and immediately propped his feet up on my desk while Bristol and I sat in the chairs on the other side. "So, tell me about Charlotte," I said.

"Well, you already know we had that event conflict last night," Ron said. "I had to be here in Durham for my DC-OSP interview."

"Obviously," I said. "No interview, no endorsement. By the way, Jack said it went well last night."

Ron nodded. "So Bristol went to Charlotte as my surrogate," Ron said. "No big deal since it was just a meet and greet."

"Right," I said.

"Not right, it turns out. Bristol walks in at six o'clock and within five minutes runs into Jane."

"Jane? What in hell was she doing in Charlotte and not Durham? Her DC-OSP interview was scheduled for four o'clock."

Bristol smirked. "That's the million-dollar question."

"So Bristol starts . . . well, I'll let her tell the rest."

"I'm freaking out wondering what's going on," Bristol said, rising from her chair. "Carmichael was beside himself—I mean really losing it. Then he and I walk up to Christian Tate and chat him up."

"Tate went to high school with Casey's mom," Ron said. "Casey filled Bristol in the night before."

"That's right," Bristol said. "So Tate asked me why Ron wasn't there, and I explained that Ron and Jane were both scheduled to have their interviews with the DC-OSP early that evening—Jane at four and Ron at six—and that neither would be able to get to Charlotte in time. Tate says, 'Well, I guess this event was more important to Jane than that interview.' Then Bill walks in."

"What?" I exclaimed.

"Chess, not checkers," Ron said, gazing at the ceiling.

"Carmichael turned bright, bright red," Bristol said. "Then Tate says, 'Well, one of you will just have to stand in for Ron. We're going to start the candidate's forum in fifteen minutes.'"

I slumped back in my chair. "What happened next?"

"I didn't have a choice," she said. "Carmichael and I worked the room, and when it was time, I took my seat on the stage."

"Wait, wait, wait," I said. "You're telling me you debated Jane *and* Bill. How can that be? We saw Bill walking into DC-OSP as we were leaving Ron's interview."

"No, just Jane," she said. "Bill scurried off just before the debate started . . ."

"And beelined it for Durham in time for his interview," I concluded.

"How do you like that?" Ron said.

"You're telling me the black PACs in Durham and Charlotte got together and arranged it so Bill and Jane could appear in Charlotte *and* make their interviews in Durham?" I said.

"I'm just telling you the facts," Bristol said.

I shook my head. "Unreal. Okay, okay. So you and Jane duked it out. How'd you do?"

"Great," she said. "I was nervous before it started, but there wasn't one question I couldn't answer."

I snickered. "You aren't a two-time moot court champ for nothing. And they thought they were getting over."

"The best part was when one of the panel members went off script and asked Jane why she's the best candidate to address issues of importance to the black community."

"Let me guess . . . she talked about how black her staff is?"

"Exactly," Bristol said. "She said, 'I have more African Americans working in my office than anyone else on the Council of State.'"

"Did you have a chance to respond?"

"Absolutely. I said, 'It's great that Jane has so many African Americans working in her office, but that shouldn't be the measure of how attentive a candidate will be to issues specifically impacting the black community. How does the fact that she employs black folks explain how she'll expand opportunity to the thousands of African Americans in this state who cannot afford college tuition? How will that help the disproportionately high number of blacks currently living below the poverty line? Ron's been working to expand opportunity to African-American communities his entire career, whether by helping to get black-owned small businesses off the ground or by using the low-income tax credit to spur the development of livable, affordable housing in previously forgotten and impoverished areas of Raleigh, Durham, and right here in Charlotte.'"

"Like a boss!" I said.

Bristol smiled broadly. "So this morning, Ron and I attended the

Lillian's List PAC breakfast in Raleigh, and of course Jane was there. She said, 'You did one heck of a job last night.' And then she turned to Ron and said, 'It's probably better for you that you weren't able to come. You're pretty good, but she's better. I got shellacked down there.'"

I let out a low whistle. "You really gave them a show, huh?" I said.

"It was one for the books, Al," she said, returning to her seat. "You would've loved every minute of it."

Ron pushed himself up and went to stand by the window. After a moment, he turned to face me. "We were lucky this time, Carp, but the writing's on the wall: this thing has officially gotten too big for us." Just then, Casey came into the office. "You're just in time, Casey," he said. "I was just filling them in on the additions we discussed."

"Great," Casey said.

"It's time to hire a campaign manager," Ron said.

"No arguing that," I said. "But I'd like to know where you found a pot of gold so I can get some for myself."

"There's no gold," Ron said. "We've been doing well enough for long enough that we can afford to bring someone on cheaply. I've got somebody in mind who'll do it for substantially less than the going market rate."

"And why would they do that?" I said.

"Because he needs a job," Ron said. "And frankly, he's built a reputation for being so demanding that he's been informally blacklisted even though he's never lost an election."

"Well, demanding's fine as long as he gets results," I said. "While you're giving out jobs, how about hiring a political director too."

Casey leaned against the wall. "Couldn't agree more," she said. "Carmichael's done a great job, all things considered, but we need someone who's already connected, particularly with black electeds and other political power brokers across the state. We've got to get surgical with the political outreach piece, and fast."

"Casey and I have someone in mind for that job too," Ron said.

"Who's that?" I asked.

"Wilkins," Ron said.

"Roger Wilkins?" I said. "He's fantastic! Knows everyone and is loved by everyone, and from what I've seen and heard, the guy can get a meeting with just about anyone."

"Exactly," Ron said.

"So why would he work for pennies?" I said. "He's got bills. Isn't he in grad school over at State?"

"He's wrapping up his master's of public administration this semester, then it's off to Duke Law," Ron said. "Did his undergrad at Chapel Hill. Anyway, I had a meeting with him the other day. He expressed a strong interest."

"I see," I replied.

"And I expressed an interest in having him come on for next to nothing," Ron said. "He said the money's not important because he believes in what we're doing. I told him I'd run it past the team and get back with him quickly. Sounds like I'm not hearing any objections."

"Bring him on," I said.

"I love him already," Bristol said. "I think Al and Roger will make a great tag team out there."

"And what about the campaign manager?" I said. "When do I meet him?"

"Maybe tomorrow," Casey said.

"That's right," Ron added. "I'm going to make an offer tonight. He and I have already met multiple times to discuss the potential of him coming on."

A terrible thought suddenly occurred to me. "Wait a minute. You're not talking about Shane Reese are you?"

Ron smiled. "I am," Ron said. "The Redheaded Dread himself."

"Wait, he's white?" Bristol said.

Ron snickered. "As of the last time I saw him."

For the second time in less than ten minutes I was floored. Shane Reese, the five-foot-five, fiery, red-coifed campaign fixer, was never hired as a first option. You didn't go to him unless you were desperate. And it wasn't because he was less competent than his peers—after all, he had none. Ron was right; he didn't have a single loss to his name. He also had no friends to speak of. With each victory, he left a trail of people he'd trampled, careers he'd destroyed, and personal relationships he'd ruined with indifference, and all this before the age of thirty. At the ripe old age of thirty-two, Reese was a legend, though a guy like me would never openly admit to admiring him. Privately, however, I couldn't help but appreciate his tenacity. I finally said, "I've heard the horror stories. J. C. Lockhart told me how ridiculous he was on Jane's last campaign."

"I'm not interested in popularity contests," Ron said. "My interest is in winning. Besides, aren't you always saying we need the kind of structure and discipline that only a seasoned manager can bring?"

"True, but I don't do well with micromanagement."

"Don't worry about that," Ron said. "You'll still only answer to me."

"Does Shane know that?" I asked.

"Not quite," he said, returning to his chair. "I told him you occupy a special role, and he said he'd be open to whatever arrangement we thought best." Ron leaned forward and locked eyes with me. "I know you're not crazy about Shane, but we're playing to win. I need your support on this."

"Whatever it takes," I said. "Whether you choose Shane Reese or Donald Duck, I'm on board."

"Why don't you take the afternoon off," Ron said. "You've been going pretty hard. Go clear your head." Bristol leaned against the wall next to Casey, looking pensively in my direction.

I rose to my feet. "Okay," I said. I packed my laptop, stuffed the stack of papers on my desk back into a Redweld, and left Ron, Casey, and Bristol in my office. Outside, in my car, I sat motionless a few moments before starting the engine. This was my last day as de facto manager of Ron Johnson's US Senate campaign. I'd always looked forward to this day because I knew hiring a campaign manager was the only way we'd have a prayer of competing against Jane and a potentially DSCC-backed Bill. But in those solitary moments, I could only focus on what I'd lost rather than on what the campaign had gained. As I dug deeper into my thoughts, I found the true cause of my sorrow: I'd never lost something this significant in my life, and the fact that the thing I'd lost was never mine to lose only deepened the pain. I tried and failed to block the memory of that shoebox and its contents, the only physical evidence I had of his existence and a constant reminder of his exit.

Ordinarily I'd seek Darden or Simmons's counsel at a time like this. But I didn't want to speak with either of them. What comfort could they provide to soften the blow of losing nothing? So I called Uncle Tom, and on his recommendation we spent that Monday afternoon doing what men in my family do to wash out life's setbacks—play golf. As always, we passed the time between shots sharing stories. His were usually better than mine.

*****

"It was seven thirty," I began as Uncle Tom and I approached the fourteenth tee box. "On the first Friday night after Obama's election."

I decided to have a cup of peach tea before showering. I removed the new Miles LP from the turntable, quickly inspected the vinyl for blemishes, and, finding none, replaced it with Coltrane's *Ballads*. I took my tea to the couch and settled in. McCoy Tyner's piano introduction to "I Wish I Knew" came pouring from the speakers like honey. Then, some fifteen minutes later, my vibrating phone startled me from an unintended nap.

"Sup?" I muttered into the phone.

"Carp!" Darden said. "What time should I come through?"

"Let's say nine-ish. I still need to shower and dress."

"I really need a release tonight," Darden said. "Roxi has been stressin' me all week."

"I thought you were breaking things off with her this week."

"Brotha, the week isn't over."

"Valid point. Let me go get dressed."

I shaved, showered, and dressed. Stevie's *Songs in the Key of Life* provided the soundtrack. I had just finished buttoning my shirt when Simmons phoned to say he was en route. After switching off the record player, I cued up one of the several neo-soul and hip-hop playlists on my ThinkPad. About fifteen minutes later, Darden buzzed my apartment from downstairs. I could hear Simmons laughing in the background.

Upon entering my apartment, each prepared a cocktail. I had just poured a bourbon on the rocks. Simmons was also a bourbon guy, and I just happened to have a half bottle of Simmons's favorite, Eagle Rare, left over from the prior weekend. Darden took his usual vodka soda, and we all settled into our preferred seating arrangement: Darden on the end of the couch closest to the window and Simmons on the other end. I sat at my desk.

"Did I tell you guys what happened on my walk home from Simmons's Tuesday night?"

"No," Darden and Simmons said, in that order.

"Hilarious," I said. "I was almost home, and I was thinking about how crazy it was that a black man is about to be living in the White House and running the free world. I shouted some curse word—who knows what I said—and this woman starts screaming at me. At first I thought she was pissed because her two kids were right there, but then it became clear she was mad about Obama."

"Why do you say that?" Darden said.

"She said something like, 'Now you people think you can do anything.' There was no reason for her to say that, other than the fact that Barack had just been elected."

"That's slightly unbelievable," Simmons said. "I know some folks are still living in 1955, but usually that stuff gets manifested in more passive ways, like hiring a white person for a job when the black guy was clearly more qualified."

"Let me check the calendar," I said. "Yup, November 7, 1955."

"Can you imagine what would've happened if Barack didn't win this thing, given how far ahead he was in the polls?" Darden said. "Black folks would've been rioting in the streets!"

"Part of me thought that a lot of the white support Barack was getting was some whacked-out Bradley effect stuff," I said. Simmons stood and walked toward the kitchen.

Darden raised his eyebrows. "Bradley effect?"

"Remember that black mayor from L.A. who ran for governor of California in 1982?" I said. "A lot of voters were saying they were going to vote for him, but when the election came around, they ended up voting for his white Republican opponent instead."

"I read this column a few weeks back," Simmons called from the kitchen. "It didn't specifically refer to Bradley, but the point was that this sort of thing might be in play for Obama and McCain. I didn't buy it, though. There was no way Obama was about to lose to McCain."

"Well, Barack did have one big thing going for him: Bush," I said. "Without that administration's complete bungling of the WMD-Iraq situation, not to mention tax cuts for the wealthy in the face of record deficits, Obama wouldn't have had a shot in hell."

"That's . . . probably right," Darden said.

Having inbounded the ball, I left it to the gentlemen from Virginia and New York to bring it up the court, periodically cycling in and out of the discussion while manning the music. The quality of the music usually determined the rigor of our conversation. The music had been stellar so far, drawing heavily from Erykah's most recent album, *New Amerykah Part One (4th World War)*. But we were still ramping up.

"My biggest concern going forward," I said, "isn't how Obama haters will frame this election and ultimately try to discredit every major decision he makes—and rest assured, they will do just that. Far more critical is how blacks will respond to his presidency—and whether we'll keep Obama's feet to the fire when it comes to making progress on our issues. They definitely gave candidate Obama a pass on Reverend Wright."

Simmons snickered. "Black Democrats had no real choice but to give him a pass. That situation almost obliterated Obama's support in the white community. It dug up deep frustrations within the black community that usually only come out in the privacy of church every once in a while."

"No question," I agreed. "At some point over the last generation, we came to a sort of tacit understanding with white America: we won't publicly complain about the institutional legacy of three hundred years of slavery anymore, at least not ad nauseam, and you won't publicly complain about affirmative action."

"At least not ad nauseam," Simmons said. "They're still complaining."

"You're right about Reverend Wright," I said. "He voiced concerns about economic and racial disparities that some white folks didn't—and still don't—want to hear. These are some of the same white folks who're among the legions of Obama supporters. America is nowhere near postracial, but the mainstream discourse *has* become virtually postracial. Wright was in clear breach of the tacit agreement."

Simmons snickered. "My man went to town at the National Press Club!"

Darden slowly shook his head. "I wouldn't have believed it if I didn't see it with my own eyes."

"Let me ask you this," Simmons said, leaning in. "Do you think Obama's people got together with Wright and staged that performance to give Barack an out?"

"Definitely plausible," I said. "Obama couldn't really get away with canning Wright until the press could frame him as a complete nut job, which he isn't, by the way."

"Wright said the things I think Obama wants to say but obviously can't," Darden said.

After a thirty-second timeout, we got back after it.

"Here's a question: Do you think blacks will stay engaged in the political process?" I asked. "Getting Obama in was huge, but it won't mean a damn thing if we don't continue to exercise our power as a voting bloc."

"How can you even ask that?" Darden said, sitting up and leaning forward. "Having a black man in the White House will change the entire mental framework our people bring into the political process. The starting point is no longer, 'How can we make sure we're heard?' It's 'How do we use our power to influence decisions at every level of government?'"

"I don't think it's inevitable," I said. "Things will go back to the status quo very quickly unless exciting black candidates get out there at the state and local level *and* black people vote. We need both. Voters across the board need to see more viable black candidacies for this moment to mean anything. My gut is that a lot of folks think Barack is a once-in-a-lifetime deal."

Darden leaned toward me. "Since we're on the subject of exciting black candidates . . . when are you running for mayor?" Darden said.

"DC's not ready for me to come back anytime soon," I said. "At least not in that capacity. I think another three cycles. Maybe 2018."

"And you, Simmons?" I said. "When can New York expect to have its first black Republican governor?"

"I'm in the same boat as you, son," he said. "There's a lot I have to do between now and then, so I'm not quite sure when 'then' is."

"Plan to win," I said, raising my glass. Darden and Simmons joined me right on cue. "Well, I can't wait to get on the horn," I said, "and ask the governor to shoot down to DC and help me figure out how to get us a vote in Congress."

"And help you convince Congress it's in their interests to do it, even though it isn't," Darden said.

"That's gonna be one hell of a tough sell," I said.

As was customary whenever "Other Side of the Game" played during one of these evening truth-seeking sessions, Simmons closed his eyes and joined the Queen for the final seconds of the track. As the drummer and his cymbal faded gently into eternity once more, Simmons opened his eyes before drinking deeply from his bourbon, scanning the room, and nodding with an unabridged smile.

"Looking forward to that phone call, brother," Simmons said in the unvarnished manner a person utters the morning's first words. "Jesus—I've come a long way from that knuckleheaded kid from Soundview."

"South Bronx in the building," I said.

"We've all come a long way," Darden said. "Strong moms. They did a great job."

"Proof positive that men have *nothing* on women," I said. "Don't tell Bristol I said that."

Darden chuckled. "You'd never hear the end of it," he said.

"Three peas in a pod who beat the odds," I said. "My dad left when I was five. I wonder how different I might've turned out if he'd stuck around."

"I hear you on that one," Darden said. "I was just a year older."

"I was five too . . . when he left," Simmons said. His eyes suddenly went glassy. "I remember one summer afternoon at Soundview Park. I was thirteen . . . must've been a hundred degrees out there. It was one of those days where even the most minor disagreement had the potential to explode into World War III. Me and the boys were hoopin' when this kid, Rick—Slick Rick, they called him—fouled me hard as I was driving to the basket. I got up slowly, staring him down the whole time. Everyone was laughing hysterically . . . you know how it goes, son. My fresh J Tens were scuffed up, shorts ripped, and my knee was bleeding like crazy. I had to do something or my rep was done."

"Around the way girls on the sideline watching?" I asked.

Simmons's eyes twinkled. "Oh, you know it. I *had* to retaliate, and Slick Rick knew it, so he just stood there a few feet away, waiting to see what I'd do. And Slick Rick—well, everyone knew he never left his house without a piece."

Darden shook his head. "Crazy. It's like you're telling a story from my teenage years."

"Mine too," I said. "So what'd you do?"

"My whole life flashed before me," Simmons said. "I mean, the life I wanted for myself—graduating high school and college, gettin' out of the hood, and having a real family. Slick Rick said, 'Make your move.' So I did. I stood up slowly with my hands raised in the air so he wouldn't think I was reaching—and I walked away. Before heading home, I tossed my piece into the river. I turned it all around after that. Stopped skipping school, started doing the work, studying, the whole nine. I never knew how smart I was until I started trying. I didn't have any male role models who'd done anything with their lives. All I knew was the streets. The other kids in school called me every name in the book for the next year. It goes without saying, but I never set foot on that court again."

"You couldn't," I said. "Not safely, anyway."

"And your rep was a wrap-a-saurus," Darden said.

"Also explains that weak jump shot of yours," I said.

"Wiped out," Simmons said. "And it's a good thing too, 'cause I lived to tell the story. I can't tell you how many friends from Soundview died because they refused to walk away."

"RIP indeed to your jump shot . . . it's literally trash," Darden said. "But you probably never would've become state tennis champ if that didn't happen."

"Truth," I said. "And I hate to say anything that might further inflate that morbidly obese ego of yours, but you've got a *killer* forehand, brother."

"Face it," Simmons said. "You just happen to be close friends with the most talented man alive."

"Here we go," I muttered.

"It's true," Simmons said, shrugging. "Facts are facts."

"So what became of his Slickness?" I asked.

"His rep was golden through high school. He's doing life for murder at Sing Sing."

"Walking away is so much harder than just going with your gut in situations like that," I said. "What you did took real courage. And look at you now: a black Republican with a highly questionable jump shot."

"It's not highly questionable," Darden laughed. "It's hideous."

"'Hideous' is debatable," Simmons fired back.

"Simmons's arrogance, however, is not," I offered conclusively.

Simmons snickered. "Then I'm in very good company."

"He's got a point there," Darden said.

As the bass line on Tribe's "Bonita Applebum" dropped, there were three rapid knocks at the door. My first thought: *Have we been yelling at each other over this music the whole time?* Second: *I know those knocks.*

"Who's that?" Simmons said.

"Who is it?" I yelled.

"Open the damn door!" she said. "Why is it locked?"

Darden and Simmons turned to each other. "Bristol," they said in chorus.

"One second," I said. I rose from my chair, eased over to the door, and undid the deadbolt. Catherine the Great whisked past me and into the living room without so much as a hello, her left hand gripping a bottle of champagne and her right hand a hunk of brie. She wore a pithy little black dress that showcased just over an inch of cleavage. Jennifer, about three inches shorter than Bristol, followed closely behind wearing a form-gripping burgundy number cut about twelve inches above the knee. Naturally I did what any respectable, red-blooded American man would do in a situation like this: steal as good and as long a look as possible without appearing to stare. Though Jennifer bared very little skin above her waist, the imagination didn't have to do much work.

"You black men are loud as hell over here!" Bristol proclaimed.

"What of it?" I asked, shrugging. "Did you descend your throne merely to note the obvious, or has the noisy proletariat done something to pique your queenship's interest?"

"Both!" she said, a smile sneaking forth. "Why don't you go sit yourself down somewhere, lightskin."

I shook my head at Darden, who grinned back at me. "Are you ladies rollin' to this party tonight?" I asked.

"Looks like it," Jennifer said, rolling her eyes at Bristol. "I convinced Old Mother Hubbard here to leave the house tonight." This was no small feat; Bristol rarely went out. Jennifer hugged me, then Simmons. She embraced Darden last, even though he stood closest to her when the hugging ritual commenced.

"Simmons!" Bristol said, midhug.

"We missed you at the watch party on election night," Simmons said.

"Yeah, I was down in North Carolina fighting the good fight,"

Bristol said.

"Looks like that door knocking paid off," Simmons said. "Obama only won NC by a nose."

"Yup," she said. "Long time no see, sir. What you been up to?"

"The usual," Simmons replied. "Doing my best to avoid getting any work done. And yourself?"

"Trying to get work done but with no success," she replied. "The infamous 3-L slump is in *full* effect. All I wanna do is eat and sleep."

"I think we've earned the right to be a little lazy this year," Simmons said.

"Abbbsolutely," I said. "We worked our butts off 1-L year."

"Before we started law school," Simmons began, "I remember asking 1-L friends just how bad it was."

"And they couldn't put it into words, could they?" Bristol said.

"Not at all," Simmons said. "Just like we had trouble explaining it to our friends and family who didn't understand why we couldn't spare five minutes to talk on the phone."

"1-L year is the relationship-killing year," I said. "That's how I explain it. If you're in one, get out before you start school; at least they won't end up hating you that way."

"The man speaks the truth," Simmons said.

Bristol snorted. "Class all day, then reading cases all night," Bristol said. "If I could do it all over again, no way I'd go to law school."

"Good thing for law schools that the hell of 1-L is impossible to explain," I said. "If it were explainable, no one would come."

Over on the couch, Darden and Jennifer sat together chatting at a safe volume. They'd been off and on during 1-L year, and from time to time thereafter, I think, in love. I don't think Bristol or Simmons knew. Jennifer Bertelsmann was the daughter of Andreas Rafael Bertelsmann, CEO of media megaconglomerate Bertelsmann & Company. Her mother, Vickie, the daughter of two African-American Atlanta schoolteachers, was a jet-setting foodie and fashionista who split her time between New York, Los Angeles, and Western Europe doing, as Jennifer frequently put it, "whatever and whomever her little heart desires." During our group's fall 2006 weekend retreat to one of the Bertelsmann homes—this one the sprawling fifteen-thousand-square-foot mountaintop showplace in Orange County, New York Jennifer casually referred to as "Daddy's Playhouse"—I'd stumbled on Darden and Jennifer knockin' boots to "12 Play" during my late-night, quarter-mile search for a bedroom.

"Can we stop off at Starbucks first?" Bristol asked. "I'm dragging a little."

"It's already quarter to ten," I said.

Then came the puppy eyes. "But I want to go there first," Bristol said. "Can we?"

"You can do what you want," I said. "I'm going to Boston."

"You're such an ass," Bristol said.

I turned to Simmons, who was standing next to me. He grinned. "Will you two cut the charade already?" he whispered.

We gradually spilled into the hallway during the next several seconds. By the time Darden and I reached the threshold, the others were already standing in front of the elevator at the other end of the hall.

"Why don't you just go ahead and do it?" Darden said, laughing. "That would eliminate all this fighting."

"Yeah, and create ten more problems to replace the one it fixed," I said.

"You're probably right about that. That's a damned shame . . . she's one of the baddest women at Harvard. You two would make quite the power couple."

I eyed Bristol intently. "No, I couldn't, and she wouldn't. It would be too complicated. And more importantly, I actually care about her."

During the brief ride down to the lobby, Bristol and Jennifer stood before us chirping about a 1-L who had recently snagged some "beautiful man" at Harvard Business School. The elevator door produced three cuties on the ground floor. As we slid past these potentially undiscovered neighbors, Darden, Simmons, and I followed them still, averting our eyes only after it seemed socially unacceptable to continue. As the automatic lobby doors swung open and we entered the frigid night, Simmons, Darden, and I could no longer hold back the uncontrollable urge to laugh. Bristol, who had been walking directly in front of me, turned and stopped abruptly, making collision unavoidable.

"What?" I said.

"Will you grow up!" she said. Before I could respond, she stormed off ahead of the group toward the car.

Jennifer chased after her, as the rules required, but not before accepting the wool overcoat in Darden's outstretched hand. "Thank you," she said, fluttering her eyelashes. She turned to me. "You and Bristol obviously have some unresolved issues. Work it out my brotha."

"We're fine," I responded.

She snorted. "And it wouldn't hurt to scan your living room for unmentionables before having people over," she continued, surreptitiously pulling a purple lace article from a small slit in the side of her dress and sliding the same into my breast pocket. "These were in the corner of your couch." Before I could respond, she'd jogged ahead to Bristol.

"Jesus," I muttered. I can only speculate, but I've since concluded that the next few seconds of silence must have been attributable to what can only be described as the natural reaction of three men watching a woman—at her physical peak, mind you—jog in three-inch heels. To date, I've seen nothing like it. God bless African-America.

The five of us cruised down Storrow Drive toward Boston, the Charles River glistening below the lights lining the highway while a sparkling downtown Boston beckoned in the distance. I cracked my window just enough to keep the others from fogging, and a constant stream of frigid air poured into the car and against my skin. The star-speckled, moonlit sky was cloudless.

We exited the highway at Copley Square. After narrowly escaping a few red lights, we made the familiar left turn onto Commonwealth Avenue. The stately homes of Boston's wealthy elite rose up on both sides of the grand thoroughfare. At length, we entered the theatre district. Then came the familiar sight of Boston's cold-weather, partygoing female faithful, their legs exposed, their heels high, their coats and makeup heavy. Once we crossed Charles Street, we found ourselves in the thick of the usual bumper-to-bumper Friday night traffic caused mostly by the excessive jaywalking of intoxicated pedestrians.

We lucked out and found a parking space just a block away from Tryst, where at least fifty shivering souls stood in line. We claimed a place at the rear.

I turned to Simmons and Darden and whispered. "Five, four, three, two—"

"Oh hell no!" Bristol said, right on cue. "It's cold as hell out here. I'm not waiting in this line."

The boys laughed heartily, and even Jennifer cracked a smile. "I'm not waiting either," she said. At that, our two female friends whisked past us.

"This should be interesting," I said. "Twenty bucks says they get in within the next minute."

"I'll cover that bet," Simmons said. "My man, the cold is finally getting to you. Look at the talent in this line."

"You, counselor, severely underestimate Bristol's talk game," I said. "Those two will be wrapping up their first round of bubbly before we see the inside."

"Bet," Simmons said, shaking my outstretched hand.

We watched closely as Bristol and Jennifer commenced opening arguments with the bouncer. The conversation between the two girls immediately next to us and the cacophony of shouting, car horns, and wind scrambled the report of Bristol's voice. The six-foot-eight bouncer leaned forward at Bristol's manual request, at which point the dynamic duo began whispering sweet nothings in his ears. Bristol did most of the litigating. In mere seconds, the grinning bouncer executed a convoluted series of hand gestures in the direction of the woman collecting money just inside the door. At that point another tall, well-fed gatekeeper emerged and unhooked the velvet rope. Simmons shook his head in defeat as Bristol and Jennifer vanished behind the sleek, shiny black doors.

"I'll take a Rémy Martin on the rocks, splash of ginger," I said.

"Yeah, yeah, yeah," Simmons said.

"I should've gotten a piece of that bet," Darden said, "but there are way too many attractive women in line to merit letting Bristol and Jennifer in like that, even if they're *arguably* better looking."

"It's the free market at work," Simmons said. "Laissez-faire, son. They leveraged their assets to get what they wanted. It's the American way." He wrapped one arm around my neck and the other around Darden's. His eyes glimmered in the moonlight. "I've got zero plans of losing tonight," he said.

"Plan to win," I said.

"Let's make it a good night," Darden added.

"Don't sell it short," Simmons said. "Better to make it a championship night."

A firm believer that a man's attire should say far less about him than the man himself, Simmons wore a black merino wool sweater over a white oxford shirt, dark blue jeans, and black loafers. Darden wore a fitted black velvet blazer over a white V-neck T-shirt, dark blue relax-fit jeans, and black hybrid sneakers. I wore dark blue skinny jeans, a white Ralph Lauren Black Label dress shirt with French cuffs, and a black pinstriped sport coat. Each of us had visited our respective barber within the last ten hours and had the fresh lineup to prove it.

I handed my identification to the bouncer who'd so eagerly removed the velvet rope for Bristol and Jennifer twenty minutes earlier and stepped inside. Darden and Simmons were waiting at the base of the steps. The walls were lined with plush red velvet upholstery, and the lights were just bright enough to permit safe movement from the small foyer and up the stairs. Sliding over to the others, I could feel that familiar tickle in my stomach, the onset of supreme excitement. It was about two notches down from the feeling a man has when he's on his way home with a woman he really likes, has only recently met, and with whom he knows with almost absolute certainty he's about to get lucky.

We swaggered up the marble stairs, turned right, and entered the club's grand arcade, which culminated in a twenty-five-foot-high glass skylight running the length of the oval room. The supple artificial lighting running intermittently along the golden walls supplemented the constellation beaming down through the glass ceiling, while a beautifully engraved bronze railing provided a protective barrier around the terrace overlooking the marble dance floor. Here and there, patrons leaned over, drink in hand, to take in the view while others ascended and descended the spiral staircases at either end of the oval. The dance floor some eight feet below us was already near capacity, and the flashing, multicolored spotlights slashing back and forth in every possible direction revealed discarded sport coats and sweaty brows. We stood there in a row, imbibing this grand visage and blocking the entryway. The sunken bar just a few feet ahead of us was exquisitely mobbed with an abnormally high percentage of well-appointed, attractive women and competently attired gentlemen. Something unmistakably special fluttered in the air that night. It was a complex potion of serendipitous possibility and pubescent exuberance that I'd like to believe everyone experiences at least a couple times in life.

"First round's on me," I said, continuing to assess the crowd. I stepped down to the corner of the bar and made eye contact with a bartender I knew from around town. She winked in my direction, finished her pending transaction, and, to the dismay of the two dozen other cocktail seekers, took my order.

"What'll it be good sir?" she said.

"Three tequila shots, please, salt and lime." I turned and found Simmons applying his right forefinger and thumb to the outstretched chins of two Nubian goddesses. A few seconds later, I distributed shots and, raising mine toward the stars, said, "Plan to win!"

We made our way to the south staircase just behind the bar and down to the dance area to make our initial rounds. The-Dream's "Rockin' That Thang" welcomed us as we entered the fray. That familiar, trancelike expression swept across the countenances of seemingly every woman on the floor, their bodies absorbing and processing the hypnotic rhythms completely and with utter efficiency. The men bore the look of so many seven-year-old boys on Christmas morning, enthralled by boxes whose precise size portended their content. Both sexes were at once possessed and perfectly tranquil. I put my hand on Darden's left shoulder to briefly borrow his attention, and said, "Life is good."

Located at the other end of the room, on the same level where I'd purchased shots, was the central, obscenely large VIP area overlooking the dance floor. From my vantage point far below, I could clearly identify a bottle of Grey Goose and two bottles of Perrier-Jouët, all on ice. Lording over these were two men I didn't know, both sitting on a half moon–shaped couch with Bristol and Jennifer. The foursome raised their flutes toward the stars, smiled, and touched glasses. I nudged Simmons and pointed toward the theatrics above. He rolled his eyes, shook his head, and smirked as we continued across the dance floor toward the bar below the VIP area.

As I approached the bar a few moments later, I turned and spotted Darden dancing with a cute caramel-hued young lady. Simmons had set up shop next door with a drop-dead gorgeous Puerto Rican woman he'd previously introduced to Darden and me. Her name was Cassandra. I intercepted Simmons's line of sight as he danced behind her, both of them facing me. Without missing a beat, he mouthed to me, *I'm going to marry her.* I smiled and mouthed back, *I'll believe it when I see it.* I leaned comfortably against the bar, which was far less crowded than the one near the entrance. Then I turned to my left. "Merciful Christ!" I muttered. She was about five ten, call it 135 pounds, 36-24-36, with light-brown almond-shaped eyes and rich, caressable caramel skin. She wore a green micromini dress, but she carried herself in a way that made it clear she wasn't easy. My guess was that she'd bought the dress, aware of the attention she'd garner, purely for her own amusement. She had a swagger of consequence about her, the rare fruit springing forth from a purity of confidence that eschews arrogance. I scanned the faces around her and concluded that every guy within fifteen feet must have believed that he, like me, was hopelessly in love.

She looked my way from the other end of the bar, then quickly shifted her focus when she noticed my eyes on hers. We played this game for the better part of three minutes before I decided to make a move. But before I could take a step toward her, she began walking my way. Then there was a tap on my right shoulder.

"Bristol, what are you doing down here?"

"Am I not allowed?" she said, peering over my shoulder. I watched as the woman in the green dress turned and disappeared into the crowd.

"Did I interrupt something?"

"No . . . I, ah, it's no big deal. What brings you down here amongst the commoners?"

"I needed a break."

"A break from expensive champagne? I'm sorry, and your name is?"

Bristol grabbed my hand and pulled me onto the crowded dance floor.

"You must be drunk," I said. "We don't dance. Well, actually, that's pretty much all we do. But it manifests as fighting. Constant warfare. Truth intractably engaged with denial. The—"

"Will you just shut up and dance?" she said. "We can get back to fighting tomorrow."

"Lunch tomorrow?" I asked.

"Yes, Alex." Then, for the first time in the two years I'd known her, we danced. After a few moments I spotted Simmons coming toward me.

"We live in the best of all possible worlds, don't we, brother?" I said as Bristol continued dancing with her back toward me.

"What's happening here?" he said, rapidly moving his right forefinger between Bristol and me.

"We're dancing," I said.

"Yes, I can see that you're dancing, but how did this happen?"

"Ms. Davis is having a moment of weakness," I said. "It'll pass."

Simmons leaned in and said something to Bristol. She turned back toward me as Simmons meandered toward the bar. Meanwhile, Darden and Jennifer embraced warmly just a few feet away.

"Are Darden and Jennifer—"

"I thought *we* were dancing?" I said. I leaned in toward her lips without a conscious thought, but she blocked the landing with a firm right hand to my chest. "Al, we can't just—"

I shook my head vigorously. "You're right."

"I just need to know what's going on."

"I suppose your friends up there in VIP are wondering the same thing."

She sighed heavily. "You're impossible."

"Now there's something we have in common," I said. Bristol stood perfectly still for a few seconds, her head hung in defeat. Then Total's "Can't You See" commandeered my existence with the warmth of yesteryear's most unforgettable junior high school crush, so Al Carpenter stepped toward her. Slowly, reluctantly, she draped her arms around his neck, and he placed his hands on the small of her back. They shuffled side to side, two twelve-year-olds unsure of exactly what to do or how to do it but instinctively doing it anyway.

The awkwardness of their untutored foray into the world of bees and birds was soon supplanted by a smooth, almost elegant familiarity. She gently dug her head into his chest before looking up and into his eyes. She spoke without uttering a single word. *I'm sorry for all the rings of hell.* Then he pulled her closer.

"We did good," he said. Al Carpenter would never forget the way she looked at him after he uttered those three words. The moment seemed to endure for hours.

"We did, didn't we?" she said.

*****

"WHAT HAPPENED NEXT?" Uncle Tom begged as I tapped in a short par putt on the eighteenth hole.

"I'll save the rest for the next round."

"Alright," he said. "We're playing again in two weeks. Don't forget."

"Of course," I said.

"Stop playin' and finish the story, nephew."

"If you insist."

"My man."

*****

SIMMONS HAILED a taxi for Cassandra, then he, Darden, and I plopped into my car. While starting the engine, I recalled that I hadn't seen or heard from Bristol or Jennifer since they returned to the VIP area.

"Has anyone seen Jennifer or Bristol?" I said.

"Last time I saw them, they were with those cats up in the VIP," Simmons said.

"Same," Darden said.

I called Bristol and asked Darden to call Jennifer. Neither answered their phones. "Should we just head back without them?" I said.

"Let me try Bristol," Simmons said, pulling out his iPhone. "I'll put it on speaker."

She picked up after a few rings. "Hello?" Her voice was partially obscured by music and voices in the background. "Simmons?"

"Yeah, it's me. What happened to you and Jennifer?"

"We left with two of my friends from grad school. I know one of them from back home too." I'd almost forgotten that Bristol picked up a master of arts in politics and global affairs from Columbia's Journalism School right after graduating from Chapel Hill. "My boy Rob's about to move back to North Carolina from New York to start a new job, so we're catching up."

"Ask her which one was Rob," I whispered.

"Which one was Rob?" Simmons asked.

"The one in the white T-shirt. Look, we're eating at Starlight Café. Meet us here?"

We looked at each other and shook our heads. "Nah," Simmons said. "I think we're gonna head back."

"Okay, talk later," Bristol said.

"Be safe," Simmons said.

After making an illegal U-turn on Kneeland, we traveled back northwest toward Cambridge. Darden and Simmons both passed out within seconds after the call with Bristol ended. I rolled my window down halfway and turned on the radio. *Who's this Rob character?*

"IHOP, anyone?" I asked as we crossed the Charles River, reentering Cambridge.

"I'm good," Simmons muttered. Darden was still out cold in the backseat.

"Okay."

Within a few minutes, we were idling next to Simmons's apartment building. "Gentlemen," Simmons said, opening the door. "It's been a distinct pleasure."

"Alright, man," Darden said.

"Night, brotha," I said. As soon as the door closed, I made a quick U-turn, dropped Darden off, and headed home.

Riding the elevator up to the third floor, I thought about what had happened with Bristol earlier that night after we got off the elevator—and our first dance at Tryst. Then the elevator door slid open. As I stepped into the bright corridor, I saw Bristol and a man I didn't recognize embracing affectionately at the other end of the hallway.

Stepping back into the elevator to avoid being seen, I pressed the button activating the rear door, stepped out, and walked around the corner. I leaned uncomfortably against the wall's edge, positioning myself just beyond their line of sight. Peeking around the corner, I identified Bristol's T-shirted companion as Rob. There was no way to get to my door without being seen. My watch read 1:50 a.m. *How much longer can they possibly stay in the hall?* I peered around the corner again and saw Bristol inserting her key into the lock. He kissed her forehead and quickly disappeared behind the stairwell door. Bristol fell back against the wall next to her apartment door and raised her eyes beyond the skylight and into the company of the stars. Upon hearing the fastening of the deadbolt, I walked around the corner toward the end of the hall. As I turned the doorknob, Bristol opened her door.

"Early night?" she said.

"I don't think two in the morning qualifies as early in Boston. What happened to your boys?"

"They dropped me off and went to their hotel."

"How long you been back?" I asked.

"Not long. Lunch tomorrow?"

"Gotta eat."

"What did you guys do after Tryst?"

"Stopped by Governor Patrick's place, watched some public television, and caught up on some Trusts and Estates reading . . . the usual."

She snickered. "Right. Home alone tonight?"

"Looks that way, unless you're interested in drastically changing the nature of our relationship," I said, raising my eyebrows.

Bristol shot me a side-eye before looking down at her furry pink slippers. "I'll pass."

"Good girl," I said, opening my door. "Love the look, by the way. Black freakum dress, pink bunny slippers. You may have something here."

"Night, Al."

I turned to face her. "Good night . . . Rob."

Bristol snapped her neck around so quickly I thought her head might fly clear off her neck. "Whatever, Al," she said. Before she could close her door, another one creaked open at the opposite end of the hall across from my now abandoned stakeout position. We both waited eagerly for the culprit to come into the light. I had difficulty seeing clearly through my dried-up contact lenses, but it didn't take perfect vision to recognize that hair and those legs.

"Angie?" I said involuntarily.

"*Angie*?" Bristol said.

"Alejandro?" Angela said.

"What are you doing in my building?" I asked as she walked toward us.

"Mary and I came here for a preparty. We lost track of time."

"Angela, this is my good friend, Bristol Davis. Bristol, meet my dear friend from college, Angie—I mean, Angela Rodriguez."

"Nice to meet you," Angela said.

Bristol smiled and softened her eyes. "Nice to meet you too."

I turned to Angela. "So, did you, ah . . . wanna come in for a bit?"

"I don't want to interrupt you guys," Angela said.

"Oh no, you're not interrupting anything," Bristol said. "I was just about to go to bed. You guys go ahead. I'm sure you have a lot of catching up to do."

"See you tomorrow, Bristol," I said.

"Nice meeting you, Bristol."

"Have a nice visit," Bristol said, closing the door gently behind her. Angela's black curls brushed my face as she walked past me into my apartment. I followed her into the living room.

"You have a really . . . clean place here. Still the same neat freak you were in college."

"Old habits."

"Speaking of old habits . . . why didn't you call me tonight?"

"I figured you said it to be polite."

"Well, I meant it."

"I'm sorry. Things are just so different now. I mean, you're engaged. Freakin' engaged! I still can't wrap my brain around that concept. How is he, by the way?"

She released a deep breath. "Let's not."

I'd been fiddling with some papers on the kitchen counter when I looked up and found her staring at me from across the room. She didn't avert her eyes. I felt a category 7 brewing in my gut.

"Alexander, I'm so happy we've been able to stay friends in spite of all that's happened."

"Amazing, isn't it?"

"Miraculous."

I looked at my feet. "I wasn't good to you back then. I mean—"

"You were young," she said.

"True," I said, returning to her eyes. "I was a know-it-all from DC. Couldn't tell me anything. But you were a piece of work too. And opinionated as all get-out. We still hadn't seen the world. Look at you now. A political activist. A real grown-up. You've got this whole counterculture, Angela Davis thing going on. I guess that's not a total shock, though . . . your momma was sharing her Black Panther stories before you could walk."

She laughed. "We were *both* young . . . and immature. I wasn't ready for what was happening between us. I also did some things I'm not proud of. Our paths just crossed too early in life."

"Is that how you deal with it?" I asked.

"Deal with what?"

"Your feelings."

"Please don't, Al. Please." The quarter moon orbiting the world outside my window bathed the room in an easy, subtle shade of light blue. We didn't need much light. I'd long ago looked into the depths of her soul, and she into mine. But at this stage in our lives, at this hour, the light was our greatest adversary. It could only remind us of the things our circumstances required us to forget, like those frigid New Haven nights where the warmth of our embrace, and this light, seemed to save us from a world that must have been totally frozen over. I felt I knew her better than him, but I clung to the memory of a person whose heart had stopped beating long ago. I stared into her eyes, searching for the old girl. At length I found her, and I couldn't bear seeing without touching. I longed to recline with her again in some late afternoon, the falling sun bright in our eyes and the pure, cool September air swimming around us as we dreamed about tomorrow.

We sat on either end of the couch, staring into each other, totally unsure of what we'd do next and beating back still fragrant, lush flowers of craving.

"Why do we do this?" she asked.

"Because you're Angie and I'm Al."

At that, she stood, walked to the kitchen counter, and prepared a drink I'm sure she didn't want. "You always had an answer for everything," she said. "It frightened me . . . but it was also . . . comforting. I always felt safe with you."

"That's what a man is supposed to do."

She snickered. "A man? You were an eighteen-year-old boy with all the answers." She scrunched her pink lips together while staring into the sultry Southern evening depicted in the lithograph on the opposite wall: a man placing a single flower into his virgin lover's hair as she leans in, eager to receive it.

"I noticed a little tension out there in the hallway," she said, returning to the couch. "What's the deal with you guys?"

"There's no deal," I said.

"She's really pretty."

"I'll put in a good word for you if you like."

"Well, I think you should make a move."

"Why does everyone keep telling me that? It's a terrible idea."

She smiled. "You'll be lonely when I'm gone. You need someone to take care of you."

"You've been gone a lifetime already," I replied. "I take care of myself. I don't need anyone else."

"You never could let anyone in. Does anyone really know you?" My phone vibrated on the desk. "Is that why you didn't call?" she asked. "Is there someone coming over?"

"It's Bristol," I said. "She wants to know what time I want to get lunch tomorrow."

Angela turned her gaze toward the courtyard. "It's after two in the morning. She's not texting to schedule lunch." She sipped her vodka cranberry slowly for the next minute or so, continuing until it was finished. Rising once more, she seemed to float toward the bedroom. Her dress fell gradually to the ground during the journey, exposing that angelic frame I hadn't seen in eight years. She'd filled out substantially in the hips and thighs since then, but her stomach remained flat—it was the black man's dream come true. She requested my company with a slow, deliberate, repeated curling of her right forefinger, and on the wings of her scent and ancient memories, I came to her.

Standing face to face, she undressed me meticulously, as though unwrapping a gift covered in fine tissue paper she wanted to keep and perhaps even reuse at some later date. My lips touched her forehead, and my hands moved patiently down her back. At length, I lifted her triumphantly into the air. I turned, sat down on the bed, and reclined on my back. As she leaned over, kissing me indulgently on my neck, that familiar New Haven chill poured into the space around us only to be neutralized by the fire emanating from our conjoined bodies. I closed my eyes and drifted off into her soul. And there we were cheating time again, osculating sleeplessly for hours, fulfilled entirely in the tangle of our embrace.

At seven o'clock, chilly New Haven took its leave as the merciless light of a new day came rushing in. I sat up in a frenzy. *Oh my god!* I thought. I looked down to my right and released a deep breath when I found two fluffed pillows and my discarded undershirt. Still, I sniffed the pillows just to be sure. Then three rapid knocks. Startled, I wandered into the living room and past the kitchen to the front door.

"Good God, Carpenter, you look horrible," Bristol said. "Are you sweating?"

"Good morning?" I said.

"Try afternoon."

"Are you serious? What time is it?"

She checked her wrist. "Twelve twenty."

"Give me a few minutes to wash up and I'll swing by."

She cleared her throat and looked down the hall. "How was last night?"

"Last night . . . what do you—ooooh, yeah. It was fine. We had a quick drink, then she left."

She returned her eyes to mine. "I see. Well, chop chop, counselor. I'm starving."

"Of course." I closed the door slowly until it clicked shut, then I downed an entire bottle of cold water. As I entered the bathroom, I stopped in front of the sink and studied my reflection. *Thank God nothing happened.* Then I saw her looking back at me, waving good-bye as she had just hours before—right after finishing her vodka cranberry.

*****

"ANGELA RODRIGUEZ, huh?" Uncle Tom said. "The one that got away."

I snickered. "I guess you could say that."

"I'm proud of you—both of you—for doing the right thing that night."

"Me too, although I'm still not sure how we managed it."

"People grow up . . . even boys!"

"I suppose."

"Nephew, that story wasn't half bad."

"Not half bad?" I exclaimed.

He downed the last of his beer before tossing the spent can into the golf cart. "Next time we play, remind me to tell you about the time I went to St. Maarten. I was about your age. Imma tell you like this—when I'm done with my story, you won't remember the one you just told me."

"Is that right?" I said, raising my eyebrows.

He winked at me. "That's Old School," he said. "Old School beats the New School every time."

"Not on the golf course," I said.

"Please. If you don't figure out how to keep that driver in play over the next two weeks, you won't break a hundred."

"I'm not too worried about that, *Old School*. Your short game was mad suspect today."

"Whatever," he said, tossing his golf bag into his trunk. "We'll see. That's why you play the game. You never know until you add up the numbers at the end."

"That's what I keep telling myself about this campaign."

"I guess you forgot what I told you and your boy Harlan back in Cambridge."

"I wouldn't say I forgot," I said. "I'm just hoping you're wrong."

"Sometimes you gotta learn the hard way. That's why I didn't object when you said you were coming down here to work with Ron."

"So you want me to fail?"

"I want you to learn. You don't learn nothin' from winning."

"So what did you learn from the butt whipping I put on you today?"
He smiled. "That change is coming."

CHAPTER THIRTEEN

FEBRUARY 2010

FEBRUARY 4, 2010, was the beginning of a new era for the Ron Johnson campaign. It was the day the team was formally introduced to its two newest members, Shane Reese and Roger Wilkins. And for everyone on the team except Ron and Casey, it was the first time we set foot inside our new, significantly larger downtown Durham offices.

"Wow," I said as we walked into the large, high-ceilinged, rectangular common area. "This is going to be great for phone banking and meetings with volunteers."

"And rallies," Ron said.

"Al, that's exactly what Ron said when we first saw this place," Casey said.

"Great space," Bristol said.

"Where are the offices?" Carmichael asked.

"Back in the hallway," Ron said. As we turned to follow him, I heard the front door open. We all swiveled abruptly.

"Good morning!" Shane said, holding the door open for a good-looking, brown-skinned man of average height and a hefty build. "Look who I found in the parking lot." I was immediately taken aback by how closely Shane's accent mirrored my grandparents', despite his attempt to mask it. Shane walked toward the group with unnecessary speed. As anyone who's ever met Shane will tell you, his speedometer—whether walking or talking—had only one reference point: fast.

"We pulled up at the same time," Roger said, jogging to catch up with Shane.

"Perfect timing," Ron said. "You two are obviously going to work well together. Team, I'd like you to meet Shane Reese and Roger Wilkins." We remained planted near the center of the common room as our two newest team members joined the circle.

"Al Carpenter," I said, shaking Shane's hand. His squeeze was excessive.

"Good to meet you, Al," Shane said. "I've heard a lot about you. Looking forward to working with you."

"Same here," I said, studying his eyes closely.

"Mr. Carpenter," Roger said, winking. "Nice to meet you. Ron tells me you're gonna be a senator yourself one day."

"Ron's brain is scrambled from begging for all that money," I said, glancing at Ron. "The pleasure's all mine, Roger. It's good to finally meet the legend himself."

He raised his eyebrows sharply as we shook. "Legend?" Roger said. "I don't know who told you that." Then he leaned closer to me and whispered, "I'm just another black man tryin' to make it in a white man's world."

"My man," I said. "Good to have you on the team."

At only thirty years of age, Roger Wilkins was among the most well-respected political hands in the state. Due in no small part to his long and loud track record of fighting systemic inequities in the sentencing of African-American drug offenders, he had a Rolodex that was the envy of political operatives throughout the Southeastern United States. The folks I'd venture to call his political peers—there were only a handful—were nearly twice his age and reportedly referred to him behind his back as "Little Roger." I guess it's true what they say: you haven't truly made it until you've acquired a critical mass of haters. It likely didn't help his cause among those haters that, next to Congressman Darling, he was probably the best-dressed politico in the state. His immaculately tailored suit was a gorgeous charcoal gray, accented with a muted pinstripe pattern and topped off with a pearly white handkerchief, freshly pressed white shirt, and navy-blue bow tie.

After introductions, Ron and Casey took us on a guided tour of the offices. The enclosed hallway running next to the common area led to five offices. Ron led us to the far end of the hallway first. On the way, Roger leaned in and whispered, "Have you heard a rumor about Preston Roberts getting into the US Senate race?"

I raised my eyebrows and turned to him. "No. Think it's true? My guess is it was planted to screw with black voters."

"That was my first impression too, but I'll do some digging to see if I can't figure out the source of this nonsense."

"Sounds good."

"Shane, this will be your office," Ron said as we entered the room. A weathered, gray metal desk and wooden chair furnished the otherwise barren room. "We'll obviously be putting some furniture in, but you get the idea."

"No need for that. This'll do just fine. I'm sure folks won't mind sitting on the floor during meetings. It'll build character."

Ron and Casey laughed nervously. "Well, let's have a look at the rest of the offices," Casey said.

Bristol and I were last to reenter the hallway. "What do you think?" she said, wrapping her arm around my shoulder.

I began shaking my head as I closed the door behind me. "Jesus be a fence around me . . . and him. We might not both make it."

*****

"That wasn't a bad game," I said.

Grandma set her coffee down after taking two audible sips. "That Drew Brees is something else, isn't he?"

"Ahhhh, you don't know what you're talking about," Grandpa said. "You haven't watched a single Saints game all season!"

Grandma turned toward him with narrowed eyes. "Charles, you don't have a clue about what games I've watched."

"*I'll* be damned," he said, winking at me. Bristol chuckled.

I grabbed a handful of popcorn. "Great game," I said.

"It *was* really competitive," Bristol added, "but the Saints' offense dominated the fourth quarter."

"Yeah, that Brees is something else," Grandpa said.

"And that Manning interception was a killer," Bristol said. "He doesn't throw interceptions in the fourth quarter of big games."

"Well, Tracy Porter made one heck of a play on Manning's pass," Grandma said, winking at Grandpa.

"Here she goes again," Grandpa said.

"I'm just hoping the Panthers have a better season next year," Bristol said. "This one was a huge letdown after last year."

"They'll pull it together in the off-season," I said. "Sadly, I think they need to do a little worse before things will get better. They need a top draft pick."

Bristol looked at her watch and whispered to me, "It's getting late, Al, and we've got a busy day in the office tomorrow."

"Well, Grandma, we should be heading back," I said.

"Time flies," Grandpa said. "Bristol, you make sure to get this young man back over here within the next few weeks."

"You got it, Mr. Carpenter."

"Oh, before you go," Grandma said, "let me pack you two some to-go plates. Tom won't be able to eat all this food himself."

We all rose to our feet. "I'll help you, Mrs. Carpenter," Bristol said.

"Oh, it's no trouble," Grandma said.

"I insist," Bristol said. "My mother would have a fit if she knew I didn't help."

Grandma grinned. "Well, thank you. You're such a doll."

"We'll be outside," Grandpa said. I grabbed my cell phone and headed toward the front door with Grandpa. "Where's your coat, boy? It doesn't make any sense, you parading around outside with no coat on. You're liable to catch the flu."

"I'll be fine," I said, stepping into the frosty night.

"So, how are things going with the two of you?"

"Pretty good, though I'm still getting used to the new Bristol. We used to fight like cats and dogs in law school. She's totally different now."

"Why do you think she's changed?"

"Not sure. Maybe the stress of law school brought out the worst in us."

"I think she's changed because you've changed. Tell me, how many women are you seeing right now?"

"To tell you the truth, just Bristol. We're not official or anything, but I cut the others off over the last few weeks. Bristol and I finally had *the talk*."

He studied my eyes intently. "I see. Well, don't screw it up. Good girl, that one."

"I know," I said as we approached my car.

He snickered. "If I wasn't happily married and old as dirt, you'd have to watch out for me."

I laughed. "Of that I have no doubt, Grandpa."

"How's the campaign?"

"Just brought on a campaign manager a few days ago."

"Shane Reese, I know. Taught his father calculus in the twelfth grade."

"How did you—"

"We have newspapers in Rock City, you know."

"I was going to ask how you remembered teaching his father."

He snickered again. "I'm old, but my memory is still spry. I wonder if Shane is as difficult as his father."

"He's a pain, but he's got a pristine track record."

"Well, check your ego at the door, boy. You came here to win an election. That's your focus. Keep working hard. Your time will come, but until then . . . prepare to be lucky."

Prepare to be lucky. "Got it."

As Bristol approached with two plastic bags full of food, he leaned in. "Make good decisions, and don't make excuses. I'm not gonna be around forever to keep reminding you." I shook his outstretched hand as he stared into my eyes.

"This looks like an unholy alliance if I ever did see one," Bristol said. "Your wife and your grandmother just told me to watch out for you boys." She stopped in front of us, grinning while examining our faces. "Yep, always up to something."

The two of them hugged while I looked on. "You keep him in line, you hear?" Grandpa said.

"I'll do my best."

I spent most of the hour-long drive back to Raleigh listening to the radio while Bristol slept. About five minutes from Bristol's apartment, she was roused by the stop-and-go of traffic lights once we'd exited the highway.

"We're almost back," she said.

"Good nap?"

"Food-induced coma is more like it," she said. "You were eating like that every summer, every night?"

"That's right."

"I'm jealous. Your grandmother is a genius . . . and that lemon meringue pie . . ."

"Ridiculous, right?"

Her expression suddenly turned. "Al—I think we should talk."

"About?"

She sat up slowly in her seat. "Us."

"I thought things were going fine."

"They have been. We've been spending all our free time together, and it's been great. But we need to discuss Jessica."

My stomach dropped. "Jessica . . . I don't believe I know anyone by that name," I said.

"Al."

"Okay, okay," I said. "What about her?"

"I know you two hang out from time to time."

"How do you—I mean, well, yes, we've gotten drinks a few times." She narrowed her eyes. "Al."

"Bristol, what do you want? A play-by-play?"

"No, Al, but before any of this started, back when you asked me to join the campaign, you agreed that if things between us progressed, you wouldn't see anyone else without letting me know."

I released a deep breath. "You're right. But nothing's happened between Jessica and me since the talk you and I had a few weeks back."

"The rumors have been flying, and I just hate hearing them."

"I'm sorry, but I can't help what others say. You want me to stop talking to her? That's complicated. She's a reporter, and I've been trying to work her to help the campaign. Dropping her doesn't make business sense. My personal relationship with Jessica will hopefully lead to some good press coverage for the campaign."

She released a deep breath and turned toward the passenger window. "Remember back at Vance-Aycock, when we ran into Darling—and Jessica Parker?"

"Of course."

"I was starting to tell you something about her."

"Okay."

"We went to the same high school. When I was a senior, she was freshman."

"Small world."

Her breathing became mildly labored. "I was . . . dating this guy. He was captain of the football team. We'd been dating for almost the entire school year when it happened."

I turned toward her, keeping one eye on the road.

"Remember the guy who dropped me off that night after Tryst?"

"I do. Rob. Did you guys get back together?"

"That's why he was in town . . . he wanted to try again."

"Timing seems odd. Wasn't he about to move back here?"

"He tried to sell me on doing the long-distance thing until graduation in June. After that, I'd be back in North Carolina with him."

"Ahh."

"We were off and on back in grad school at Columbia. It was one disappointment after another. He ended up disappointing me again when he came to visit that weekend in November after the election. Turns out he had a girlfriend."

"I see. So what happened in high school?"

"Jessica decided she wanted him, so she turned on the Parker charm and got his attention."

"He cheated on you?"

"No." A tear streamed down her cheek. "She spread a rumor that I'd been cheating on him with his best friend."

Just then we pulled up to her apartment complex. I kept both hands on the steering wheel and stared straight ahead as she began to cry.

"She ruined our relationship, and he lost his best friend of ten years."

I still couldn't bring myself to look her way.

"So I'm asking...no, begging you, Al—be careful. My heart cannot take another episode like that. Back in August, maybe I wouldn't have cared. But now I do."

I finally turned toward her. The street lamp outside revealed smeared mascara. "What do you want me to do?" I said.

She turned her head sharply toward me and pierced my eyes with a gaze I knew, in that moment, I'd never forget. "If you want her, please, just tell me now. It'll hurt, but not as badly as if I stick around for what I know she's capable of."

I cleared my throat. "It's like I said, we had something for a minute, but it was nothing serious and nothing has happened since we had *our* talk."

"I know I agreed that we wouldn't put an official title on it, and frankly, I don't need that. I just need to know you're not going to make a fool of me. This is where I grew up, Al. A lot of the same people are still here, and they've seen this movie before. I can't go through all that again."

"I hear you, and I won't let that happen."

"If you need to deal with her socially to help the campaign, then do that. I just ask that you remember what I told you tonight. And with that, the Bristol sobfest is over." She abruptly opened the door and stepped out of the car.

"Don't forget your food," I said.

"Good Lord. That's how messed up my head is right now. I wouldn't have seen this food again if I let you take it home."

"Not a chance."

"Night."

"Bristol—I heard you loud and clear. Don't worry about it."

"Al, do you remember Professor Jackson's last piece of advice to us on the last day of our ethics class?"

I chuckled. "'When you stop sweating the details, it's time to get out of the law.'"

She tendered a tight-lipped smile. "Good night, counselor."

"Night, Bristol."

*****

I ROSE LATE on Sunday, February 21, around eleven. For the first time in months, I cooked myself a proper breakfast of pancakes, eggs, and bacon. I was scheduled to meet Casey for coffee in downtown Durham that afternoon to catch up on the status of her outreach with the North Carolina Association of Teachers. That meeting was supposed to start just an hour before the DC-OSP meeting at First Baptist Church. The purpose of that day's DC-OSP meeting was the annual installation of its executive officers. Ron, Shane, Bristol, Roger, and Carmichael were all in Charlotte attending church services that morning and afternoon and wouldn't return until late evening.

As I neared the bottom of my final cup of coffee, Casey called to say she wouldn't be able to meet before the DC-OSP meeting because the person she'd hired to drive her children to their various appointments that day cancelled at the last minute.

"Why don't you just hire a permanent driver for your kids?" I quipped.

"Ha . . . if you want to bankroll it, I'm down," Casey replied.

"I'll have to pass."

"I'll meet you at First Baptist at 4:45," she said. "Starts at 5:00 p.m., right?"

"Yes, starts at five. See you at quarter 'til."

I pulled up to First Baptist Church at 4:43 p.m. Not surprisingly—she was habitually late—Casey was nowhere to be found. After chatting with a few familiar DC-OSP members, I ran into Jack Monroe. From what I'd heard about him during my time in North Carolina—and based on the substance and tenor of our weekly phone calls, which I suffered for the sole purpose of locking down the DC-OSP's endorsement—Jack was a decent enough guy. He'd had humble but solid beginnings in the backwaters of eastern North Carolina. After a rocky start in grade school, he began to show serious academic promise in high school and went on to graduate with high honors from the University of North Carolina at Chapel Hill just a few years back. It was during his time at UNC that he discovered his interest in—and significant talent—for politics.

To be sure, and I suspect that anyone who's met and spoken with him for even a few moments could confirm this, everything he said and did could be tied back to his ultimate aspiration to insert himself into the cast of statewide players in North Carolina power politics. An important first step, he believed, was obtaining a position in the executive ranks of the Young Democrats of North Carolina, a goal he'd achieved a few months earlier when he was elected vice president. To beef up his policy bona fides, he'd vigorously lobbied for and obtained appointment as the DC-OSP's director of affordable housing policy. Jack had been remarkably strategic in plotting his path to success, he was making all the right connections, and at the tender age of twenty-five, he'd put together a formidable résumé.

That Sunday marked the occasion of my fourth in-person interaction with Jack. This time I hoped to engage him in something more than the usual awkward Q&A, but before we could dig in, Dalia Greenway, a longtime DC-OSP member and the only member of the party executive establishment in the tank for Ron, grabbed my arm and led me briskly down the hall. "Hurry," she said. "You need to meet Dr. Creedmoor today. It's been long enough as it is."

Dr. Olivia Creedmoor was the long-time executive director of the DC-OSP. Though I hadn't met her before that day, I'd heard enough to understand why black folks in North Carolina harbored such mixed feelings about her. The vast majority found her cantankerous at best and intolerable at worst, but almost all held her in the highest esteem in light of the indisputable dedication she'd shown the African-American community in Durham County during her thirty-five years of service.

As Ron liked to say, Creedmoor obtained her doctorate in Whippoorwill Park, the site of her now infamous 1999 speech during which she successfully demanded a hike in state spending on affordable housing in Durham County. According to local legend, Creedmoor spoke with such tenacity and displayed such a keen understanding of the issues that people just started appending "Dr." to her name. Ron said that behind the rough exterior was a gentle old lady who loved Durham and fought like nobody's business for the blacks in that county.

As Dalia and I weaved through the nearly empty rear corridors of First Baptist, we gradually saw more people until, as we stood some ten feet away from a door marked "Pastor Leeland," we could move no farther. Dalia, by no means a small woman, ripped a path through the crowd of folks waiting to get messages to and make requests of Dr. Creedmoor. "She's working just behind this door," Dalia said.

As we pushed past the threshold, I heard an elderly, menacing voice. "Did you, in fact, order enough programs, child?" Within a few seconds, we were upon her. It was like walking into a concert hall to see a band you'd never heard—I could tell who she was because everyone was looking in her direction. They all stood waiting for instructions and preparing to be chided for some inevitable failing.

"Dr. Creedmoor," Dalia began as she pushed a few more people out of her way, "please meet Al Carpenter."

From behind Pastor Leeland's desk, the diminutive, white-haired Dr. Creedmoor squinted at me through her bifocals.

"He's Ron Johnson's senior advisor," Dalia added.

"How nice for both of them," she said. "Boy, what in tarnation do you want?"

"I just wanted to meet you in person," I said.

She looked me up and down, then straight through me. "Ron has some nerve sending an aide to talk to me."

"Ron's extremely sorry he couldn't be here today," I improvised. "And I can assure you that—"

"Step aside, boy." She stood and pushed past me out of the office, a dozen or so hangers-on trailing behind her. Within a few seconds, Dalia and I were alone.

"Well that was, ah, memorable," I said. "Is she always like that?"

"Like what?" Dalia replied.

"So . . . dismissive."

"That was nothing," she said. "You should see how she acts when she *doesn't* like someone. She loves Ron like a son. He's worked with her on lots of issues in Durham over the years, and she hasn't forgotten his loyalty. She just doesn't like being disrespected."

"Of course."

"Don't worry," she said. "She couldn't deny Ron the endorsement if she wanted to, and she doesn't."

"That's good to know, Dalia, but it's a question of speed," I said. "We needed it yesterday."

"I know," she said. "Roger's been pressing me and Jack pretty hard. But it won't come until early April, late March if you're really lucky. That's when all the black PACs usually endorse."

"Any chance we can speed that up?"

"Nothing short of a request from Obama himself could make that happen," she said. "And come to think of it, he's not on her good side these days either."

"Why is that?"

"She thinks his people are exercising too much influence in the Senate race against Ron."

"Wow," I said. "I guess I misjudged her."

"Come on, let's get out there. The program's gonna start soon."

When I returned to the sanctuary, I found Casey sitting near the back. "Your friend Jack Monroe is a trip," she whispered while lifting her jacket from the adjacent chair.

"My friend?" I asked.

"Yes, your friend," she replied. "He says he's been trying to catch up with you in person, but each time he runs into you, you just run off. He also said he wants to be as helpful to the campaign as possible and that he'll use his influence within the DC-OSP and the Young Democrats to help us out."

"And you trust him?"

"Who cares about trust? You and Roger need to pump him for as much information and as many contacts as you can."

"Got it."

"Sorry I'm so late," she said. "I had to get a ride over here. The van broke down."

"Again?"

"Yes, again. But that's not important. What's important is getting Darling's endorsement. Where are we on that? Ron says you've still been working on that even though he blew the deadline."

I let out a deep breath. "Darling and Randolph are MIA," I said, unable to make eye contact. "I can't get Jim to return my calls to save my life. I'm sorry."

Her eyes softened. "I was afraid this might happen. But it's not your fault, so don't stress it. Okay?"

"Well, that's all water under the bridge," I said in a rush. "He gave his word and he broke it. Now I've gotta apply some pressure."

"What kind of pressure?"

"The kind that hurts," I said.

"What does Shane think?"

"He thinks I shouldn't waste any more time on Darling." *Of course he thinks that. He doesn't know what I have on Darling, and neither do you.*

"Maybe he's right."

"I'm not ready to give up just yet."

She gripped my arm. "You be careful," she said. "We'd obviously love to have the endorsement, but there's such a thing as too high a price. When this is all over, win or lose, you need to be able to walk away intact. Don't let this Darling thing get personal."

"I'll be careful. Don't worry. I won't do anything stupid and jeopardize the campaign." *It's already personal.*

We stopped chatting and listened to the ceremony for a while. The entire slate of executive officers was reinstalled. About midway through, my phone vibrated. It was a text from Roger: *Bad News. Jack Monroe's signed on as Bill's deputy campaign manager.*

What? I tapped out. I'd known Jack wasn't as firmly behind Ron as Dalia, but over the past few months he'd done me several favors, including making introductions to black political operatives from the eastern part of the state, where we lacked a meaningful organization, and promising to "push hard" for Ron in the halls of the DC-OSP. To have him join Bill's campaign, and to find out this way, was a slap in the face. After I recovered, I texted, *That's a surprise for sure. But it doesn't change things for us.*

Roger's response came almost instantaneously: *That's not the worst of it.*

What else?

In seconds, the news we'd all hoped would never come flashed across my phone: *The DSCC's backing Bill.*

*****

THE FOLLOWING SUNDAY, Ron, Carmichael, Roger, and I traveled to Winston-Salem for its annual Black History Month celebration. We figured this would be a golden opportunity for Ron to appear in his hometown and excite our African-American base. In December, Ron committed—without checking his schedule—to being in Greensboro that morning to deliver the keynote at a breakfast meeting of the local black bar association. Although timing would be tight, we calculated that we could do the breakfast, get Ron to the main event in Winston-Salem by twelve thirty, and leave by two since he had to be back in Raleigh by five for an in-studio candidate profile taping at Channel 5.

In anticipation of this weekend, we'd spent the prior several weeks working to secure the informal endorsement of the Commission, the most politically influential ministers in Winston-Salem and the surrounding towns.

Just two days before our trip, the Commission's most prominent member, Reverend Carlyle, called Ron directly to communicate that they'd agreed on Ron and would inform their respective flocks in the appropriate manner and time. This endorsement, informal though it was, was a major coup for us in a critical region. Over the course of the campaign, I'd learned that few things hold more sway over the hearts and minds of voters than the endorsement of the preacher who addresses them from the pulpit every Sunday.

"Spoke to our guy down in Pitt County last night," Roger said while applying the finishing touches to his forest-green bow tie—as always, without the aid of a mirror.

"Oh yeah?" Ron said from the back of the Tahoe. "You finally got a hold of old slippery Jimbo Frazier, huh? What's the latest?"

"Actually, he got a hold of me," Roger replied. "Wants to know when we'll have yard signs for him. He says folks have been, and I quote, 'knocking my damn door down looking for yard signs.'"

"We can't afford yard signs," Ron said. "We're just barely making ends meet. I got you and Shane on the cheap, Roger, but you two aren't *that* cheap."

"I spoke to Shane about the signs this morning before we pulled out of Durham," Roger said.

"And what did he say?" Ron said.

"Said we're not gonna have the cash to do yard signs until a few weeks before Election Day, if ever," Roger replied. "Told me to stall Jimbo and anyone else asking about yard signs or anything else not already in the budget."

"That's why I pay Shane the big bucks," Ron said. "Stall old Jimbo!"

"Aye aye," Roger said.

"Jane and Bill aren't exactly making it rain either," Carmichael said. "I haven't seen any yard signs from them." He parked the car in a lot a few blocks from the Benton Convention Center.

I tightened my necktie and slipped back into my suit jacket. "You've been reading FEC reports again, haven't you?" I said. "What did I tell you about trying to read above your grade level?" I grinned as Carmichael snorted.

"What's this event again?" Ron asked as he stepped out of the car and into the blazing sun.

"It's just your basic Black History Month program put on by the local Black History Month committee," I said.

"My father used to serve on the committee," Ron said. "Should be a lot of familiar faces at this thing."

"Reverend Carlyle is also on the committee," Carmichael said.

Ron snickered. "The Reverend *Doctor* Carlyle?" he said.

"The one and only," Roger said.

"Beautiful, beautiful, beautiful," Ron said. "Am I speaking?"

"Not speaking here," Carmichael said.

Ron sucked his teeth. "You guys have got to get me more speaking engagements. This is the fourth quarter. I need to be speaking everywhere I go. Carmichael, what churches are scheduled for next weekend?"

"Trying to get you back to a few churches here in Winston. Reverend Carlyle is helping me with that."

"Great," Ron said, using his reflection in the car door window to straighten his tie. "I need to be in two or three churches every Sunday, speaking if possible."

"Understood," Carmichael said. "I always make that ask, but some of them just won't allow it."

"Well, I should at least be recognized at each service," Ron said.

"Definitely," Carmichael agreed, now visibly frustrated.

Ron pulled at his shirt cuffs so that they sat the proper distance below his suit jacket sleeves. "Alright, let's go," he said. "Roger, walk with me please. I need to follow up with you on a few items." Ron and Roger walked ahead while I waited on Carmichael to grab his jacket and lock the car.

"Jesus!" Carmichael said.

"I know, I know. But you've gotta remember, he's in the pressure cooker, and he can't see past his own nose sometimes. That's the nature of the bubble he's in."

"I know," he replied. "It just gets frustrating as hell. I spend hours and hours on end trying to get him speaking spots at these churches, in addition to driving him around and taking stupid phone calls from Shane all day asking where we are and if we're on time for the next event. We have those ridiculous conference calls every night . . . those are a total waste of time. And then, when the day's finally over, I've got to take him back to Chapel Hill before driving the forty minutes back to Raleigh. Do you know that on the way home, I roll the windows down and blast music just to stay awake? I rarely get to bed before two in the morning."

"What kind of music do you listen to?" I asked.

"What?" he shrieked. Though Ron and Roger had a big head start, Carmichael and I were swiftly gaining ground.

"You know, when you're driving back to Raleigh," I said.

"I don't know, whatever's on the radio."

"No, no, see, you've got it all wrong," I started. "You've gotta play something you really like. You know, maybe some Neil Diamond, or better yet some of that Barbra Streisand you love so much."

"Go to hell, Carpenter," he said, shaking his head while battling unsuccessfully to keep a burgeoning smile at bay.

"I'm already in it," I said. "Traveling around the state all day having to look at your ugly mug *is* my personal hell."

"If you look up the word *hell* in the dictionary, you'll find your picture."

"Wow, that was absolutely horrible. You must really be tired."

"Got four hours last night."

"Ouch!" I said. "And don't you have to drive Ron to DC and back tomorrow for that fundraiser?"

Carmichael let out a deep breath. "What happened to my life? It started with such promise."

Like many Southern white men I knew between the ages of fifteen and thirty-five (particularly the ones I knew who'd attended college in Virginia), Carmichael had seen fit to attach one of those neck straps to his sunglasses. Despite my burning inclination to comment on his beloved little convenience mechanism, I decided that it would be in the best interest of his continuing sanity—and my own—to hold this particular punch.

Jack Monroe was leaning dispiritedly against the rear wall of the auditorium as we walked in. On either side of him were staffers wearing T-shirts that read "Bill for U.S. Senate." As Ron passed by, he shot Jack the same look of disgust he usually reserved for Bill.

"There's ol' Jack Monroe," Carmichael said. "He hasn't grown more than a few inches since our days at the Y."

"I'll bet he's put on some weight though."

"I'll say. He's gotta be 220 pounds, but he's only five eight."

"Carmichael, we can't all be six-foot-six like you."

Carmichael winked. "That's a shame. Hey, don't you think Jack sort of favors MLK?"

"I'm gonna pretend you didn't say that."

"No, really," Carmichael said. "I think it's because of the mustache."

"His shoes aren't polished," I said. "His shirt is wrinkled, and one of the collar buttons is undone. MLK wouldn't have left the house lookin' like that."

"Yeah, he's lookin' a little rough."

As Carmichael and I approached Jack, I reached out to shake his outstretched hand. "Monroe . . . don't tell me you're already bored," I said. "You usually make it through the first hour of these things showing at least a semblance of interest."

He sighed. "Not so much bored as tired."

"What the hell were you thinking joining Bill?" I asked. "There are much cleaner ways to commit suicide."

"Come off it, Carpenter," he replied dryly. "I don't have the strength today."

"But seriously," I said, "if I'd known you were looking to get into the campaign business, we could've made some room for you on our team. We've got a lot less money and a much smaller staff than you guys, but if you were with us, at least you'd have some motivation to keep going past—what time is it?—12:45 p.m." I motioned toward the exit. "Whatta ya say we grab a cup of joe, on me? Ever been to the Times Café across the street? Best cup of coffee west of Durham."

"I can't just walk out of—"

"It'll be good for you," I said, wrapping my arm around his

shoulder. "We won't miss anything. This'll drag on another two hours or more. You know our folks—I mean, *my* folks. Word on the street is you lost your card when you joined Billy Bob."

"I thought they taught the art of persuasion in law school," Jack sniped. "Either you skipped a lot of classes or Harvard isn't all it's cracked up to be."

I laughed. "If you taught a course on politics, Jack, it would meet once and there'd be just one assignment: sleep tight and don't let the bed bugs bite. Carmichael, you've got the bridge."

"Aye aye, captain," he said, tendering a brusque salute.

With difficulty, Jack and I dodged the unusually heavy weekend traffic and scampered across the street and into the Times Café.

"Good . . . it's nearly empty," I said. "I can't afford to be seen with you."

"This was your idea Carpenter."

"I'm doing this for you! You were two-point-two seconds from hitting the dirt back in there. Don't get me wrong Jack—we want to win, but not that way." I nodded to the waitress—"Two large coffees, please"—then turned my attention back to Jack. "What's got you down, Jack? Is it the guilt?"

"Save it, Carpenter. I'm sure this won't surprise you," he said stiffly, "but there are people other than you, important people, who aren't happy with my decision either. I got an earload from Dalia Greenway a few minutes ago."

"Dalia's just trying to look after us," I said. "I speak to her frequently, even more now that she's got your old job over at DC-OSP. You know, when the news about your resignation dropped, she called me and didn't stop screaming for ten minutes."

"Jesus," he said, scratching his head.

"Come on, you knew black folks were gonna run your narrow behind through the wringer when you signed up for this."

"Actually, I didn't," he said. "Believe it or not, I did my homework before I pulled the trigger. I asked around. Besides, what do you care? When this whole thing is over, you'll be gone, sitting behind your fancy desk at your fancy law firm. This right here, politics in this state, this is my future, and I've got to start preparing for it." He slumped back in his chair. "You think I don't know what people are saying about me going to work for Bill when there's a solid black candidate in the race?"

I snickered.

"Look," he continued, "when Bill's people came to me, of course my gut instinct was to say no. But it's a great opportunity. I don't know if he'll win, but that's beside the point."

"So what's your angle? Because I don't see how you recover from this."

"Well, I just launched my own political consulting business. This was as good a chance as any to get my name out there. Would I have preferred to work for a black candidate? Obviously. But that's even more of an uphill battle. You know better than anyone else right now just how screwed up the black political infrastructure is in this state. Everything has to go through Preston Roberts and his crew at the party. That's why you guys are having such a tough time gaining traction with blacks. The activists, the grass tops, the ministers, the PACs, the electeds . . . so many of them are in the tank with Roberts. Even the ones who say they're with you, right to your face, are doing the same song and dance for Bill or Jane. At least with Bill I'm not nearly as beholden to those folks as you are. Quite candidly, they aren't actively working against Bill the way they're working against Ron."

My eyes narrowed. "Speaking of Preston, what's this I hear about him getting into the race?"

Jack sat up with a jolt and averted his eyes. "That's not true."

"Oh, I know that. That's the genius of the maneuver."

Jack began tapping his finger softly on the wooden tabletop. "I know you're not suggesting what I think you're suggesting," he said.

"Come on, the white establishment's been doing this to black candidates for years. What better way to deflate Ron's candidacy and improve Bill's chances than to insert the idea of another black candidate into the collective black psyche?"

"That's ridiculous! I—" He stopped himself and forced a smile when the waitress returned with our coffees.

Once she left, I leaned across the table. "Wrong, it's brilliant," I said. "Preston wouldn't actually run; unlike Ron, he has no chance of winning. But he doesn't need to run for the scheme to work. Just the idea of Preston entering would make folks toss them both into the 'can't win' bucket for mathematical reasons."

"You're full of it," Jack stammered.

"I'm pretty sure Bill and Preston are working together on this," I said. "But it makes sense that you aren't in on those conversations— it's just a few bucks above your pay grade."

Jack, not rising to the bait, only stared into his mug. "This is damned good coffee."

"Don't try to change the subject."

"I'm not. But you guys are screwed. It's the black community."

"You're saying Ron can't win because he can't count on a sufficiently large black turnout?"

"Basically," he said. "But it's not that black and white, so to speak. Look, I know a lot of black folks want to be with Ron. I talk to black politicians and grass tops damn near everyday who say they want to be with Ron. But politically, it's just not worth sticking their necks out against the establishment when Ron's going to lose. They don't think Jane can win in the general, but they're convinced she's gonna win the primary. If they come out for Ron, or Bill for that matter, when Jane wins, they're stuck on the outside. Jane has a long memory. She's also got Preston and the party in her back pocket."

"See, that's the same kind of thinking black folks used to decide between Obama, Hillary, and Edwards at the beginning of the '08 primary season. Off the record, they *wanted* to be with Obama, but they just knew he couldn't win."

"But that thinking was rational, wasn't it?" Jack said. "You've gotta admit that much. Don't you remember how much of a long shot Obama was?"

"Wasn't it also rational in 1963 to believe Governor George Wallace when he said 'segregation now, segregation tomorrow, and segregation forever'?"

"The point is," Jack said, "when Bill's people came to me, I asked around. Several folks in the black community, people whose opinions I trust, told me Ron couldn't and wouldn't win."

"And what sage advice did these folks give you about Bill?"

"They said Bill's a long shot to beat Jane, but he stands a much better chance than Ron because he looks the part."

"Bill's just a new version of the old way," I said. "He's a Branford Darling blue dog progressive who'll run—and vote—as far to the right as he can get away with."

"But that's exactly why he has a chance. He's young, and he tosses out just enough progressive-sounding sound bites around the right folks to be convincing. In reality, he's not progressive at all. He'll be whatever he needs to be to win this primary. And that's what matters."

"I thought you said winning was secondary for you."

Jack smiled. "We all *want* to win. That's why you run."

"You do realize, of course, he's not going to win, don't you?"

"Bill spoke at a student rally last week in Wilmington. Three students fainted. The guy's Jack Kennedy 2.0."

"You guys can bank on Camelot if you want," I said. "But unless someone in your camp has Daddy Joe Kennedy's pockets—and I don't think the DSCC is gonna spend that kind of money this cycle—you're missing the forest for the trees."

"Hey, don't get mad at me for stating the facts," Jack said, spreading his hands wide. "Besides, it's not all bad news for your camp. I heard a rumor last week that the WC-CSP was starting to turn for Ron."

"Oh, is that right?" I said. Of course I knew about that rumor. I'd started it. For months now, I'd been in near daily contact with Keri Jameson, and I was still no closer to getting an endorsement. Since the news of the DSCC's decision to back Bill broke, many in the black community had complained that the DSCC's involvement in the race was inappropriate. We'd pounced on this angle and started a whisper campaign to make the case that the DSCC was so worried an African-American candidate might actually gain traction in this primary that it had jumped into the race to ensure Ron wouldn't raise enough money to contend. Within a few days, we began receiving calls voicing this precise concern. Roger was even able to convince a few freshman black electeds in Wake and Mecklenburg Counties that immediately endorsing Ron would all but guarantee their standing in the African-American community in advance of their own primary battles. It wasn't much, but I hoped it might draw attention to our campaign, amplify the fledgling perception that Ron was starting to gain traction in the black community, and make it at least marginally more difficult for Keri to work against us. "That'd be great, but of course you can't believe everything you hear," I said.

Jack chuckled to himself. "Yeah, I guess that's true, especially when it comes to Keri. Last night she told me she's still loyal to Bill and that she's gonna make sure the rest of the WC-CSP gets on board. Then this morning, I get a call from Mary-Jane Fenway. She says Keri's agreed to quietly orchestrate GOTV work for Jane. I think Mary-Jane's mom and Keri were high school classmates, so maybe that's how she got the intel. It's bullshit."

My stomach dropped ten stories. "Wait," I said. "'*Still* loyal to Bill'?"

"Yes," Jack said, looking up in surprise. "You ran into Keri back in early January at the Chamber Club for that CC-CSP party, didn't you?"

My mind flashed to that evening: Keri standing in the corner, watching the crowd. "Yeah, so?"

"Didn't you wonder why she was there?"

"Well, not so much why as—"

"She was there to sell Bill on the idea of paying her—secretly, of course—to deliver the WC-CSP endorsement."

Without thinking I put my head in my hand. All those calls, all those favors, for nothing. Keri was never going to back Ron. She'd planned on claiming her share of the victor's spoils no matter who took the primary.

I looked out the window. A little boy was running circles around his mother while she tried to grab him. Each time she managed to catch him he wriggled out of her grasp like a fish.

"You know, it's funny," I said at last. "You've got the Keri Jamesons of the state running around out here, dipping and ducking, making more promises than they can keep or remember, all to make sure they've got a place at the table. They're not putting their necks out because they don't see this as their battle. The ironic thing is, this *is* their battle. They'd all benefit from Ron getting in, but they're so blinded by doubt, so convinced a black man can't win, that all they can see are the crumbs Jane or Bill might throw their way. Never mind that we have a black president. Never mind that he won North Carolina. It's insanity! Why won't people stop to think about why the establishment spends so much time and energy telling them what they can't do? If it was so impossible, there'd be no need to waste time and energy convincing them."

"All valid points," Jack admitted.

"But there are people out there who are down for the cause, some of them in very high places. These are the folks you, Jack, are gonna need, and they won't forget what you did when the sun sets on this primary. I guess you're just hoping that when Bill loses, they'll forget you ever worked against Ron."

"Not so much forget as choose not to remember." Jack gave a thin, tired smile. "This is politics, Carpenter. Political winds are in constant flux. Alliances aren't permanent. I'll recover. Hey, did you hear that Jane spoke to an assembly of *all* the state NAACP chapter presidents on Thursday?"

My stomach churned. "How in hell did her people pull that off?"

"She's establishment," he replied. "Folks wanna keep their place at the table."

"You know, we couldn't even get a list of NAACP chapter presidents and their phone numbers. We spent a month piecing that list together. I'm guessing they just handed it over to you guys."

"More or less," he said, smiling broadly.

"Can I get you something else?" the waitress said.

"Just the check, please," I said.

"Ready to get back over there?" Jack asked.

"Yeah. Let's get back in there so I can fight the good fight."

"You, *Mr. Carpenter*, have the luxury of working for a candidate simply because you believe in him. And that's because the outcome of this election has pretty much no bearing on what you do next. You've got a golden parachute. If I went to work for Ron and he lost, what in hell would I do next? Plus, there's not really room for two ambitious young black men—or their egos—on one campaign." He shot me a sidelong glance. "Or so Bristol says."

"Bristol? Why on earth would someone like Bristol waste her time talking to a guy like you?"

"Don't know," he said with a shrug. "She's a North Carolina girl. Maybe she's thinking about building a future here too."

Underneath the table, my hands clenched into fists. "If you're trying to convert Bristol to Bill's side, don't waste your time. It's not gonna happen."

"Who says I'm trying to get her to join Bill's team? Maybe I just want her on mine."

At a loss for words, I returned my eyes to the street. The battling mother and child were gone. "Well, of course you do," I said at last. "She's great."

"I know. We're having lunch tomorrow," he said. The triumph in his eyes was unmistakable.

"How about that," I said. I signed the bill, thanked the waitress by name, and headed toward the door. *What do I care? She's a grown woman. She can do what she wants. Besides, it's just lunch. I trust her . . . but this still stings.* I grabbed the handle, turned, and said, "Well, I hope you get some sleep before then. You can't go out with Bristol looking like this."

Before Jack could respond, I darted back across the street, narrowly avoiding oncoming traffic. After stopping briefly to tighten my tie, I stepped back into the auditorium. I suffered a minor conniption when I saw Bill standing at the podium preparing to deliver remarks. I shot Carmichael a look from across the room, and he answered my unspoken inquiry with a dejected shrug. About a minute into Bill's speech Roger approached me, shaking his head.

"What in hell is he doing speaking?" I whispered.

Roger's face remained stoic. "I've been asking around since he started," he said. "His name isn't on the program." Roger had a reputation for what I called 'ostensible emotional impenetrability.' You never knew if what you'd said or done to him had upset him until he'd already busted you upside your head, so to speak—not physically, but in the way well-seasoned political artisans inflict pain: by winning. To that point in time, I hadn't seen him permit anyone or anything to provoke physical evidence of anger. But one would do well not to mistake his agreeable temperament for weakness or the absence of first-rate intelligence.

"Dammit!" I said a little louder than I should have.

"He or Jack must've pulled some strings with someone on the committee," Roger said.

"Who the hell would sanction this?" I said.

"My guess," Roger said, "and this is only a guess, is that his campaign helped to, ahhhhh, defray the costs of this year's festivities."

From the corner of my eye I caught sight of Jack. He'd reclaimed the same spot against the wall. When he caught my eye, he fired off a wink.

"As a twelve-year-old boy in . . . Kannapolis, just down the road, my father and I walked into a . . . segregated restaurant," Bill said.

"Segregated!" I whispered to Roger. "He's thirty-eight. There was no segregation in Kannapolis when he was twelve."

"I looked at my dad," Bill continued, "and I asked him, 'Why are all those . . . African Americans . . . sitting on one side?'"

"Leave it to Bill to find the one remaining segregated restaurant in Kannapolis in 1984," I muttered.

"My dad looked deeply into my eyes and he . . . grabbed my hand. He walked me over to . . . the side where all the . . . African Americans were sitting and peacefully eating their lunches. That moment is something I . . . could never forget, and it's . . . something I've worked to eliminate from . . . our society. As student body president at Davidson, I . . . marched with African-American students who were demanding the erection of an . . . African-American cultural center. We in the student government thought they deserved . . . such a center and that it ought to be built in a . . . prominent location on campus. With hard work, that building was . . . erected, right next to the football stadium."

Bill waited in vain for recognition from the crowd, a crowd that seemed to be struggling to comprehend why he was standing there speaking in the first place. He droned on for a few more minutes about the importance of recognizing the achievements of African Americans not just in February, but every day, then finished with a bold call for an end to race discrimination. The crowd rewarded him with a smattering of applause. Bill waved and smiled for the entirety of his long walk across the dais and down toward his front-row seat.

I turned to Roger, returned his ear-to-ear smile with one of my own, and shook his outstretched hand. "That couldn't have gone better for us if we'd planned it ourselves," I said. "It was even better than his performance at the Chamber Club."

Upon the formal conclusion of the program, Ron, Roger, Carmichael, and I began working the room. I was talking to Mary-Jane Fenway when we saw Jack make a beeline for Bill.

"What's got Jack all in a tizzy?" Mary-Jane said.

"Probably wants to intervene before Bill shares another gem from *Bill Billingsworth—The Civil Rights Years*. Excuse me for a second." After shaking hands with the committee members, Bill and Jack departed. I maneuvered over to Ron as he finished shaking hands with a group of voters and whispered from behind, "That went well."

Without turning he whispered back, "A few more performances like that, and we just might get that supermajority of black votes after all. Jane didn't even show. Do we have a camera here?"

"No," I said.

"That's a mistake," he said sharply. "We shouldn't be traveling without one."

I turned to Carmichael, who was standing on the other side of Ron. "Why don't we have a camera here?" I whispered.

"It's in the car, along with the dead battery."

It was already nearing 2:30 p.m., which meant we were late as usual. As Roger escorted Ron across the room to steal a few precious minutes of face time with committee members, I instructed Carmichael to make sure we got Ron out of there by 2:40 p.m.

When we left at quarter to three, we ran into our friend Reverend Carlyle. He was a short man with the thickest glasses I'd ever laid eyes on. Reverend Carlyle was, however, like most of the ministers I'd met during this campaign, always impeccably dressed and teeming with cordiality—though I must admit, in Reverend Carlyle's case, the cordiality always made me uncomfortable. From our first meeting, I'd suspected his helping hand would come, if ever, at a hefty price or, alternatively, was no helping hand at all. But I gave him the benefit of the doubt for two reasons: first, he'd never given us any reason to suspect him of pernicious motives, and second, we didn't really have a choice.

"We're so happy you could make it today," Reverend Carlyle said warmly, shaking our hands.

"Reverend, if you don't mind my asking, how on earth did Bill get on that program?" I asked.

"I'm not quite sure how that happened, Al," he said in a tone of genuine astonishment. "It was totally unacceptable for him to get the chance to speak without you also having an opportunity."

"Well, perhaps it all worked out for the best," Roger said. "I don't think it went over too well for our friend from Kannapolis."

"No, I can't say that it did," Reverend Carlyle replied. "Well look, I know you've got to run to Raleigh for that interview, so I won't keep you. It means so much to us to have you come home and be, however briefly, among friends and family. Thank you, on behalf of the Commission and the committee."

"Thanks for having us," Ron said. "And thanks for everything you're doing for us here in Winston."

"Not a problem," he said. "Roger, Al, let's keep in touch. Mr. Carmichael, I'll call you later today about setting Ron up to speak at all three services next Sunday." With that, Reverend Carlyle jogged off down the street and around the corner as fast as his wing tips could carry him.

Ron turned to us. "I'm really hungry."

"We can grab something quick at Jimmy's on the way out, but we have to keep moving," I said.

"Fine," Ron said.

Roger and I went to grab sandwiches while Carmichael and Ron retrieved the car. While we were in line, Roger leaned toward me. "Don't look now," he whispered, "but I believe the Reverend Doctor is sitting over there with Bill and Jack."

I did my best to look in their general direction discreetly. It was them alright, sitting by the window and yukking it up.

"That Jack Monroe is somethin', ain't he?" Roger said.

"That he is. The least they could've done was pick a place more than two blocks away from the auditorium. I guess Jack didn't figure we were sandwich guys."

As usual, Jimmy made the sandwiches with lightning speed, and within two minutes, Roger and I were climbing back into the Tahoe. As Roger handed out the food, I nodded toward the restaurant's window. "Guess who's having lunch in there together."

Ron turned to look. "Bill, Jack, and . . . is that Carlyle?" Ron said. He shook his head. Carmichael's jaw almost hit the gas pedal.

"How do you like that?" I said. "Something told me we couldn't trust him."

Ron laughed. "Not everyone is dirty, Carp," Ron said. "We don't even know if *Carlyle* is dirty. This is politics, and that's just a meeting."

"A meeting that looks like it's going pretty well for Bill."

"Who knows?" Ron said. "Maybe he's in there working for us. Whatever the case, this is good for you guys to see. It's a reminder that we can't be walking around . . . what is it you like to say, Al, 'blind without a cane'?"

As Carmichael drove off, I tapped Roger on the shoulder and

pointed to the storefront. Bill and Jack were now shaking hands with Reverend Carlyle.

"You should only believe half of what you see," Ron said. "Stay focused on what we're doing, and let's spend less time worrying about what everyone else is doing."

"Makes you sick, doesn't it?" Roger whispered to me, straight-faced. I grimaced while reaching down to the floor to retrieve the copy of the *New York Times* I'd purchased that morning.

Carmichael's phone rang. "Shane, you're on speaker," he said.

"Where are you guys?"

"Just heading out of Winston now."

"Please tell me you're joking, Carmichael. You're totally late."

"I'm aware of that," Carmichael muttered. Ron cracked a smile.

"Well, you're gonna need to make up the time on the road," Shane said.

"Sure thing. I'll just do ninety-five miles an hour the whole way. We'll see how that works out."

"What's your problem, Carmichael?" Shane said.

"No problem on my end," Carmichael replied. "It's not my fault we're late. The event ran over, so we're a few minutes behind."

"Well, try to make up some time now without killing everyone," Shane said. "And—" Carmichael hung up before Shane could finish.

"Doing alright there, Carmichael?" Ron asked, stifling a chuckle.

"Been better," Carmichael exhaled. "Just a *little* sleep deprived." His face had boiled to a deep, bright red.

Ron yawned loudly. "Come to think of it, I'm pretty tired myself." Within a minute, he was out cold. Carmichael looked at Roger and me through the rearview mirror and shook his head—Carmichael's breathing simulated that of a pregnant woman in the middle of a Lamaze class.

"Well played, Carmichael," Roger said. "I don't know how you do it. I'm not sure I could've made it through that one." Just a week before, I'd watched Roger silently endure a thirty-minute scolding from a powerful black mayor in Roger's hometown down east for a scheduling mix-up the mayor had caused. After Mayor Gates stormed out of the restaurant, and after Roger finished removing the mayor's spit droplets from his forehead, he turned to me and said, "I think he handled that pretty well, all things considered."

I pulled down the window shade and settled back into the leather-upholstered seat, which was still warm from the hours of direct sunlight it had absorbed as the car sat in that uncovered Winston-Salem parking lot—a perfect complement to the icy air pumping from the vent above my head. I'm no climate change expert, but eighty degrees in February seemed just a smidge abnormal to me—even in the South.

"What's in the news?" Carmichael asked.

"Did you hear about this earthquake in Chile?" I asked. "It was eight point eight on the Richter scale."

"Crazy, right?" Roger said. "Another earthquake. Folks are still trying to recover from the one in Haiti last month. How many casualties?"

"This one wasn't as devastating as the one in Haiti," I said. "Not sure on specific numbers, though. And of course the fallout from the *Citizens United* decision continues."

"If we win this primary," Carmichael said, "how in hell are we going to compete with Senator Rodney and all that unlimited money his corporate compadres will be pouring into ads?"

"I don't wanna talk about that," I said. I looked out the window just as we passed the Koury Convention Center where, just a few weeks before, Carmichael narrowly missed an opportunity to meet Jesse Jackson at a celebration of the fiftieth anniversary of the day the "Greensboro Four" executed the historic Woolworth's sit-in. While continuing to gaze into the distance, I was nearly overwhelmed with rage. Jane's unprecedented NAACP meeting, Keri's hedging activities, and Reverend Carlyle's two-timing—it seemed that while Team Johnson played by the rules (most of the time, anyway), some of the other players were cutting corners. After months of sloshing through rookie mistakes, we'd finally traded our political checkers in for chessmen. But we were still struggling to advance while our opponents crisscrossed the board. Just two months outside of the May 4 election date, the core of our campaign was a paltry seven souls, and that included Ron. By that time, it was also clear to me that virtually no one could be trusted. Even bystanders like Mary-Jane might be working an angle.

From day one of the campaign, we knew that winning would require us to leverage the smarts of a few people into a massive grassroots movement. By any objective measure, we'd already pulled off some pretty ridiculous feats: endorsements from the colorful and electorally comfortable congressman from North Carolina's First Congressional District, the mayor of Durham, and twenty-five other mayors of small and midsized cities. We also had enough money in the bank to hire a campaign manager, open a legitimate campaign office in downtown Durham, and keep the lights on. But while this was impressive for a candidate with no experience, we knew it wasn't nearly enough. And we were running out of time. We'd drawn about as much as we could from our admittedly significant store of ingenuity.

I didn't have time to lick my wounds. Whether I liked it or not, this was the hand we were dealt, and I still intended to find a way to win, if not for the causes we'd been fighting for, then to wipe that perpetual smirk off Branford Darling's face. But I wanted to do it the right way. Not by embarrassing him with a public airing of his dirty laundry but by shredding his giant ego in a manner befitting a gentleman: beating him at his own game, fair and square. There was, however, one major problem: he was an NBA All-Star, and I was a benchwarmer in the D-League.

I wasn't sure how to kick our campaign into a higher gear. So far, we'd determined that our initial strategy of winning—obtaining a supermajority of the black vote—could only be achieved by the painstaking task of piecing together a statewide organization based on relationships with black political influencers in each county. But these folks were proving more slippery than we'd anticipated, and the taxes they'd been assessing were making their services prohibitively expensive.

"You ever heard of the black-on-black tax, Roger?" I said.

"Never heard it put quite that way before, but I think I get you," Roger said. "Blacks charging their own more than they charge others."

"Why are you folks so mean to one another?" Carmichael said. "We white folks are tired of being blamed for your problems."

Roger smiled. "You're lucky I like you, Mr. Carmichael," Roger said. "I'm gonna let that one slip since you've gotta drive over four hundred miles tomorrow."

"You're a real bleeding heart, Roger," Carmichael said.

I snickered and winked at Roger. "Roger, a bleeding heart? You've got the wrong one, Carmichael."

As I dozed off, I thought of a nine-year-old boy who answered my knocks when I was canvassing in Wilson County a few Sundays back.

"Is your mom or dad home?" I asked. *He looks a lot like I did at that age.*

"No. She's at work and—" He tucked his chin into his chest. "My dad doesn't live here."

I handed him a piece of campaign literature. "Can you please give this to your mom when she gets home?"

"Okay," he said, still looking at the ground. I smiled and shook his tiny, limp hand before walking off. After the door slammed shut, I turned back and saw a crumpled handbill resting on the patchy lawn, several feet from the doorway.

CHAPTER FOURTEEN

"ALRIGHT," Ron said as Carmichael dropped us off at Bertie's, a popular downtown Raleigh lunch destination. Inside, I immediately spotted Roger waving us over. My frenemy Keri Jameson and her WC-CSP associate Raymond Brown were sitting with him at a round table situated in a dark corner in the rear of the restaurant.

"Mr. Carpenter," Roger said, meeting my outstretched hand. Over his crisply pressed white shirt he wore a Carolina blue linen suit, a Wolfpack red pocket square, and a Duke blue-and-white polka-dotted bow tie.

I turned to Roger. "Duke already won the ACC Tournament this year and is about to win another national title. At some point, you have to pick sides."

Keri rose from her chair, glided around the semicircle separating us, and embraced me for a few beats too long. "That's exactly what I told him when he walked in here," she said.

Ron laughed heartily. "I told him when he started with us that I understand and respect his allegiance to the Tar Heels, but check it at the door."

"And how's that been going?" Keri said.

"Looking at his suit today, I'd say we're making very, very slow progress," Ron replied.

"It's so good to see you, Al," Keri said. "Haven't seen you since . . . wow, I can't even remember."

"The Chamber Club."

Her eyes widened. "Are you sure?"

"Quite," I said through gritted teeth.

"When was that? February? Too long ago, anyway! When Roger and I were setting this meeting up last week, I told him to make sure he brought my good friend Al Carpenter along." She threw an extravagant wink at Roger. "Told him I needed you around in case he and Ron got rough with me."

Raymond Brown, Keri's primary minion on the WC-CSP's endorsement committee, barely raised an eyebrow throughout these introductory proceedings. He'd once been a charismatic NBA-bound basketball star at State, but his dreams were dashed on graduation eve after a bad Achilles tear during an impromptu pickup game. From his refusal to recognize us, Ron and I could safely draw two conclusions: first, he didn't really want to be there, and second, if he had to be present, he'd prefer we weren't.

"Raymond, good to see you," Ron said, reaching to shake his hand.

Raymond struggled to his feet. "Ron," he grumbled. He gripped Ron's hand for a second before falling back in his chair. The rest of us took our seats.

"It's warming up a little earlier than normal this year, isn't it?" Keri observed. "Probably gonna be an unbearably hot summer."

"I tell ya what," Ron said. "When I walked out the house this morning at ten, it must've been eighty degrees already."

"And it's only March!" Roger said. "Ain't that somethin'?"

"How nice to be leaving home at ten o'clock," Keri sneered. "I was in the office before nine."

"Me too," I said. "I guess we can't all be running for the Senate."

Keri allowed a quick, dry giggle to slip out. "Too true."

"Yeah, the good life," Roger said. "Spend all day on the phone begging friends and strangers for money, then night after night traveling the state giving the same speech. Then, if you're lucky, you get to bed before two."

"It's amazing more people don't sign up to do it," I said.

A pause of about five seconds followed, just enough to make things awkward again. Finally, Keri said, "How are Casey and the kids?"

"Doing really well," Ron said. "She's a terrific asset to the team."

"Maybe she oughtta run instead of you," Raymond said under his breath, his eyes fixed on his phone.

"And, ah, the kids have been great," Ron continued. "They've been getting over to the office to help out a few times a week."

"This process can be pretty hard on the family," Keri said.

"There's good days and bad days," Ron said. "But the fact that the whole family is dedicated to the cause has made all the difference."

Keri smiled heartily. "Well, that's great to hear."

After taking our orders, the waitress quickly returned with a round of sweet teas, biscuits, and Bertie's famous homemade sweet butter spread. Raymond devoured most of the biscuits before the waitress brought our entrees.

"So Ron," Keri continued between bites, "how's everything on the campaign trail?"

"Great. We're making real progress out there. I think our message is starting to resonate." Ron shifted a bit in his seat and forced a smile. "We have an exciting and rare opportunity to do something important. In this election, we can take the political process by the reins and ensure that going forward, things are done differently here in Raleigh and up in Washington." As Ron sat up a little straighter, I noticed Raymond gently grasping the right side of his sunglasses, pulling the frames ever so slightly down the bridge of his nose.

"This election isn't about me, and this isn't something I'm doing for personal gain," Ron continued. "A few weeks ago, we were over in Pasquotank County at an alumni event at Elizabeth City. Someone asked, 'Why would you give up a perfectly good life to get tangled up in politics?' I actually get some version of that question quite a bit. I told him, just like I tell everyone else, that I got in this race because I saw an opportunity, in the wake of what we accomplished in 2008, to do my part in making sure we continue to move the ball forward on the issues that matter to folks out here, folks who are working hard to give their children opportunities they didn't have. I want to help them realize the power they have to take decisive action, in this moment, to make a difference for our children and for all those people out here hurting—people who want to work but can't find a job. We've only got a brief window, so we've got to put a stake in the ground for change right now."

Keri didn't waste a moment waiting to speak. "Well," she said, shifting in her seat, "You know I'm with you one hundred percent. I worked hard for you during the endorsement committee sessions."

I glanced stealthily at Roger and Ron, hoping in vain to catch their eyes. This was the moment we'd been waiting for.

"Yeah, so I'm not completely sure how that process works," Ron said, feigning confusion. "Does the endorsement committee preselect a candidate and then submit its recommendation to the general body? Is that what happened?"

Keri looked at Ron with new interest. Here was her chance to show off. "That's basically correct," she said. "The committee is composed of six members, and as you know, I'm on that committee.

The proceedings of that committee—all discussions, vote tallies, even the identity of its chairperson—are secret. According to our bylaws, the only information that can come out of the committee is its recommendation. But . . ." She leaned forward and lowered her voice. "To show how much I'm in your corner, I'm gonna tell you what happened. It took twelve ballots. Each of the first eleven ballots came back in a tie between you and Jane. Before each vote, I argued in your favor. I pointed out the importance of choosing the most progressive candidate, how our membership would benefit from having an African-American senator representing their interests in Washington. But before the twelfth and final vote, one of Jane's supporters stood up and urged the committee not to vote for you, because without support from Preston, the party, and the DSCC, you'll have no chance of winning the primary. He said the WC-CSP risked losing its credibility if it endorsed a losing candidate." She sat back, shaking her head. "I'll tell ya, Ron, it made me sick to hear a thing like that, and I let him know!"

I could tell Ron was struggling to school his face. After a long moment he said, "Your loyalty is greatly appreciated, Keri."

"The next vote came out for Jane," Keri continued. "As you know, on Monday, the general body will vote to uphold or overturn the committee's recommendation."

I caught Roger's eye. His jaw twitched, but he gave no other acknowledgment of what we both already knew from another committee member: According to the same bylaws Keri mentioned, the endorsement committee chair could, at his or her discretion, break a tie if one persisted for three consecutive ballots. Second, the chair did indeed break the deadlock, after the fifth ballot. And third, Keri was the chairwoman of the committee.

"So the final vote came out four for Jane and two for Ron?" I asked, scratching an imaginary itch on the back of my neck.

"That's right," she said, tightening her lips. "Jane is well known and liked around here. She's got a strong following."

"Well, it goes without saying, but we really want and need WC-CSP's endorsement," Roger said. "What do we need to do over the next week to secure it?"

Raymond slowly removed his sunglasses, folded them, and placed them on the table. He leaned over, his cupped hands supporting his vast chin. "Tell me why I should support you," he said, his voice thick and slow. "You know, you young black politicians are always coming to me asking for my support. And I've supported lots of you people." He spotted our waitress and shouted, "How about more biscuits?"

before turning back to Ron. "But you boys don't get it," he continued. "When I do go to the trouble of getting you people in, I can't count on you for a damned thing. I ask for your help drumming up a measly thousand or ten thousand for one of my many charitable causes, and you boys develop acute amnesia. It's like you've been hit with one of those neutralizers, or neuralizers, whatever the hell those things are from that movie about men in black suits. Why should I trust *you* to do anything different?" He returned his shades to his face, securing them in place with a quick punch to the bridge with his right forefinger.

Ron's face was equal parts shock and confusion. "Well, Raymond," he stammered. "I can tell you I'm running to speak for the people, to be their advocate in Washington. I'll be a voice for progress, greater access to quality education and affordable housing, and for increasing the number of available living-wage jobs out here."

Raymond cocked his head sideways and gave Ron a withering look. He was now sure he could safely put Ron in the "Won't Play Ball" column of his mental ledger.

"We need this endorsement," I broke in. "We need it because the WC-CSP's endorsement matters. It sends an important message to voters throughout the state, and not just the black ones. It's a message that speaks not only to the quality of the candidate you select but also to that candidate's viability."

"Well," Keri said around a mouthful of collard greens, "I've been working hard to turn the tide in Ron's favor, and I'll keep on working the rest of this week. All we need to do is make sure a majority of the members don't vote to uphold. If they reject the committee's recommendation, it goes to an immediate vote of the general body. I've never seen that happen, but maybe we can pull it off this time." She looked down nervously at her watch. "Well, we working folks have gotta head back," she said. "Then after work, it's off to the gym. I'm trying to get the body to match this Halle haircut." She winked awkwardly in my direction.

"Understood, Ms. Jameson," Roger said. "Just one more thing: What would you say is the current breakdown in terms of the total membership's support for the candidates?"

Keri sighed impatiently. "This is only a guess," she said, "but I'd say forty percent for Jane, forty for Ron, eighteen for Bill, and two percent undecided.

"Two percent undecided," Roger said. "So roughly three people."

"Give or take," she said.

"Well, let's get to work on those three," Ron said. Just then, the waitress returned with the bill and, to Raymond's visible disappointment, no biscuits.

"I've got this," Keri said, reaching for the printout. "Can't let my favorite candidate waste money on lunches."

"Thank you both for taking time from your busy schedules to get together, and thanks for taking care of lunch," Roger said, rising to his feet.

"Yes, thanks so much," Ron added. He stood and shook Raymond's hand, his mouth stretched in a smile that was dangerously close to a grimace. Raymond gave Ron a sharp nod, then walked off with shocking speed toward the front door, ignoring Roger and me.

"So nice to see you again, Keri, and thanks so much for lunch," I said. After giving her a hug and quick kiss on the cheek, I watched intently as she walked ahead of us to join Raymond. When the restaurant door closed behind them, I said, "Well that was—"

"Let's wait," Roger said. "We can download later by phone. I've got to run to another appointment."

"Good deal," Ron said. "Thanks for setting that up. Confirming where she stands was important."

"I don't think *she* knows where she stands," Roger said.

"Precisely my point," Ron said. "She's going to hedge until the last possible moment. That means that not everything she says will be untrue. There's value there. In a few hours, call her and do what you have to do to get the names of the three remaining undecideds. Crosscheck those names with our mole on the endorsement committee. Then go get 'em."

"You got it," Roger replied.

Outside, on the other side of the street, a Ray-Banned Carmichael leaned comfortably against our Mystery Machine.

"Later, Rog," I said as the sun burned the back of my neck. Ron and I climbed into the car, which, thanks be to God, was as cool as the other side of the pillow. I looked at Ron and said, "Well, if you live long enough, I guess you get to see everything."

"I told you—chess, not checkers," he said, slowly leaning back in his seat. As he ran his hands over his scalp, I suddenly noticed he'd grayed significantly since the night of the Inauguration ball when he first asked me to join his campaign. "You're getting one hell of an education down here. They don't teach this at Harvard and Yale."

"True, true," I said. I chuckled to myself. "Quite a character, that Raymond Brown. He really showed his cards. He just earned a permanent invite to poker nights at my place."

Ron began laughing hysterically.

"What happened?" Carmichael said.

"I wish you could've seen it," I said. "Jesus Christ."

"Jesus made an appearance, did he?"

"Depends on who you ask," I said. "Raymond Brown . . . the guy basically said, 'Here you come with this progress and opportunity foolishness, trying to upset the natural order of things. Why in hell should I screw myself by supporting you? Are you gonna do my bidding if you're elected, because these other young black politicians sure haven't.'"

Ron shook his head, still laughing. "Most of what happens in politics is driven by money," he said. "The folks Raymond has in his pocket take care of him, and Raymond gets out the vote when they're up for reelection. Our candidacy threatens his influence and his finances—and he's not alone."

"So how do we convince people like him that it's in their long-term best interests to change things?" I asked.

"The answer is simple, though getting there isn't," Ron began. "You have to go directly to the people. That's what Barack did in the South Carolina primary. Hillary had all the bagmen and grass tops in her pocket. After all, she'd been building relationships since Bill ran in '92. Plouffe and Obama knew they couldn't win the game that way, so they went directly to the people. That's how we get around the Raymond Browns of the world. Once you get the people on board, the game changes. Then all the grass tops, the ministers, and the bagmen are forced to change teams or risk losing their influence. Their power is based on picking winners and keeping the people on their side. They can't afford to side against the people, even if they think the people have chosen the wrong candidate. If they don't get on board with the people's choice, they're finished."

"Makes sense," I said.

"The hard part," Ron continued, "is getting the kind of money necessary to maneuver around the grass tops and speak directly to the people. Obama was able to leverage a fresh message into dollars. It was a great story and a historic opportunity, and people wanted to be a part of it."

I sighed. "So somehow, within the next few weeks, we've got to reactivate the Obama Coalition without Obama," I said, rubbing the ache in my neck. "Frankly, I'm not sold on the idea that Obama could do that himself right now. A lot of people in the black community are upset with him for calling Billingsworth after the DSCC backed him."

"I don't disagree," Ron said.

"I could see if he took a hands-off approach to our race," I continued. "You know, then he could say, 'At least I didn't do anything to hurt the guy.'"

"But let's consider this from the White House's perspective," Carmichael said. "If we're honest about things, it's pretty clear that Ron's a potential problem. You've never held elected office, so they don't really have a sense for what you'd do when you got to the Senate. But they can be pretty sure that you'd be left of where Obama would want you to be now that he's in the business of consensus building."

"That's a great point," Ron said.

"And more than a year after North Carolina went blue," I said, "it's clear that 2008 did not signal a major political shift in North Carolina. It's back to business as usual here. Party power brokers in DC know it's still a pretty conservative state, and that's why the DSCC went after Bill. Victory for you this cycle, and for other progressives across the country, could lead to a backlash in 2012 that could put North Carolina and other swing states back into the red, and send the Obamas back to Chicago."

"Right, right, right," Ron said. "And the White House may just see me as some black guy on an ego trip looking to leverage the Obama brand for my own gain. They don't want anyone whose motives they don't know and whose actions they can't control going anywhere near that brand. I get it. I don't care, but I get it."

"They've got lots of moving pieces to manage," Carmichael said.

"Well, that's Barack's problem," Ron said. "We've got a few of our own down here. So let's get back to it."

"Back to the office?" Carmichael said.

"Yeah, let's get back to Durham," I said.

"By the way," Carmichael said, easing the car into traffic, "why didn't you guys bring me any biscuits? You said you'd save me a few, remember?"

"Sorry, brotha," I said over Ron's renewed laughter. "Ray Ray cleaned 'em out."

CHAPTER FIFTEEN

As USUAL, I got to work on time that morning. While navigating into the tightest parking space ever negotiated by man or woman, I received a group text from Roger saying he'd be a little late for our morning meeting. For only the second time I could remember during the campaign, I arrived at precisely the same time as Ron and Carmichael. Upon entry we were welcomed by the familiar noise of Shane rustling back in his office. Unlike the stout oak walls in our former headquarters, the walls in our newer downtown Durham offices were paper thin.

Within seconds Shane entered the common area to take attendance. "Good," he said. He was even more disheveled on that particular morning than usual. To be blunt, he looked as though he'd been rolling around in somebody's patchily turfed backyard. As he moved closer toward us, I began to suspect that he hadn't shaved or bathed during the preceding twenty-four hours.

"Do you know what today is?" Shane continued. "Seeing as how I have exactly zero seconds to waste waiting for an answer, I'll tell you. It's Tuesday, April the twenty-friggin'-seventh! Exactly one week before the election. And you're all late. Ron, I need you on the phones an hour ago making us some friggin' money!"

On that day, as had been the case for the last two weeks, the common area overflowed with volunteers who were busy cold-calling voters in our key counties. At first, Shane's not-so-periodic outbursts (usually directed at Carmichael) had a rather off-putting effect on most of our volunteers. But by that Tuesday morning, they were old hands. I don't think a single one of them flinched at this, Shane's most recent spasm.

"Well, I think we've had enough fun for one day," I said. "Ron, you should get on the phones. You *do* want to get an ad or two on television, don't you? We need at least another eighty thousand to make that happen."

"Spending eight hours a day begging for money is killing my spirit," Ron murmured. "I need to be on the trail meeting voters!"

"That's the problem!" Shane shouted. Realizing he was yelling at the candidate in the presence of the same candidate's volunteers, he lowered his voice to a whisper. "You should be spending at least ten." He turned and walked purposefully back to his office to answer his ringing cell phone.

Once Shane was out of earshot, Ron said, "There's got to be an easier way. You guys are smarter than this. Why don't you put your heads together and come up with something? It's just not gonna happen this way." This was the first time in my eight months with Ron that I'd heard him express even an inkling of doubt about winning.

"I'll think of something," I said.

Unstirred by Shane's most recent haranguing and determined to talk to anyone other than the folks on his call list, Ron stopped to chat with a few volunteers. In seconds Shane reemerged into the long hallway connecting our offices to the common area. He approached us with his hands on his head.

"Please," he said, pulling Ron away from an elderly female volunteer, "get upstairs and on the phone. I'm beggin' you, brother."

"Okay, okay," Ron said, holding his hands up. "I'm going."

"Great. Al, Carmichael, to my office, please. And where's Roger?" At that exact moment Roger slid through the front door, high-fiving a few volunteers as he moved to join us. "Perfect timing," Shane said. "You're just in time for the bad news."

The four of us walked to Shane's office single file, like second graders being herded from one room to the next. Shane was last to enter. He slammed the door behind him, walked to his desk, and picked up a single sheet of paper from his otherwise empty desktop. Bristol was hunched on the couch in the corner, poring over a ream of paper. I removed my suit jacket, hung it from the hook on the reverse side of the office door, and fell onto the couch in the opposite corner. Carmichael stood erect in a third corner with his arms crossed tightly over his chest while Roger leaned casually in the fourth corner, his hands tucked deep into his pants pockets.

Shane plopped in the black ergonomic chair he'd bought with his own cash, propped his feet up on the desk, and pulled his reading glasses from his shirt pocket. He studied the sheet of paper for a few seconds before tilting his head forward slightly. "The latest poll numbers are in, Roger," he said. "We're down two points from last month. For those of you who haven't been paying attention, that's five points we've lost over the last two months. We're at seventeen percent, Bill's at twenty-six, and Jane's at thirty-one."

"Bill's up one since the last poll, and Jane's just down slightly from where she was in January," Bristol said without looking up.

"Wait, that's only seventy-four percent," Carmichael said. "Are twenty-six percent undecided?"

"Give or take," Bristol said.

"Election's in seven days, boys and girls," Shane said, removing his glasses.

"How are we doing in the Af-Am community?" I asked.

"We're at thirty, Bill's at twenty-one, and Jane's got forty," Bristol said.

"Those numbers are bull," Carmichael said. "There's no way we're only at thirty. Where are they polling, Anson County?"

"Maybe those numbers are a little off, but so what?" Shane said. "By now we should be well ahead of Bill and Jane with blacks."

"Since I started in August, we've done everything but throw the kitchen sink at blacks in this state," I said. "They just aren't paying attention this cycle."

"That's not a valid response!" Shane snapped. "Our entire strategy is based on having their attention. Without it, we lose. It's why we're losing now."

"Are you suggesting it's my fault?"

Shane threw up his hands. "Jesus, Carpenter, could you be more self-absorbed?"

"We're doing better with progressives—over the last month, anyway," Roger said. "And some folks in the business community are finally starting to take note, but that's not gonna get it done."

"And even though Darling totally screwed us," I said, "from what I've heard, his buddy Jim Randolph has actually been doing a pretty good job of getting people in the progressive and business communities engaged on our behalf."

Shane rubbed his clenched eyes. "I think our strategy is sound," he said. "We're just not executing."

"To hell with the strategy!" I said. "If we don't get eighty-five to ninety percent of the black community excited about this campaign in the next six days, we're all going on an early summer vacation.

Somebody pull up Orbitz. Shit!"

"Spoke with Chris Knight at the *News & Observer* today," Bristol said. "He says this race is still boring him to tears—him and the five other people in this state who are actually paying attention."

"He's bored," Shane said, laughing. "That's rich. He's bored, but he doesn't cover anything we do."

"We've got a money problem," Roger said, "and it's stifling our ability to make inroads politically. People aren't taking us seriously because we don't have any money."

"And we don't have any money," I added, "because the people sitting back saying we aren't a serious campaign aren't giving us the money we need to get serious."

Shane looked at the ceiling as if scanning it for answers. "If we don't figure out a way to raise some serious cash, and right now, there's no way in hell we get on television. That's our only hope now. It's TV or bust for us."

"The election is next week," Carmichael said. "We can kiss television good-bye."

"Maybe not," I said. "We just need something big. Something that will grab headlines, drive fundraising, and get people in voting booths on May fourth."

Carmichael rolled his eyes. "Unless you've got a brother whose name is Aladdin, I don't see how we get access to a genie in the next few days. And what about early voting? That started more than ten days ago, so we're already seriously behind the eight ball."

"Turnout has been horrific so far," Bristol said. "We've got plenty of problems, but losing this election during the early voting period isn't one of them. If we do manage to come across a genie, there'd still be plenty of people left to convince."

"What we need is a gimmick," I said. "What drives people to give money and vote?"

"Extremes of emotion," Roger said.

"Right," I said. "Excitement and anger. We've got to find something that does one or the other, and then make sure it reaches lots of people."

Bristol shook her head. "Political stunts are dangerous. You can't always predict how they're gonna play out, or how the media will spin them. And you risk alienating one group while strengthening your support in another. Net-net, you gain nothing. It's a miracle we've been able to put together the coalition of blacks, business people, and progressives that we've got, small as it may be. We can't risk busting that up."

"Dammit, Bristol!" I startled her but didn't care. "We've been playing it safe since Shane walked in that door, and look where it's gotten us. Seven days until an almost certain defeat. I didn't come down here to lose. You guys want to win, don't you? Shane, do you want your winning streak to end next week?"

Shane looked down at his desk in silence.

"He's right," Roger said. "This thing is slipping out of reach. Safe mode will keep us safely in last place, and that's precisely what Jane is counting on."

"Maybe," Bristol said. "But if we bungle some harebrained rookie stunt, we'll take ourselves right out of this thing."

"And how, precisely, would that differ from where we are right now?" I said.

"Enough!" Shane shouted. He paused for a moment, as if reluctant to continue. At last he said, "I actually agree with Al on this one. We need something huge. But it has to be considered carefully and executed to friggin' perfection." He nodded in Bristol's direction. "And we've got to manage the risk too. Let's start brainstorming."

"Finally, we're getting somewhere," I said. I stood and began pacing. "Now, we know with absolute certainty we can't win without a supermajority of the black vote, right?"

"Nothing's more certain than that," Roger said.

"Blacks did their part in electing Obama, and now most of them are napping," I said. "While they nap, proponents of the status quo are working to recover what they lost in 2008, and they're playing for keeps this time. We've gotta wake these black folks up from this ridiculous dream of postracialism. We've gotta remind them that electing Obama was only the first step in transforming our politics, not the last. And when we do that—and I'm talking about the people in this room—we'll do it in a way that steers them right smack into Ron."

Shane began a slow, sardonic clap. "Beautiful, counselor. Tell me, what's your master plan to, as you put it, 'wake these black folks up'? If it's good enough, I'm prepared to hand the reins back to you. That's what you've wanted since the day I started, right?"

Ignoring him, I said, "What's the quickest way to rouse someone who's been sleeping?"

"A slap in the face always did it for me in the frat house," Carmichael said.

"That's right, and when you woke up, you were raving mad at the person who'd slapped you, not the other five idiot housemates who watched and laughed."

"What are you getting at, Carpenter?" Bristol asked.

"If we can't get blacks excited about Ron," I said, "we'll just have to get them angry about something else. And there's one surefire way I know to orchestrate a massive pissing-off of blacks, one that will not only make them angry with the hit man but also make them fall hopelessly in love with his victim."

"Well, counselor," Bristol said, "what is it?"

"We set up a fake e-mail account—a male with some obviously nonblack name—send some incendiary, racist e-mail to Ron, then have Ron bring it up at tonight's forum."

Shane's eyes widened. "Somebody call the nuthouse," he said. "Tell 'em we've got a live one here."

"Don't tell me you're seriously considering *that*," Roger said. "It's too dangerous. It could totally balloon out of control."

"Yeah, Carpenter, this is left field, even for you," Carmichael said.

"This is doable," I said.

"No friggin' way," Shane said. "No way. If it got traced back to us, we'd be done. None of us would ever find work again—ever."

Bristol was suddenly sitting erect and staring cross-eyed across the room. "It would trigger a beautiful storm of speculation."

"The press *would* have a field day with it," Roger said. "It's what they've been begging for—scandal, excitement. This could get picked up nationally."

"The AP would pick it up," Bristol said, now possessed. "Then it would hit the networks and cable news." A deep grin crept across her face.

"A national news story," Shane mused. "Money would come pouring in from all over the nation, maybe overnight. Sharpton, Jackson, Smiley, West . . . they'd all catch the first thing smokin' down here to Raleigh." For the first time in weeks, he smiled.

"And where they go, the cameras will follow," I added. "Bring on the liberal media establishment."

"And can you imagine preachers in the pulpit on Sunday morning?" Roger said.

"They wouldn't wait for Sunday," I said. "They'd call special services."

"And just like that, bada bing, bada boom—we're on TV by the weekend," Bristol said.

"That's a pretty quick turnaround for a commercial, isn't it?" Roger asked.

Bristol waved her hand dismissively. "If we have the money, it's totally doable."

"And at long last," Shane said, rubbing his hands together, "we finally reach the sleeping legions of blacks, business people, progressives, and college kids—and blast them with Ron's message."

I nodded. "That's how we win. That's how we get to forty percent."

Over in the corner, Carmichael looked queasy. "With all due respect, gentlemen and lady," he said, "and in the present moment, I use the words 'gentlemen,' 'lady,' and 'respect' in the loosest possible sense, I do believe you've lost your damned minds."

"No, I think for the first time in months we're actually using them productively and focusing on how we win with the cards we've been dealt," I said. "We've been so caught up in the day-to-day that we've lost sight of the reason we're all here: to get Ron elected."

"It matters how we get there," Carmichael said, clenching his fists.

"This is politics, not math class," I shot back. "You were a history major, Carmichael. You know as well as I do that no one remembers the losers, and frankly, people don't care if you get a little dirty on the way to the top. And why is that? Because it's the winners who write the history." I walked over to him and wrapped my arm around his shoulders. "Brett Carmichael, you know as well as I do that this is just a game. Nothing more, nothing less. If Ron wins, he gets the power— the power to make a real difference for people who desperately need him. He'll have the power to literally change lives. But you have to win the game first, and you do that by playing it better than your opponents. You didn't notice because you were too busy making those worthless minister cold calls yesterday, but Bill Billingsworth and Jack Monroe actually came down to the office and ate your lunch for you." I slapped his back before returning to my seat on the couch.

Carmichael heaved a deep sigh. "You guys do what you want," he said. "This is obviously above my pay grade. But I'm telling you, it's the wrong move. Every day we're out there on the trail telling folks that Ron's candidacy is about moving past race and doing away with all the slicing and dicing we do to one another based on our differences. You do this and you'll undermine everything we've said out there, everything we've worked so hard to accomplish, and that's the reality. This may be a game, but it's just one game within a larger, more important thing called life, and you'll have to live with it for the rest of yours if you do this."

I leaned forward and locked eyes with Carmichael. "I'm here because I believe Ron can move this state forward. He's a perfect example of the fruits that wider access to opportunity can bear. But if he doesn't win, this state will go right back to the same tired good ol' boy politics that lives on the kind of race-based slicing and dicing you want to end. That's why we're all here, right? Don't you want to help put an end to all that? Wouldn't you like to be the guy who knocks down the next domino in a line that will ultimately destroy the system that keeps the poor, minorities, gays, and women on the margins?"

"But—"

"Here's the reality, Carmichael," I said, interrupting him. "We've got a great message, great ideas, and an even greater candidate, but we're dead last in the polls. We've got seven days—six, really—to turn this campaign around, get on television, and wake people the hell up. Jane's got commercials running as we speak. Bill too. If we don't get on TV, Ron's message and our vision for progress don't exist. Period."

"He's right," Bristol said. "No TV in North Carolina, and you're out. It confers legitimacy no matter how illegitimate a candidate may be. I can't tell you how many times in the last week I've been asked, 'When is Ron going on television?' Lots of folks won't vote for him *because* they haven't seen him on television."

"They're right, Carmichael," Shane said. "If you're not on television, you don't exist."

"I'm not debating the television point," Carmichael said. "I get it, but we can't do it like this."

"It's friggin' risky," Shane said, running his hands over his head. "But I don't know that we have a choice." He turned to Carmichael. "Run upstairs to the war room and make sure Ron's on the phone, would you? And close the door behind you, please."

Carmichael cast a broiling stare at each of us before whirling around and throwing the door open. He did, despite this, close it gently. After he'd left, Shane, Roger, and I sat in silence while Bristol paced along the same route I'd taken a few minutes before. I knew Carmichael was right; in a perfect world we wouldn't need to resort to this sort of thing.

"It's risky," Bristol said, breaking the silence. "Now that I think about it, I'm more than a little concerned about how Chris Knight and the other more conservative reporters might frame something like this. And the black community's reaction might trigger a backlash among our white supporters, maybe even progressives. We can't afford to lose them."

"But we need a supermajority of blacks to be with us," I said. "This would get us there."

"How in hell would *we* respond?" Shane said. "I can't even begin to imagine how we'd have Ron address it onstage and in interviews afterward. Not to mention the possibility—no, strong likelihood—that a handful of black folks will go off the deep end with their response to something like this."

Bristol sighed. "He's right," she said. "How would we address those who go rogue without alienating a critical mass of blacks? And how would Ron address it without running the risk of offending too many white folks?"

I slumped back onto the couch. "These are problems I . . . obviously hadn't considered," I admitted.

We were interrupted by a knock at the door. Without waiting for a reply, Carmichael poked his head in. "So have you guys come to your senses?" he said.

"Sadly," Bristol said. "Too many unknowns. And too many hands potentially trying to ice the cake."

Shane let out a deep breath as he rose to his feet. "Back to work, people. Let's keep our volunteers fired up out there. In the meantime, keep looking for Aladdin. And one more thing." He gave each one of us a long look. "This conversation doesn't leave this room. Got that?"

We all nodded in assent before filing out of his office. As we walked down the stretch of hallway separating my office from Shane's, Carmichael said, "Lay off the sauce a few days. You almost set dynamite to this campaign."

"We've got six days, Carmichael," I said. "And I intend to win this thing at any cost."

When we reached my office door, I placed my hand on his shoulder, and looked him in the eyes. "You a God-fearing man, Carmichael?"

"I used to go to church pretty regularly before joining this campaign," he said. "I used to do a lot of things pretty regularly."

"That's not what I asked you," I said sharply. "I said, do you fear God?"

"Of course."

"And why do you fear God, Carmichael?"

"Why are we wasting time talking about—"

"Why, Carmichael, do you fear God?"

"I—I don't know," he said exasperatedly.

"Do you fear Him because of what you've seen Him do?" I asked.

"No."

"Do you fear Him because of what you think He might do?"

"No."

"That's right," I said. "I'll tell you why you fear God: it's because that's what you were taught."

"What's your point?" he asked curtly.

"We have to teach the liberals in this state why they ought to be afraid of the status quo."

"And how do you propose to do that?"

"I don't know exactly," I said. "What I do know is that we miscalculated this race. We thought we could win with a slightly modified version of the 2008 playbook, by stirring the emotion of excitement. We were wrong. People got that out of their systems in 2008. They got excited—blacks, whites, you name it—about an opportunity to show each other just how committed they were to the idea of change. But what's clear now is that they weren't really committed to doing anything differently. Anyone can commit to commit. But getting up every day and doing what it takes to change minds, hearts, and laws—that takes hard work, and it's the only way to move the needle. The establishment wins most of the time because so-called progressives don't really want to fight; all they want to do is talk about how hard they're fighting. Well, the time for speechmaking is over. The forces of the status quo are ready for battle. They've seen enough of what hope can accomplish, and they're poised to take back every inch of the ground we've won. How many battles in history do you reckon were won by the side who, after winning the first half and with the enemy still looking on, decides they've done enough, takes a seat, and grabs a little shut-eye? It's madness what Democrats are doing right now. Instead of slamming the door behind us and throwing away the key, we've left it right under the mat. An ape could find it."

Carmichael exhaled heavily. "Like I said, lay off the sauce. Go make some phone calls or something. You've gone postal."

"Carmichael, you've forgotten why we're here. Here's some advice for you: Spend some time thinking about how we can get Democrats raving mad about the status quo. And while you're at it, do the same for yourself. It's the fourth quarter now."

Carmichael gave me a mocking salute before continuing down the hall. "Sure thing, coach."

I stepped into my office, closed the door behind me, and approached the window. The sky was a shade of blue I'd never seen. The clouds that obscured the sunlight during the drive into work had vanished, and I gazed deeply into that vast new blue with renewed excitement.

I didn't much feel like calling anyone on my worthless call list, so I called Jim Randolph instead. This was my forty-first time calling Jim since Darling and I cut our Nashville deal. I kept track of—and took detailed notes during—each of those calls.

"Al, I've been trying to get a hold of Branford for weeks, but—"

"I don't wanna hear any more excuses, Jim," I said. "I'm done playing games with you people."

"I got him earlier this morning, Al. I finally reached him."

"Jim, I swear, if this isn't good news, I swear I'll—"

"I asked him about the status of the endorsement announcement."

"And?"

"And . . . he insisted that he had to drop off for an important meeting."

"Now Jim, you listen here, dammit. If he doesn't publicly announce this endorsement within the next twenty-four hours, I will personally see to the end of Darling's congressional career within the next forty-eight. Dammit, Jim, I mean it. I'm tired of his bullshit."

Jim sighed. "Understood, Al. I'll try to relay the message."

"See, that's the problem. Stop trying . . . just get it done, by God!" I hung up before he could respond.

*****

I SPENT THE REST of the morning and afternoon calling leaders at the various black PACs and encouraging their respective organizations to endorse Ron immediately. I also asked each of them why they'd broken with their long custom of endorsing a candidate for US Senate no later than the end of the first full week of April. I received some variation of the same response from each: "It's complicated."

Since our March 30 lunch meeting at Bertie's, Keri and our mole on the WC-CSP's endorsement committee had been as successful in eluding Roger and me as the Road Runner in discombobulating Wile E. Coyote. When I finally got a hold of Keri that day, she informed me that the WC-CSP general body meeting that was originally scheduled to meet during the first week of April to consider the endorsement committee's selection had been postponed—for the third time now— for "administrative reasons" beyond her control. Exhausted from the flurry of phone calls and months of unfulfilled promises and unrequited favors, I stepped outside my office for a change of scenery and, hopefully, the midafternoon coffee run I often made with Carmichael to Beyú Caffé on days we weren't both traveling.

My entry into the hallway coincided with Ron and Casey's descent from the war room. Since the three of us hadn't huddled up in a while, I suggested we steal a few moments in my office to catch up. We weren't there fifteen seconds before Shane reemerged from his own yelling, "Ron!"

I instinctively looked at my wristwatch. "Dammit," I said, looking at Ron. "It's six thirty. I thought it was three thirty." Then Shane knocked on my door. "Come in!" I said.

Shane stepped inside. On seeing the three of us smiling, his shoulders slumped. "Why do I always feel like the bad guy?" he said, unable to hold back a smile.

"Because that's what we pay you to do," Casey said.

"Alright, wheels up in five minutes," Shane said.

I closed my computer and threw on my blazer. "Let's go," I said. "The traffic on I-40 headed to Raleigh is gonna be ridiculous."

"Where's my tie?" Ron asked, looking around my office even though he'd come in tieless.

"Carmichael!" I screamed. A few seconds later, Carmichael strode into my office dangling a Carolina blue necktie.

Ron snorted. "I can't wear that."

"We'll just have to call a moratorium on the Duke-UNC rivalry today," I said.

"Alright, people," Shane said. "Get outta here." Shane, Carmichael, Ron, and I left Casey in my office. We wove through the volunteers and out into the early evening heat while quizzing Ron on policy questions he was likely to get at that evening's forum. He answered them quickly and crisply while struggling to execute a decent knot.

"Raise any money?" I asked.

Ron snickered. "Come up with a plan to get me a million?"

"Almost," I replied. "But it was riddled with too many question marks."

"Yeah, and would've ruined our careers," Carmichael said.

"I'll catch up with you guys on tonight's conference call," Shane said as we came to the car. "Knock 'em dead."

"Isn't Bristol coming?" I said.

"No way," Shane said. "I need her here. We're gonna need to prepare a press release on the forum as soon as it's over."

Above us, thick cumulous clouds racing eastwardly across the dingy gray sky portended a downpour. I felt the first few drops on the back of my neck as I opened the front passenger door.

"What should I say in my opening statement?" Ron asked.

"Give them the usual spiel," I said. "But slow it down a bit, and make it forceful. This is the last debate."

"Who's sponsoring this one?" he asked, still fiddling with his tie.

"The North Carolina Association of Teachers," I said. "You'll each have two minutes of intro, followed by forty-five minutes of Q&A with the moderator and another two minutes each for final statements."

Ron snorted. "Are we actually going to debate this time, or are we still not allowed to address the other candidates?"

"We got explicit instructions that candidates are not to pose questions or otherwise speak directly to one another," Carmichael said from the driver's seat. "Can't have you fracturing the party by highlighting the candidates' differences."

"Preston and his minions have almost reached their goal," I said. "They aren't about to start taking chances this late in the game."

The typically snarled early evening traffic on I-40 was worsened by the heavy rain shower we'd brought from Durham. We made a left turn onto a construction-riddled Hillsborough Street at seven thirty, twenty minutes behind schedule. As we pulled up to the main entrance five minutes later, I was shocked to find a throng of Ron Johnson supporters lining both sides of the walkway leading to the building's double doors.

"What the hell is this?" I said, squinting at the cheering crowd. "And when did we get T-shirts?"

"Last week," Carmichael said. "And this minor spectacle was orchestrated by our Wake County field director."

"Not bad," Ron said. "Do we have a camera?"

"We've got three volunteers taking pictures," Carmichael said.

"Beautiful, beautiful, beautiful," Ron said. "Alright, let's go."

"Wait!" I said. Bill Billingsworth, mobbed by twenty or more supporters, had just turned the corner and was advancing toward the same walkway. About fifty feet behind Bill and company, on the other end of the parking lot, there were news trucks from all the major local stations.

"Looks like the press finally got the memo that there's an election next week," Ron said.

"Let's wait until Bill's in before we get out," I said. Exhilarating chants of "Let's go, Ron! Let's go, Ron!" were audible from inside the car.

Ron laughed. "At least they know my name," he said. "I wonder if Jane's already inside."

"Yes," Carmichael said. "According to one of our volunteers, she's been inside for fifteen minutes. She and Bill wanted to clear the stage for you."

"Okay, Bill's in," I said. "Let's go."

Carmichael got out and walked around to open the back door. "What do you have planned for tonight?" Ron asked.

I shrugged. "Probably just a quiet evening with Bristol. Dinner, movie maybe."

"Getting a little restless, aren't you?" Ron said.

"How do you—I mean, I guess you're—"

He snickered. "Let me tell you something. I know it may be hard to see it now, but the fun you think you're missing out on sitting at home with Bristol . . . it's an illusion. I don't want you to do anything you're gonna regret."

I chuckled. "You've been talking to my grandfather, haven't you?"

He grabbed my arm tightly. "Just remember this: Life comes at you fast, and there's no rewind button. Old fools were once young fools. Trust me."

I smiled. "I think I understand, Ron."

When Carmichael opened the door, the chants for Ron grew louder. "Plans tonight, Carmichael?" Ron asked while stepping out of the car.

"Nope," he replied. "Just driving you home, then myself."

"Well, make some," Ron said. "Casey can take me home. Find something fun to do."

Carmichael turned to me with raised eyebrows. "Okay, Ron. I'm gonna park the car. See you guys inside."

The scene was frenetic. Since our arrival, another thirty or so T-shirted Johnson supporters had joined those already assembled and were screaming at the top of their lungs. Cameramen from Channels 4, 5, and 7 each captured Ron's slow ascent up the walkway and four stairs immediately fronting the doors. He took time to shake hands and wave. He even found a baby to kiss. In this heretofore sleepy US Senate primary race, this was by far the biggest crowd we'd seen outside an event. While struggling to keep Ron within reaching distance, I spotted Chris Knight in the crowd, scribbling notes on his iconic yellow notepad. I nodded in his direction, and he winked in acknowledgment.

Inside we were immediately greeted by Florence Gardner, the longtime president of the North Carolina Association of Teachers. Though we'd funneled most of the campaign's communications with NCAT through Casey and Bristol, I'd shared several phone conversations with Florence since January and engaged her in person at two prior Wake County events.

"It's so nice to see you again, Flo," I said. "Where do you want him?"

She cocked her head to the side and smiled. "Good to see you again too, Al, Ron," she said. "Follow me." She led us into the amphitheater complex on the other side of the hallway. With difficulty, we weaved through the voters crowding the aisle leading to the stage. Above the amphitheater doors was a sign that read "150 Maximum Occupancy." There must have been upwards of three hundred people packed into that modestly sized room.

"Looks like somebody got the word out that there's a US Senate race going on," I said to Florence over the din of buzzing voices.

"We've spent the last month pubbing this event hard," she said.

"What's your secret?" I said.

"Not a large endowment, I'll tell you that much!" At that, Florence broke into hearty laughter while Ron and I shared a couple of nervous chuckles.

As we neared the front of the room, I spotted Jack Monroe standing and chatting with Jessica Parker in the second row. It had been over a month since I'd seen her. She'd texted a few times for drinks, but I'd replied with a plausible excuse on both occasions. She shot me a quick, salty glance before turning back to Jack. I hadn't seen him since our coffee date in Winston-Salem back in February. Looking just as fatigued as he had then, Jack corralled what little energy he had to nod in my direction. His March 1 lunch with Bristol hadn't panned out the way he'd envisioned. Bristol had shared the story later that evening over dinner.

As they pulled up to our offices after lunch, Jack asked her, "Why did you accept my invitation?"

Bristol opened the passenger door and said, "I thought you might have some information that could help Ron's campaign."

"But I'm working for Bill."

"And? Come on, Jack, you're smarter than that. Who you're working for and what information you're willing to share are two different questions."

"I see," Jack said. "So I guess I'd be wasting my time asking you out again?"

"Unless you plan on developing a severe case of diarrhea of the mouth. This wasn't a date, Jack. It was lunch. Thanks for getting the bill."

Meanwhile, Bill Billingsworth stood at the foot of the stage reading from a solid white sheet of 8½ by 11. Up until a few short months ago, he'd made a production of shaking my hand and speaking every time we met. Since running into him at the Chamber Club just before he announced his candidacy, he'd adopted a firm policy of avoiding all eye contact. Bill gave me and Ron his back as we approached and timed his turn to ensure we knew we were the cause.

Once Ron was seated on stage, I descended the stairs and nearly tripped over a cord. It belonged to a camera held by a man in all black who was standing beside the foot of the stage. Next to him was a five-foot-seven, stocky, dark brown–hued man holding a Channel 7 News microphone and wearing a jacket and tie. He appeared to be about twenty-eight years of age. He looked vaguely familiar, but I couldn't pin down if I'd met him. All the other cameras and reporters were camped out in the rear of the room.

After gathering myself from my near tumble, I walked back toward the amphitheater doors and stepped into the hallway. I immediately spotted Carmichael chatting with Jack just a few feet away.

"So who do ya like in this race, Jack?" I asked as I approached them. "My money's on Bill." Looking at Jack, it struck me that I'd rarely seen his hands outside of his pockets—when he needed his right to shake a hand or his left to write, but that was about it.

"I don't know, Al," Jack said. "I like sleepers. I think Ron's got it in the bag—it's just that no one knows it yet."

"You guys are both way off," Carmichael said. "I've got this thing all locked up."

"So," I said, turning to Jack, "what's the latest over at Billingsworth central in Guilford County? I hear your people are backing off that DSCC, handpicked angle like you stole something. That whole thing didn't backfire, did it?"

"I don't know about all that," Jack replied. "But we've been keeping pretty busy ducking all the mud you guys are slinging our way. Never thought you guys would go negative. You must be getting pretty desperate."

"Carmichael, was Jack this much of a complainer on the basketball court back in the day?"

"No one called more phantom fouls than this guy," Carmichael responded.

"Jack, you took the words right out of my mouth," I said. "I never thought *you guys* would go negative. That's what candidates in last place do."

"Well, you certainly are in last place," Jack said. "I see you haven't totally lost touch with reality. I guess your delusions kinda go in and out, huh?"

"Good one," I said.

"Hotter than hell in there, isn't it?" Jack said, tugging at his collar.

"You think I came out here just to shoot the breeze with you, Jack?" I said. "It's a sauna in there."

"Last forum before the election," Carmichael said.

Jack snickered. "Right . . . I'm really gonna miss these things."

"Seriously," I said. "These things are worthless. Who the hell wants to see these guys answer the same stupid questions over and over? People wanna see them debate each other, take the gloves off."

"That's not what Jane's camp wants, or the party," Carmichael said. "They've stuck pretty well to their strategy, haven't they?"

"Yeah . . . run out the clock," Jack said.

"Well, enough fun for one night," I said. "It's naptime. Shall we?"

"Yeah," Jack said. "Let's get back in there."

I reached my arm out to stop his progress. "If I don't see you again before Tuesday, best of luck, Jack," I said, extending my hand.

"Same to you," Jack said. "Al, Carmichael." He quickly shook our hands before disappearing behind the amphitheater doors.

Carmichael shook his head. "It's amazing," Carmichael said, "how you two idiots can shift from street brawl to bar-side commiseration in the space of a second."

"Misery loves company," I said.

Carmichael opened the door just as Ron was finishing the first sentence of his opening statement. From the ease of his cadence and the broad smile plastered across his face, I knew he was finally starting to enjoy these things. I shot Carmichael a grin. As Ron neared the end of his opening, I left Carmichael and walked toward the stage.

I looked on from the foot of the stairs next to the stage, beside the reporter I'd seen earlier when I almost tripped. "This race isn't about me, or any other candidate here tonight," Ron said. "It's about whether we're willing to move boldly forward together, and make the tough decisions that for too long now have been kicked down the road for others to deal with. I'm asking for your vote, and I'm asking you to stand with me in this election. Let's put a stake in the ground for the expansion of opportunity to every citizen in every corner of our great state. Thank you."

A roar burst from the crowd. Within seconds, supporters across the room began chanting "Get Ron in! Get Ron in!" It was by far the greatest ovation Ron had seen during the campaign. Just as the grand ovation began its denouement, I heard four words that would change the course of the campaign. They came from an elderly black man sitting in the second row, two seats in from the aisle where I stood.

"A nigger can't win."

I instinctively scanned the faces of the folks around him to determine who had heard and seen him. The seats on either side of him were empty. The woman sitting directly in front of him turned and put her hand to her mouth, but I could tell by the confusion in her eyes she hadn't identified the culprit. In no time, the uproarious applause gave way to an almost equivalent volume of mumbles and whispers. Here and there, people pointed in the general vicinity of the second-row bigot. Word spread like waves in a pool in the wake of a cannonball. Though it seemed like an eternity, within thirty seconds, I received a text from Carmichael: *Did someone down there say the N-word?*

I kept a straight face and stood perfectly still, trying not to draw any attention to the location from which the Molotov cocktail was thrown. Oblivious to the uproar he'd caused, the elderly man read that morning's *News & Observer* like he was sitting at home, alone in his favorite chair. Onstage, Jane commenced her opening statement, unaware of what was happening in the audience.

Suddenly I remembered the Channel 7 reporter I'd seen earlier. He was right where I'd left him, standing a few feet behind me and inspecting the side of the camera perched atop a tripod.

"What happened to your cameraman?" I said.

The reporter turned around. "Nature called, but the show must go on," he replied.

"So, did you get that old guy on camera?"

A devilish grin came over his face. "I sure did."

The mumblings and whisperings of a few moments before were replaced with the collective hum of conversation. People in the crowd began moving feverishly up and down the aisles, streaming in and out of the amphitheater doors. By then the three candidates and the moderator knew something was amiss. Having lost the crowd, Jane returned to her chair. Ron looked at me and mouthed, *What's going on?* I shrugged and turned back to the reporter.

"What's your name?" I said.

"Rob Williams. So, you caught that little disturbance, huh?"

I cleared my throat. "I did."

At that, he craned to look over my shoulder. "Jesus Christ, he's gone!" he exclaimed. "I needed to interview that guy. Dammit!"

"That's a shame," I said. "Listen, were you able to get sound on that guy or just video?"

"Both," he said triumphantly.

I had to think quickly. I gathered myself before leaning over to speak directly into his ear. "My name's Al Carpenter. I'm one of Ron Johnson's top advisors."

"Ron Johnson," he said. "Doesn't Bristol Davis work on that campaign?"

"Yeah, why? You know her?"

His eyes misted over. "You could say that. We dated on and off . . . she was the one that got away, so to speak." He shook his head.

While Rob reminisced, I watched as the man of the hour slowly folded his *News & Observer*. Then, amid the cover provided by the increasing confusion in the audience, he carefully stepped between the narrow gap separating the two seats in front of him and made his way across the walkway fronting the stage and out the side door into the night.

"Anyway, what can I do for you?" Rob said.

"Rob, I'm sure you can appreciate how delicately a situation like this needs to be handled, with it being the South and all."

"Of course. And just a week outside of an election."

"Precisely," I said. "Then you can also appreciate how something like this might have an . . . ah . . . untimely and unfortunate impact on my guy's chances?"

"Absolutely."

"Great," I said. "So, what can we do here? The only thing I can think of is to hold off on the video. The audio we can live with, but—"

"I'm running this tonight," he interrupted. "Sweeps started today. Plus, there's an anchor spot at my station I'm gunning for."

"Rob, I don't think you fully understand the magnitude of this moment. You and I, we can change the course of Southern politics. I'm just asking you to hold off for one day."

He searched my eyes for a long moment. "Well . . . I suppose we can work something out," he said.

"Great," I said. "So, can I have your word that you won't run the video tonight?"

"Slow down, man. I've got bosses, demanding bosses, and a career to think of. I'm under major pressure to break the next big story. To hold something like this back is, ah . . . well, it's expensive."

I sighed. *Should've known it wouldn't be easy.* "How much?" I said.

"Oh, I don't know. I think fifteen large should cover it."

"Fifteen!" I exclaimed. "For one day? Look, I appreciate your situation, but—"

"Listen, Al, I'm itching to run this thing. Like you said, this is history we're talking here."

I looked at Ron. He was still sitting onstage, where they'd recommended the forum. "You won't tell anyone you have it?" I said. "I'm talking video and audio."

"You're the only one who knows."

"Okay, you've got a deal," I said.

"Great," he said. "I'll meet you tomorrow at that coffee shop on Fayetteville Street near the capitol."

"Sandra's?"

"Yeah. Sandra's at four thirty."

"No, sir. I want a day—the full day." I looked at my watch. "You're gonna give me until eight thirty tomorrow."

"That's too late," he said. "I've gotta get this thing on the six o'clock news."

"Fifteen for a day," I said. "Let's be reasonable here."

"You drive a hard bargain, Carpenter."

"Eight thirty, Sandra's?" I confirmed.

"In and out, Carpenter. I don't want any funny business. And cash."

"Of course," I said, offering my hand. Our business concluded for the time being, I walked up the aisle toward the rear of the amphitheater as the moderator posed a question to the three candidates: "As you all know, there's a great deal of discussion among conservatives and some Democrats in Washington about scaling back, or doing completely away with, the so-called 'carbon bill' signed into law by President Obama last summer. If the question comes before the US Senate during your tenure, would you vote to scale back or repeal the American Clean Energy and Environmental Protection Act of 2009, and if so, why?"

Carmichael stood frozen by the doors. Through the glass, I saw a sea of people milling about the hallway.

"How's it going out there?" I said.

"Everyone's talking about what happened."

"What are they saying?"

"Word is some guy said, and pardon me for saying it, 'A nigger can't win.'"

"Let's go," I said. "I need a ride to my place."

Carmichael raised his eyebrows and looked at me, wide-eyed. "What? But someone needs to stay here to see what happens!"

"This forum was worthless from the beginning," I said. "Quietly spread the word among our volunteers to keep their eyes peeled and text you if anything interesting happens. You're coming right back here after you drop me off."

"Okay, but—"

"And have one of them wait near the front where I was," I interrupted. "As soon as the forum is over, I want that person to quietly tell Ron not to answer any questions from the press. I don't care if they ask him if he knows his first name."

Carmichael scowled. "Anything else, *sir*?"

"Yeah—if *anyone* screws up, I'm going to beat you like you stole something."

Carmichael rolled his eyes, then walked briskly toward a college-aged female volunteer standing several feet away. He whispered into her ear, then returned. "You were down there," he said. "Who said it?"

"I'll tell you outside." We walked slowly through the hallway and out the front doors. As soon as they shut behind us, we began jogging toward the car.

"So? What happened?"

"A guy sitting in the second row no more than eight feet from where I was standing said—well, you know what he said—during the applause after Ron's opening. There was a reporter with a camera next to him."

"Did he—"

"Yes," I said. "He got the footage."

"Are you kidding?" he said. "This'll be all over the ten o'clock news!"

"Yeah, the fact that *someone* said it will be on the news, but not the footage. I cut a deal."

"What kind of deal?" Carmichael asked.

"He's gonna table it."

Carmichael's eyes widened. "And what does he get in return?"

"Nothing."

"What do you mean, *nothing*?"

"I mean nothing."

"Okaaaaay," Carmichael said as we climbed into the car. "What does he *think* he's getting?"

"You don't wanna know," I said, clenching my jaw. "Carmichael, come hell or high water, Ron Johnson is going to be the next senator from the state of North Carolina."

*****

My APARTMENT was just a short ten-minute drive away. "Alright," I said as we pulled up to my building. "Head back. Gather intelligence, don't provide any."

"And what are *you* going to do?" Carmichael asked.

"Get Ron on TV." I jumped from the passenger seat and slammed the door shut. As Carmichael turned the corner, I finally released the smile I'd been holding back. I called Shane as soon as I was inside my apartment. "Shane, you need to get over here, fast."

"Slow down. What's going on?"

"No time to explain. Just get over to my apartment." I left him listening to the dial tone. I grabbed a cigarette from Billy's pack and lit up. Then I called Bristol's cell. While waiting for her to answer, I jogged upstairs to the loft, stepped onto the balcony, and took in the downtown Raleigh skyline. The lights shined a little brighter than usual that night, and I felt a happy New Haven evening chill race through my body. All was eerily quiet below.

I was about to hang up when she came on the line. "Al, how'd the debate go?"

"It's complicated. Are you alone?"

"Yeah . . . Shane just ran out of the office, but he didn't tell me where he was going. I'm just catching up on e-mail. How are things there?"

"Well, we're a week outside of the election and two months outside of July Fourth. I don't know whether I should call *tonight's* fireworks late or early."

"What happened?"

"Why didn't you tell me your boy Rob is a TV reporter?"

"Rob who?"

"*Rob.* From high school *and* grad school. You know who I'm talking about."

She let out a long breath. "Oh, *that* Rob. I don't know. I guess I didn't want to dredge up bad memories. I haven't even seen him since that night in Boston. Anyway, what's Rob got to do with anything? Was he there tonight?"

"He was," I said. "He and I made quick friends."

"How so?"

"He has certain information, information that may well determine the outcome of this election."

"What are you talking about?"

"What I'm about to tell you is highly sensitive," I said. "Please don't take this request as an affront to our friendship, but I need your word that you won't repeat what I'm about to tell you."

"My *word*? Al, what the hell is going on?"

"I just left the forum. Some random—or maybe not so random—older man in the audience used the N-word, and Rob got it on tape. Based on where he was standing, I'm sure his was the only camera that could've gotten it."

"An exclusive, huh? What exactly did the guy say?"

"'A nigger can't win.'"

She gasped. "Stop it! You're *not* serious."

"Dead serious. Shane's headed to my apartment now to strategize our response. This is potentially a very good thing for us, but it has to be managed carefully."

She snorted. "What do I know? I'm just the press secretary."

"Don't worry, we'll keep you in the loop."

"Gee, thanks. Wait! Was it a white person?"

"No."

"Oh . . . my . . . God! How exactly did this happen?"

"Ron had just finished his opening statement. It happened just as the applause was starting to die down."

"So the audience heard it?"

"Yes," I said. "But I think the applause made it hard for people to tell *who* said it. Even the woman sitting in front of him wasn't sure. The story spread around the room pretty quickly, and of course reporters from every major local TV station and paper were there. It'll definitely lead the ten o'clock news tonight and hit the morning papers."

"So, Rob's gonna run the story tonight?"

"The story, yes," I said. "But not the footage. He's holding off for a day."

"Why? This is a huge op for him."

"So that he comes swooping in with an exclusive—the actual footage—while all the other stations speculate about whodunit. After tomorrow, Rob and his exclusive will be as big as the story itself."

"Crazy," she said. "Well, at least we have a day to figure out how to respond to that unfortunate visual once it's out there."

"I intend to keep that visual off the air entirely," I said. "And I'll be spending the next twenty-three hours figuring out how."

"I see. And just how do you plan to pull that off, counselor?"

"Rob and I came to . . . an agreement of sorts. But I need your help to make sure it sticks."

"An agreement? What kind of an—"

"I assure you, you don't want to know."

"But—"

"Bristol! Please . . . just take my word on this. But I need your help."

"Tell me what you need."

"I need some leverage over Rob." I paused. "I've got something in my back pocket, but I want more, for added insurance." I immediately regretted lying to her.

"Leverage?" She was silent for several moments. "Al, tell me the truth: Are you thinking of blackmailing him somehow?"

"Whooooooooa!" I said. "Now wait a minute. Blackmail? That's such an adult word."

"Well that's—"

"Here's how I see it," I interrupted. "If managed correctly, this little incident gets us a couple hundred thousand or more in online contributions over the next two days. If we push hard, we can produce content and get on TV and radio by Friday. Two hundred thousand bucks will cover radio and TV buys for the five days between Friday and Tuesday's election."

"Go on."

"If the video from Rob's footage makes it onto television, it's over. White folks will see it and say, 'Johnson doesn't even have the black community. He's got no chance.' And then there's the black response. Lots of them have already bought into the logic underlying what happened tonight. It's the same old two-step white politicians and their black henchmen have been using to strip us of electoral power for more than half a century. Step one: 'Lots of folks are still racist, and they just won't vote for a black guy.' Step two: 'A vote for a black candidate is therefore a wasted vote, so vote for my guy. He'll do for you what the black candidate would do if folks weren't still so racist.' If this video gets out, the public—the nation—will see a *black man* echoing that very message. I think you know what happens next."

"Game, set, and match, Jane Woodall," she said. "So, what can I do?"

"I need you to close the deal. Nothing illegal, just a little old-fashioned coaxing. He's clearly still carrying a torch for you. It shouldn't be hard to fan the flames."

Bristol released a long, anxious breath. "And what if I can't convince him?"

"You will."

"Alexander, I know you. You're impulsive, but not when it comes to business. You're not going to bet this election on the off chance that an old flame still has feelings for me—on something you can't control. If you've got something you know will make him bend, why not use it?"

"I hate to throw my trump card unless it's absolutely necessary. Plus, I may need him after the primary is over. The question is, will you?"

"I see," she whispered. In her voice was deep disappointment. It was the one emotion from Bristol I didn't know how to process.

"You know what the stakes are here as well as I do," I said. "We need Ron in office to—"

"Save it, Al! I'm not some coed you can dazzle with a few lines from a speech!" After another pause, she finally spoke again, more quietly now. "I'll take care of it first thing tomorrow. Maybe even tonight. What you're asking me to do . . . well, let's just say I won't be putting this on my résumé."

"Thank you, counselor. This means more to me than you know."

"You're welcome. But so *you* know, your account with the Bank of

Bristol is officially overdrawn."

I chuckled. "Noted. Good ni—"

"Hey, before you go," she interrupted. "Remember that advice Professor Jackson used to beat us over the head with for solving a seemingly insurmountable ethical dilemma?"

"Of course," I said. "You bring someone else into the soup with you and make your problem their problem too."

"Why do I feel like I'm swimming in a pool of your chicken noodle soup?"

"Good night, Bristol. Thanks again."

"Night. Talk to you in the morning."

I hung up and looked at the clock on the TV cable box: 9:30 p.m., a mere thirty minutes before that night's fireworks would reach into homes all over the state. Suddenly there was a knock at the door that made me jump from the couch. "Took you long enough," I said. It wasn't until I'd opened the door all the way that I realized it wasn't Shane, but Jack Monroe.

"Jack, what the hell are you doing here?"

He smiled nervously. "Well, I was driving up Glenwood on my way home from the forum and figured I'd stop by."

I stood in the doorway, hoping in vain that a lack of hospitality might hasten his departure. It goes without saying that Jack had never been to my apartment, but of course in this age of the interwebs, it's disgustingly easy to figure out where someone lays his or her head at night. "Did you want to come in or something?" I finally said.

"How big of you to ask." Jack slid past me and meandered over to the floor-to-ceiling living room windows. "Nice place, Carpenter. Great view of downtown."

"Well thank you, Jack," I replied as he looked around the room, nakedly appraising every detail. "Can I get you a drink? I've got scotch, vodka, cognac, gin. I'd have to check on this, but I think I've also got some cyanide."

He didn't flinch. "What kind of scotch, Carpenter?"

"A fifteen-year-old out of Islay."

"Not too shabby, Carpenter. Where'd you acquire such a refined pallet? Harvard? Yale?"

"Your mom's house, actually," I replied. "She has one hell of a taste for scotch." I reached into the deep recesses of my liquor cabinet (where I attempted to hide the good stuff from Billy), poured the drink, and walked it over to Jack, who was still admiring the view. While making the handoff, I heard a series of knocks.

Jack raised his eyebrows. "Lady friend?" he said.

Shane didn't wait for me to greet him before bursting in. "Okay, I—"

"Shane, you're a little early," I said loudly. "Poker doesn't start 'til ten thirty tonight." Shane responded to my incessant winking with a look one might give to an acquaintance who's just escaped the local sanitarium. Then I mouthed, *Jack Monroe is here.*

"Oh, damn," Shane said loudly. "I'm sorry, I must've mixed up the time."

"Shane Reese, is that you?" Jack said. I turned and found him still facing the skyline.

"Jack 'the Hack' Monroe," Shane said. "You're the last person I expected to see here tonight."

Jack slowly turned. "I would say 'likewise,' but we both know that's not the case." He took a few steps toward us, sipping his drink. "Well, it certainly has been a night of surprises, hasn't it, boys?"

"How do you mean?" Shane asked.

"Well, with what happened at the forum tonight."

"And here I was thinking you'd just stopped by to see an old friend," I said. "Drink, Shane?"

"I've always enjoyed mixing business with pleasure," Jack said. "After all, business is nothing more than the furtherance of personal ends by other means."

"A vodka soda would be great."

While I prepared Shane's drink in the kitchen, I watched him take a seat as far away from Jack as possible on the opposite side of the living room.

"Let's get down to business, shall we?" Jack said.

"Yes, let's," I said from the kitchen.

"Gentlemen," he started, "what happened at the forum tonight was, well . . . unfortunate. But it happened, and now we all have to deal with it."

"Agreed," I said. With my back to the living room, I took out my phone and texted Shane: *Have u heard what happened at the forum? If not, leave and call Carmichael.*

"I think it's important we all unite on this matter," Jack continued, "and that all three campaigns speak with one voice. We should respond jointly."

"Is that a fact?" I said, handing Shane his cocktail.

Shane's phone vibrated when the text came through. He looked down, his eyes widening as he read it. "Sorry, I have to make a call. Be right back." He rose from the couch and went into my bedroom, shutting the door behind him.

I turned to Jack. "Have you talked to Jane's people?" I asked.

"Not yet. We wanted to get your commitment first."

"And you figured we'd just jump at the chance to do a joint response," I said.

"It would be good for the party. God knows this primary has split us up."

"Let's wait for Shane to come back before we get too deep into this," I said. "He is, after all, the manager." I glanced at the cable box again: 9:45 p.m. I had to get him out of there before ten. I had no interest in watching the news with Jack in the room.

"All done," Shane said, emerging from the bedroom.

"Welcome back," I said. "Jack was just saying he hadn't spoken to Jane's people yet about doing a joint response."

"There's also another option," Jack said, gazing deeply into his scotch. "If you saw some value in it, our two campaigns could band together on this and leave Jane out of it."

"Jack," Shane said, "I appreciate you coming to us. But I'm sure you can appreciate our hesitation to rush to a decision. Frankly, I think it would be in each camp's best interests to wait a few hours and see how this unfolds. After all, it may not end up being a huge deal."

Jack's eyes said it all. He knew he'd fumbled the ball miserably. "Well, I . . . I just wanted to run it past you," he stammered. "I think voters would appreciate us putting politics aside on this one." He stood and slumped toward the front door. "I should be going," he said. "I'll call you tomorrow, once you've had time to think it over. Thanks for the scotch, Carpenter."

"Anytime, Jack," I said. I shook his hand and closed the door behind him. "Damn," I said. "He's something, isn't he?"

Shane narrowed his eyes. "Why didn't you tell me what happened when you asked me to come over?"

I joined him on the couch, facing the skyline. "I was in a hurry. As soon as I hung up with you, I was back on the horn making moves."

"Oh yeah?" he said. "And what has my deputy campaign manager come up with?"

"Wait, have you heard from Ron?" I asked.

"Carmichael's got him. They're headed back to Chapel Hill."

"How much did Carmichael tell you?"

"He told me some idiot said—"

"That's good enough," I said, raising my hand. "Well, a Channel 7 reporter got that idiot on tape. Our idiot is black."

"Got it on video?"

"Yes."

"Dammit!" he shouted. "Did any other cameras get it?"

"Not a chance. And luckily I was right there when it happened. I spoke to the reporter and got his agreement to table it for twenty-four hours."

"How the hell'd you do that?"

"Don't worry about it."

Shane furrowed his brow. "Whatever you promised him, it's not in the budget. You know that, right?"

"Have I asked you for money?"

"No," he conceded. He sat back heavily and gazed out the window. "So, what's your plan? What're we gonna do when the twenty-four hours is up?"

"I happen to be very close with one of this reporter's good friends."

"So?"

"So . . . let's just say I'm confident we'll be able to get what we want."

"That footage would kill us."

"The video would but not the audio," I said. "I heard the guy. He doesn't sound black."

"Doesn't *sound* black?" Shane exclaimed. "Are you serious? What does *black* sound like?"

"What are you, fresh off the boat from Antarctica?"

Shane cast me a suspicious glance, rose from the couch, and walked to the bar, where he poured himself a scotch. "If I didn't know any better," he said, "I'd swear you set the whole thing up."

"But you *do* know better," I said. "If I'd set this up, would I have chosen somebody who looks like my grandfather?"

"No, I suppose not. When will you know what we can expect this guy to air, and when he'll air it?"

"First thing tomorrow morning," I said.

Shane sat back down and faced me. A euphoric smile slowly spread across his face, then he extended his right hand toward me. "Well, assuming you've got the juice you seem to think you've got— and that's a huge assumption—it looks like we're back in business."

"We're definitely in the mix," I said, gripping his hand. "The news'll be on in a minute."

"You think Jack bought the poker bit?" he said.

"Doubtful," I said. "There's not a soul in this state who'd believe you and I would spend our personal time together, even for a second." I rose to pour myself a scotch. "He's got some nerve coming here with that joint response foolishness," I said. "We gain nothing from working with Bill or Jane at this point."

"He was never going to bring that plan to Jane," Shane said. "That was just a ploy. He wants to use this incident to give Bill a boost with black voters, and for that he needs us, not Jane." He leaned forward, his elbows on his knees. "This is a game changer for us. It's probably the only way we can come close to getting a black supermajority by Tuesday, and it may still be too late."

"Well, there's one bit of good news," I said. "Jack obviously thinks a white person said it. Let's hope the rest of the state thinks so too."

"Agreed." Shane looked at his watch. "It's almost ten, time to turn it on. I'll text Bristol and tell her not to respond to any inquiries until we've all had a chance to see what angle the press takes."

"Right," I said. I turned on the TV and flipped to Channel 7. The candidates' forum was the lead story.

"Good evening," a female anchor said. "Tonight the three major US Senate candidates vying for the Democratic Party's nomination met in Raleigh to talk jobs, education, and the environment. There have been few fireworks over the course of this humdrum primary season, but that all changed tonight. Channel 7's Robert Williams reports."

The screen cut to a panning shot of the forum audience. Then Rob's voice: "Things got off to a quiet start at tonight's forum, the final debate ahead of next Tuesday's election. However, just after upstart US Senate candidate Ron Johnson, seen here, concluded his opening statement, a man sitting near the stage reportedly yelled a racist slur. Though the candidates continued with the forum, by all accounts the crowd became irretrievably distracted. I caught up with one audience member to get her impression." Rob appeared onscreen standing next to an elderly black woman. "Ma'am," he said, "you were inside the hall when the drama unfolded. Would you please tell our viewers what happened?"

"Yeah, I was sitting six or seven rows behind the fool who said it," she said. "I won't repeat exactly what he said, but it was something like 'A N-word can't win.' I liked to slap the stew out of him for sayin' something so ignorant. Some people say racism is dead now that we've got Obama, but clearly this kind of ignorant thinking is still alive and well."

"Ma'am, had you decided on a candidate before tonight, and if so, has your decision changed after tonight's events?"

"Before tonight, I was behind Jane," the woman said. "I didn't meet Ron Johnson until tonight. Honestly, I couldn't have picked him out of a lineup. But I was impressed by what I saw and heard. He spoke a lot about getting back to basics and spreading the wealth, which is exactly what people around here need."

"So you're supporting Johnson?" Rob asked.

"Yep, that's right."

"Did tonight's racially charged comment have anything to do with your decision?"

Her eyes widened. "Not at all!" she said. "It was getting to hear Mr. Johnson speak in person that changed my mind."

"I see. Just one more question, ma'am: Johnson's been a distant third in the polls for months now. With the election less than a week away, do you think he can turn it around and win on Tuesday?"

"Yes, he can! Folks haven't been paying much attention to this race. I know I haven't had time. But now that I know we've got a smart young man, an attorney that knows the laws running for the Senate, I'm gonna make sure everyone I know votes for him."

"Thank you, ma'am." He turned to face the camera. "Well, Marie, that's the latest from Raleigh. It would appear this once sleepy primary is finally up and kicking."

"Robert, have you spoken to many other voters tonight, and if so, were their perspectives consistent with this voter's?"

"I've spoken to about ten people, both black and white, since the forum ended, and every one expressed disappointment and anger about what was said. I'd say there's also a widespread sense that people haven't given Johnson a chance until tonight."

"Do we have any idea who made the controversial comment?"

"We don't know at this time," Rob said. "Given the commotion immediately following the comment, it's certainly possible no one was able to identify the man."

"Where you able to speak with any of the candidates after the forum?" Marie asked.

"Unfortunately not," Rob said. "All of them declined my request for an interview."

"Well thanks, Robert. I'm sure you'll have more for us as this story continues to develop."

"Thanks, Marie."

I turned down the volume and looked at Shane, who was shaking his head in disbelief. "This is unreal," he said.

"We've got to turn this into money while it's hot," I said. "Let's send out an e-mail tonight to drive online fundraising."

"Yeah, that and something bigger," he said.

My phone rang. It was Ron. "Senator Johnson," I said. "Did you catch the ten o'clock news?"

"I did."

"What do you think?"

Ron chuckled. "I think I like our chances," he said. "Have you spoken to Shane about our response?"

"He's at my apartment now. Would you believe Jack Monroe came by here suggesting we do a joint response with Bill?"

He chuckled again. "There's no value for us in that scenario. They must be scrambling."

"I know," I said. "We let him down easy."

"Al, this whole thing must be handled with an extraordinary degree of care."

"Of course, that goes without saying," I said.

"Good. I look forward to seeing what you guys come up with. I'll weigh in once I've seen your plan. What time will you be in the office tomorrow morning?"

"Eight o'clock."

"I like it. See you tomorrow. And don't you guys stay up all night. There won't be much time for sleep over the next week."

"Good night, Ron."

"Good night."

Shane and I stayed up half the night strategizing, periodically taking calls with Bristol. We also drew up a list of leaders, African-American and otherwise, to call in the morning to seek their advice, whether or not we actually needed it or intended to use it. Sometime around one thirty, we settled on holding a press conference in the afternoon. While we worked through the early morning hours drafting Ron's remarks, I worried about the news I'd get from Bristol.

Shane left around three thirty, but I couldn't sleep. I felt the weight of the entire campaign on my shoulders—it was simultaneously exhilarating and terrifying. It didn't help that my phone was still ringing off the hook at four—reporters, political operatives, friends, and family were all trying to find out more about what had happened. Simmons texted, *Saw the news from Raleigh. Blacks are pissed. Just gave $50 more online.* Other friends from across the racial spectrum sent similar messages, giving me hope that the story was picking up steam across the country.

But above my happiness hovered a cloud of regret. I was disappointed that we hadn't been able to excite voters on Ron's merits.

I was still tossing and turning as the birds began chirping outside. Sometime around quarter to six, I gave up the charade of sleep and walked to my bedroom window. Something about the pitch of the darkness outside reminded me of the night Ron and I rode back from a campaign stop in Charlotte in the fall. Just after we pulled out of the hotel parking lot, Ron asked if I knew North Carolina's state motto. I didn't, but I'll never forget it. He said, "'Esse quam videri,' which means, 'To be, rather than to seem.'" In a few short hours, Ron would deliver the most important speech of his life, and not long after, I'd participate in the most important meeting of mine.

CHAPTER SIXTEEN

I ROSE at 7:28 the next morning. I quickly showered, dressed, and drove to my neighborhood coffee shop to pick up my first cup of joe and scan the morning papers. The sun was already hot on the back of my neck as I stepped out of the car and slammed the driver's door shut. Inside, sitting in racks below the counter, I saw the glorious headlines atop the *New York Times*, the *Washington Post*, and the *News & Observer*: "Bigot May Propel Unknown N.C. Democrat Through U.S. Senate Primary Battle"; "In North Carolina U.S. Senate Primary, Unknown Democrat Ron Johnson Takes Center Stage"; "In Final U.S. Senate Primary Debate, Race Steals Show." The die was cast.

As the barista slid my large coffee across the counter, I received a call from Bristol.

"Good morning," I said.

"Morning. Did you get any sleep last night?"

"Not really," I said. "You?"

"A few hours. I just got off the phone with Rob."

I took a deep breath before continuing. "How'd it go?"

"Good news: He agreed to hold off on the video until after the primary. The audio will run tonight. Said he'd meet you at the planned time and location to discuss details."

"That's great news!" I said. "Look, I'm really sorry about this whole thing."

"It's fine," she said. "I think I might've been a little too hard on you last night. Chalk it up to campaign stress. Anyway, we're both here to do what it takes to help Ron win. I'm glad I could do my part in rewriting history."

"Ron and I owe you."

"I didn't do it for Ron," she said. "Until a few months ago, I didn't know him from Adam. I did it for you."

"Well, thank you."

"Get off this damn phone and go win this primary."

"See you in a bit, Bristol."

"Bye."

"Wait!" I said. "One more thing."

"What?"

"If you don't mind me asking, how'd you get him to agree to delay the video?"

"I'm a black woman and a lawyer, Al. I could sell water to a well."

I chuckled. "I'm pretty sure I've seen you do that already."

"See you soon."

"Bye."

*****

AT 8:15 A.M., I streaked past an unusually hefty complement of volunteers in the common area and into Shane's office. There I found Ron, Shane, Casey, and Carmichael poring over copies of the latest draft of Ron's statement. As Bristol stood in the corner shouting into the phone, we studiously avoided eye contact. "I need one hundred points a day in all three major markets, and I need the backwaters too," she said. "No excuses, just make it happen, Morrison!"

"Dammit, Carpenter," Shane said. "Where the hell have you been?"

"Playing hopscotch," I said. "You?"

"Funny," he said. "Look over the revised statement. The presser starts in less than two hours."

"You scheduled it for ten o'clock?" I said. "I thought we said afternoon?"

Shane shot me a withering glance. "And how many things have gone as planned during this campaign?"

"Point taken," I said. "Any other news this morning? What about the phone calls we discussed last night?"

"Knocked 'em out already," Shane said. Then to my surprise, he grinned. "Preston Roberts just called. He asked—no, *begged*—us not to talk about last night until the party issues its statement."

"Oh, I bet he'd love that," I said. "What did you say?"

"I thanked him for choosing this as the occasion for his first and only direct communication with our campaign and told him not to let the doorknob hit him where the good Lord split him."

"Are you hard of hearing, Morrison?" Bristol continued, waving her arm. "I said I need one hundred points a day through Tuesday! And call your national guy—I want the cable news channels too."

"Sounds like we made some money last night," I said.

Carmichael grinned. "Just a bit."

"You might want to sit down for this," Casey said without looking up from her copy of Ron's statement. "We've raised just over four hundred thousand dollars since midnight."

My knees did their best to give way. "What?" I shrieked. "From where?"

"All over the country," Ron said. "New York, Chicago, Los Angeles, Houston, DC, you name it."

"God, I love the Internet!" I said. "What about here in North Carolina?"

"About $115,000," Carmichael said.

"We're going to shoot, edit, and wrap a commercial today," Shane added.

"Bristol's the expert on this stuff," Ron said, "but I'm pretty sure the fastest any station will air a commercial is seventy-two hours, right?"

Bristol put a hand over the phone—"Forty-eight"—before returning to battle.

"So, we can be on TV by what, Saturday morning?" Ron said.

"Sounds like it," I said.

"Bristol's been reaching out to her media contacts to give them the heads up," Shane said.

"How do the avails look?" Bristol said to Morrison.

"What language is she speaking?" I said.

Carmichael snickered. "You're so far out of your league right now, Carpenter, it's embarrassing. Please leave the media stuff to the professionals in the room."

"Oh, Bristol and *you*?" I said.

"I took a mass media class at Carolina," he said. "An avail is an available time slot. TV commercial buys are priced on the basis of the number of points you purchase for a particular time of day."

"Forty-eight hours still seems quick," Ron said. "Don't the stations' lawyers have to sign off on the content?"

"Money talks, Ron," Shane said. "With the cash pouring in, and given how close we are to Election Day, we can speed the process up a lot."

"Al, let's chat in your office for a second," Casey said while nodding toward the door.

"But we need him in here reviewing these changes," Shane said.

"We'll just be a minute," she said, smiling generously while pushing me toward the door and into the hallway.

"What's up?" I asked as we stepped into my office. She shut the door as I unpacked my laptop and switched on the desk lamp. I removed my jacket and hung it on the hook behind the door. Casey settled into my chair and I took one of the seats on the other side of the desk.

"Who wrote this speech?" she asked, sliding the stapled sheets toward me.

"I haven't seen it for a couple of hours," I said, "but I assume it's still part me and part Shane." I scanned the speech. "It looks like a large chunk of this has been rewritten."

She leaned forward and laced her fingers together. "Al, this is subpar. What in hell is Shane doing writing a speech on race?"

"Shane's the manager. It's his ship."

"Al, what are you talking about? We've got one shot at this. We can't afford any mistakes now. *You* should've written this, or it should've been passed along to me."

"But Ron said—"

"Ron doesn't have time to make these decisions. He's gotta focus on executing, not strategizing. It's too late in the game to bother him with Xs and Os."

"This presser is less than an hour and a half away," I said.

"Then we'd better get going on the rewrite," she said. "This is going to be aired all over the country. This speech will define Ronny's candidacy. It has to be perfect. That's all there is to it."

"Let me read it first," I said.

"Quickly," she said.

Casey sat in silence for the five minutes it took me to read that latest draft. She was right—it was serviceable but uninspiring. When I was finished, I looked up. "Casey, we don't have time to start from scratch. This isn't all that bad."

"*Isn't all that bad*?" she said. "Dammit, Al, since when did *isn't all that bad* become good enough for you? I swear, sometimes I think we were better off back when you, me, Ronny, and Bristol ran the whole damn thing ourselves. This operation *looks* a lot more like a campaign than it used to, but we're too focused on process instead of substance. Shit! I'm gonna get Ronny." Within seconds, she returned with the candidate.

"Al, would you give us a second, please?" Ron said, utterly failing to conceal his exasperation with Casey. I watched Ron walk to my desk chair, plop down, and prop his legs up on my desktop. Casey took the seat I'd just vacated.

"Of course," I said before leaving. I shut the door behind me.

When I returned to Shane's office, Shane, Carmichael, Bristol, and now Roger, were all present. Each of them—except Bristol—wore the same shell-shocked expressions they had on the two prior occasions Casey Johnson temporarily hijacked the campaign.

"What the hell is going on?" Shane asked.

"Judging from your face," I said, "I imagine you already know what's going on."

"This isn't the time, Carpenter," Shane growled.

"Well, it's not totally clear," I said, "but it appears Casey has declared martial law. I wouldn't cross her or Ron for the next hour and fifteen minutes."

"But we need him in here to finish prep!" Shane said.

"Don't hold your breath," Roger said.

Shane fell back on his favorite couch and massaged his forehead with his fingertips. "At least they pay me," he said. "At least I'm being friggin' paid."

The landline on Shane's desk began squawking, and Bristol raced to pick it up. "Has that phone stopped ringing this morning?" I asked.

"Only when Bristol's on it," Carmichael said. He closed his right eye tightly and threw the paper airplane he'd been working on for the past minute toward me. "Should we even bother looking at this speech anymore?"

"No," Shane said. "It's clear Casey doesn't like it, and Ron doesn't have the time or energy to fight her right now."

I chuckled. "I'm not so sure he *should* be fighting her," I said, tossing the plane back to Carmichael. "I worry about a lot of things in this campaign—whether or not Casey knows what she's doing isn't one of them."

Shane scowled. "We're better off planning our media strategy."

I clapped once. "Then what are we waiting for?" I said. "Let's get to work."

While Bristol fielded incessant calls from the media, the rest of us spent the next hour and change developing ideas for TV and radio ads. At 9:15 a.m., forty-five minutes before showtime, Bristol left the room to greet the press. Fifteen minutes later, Shane turned to me. "You think we should check on Ron and Casey?"

"I wouldn't," I said. "Unless you have a death wish. If they know nothing else right now, they know what time it is."

Shane rose from the couch, threw on one of the several blazers straddling the back of his desk chair, and approached the door. He grabbed the doorknob and turned to face us. "Well? You guys coming or what?"

I smiled giddily. "Why?" I said. "Something special about to happen?"

"Yeah," Shane replied. "There's this black guy running for US Senate in North Carolina, and he's about to give the speech of his life. You're gonna want to see this."

"I'm told his wife wrote it," Roger said.

"She any good at speechwriting?" I said, slapping Roger on his back.

He winked. "As good as they come, bruh."

We found a crush of media waiting for Ron as we walked into the common area. The handful of volunteers present had pushed all the tables against the rear wall and arranged the chairs into six rows of ten. Lined up just in front of the tables were at least ten TV cameras, and milling between the rows of chairs were Chris Knight, other reporters from around the state, and several national news correspondents I never dreamed I'd see in Durham. The podium at the front of the room overflowed with microphones bearing the marks of local and national cable news channels, as well as those of a few cable outlets known more for their provision of entertainment than for news coverage.

Bristol stepped to the podium. "Ladies and gentlemen," she said, "I'd like to thank you again for adjusting to the last-minute schedule change. Mr. Johnson will be out shortly to deliver a brief statement."

At the conclusion of Bristol's announcement, I watched Shane emerge from the hallway and move toward the back of the room. Once there, he claimed a spot against the wall and crossed his arms, as was his penchant on the rare occasions he attended campaign events. Meanwhile, Bristol, Carmichael, Roger, and I worked the room. In addition to thirty or so reporters, I counted close to one hundred other citizens, two-thirds of whom I'd never seen, forming a rough semicircle around the rows of chairs and caucusing journalists. I spent a couple minutes with Chris Knight, as the rules required, a few more with a handful of voters, then three unforgettable minutes answering questions on camera with CNN's most prominent evening news anchor, a man who happened to share my initials.

I left the throng in the common room just before ten and went to my office. I knocked first before poking my head inside.

"Come on in, Al," Ron said. They'd switched seats since I exited the room, and I noticed that the fourth button from the top of Casey's blouse was unfastened.

"Lots of press out there waiting to hear from you," I said. "What did you two decide?"

"Casey and I have just been spending the last hour . . . ah . . . talking through the issues and . . . ah . . . trying to hammer down our message."

I lowered my head to hide the smile sneaking forth. "And what about the speech?"

"Sorry to blow up earlier," Casey said. "What you and Shane came up with isn't horrible. In fact, it's actually pretty good. But something about using prepared remarks for something like this just rubbed me the wrong way. Robert Frost could've written it, and my response would've been pretty much the same. This is the kind of thing you can't really prepare for in a few hours, so we decided that Ronny just needs to get up there and speak. He doesn't need a speech. He's been living this issue his entire life."

I stood frozen for several moments. When I found my voice, I said, "You ready to go?"

"Is our president black?" Ron replied.

"Having mixed feelings, huh?" I said, smiling broadly.

"Let's go get it in, Carp," Ron said with a smile just as big.

"I'd be remiss if I didn't tell you the whole country will see this," I said. "Welcome to the twenty-four-hour news cycle. You win this primary right now with this speech."

"I know," he said, rising from his chair. He scanned the room as if mentally bookmarking this space in time so he could retrieve the details at some later date.

"Casey, I was thinking you should wait until Ron reaches the podium before you come out and take a place in the crowd," I said. "We don't want to overdo this, or it might look like pandering."

"I agree completely," she said. "You walk with him."

"You sure?" I asked.

"Positively." Casey kissed Ron and wrapped him in a massive hug. They touched foreheads for several moments as Casey whispered. He smiled and tapped her on the small of her back three times. After she helped him slip into his suit jacket, Ron dropped his arms to his sides and jerked them slightly to ensure it sat properly on his shoulders. I leaned toward Casey and whispered, "Your button." After fixing her blouse, Casey walked quickly to the door and opened it for us. Ron and I stepped through and, side by side, started down the hallway and into the blinding lights. The large common room was soon inundated by a symphony of clicking camera shutters, the buzzing of spent flashes, and heavy applause.

Looking into the crowd as we walked toward the podium, Ron said, "Beats the hell out of practicing law, doesn't it?"

I nodded. "Not a bad way to spend a morning."

"Having fun yet?" he asked as we reached the podium.

"Bored to tears," I said with a wink. I took an empty seat on the first row. Just seconds later, I felt a tap on my shoulder.

"Imagine finding you here," a voice said.

I turned slightly to confirm my suspicion: it was Rob. "Yeah, imagine," I muttered.

"I'm planning a trip to Paris next month with the girlfriend," he said. "It'll be our six-month anniversary. With my newfound wealth, we can afford to travel first class."

I turned back toward Ron. "Is that right?" I said. "Did you win the lottery?"

"You could say that."

Ron placed his hands on the podium before gazing into the crowd. "Last summer, I got into this US Senate race because I wanted to make a difference. I saw an opportunity for all of us to move forward and forge the kind of progress and opportunity so many of us have worked so long and hard to bring to the often forgotten, hardworking citizens of this great state. As a child, my parents, both schoolteachers who lived through the torrents of the civil rights era, taught me the importance of standing up for what's right and working to bring people together, especially in the face of those who'd seek to drive a wedge between us. This is what I've tried to do my entire life: help bring folks together into partnerships that foster the forward movement and prosperity of entire communities of North Carolinians.

"There have always been, and unfortunately there will probably always be, those who try to divide us and promote confusion and hateful discord on the basis of class, gender, sexual orientation, religion, and yes, race. But our resolve to rise above this hate must not be weakened, and our determination to define each other on the basis of our substance and our contributions to our communities and to the world must not be compromised. Our enemies know as well as we do that strength is found in numbers. They know the power we can wield when we look beyond the few areas in which we differ and instead focus on the ties that bind us, and the reality that our success as a nation can only be measured by the success of the most unfortunate among us. That's why I'm in this race, to help keep the ball moving forward, to promote progress, to increase access to opportunity, and to build stronger communities.

"Bill Billingsworth, Jane Woodall, and I spend our days and nights fighting hard to win this race, but when it's over, we *will* come together to make sure our state moves forward, not backward. Much blood was spilled and many lives lost in the hope that you and I would be judged not on the basis of meaningless physical attributes, our religious beliefs, or our sexual preferences, but on the basis of the character informing our actions. Now is not the time to retreat from that hope. I will not retreat. We must push on, because if we retreat, we dishonor the legacy of all those folks—men and women, black and white, gay and straight—who fought for and dreamed of the opportunities embodied by this campaign and this moment in our nation's history. In my estimation, there's only one victory next Tuesday that matters: one that brings the people of this state together to build on that legacy.

"There are those out there who would probably have me indict the man who spoke those hateful words last night. I won't. I won't because such action does nothing to prevent it from happening again and again. Until we pull out from behind the shadows of the frustration, the hatred, and the pain that lies behind those words, we're doomed to repeat moments like these. Let this be the beginning of a real discourse about the lingering effects of racism in our country. Indictment isn't the answer. Instead, we must meet this anger with understanding and love, not ostracism and hate. Until we look past the words and focus on the anger underlying them, we will only relive in the future the mistakes of our past.

"So today I ask that you join me in the work of building each other up rather than tearing each other down. Stand with me. Let's show this nation what communities can achieve when they grow stronger in the face of those seeking to divide them. Let's show this nation that North Carolinians stand on the front lines of the battle to define the New South. God bless you all, and may God continue to bless the great state of North Carolina."

The crowd erupted into applause and shouted questions. Ron looked out solemnly into the audience for a few seconds before making his way off the dais. Per my texted instructions, Carmichael bolted from his second-row seat and led Ron out of the common room and into my office; I trailed closely behind. Meanwhile, Bristol returned to the podium, thanked the press for their attendance, and began fielding their questions.

Just a few seconds after I closed my office door, Shane entered. "That was perfect!" he said. "It had the polish of a rehearsed speech but didn't sound rehearsed."

"He's right," I said. "And guess what? I got a call from Keri Jameson during the speech."

"Voicemail?" Carmichael asked.

"Yup," I replied.

"I'll take a shot in the dark," Shane said. "The WC-CSP is endorsing us."

"Not only that," I said. "The WC-CSP and the other three major black PACs we've been stalking for the last nine months will endorse us later today at a joint press conference to be led by—"

"Olivia Creedmoor," Ron said.

"*Doctor* Olivia Creedmoor," I said.

"How'd you know?" Carmichael said.

Ron gave a wry smile. "A shot in the dark."

Shane sighed. "Less than a week before the election," he said. "Great."

"I know," I said. "These endorsements are basically worthless now."

"They know that," Ron said. "Let's just hope they've learned an important lesson. Shane, go ahead and call the PAC chairs and thank them for endorsing. All except Keri Jameson and Dr. Creedmoor."

"Will do," Shane said.

"Al, you should obviously call Keri back," Ron said. "I know these endorsements are of very limited value now, but it's the right thing to do. We're going to take the high road."

"And what about Creedmoor?" Carmichael asked.

"That call's got Ron Johnson written all over it," I said.

Ron nodded. "The other chairs won't like it, and that's precisely why I have to do it."

"She's gonna be your best friend in the world," I said. "For the next six days at least."

"Everyone's gotta pay their taxes," Ron said. "Even the great Olivia Creedmoor."

"Do you think there was any chance that WC-CSP would've endorsed us if yesterday hadn't happened?" Carmichael asked.

"Not based on that meeting we had with Keri and Raymond," I said.

"And on top of that we know Keri's working for Jane *and* Bill," Shane said.

"I think it's a little more complicated than that, boys," Ron began. "It's a black PAC. Notwithstanding our third-place status, they would've had a very difficult time explaining to black folks why they didn't endorse one of the first legitimate black candidates for statewide office probably since . . . probably—"

"Harvey Gantt," I said.

"There have been a few others," Ron said.

"So you think it was all a charade?" I said. "That whole song and dance at Bertie's about the endorsement committee picking Jane?"

"Maybe Keri figured we'd offer to pay her to deliver the final general body vote," Shane said.

"She never asked, but then again, why would she?" I said. "We made it pretty clear we weren't willing to play that game."

"In the end, they were all probably going to go for us," Ron said. "It was just a matter of when they'd endorse and how much money they'd spend to help us win the primary. My guess on the latter question is very little indeed."

"And given their timing, and the national attention we're getting, they can easily argue they don't really need to spend any money," Shane said.

"My God," I said. "That's exactly what they're gonna say."

"At the end of the day, they can still say they endorsed us, whether we win or lose," Carmichael added.

"And without spending any significant money to help us get there," I said.

Shane looked at his watch. "Oh shit, you're late! Carmichael, Ron's gotta be in Raleigh for a rally in less than an hour. Take him out the back."

"Are you kidding?" I said. "We've got news media from all over the country out front!"

"Looks like pandering," Shane said. "Ron just gave this magnanimous speech on race and when it was over, he refused to answer any questions—good job, by the way. How do you think it's gonna look if he's back in front of cameras a few minutes later?"

"It's going to look like another few minutes of free publicity," I said. "We've been dying for earned media. Now they're banging down our doors. I want everything Ron does to be on camera. I don't care what he's doing. If he's licking a stamp, I want that on camera too."

"He's right, Shane," Ron said. "Let's go."

Ron and Carmichael exited, leaving Shane and me standing face to face. He snorted, then sped out the door. "Get in your car and meet them in Raleigh," he said as he entered the hallway. "Can you manage that?"

I grabbed my jacket, walked past the crush of supporters, reporters, and cameras mobbing Ron and Carmichael, and hopped in my car. As I turned onto Highway 147 toward Raleigh, I allowed myself to briefly consider what a Ron Johnson victory would mean for North Carolina—and the South. Could his election, in tandem with Obama's 2008 win, do what so many assumed the latter would achieve all by itself? Would North Carolina's election of its first black senator—and the first in the South since Reconstruction—finally signal that America had at least crossed the threshold into a world where the accidents of one's race, gender, and sexuality are no longer granted untoward significance in the analysis of one's qualifications to serve? Or would the victory itself say far less about the state of affairs in the South than the explanation for how the victory was attained? Uncle Tom and his can of beer weighed heavily on my mind that day.

*****

WHEN I ARRIVED at Sandra's that night, I found Rob reading the *Wall Street Journal* at one of those tiny circular wooden tables you only find in coffee shops. He was the picture of comfort. I was halfway to his table when he noticed me.

"Carpenter," he said, rising to his feet like a defendant in a courtroom when the judge enters.

"Hope I didn't keep you waiting too long," I said.

"Let's make this quick," he said sharply. "I've got to get back to the studio ASAP."

"What's your rush?"

"Good one," he said. "By the way, Carpenter, I should probably thank you for having Bristol call me. If it weren't for you enlisting a woman to clean up your mess, I probably wouldn't have heard from her for the rest of my life. So—where's the cash?"

My heart raced, and my knees felt weak. "You may as well forget the footage, Rob, and that little trip you've got planned."

"I warned you, Carpenter," he said, his voice now bubbling with repressed rage. "No funny business. We had a deal."

"Gentlemen make deals," I said. "And we both know you're no gentleman."

"What the hell are you getting at?" he growled.

"May I sit?" I said. "You might want to take a seat too. You're gonna need it."

He stood pat, saying nothing.

"Suit yourself," I said. "I recorded our conversation last night at the forum."

Rob's skin color, generally in the ballpark of a Sean Combs, was in that moment more in the realm of a Terrence Howard.

"Look, I don't have anything against you personally, except for the fact that you tried to extort thousands of dollars from me. But I'm willing to look past that as a momentary lapse in judgment in an otherwise sterling journalistic career."

An expressionless, blank horror overcame his countenance, and his legs began shaking vigorously as he slowly lowered himself into the chair where just a few minutes before he'd been reading so peacefully.

"You backstabbing son of a—"

"Backstabbing?" I said. "Hardly. I don't even know you. So, you'll go ahead and run the audio tonight. Get rid of that video."

"You've got it all figured out, don't you?" His voice trembled ever so slightly. "What happened last night at that forum is finally gonna get your boy enough money to run commercials, probably by Saturday or Sunday. With just the audio, no one will know that guy was black."

"You make it sound so simple," I said. "Like I haven't had to do any legwork."

"I hope you rot in hell."

"If I so much as hear someone even suggest that you might've told them about the footage or our arrangement . . . well, I don't think I need to tell you what happens next."

"How do I know this is all I have to do to keep you from coming forward with this recording?"

"You have my word," I said. I rose from my chair, slid past Rob, and took in the view from the window behind him. "And when it comes down to it, a man's word is all he's got. For your sake, you better hope mine is worth a whole hell of a lot more than yours." I watched a black sports car peel off so quickly down Fayetteville Street that I couldn't make out its make, let alone its model. I turned around and stepped back to that minuscule table and its defeated occupant. I plucked a twenty-dollar bill from my money clip and placed it on the table so that it stood like a tiny camping tent. "For your gas," I said.

Rob didn't muster a response. His body was fixed in a disquieting state of motionlessness the likes of which I'd never seen from a human still possessed of life. Then he pulled his hands from his face and looked up at me. "No deal," he growled. "I'm running this footage. This is my career. I'll take my chances with you and whatever you've got on tape—assuming you've got anything at all." As he began scrolling through messages on his phone, a new horror spread across his face. After pounding the table with his fist, his eyes began overflowing with tears. "Get out," he whispered.

"What's . . . what's wrong?"

His eyes narrowed. "I can't . . . I'm not running any of the footage," he said, wiping his face. "Not the audio, not the video, none of it. Just get out of here."

"But—"

"Go!" he screamed. At that, I turned and began walking back toward the door.

It was 8:45 p.m. when I reentered the stickiness of that spring evening. I'd just stepped off the sidewalk when Jessica Parker texted, *I have to see you. Tonight. Meet me at Dominic's in half an hour.*

Without thinking, I hopped into my car and drove to the restaurant. When I walked in, she was already seated, a lipstick-stained, half-full glass of red wine in front of her. "I'm sorry," she said with a smile. "Did I pull you away from something important? I know you've got an election in a few days."

"It's just an election," I said. "You're far more important."

"Yeah, right."

"Didn't buy that one, huh?"

"Not for a second."

She was radiant. It was the first time I'd seen her completely decked out. Her makeup was applied tastefully, used to accentuate rather than conceal. She wore a simple, elegant black dress. After I'd settled into the booth, she abruptly excused herself to go powder her nose. She paraded across the room with the precision of a runway-seasoned model. She'd probably spent hours of her life perfecting that walk, likely on the advice of some trusted woman who'd turned her on to the powers of persuasion properly tutored women can exercise without uttering a single word.

A tornado of thoughts began swirling through my head. *Why did he suddenly decide not to run the footage? Even if I've gotten rid of him and that video for the time being, how can I be totally sure that the footage—or word of its existence—won't see the light of day? And what about the man in the footage? Who is he? And what if he comes forward?*

Suddenly, I allowed myself to entertain a thoroughly non–Al Carpenter thought: *So what?* In that moment, maybe for the first time in life, I fully resigned myself to whatever fate the universe had in store. Maybe my lucky streak was finally nearing its end, and if so, I reasoned, why spend another second of it doing anything but marveling at the utter ridiculousness of its length?

I turned toward the television mounted above the adjacent bar to find Bill Billingsworth doing his best Bill Clinton impression in an interview with Rich Gordon, Jessica and Rob's bearded colleague from Channel 7. I asked the bartender if he wouldn't mind raising the volume for a moment.

"It's a shame we're . . . still having these types of discussions about race in America," Bill said. "What happened at last night's forum was an . . . unfortunate distraction from the issues that matter to North Carolinians: jobs, education, progress, and . . . increased access to opportunity. We believe we're going to win this election because . . . we've got a message of unity that's . . . resonating with voters."

I was happy to know Ron's message was resonating so deeply with Bill and his handlers. If I didn't know any better, I might've concluded that Bill would soon endorse our campaign and cast his ballot for Ron on Tuesday. Then came Jane's latest commercial: "I've been an advocate all my life for promoting diversity and opportunity across the board," she said. "Just look at my office. I've got the most diverse office, top to bottom, in the whole Council of State when it comes to race and gender. It's too bad some people are still so caught up in our differences and not focusing on our similarities. We've got to move beyond that way of thinking, and I'm going to make that a priority when I get to Washington."

Jessica appeared on the screen several seconds later and noted that although no official polls had been conducted since the forum the prior evening, that Ron Johnson had benefited from last night's "now infamous racial outburst" was undeniable. She added that the Johnson campaign had received "hundreds of thousands" overnight and entered media buys for television and radio spots in every major media market.

"I hear she's good," Jessica said on returning to the table. "So tell me, anything interesting happening in a certain North Carolina US Senate primary?"

"Well, it seems all the momentum is with some unknown named Ron Johnson."

"Well, one thing's for sure: he's not unknown anymore," she said. "Overnight, he's become a household name. And all this because of some anonymous racist. You've gotta admit, the whole thing is pretty ridiculous." She took a sip of wine. "Let me ask you something, Carpenter, off the record of course: Do you think Ron will win?"

"If we had another two weeks, there'd be no question," I said. "But there's no substitute for time spent campaigning. I just don't know if three days of ads is gonna be enough to turn the tide. Jane's starting from a huge lead."

"Well, you've done your part," she said. "You've been working like a dog."

"I've never liked that saying, 'work like a dog,'" I said. "People use it like it's a compliment. Dogs don't work."

"Have you always analyzed the snot out of *everything*?"

"Probably," I replied. "Have you always given men such a hard time?"

"My father taught me that the only way to measure a man's interest is to test how hard he's willing to work to get you. Once a man has a woman—that is, once she's given herself to him—she completely loses hand in the relationship."

"He's right, though I feel like I'm somehow breaking guy code by admitting that."

"Your secret's safe with me."

I snickered. "Thanks. The question is, are you okay with losing hand in a relationship?"

"I pick and choose my battles. I've decided that's not one worth fighting."

"My, my," I said. "Now and again, you do show brilliant flashes of wisdom, Jessica Parker. Maybe you'll get that promotion after all."

The waitress had been hovering near our table for several seconds, waiting for an appropriate break in the conversation. "May I take your drink order, sir?" she said.

"Yes, please," I said. "We're celebrating. How about some champagne?"

"I've got a nice Perrier-Jouët," she said.

I winked at Jessica. "I suppose that'll have to do," I said.

"Wait a minute!" the waitress said, staring at Jessica. "I know who you are! You're that reporter on Channel 7. My roommate at UNC told me all about you. She's a media and journalism major."

"What are you studying?" I asked.

"Other than you?" Jessica mumbled.

"History," the waitress said energetically. "I'm a junior."

"That was my major," I said.

"How nice for you both," Jessica said.

The waitress, not picking up on Jessica's sarcasm, merely beamed. "I'll be right back with your champagne!"

"So, Carpenter," Jessica said, "what are your thoughts about that guy from the forum last night? Have you guys been able to ID him?"

"Isn't that your job?"

"No one in the media has been able to track him down. The guy pulled a Houdini."

"Well, I obviously don't know the guy, but I love him to death," I said. "If I ever meet him, the first ten rounds are on me."

"Maybe it's the conspiracy theorist in me," Jessica said, "but I can't help but think the whole thing worked out a little too well for you guys."

"You think we're behind this?" I said.

"I'm not saying you are, but I'm not convinced you aren't."

"Are you someone I need to convince?"

"No, but don't you think it stinks just a little? I mean, it's a story straight out of Tinseltown. And here you are right in the middle of it. Don't think for a second I don't see it in your eyes. You intend to ride this dog and pony show all the way to the White House."

I smirked. "Can we win the primary before you start talking Pennsylvania Avenue?"

The waitress returned with the iconic green bottle and a bucket of ice. After uncorking the bottle and pouring two glasses, she scurried off.

"What are we toasting?" Jessica asked, raising her glass.

"'May all your enemies' dreams fail miserably,'" I said.

"Cheers." Her eyes softened as we touched glasses. "Wow, that took me back."

"Long time ago, right? How about for one night, you pretend you're not a reporter and just have a drink with me?"

Jessica pulled an invisible hat from her head, took a long sip, and tendered a toothy smile. "You know, the hat would've come off on its own after I finished my first drink," she said.

"I know, but why wait?" I said. "Every passing second brings us closer to death, right?"

She arched her left eyebrow. "You mean every passing second welcomes another we get to live."

"Jessica Parker the optimist?" I said. "Who'd have thunk this transformation could be possible?"

Her eyes softened again as she grinned.

"Maybe being around me hasn't been a total waste," I said, raising my glass. "To every passing second."

"No," she said. "To passing these seconds with you."

I had the lobster, and she had the filet mignon cooked rare. The food was great, but the company was better. *I wonder what Bristol's up to?* I thought as I finished my second glass of bubbly. Then I turned toward the television above the bar. Channel 5 was reairing Ron's candidate profile from late February.

"You gonna take your Ron Johnson hat off or what?" Jessica asked.

"Check please," she said, raising her hand to get the waitress's attention. Jessica's complexion had turned plum red, a hue that reminded me of a program I'd watched years ago on National Geographic. The subject

WE HOLD THESE TRUTHS

matter was mating, and one particular segment surveyed how certain animals use bright colors to attract partners.

The waitress left the check in front of Jessica. Before I could grab it, she picked it up.

"It's on me," I said.

She laughed, waving her fork at me. "But I asked *you* to dinner. I've got to disabuse you of your preconceived notions about gender."

"Is that right? Well, I'm a willing student, but do you think picking up one check will do the trick?"

"Maybe not, but it'll make me feel better."

"Better about what?"

"Just better, that's all!"

"I insist on paying," I said. I snatched the portfolio from her hands before she could comprehend the theft.

She groaned. "You're impossible!"

"Yes, I am."

"Let's go," she said.

"Where to?" I said. "It's getting late."

"To your place."

I averted my eyes. "I, ah, don't know if that's such a good idea."

"Oh calm down. Just for a nightcap. You know, the way we used to do before you and Bristol got all serious."

"How did you know about—"

"Carpenter, I'm a reporter. Don't insult my intelligence. Plus, I'd like to run an idea by you. Could be helpful to Ron's campaign."

I scratched the back of my head. "Nightcap it is. You okay to drive?"

"Abbbsolutely."

*****

I DREW BACK THE CURTAINS when we returned to my apartment so that the moon-kissed skyline smiled delightedly into the living room. Then I went to the kitchen and wasted no time pouring myself an unnecessary drink. Glancing up, I found Jessica parked in the exact spot Jack Monroe had stood in the night before. I walked to the record player and removed *Ballads* from its cover. The vinyl embraced the needle in that familiar, euphonic union that precedes and follows the release of each capsule of sound. Once I'd gathered my liquid medication, I carried it to the window, where she stood casting a sharply defined, pitch-black shadow. We stood in silence for a time as our eyes embraced the moon and stars.

"Enjoying the view, Ms. Parker?"

She sighed. "I wish you could live here forever."

Though we'd had multiple nightcaps at my apartment, this was her first sober visit. It was also the first since Bristol and I had our talk. *How nice it'll be*, I thought, *to communicate with her as sober people do, rather than in the manner employed by characters in* Lost Generation *novels.*

"You're remarkably lucky," she said. "Do you know that?"

"I don't believe in luck," I said.

"That's because you've been blinded by your education, your friends, and your fabulous life. Luck doesn't discriminate against success, you know." She turned her gaze away from me and refocused on the night's light.

"There's no such thing as luck," I said. "Only preparedness—"

"Meeting opportunity," she interjected. "Yes, I know what you think about luck. Your problem is that you're so focused on being grown that you've forgotten what it's like to be young. There must've been a time in your life when you basked in youth, savored every minute of it, and believed in—even longed for—luck. That's what being young is all about: believing in the impossible, the unexplainable. At some point in life, we stop believing in luck and start talking about karma. We start reducing everything to inputs and outputs. That's what you've become. You've become an adult."

"Yeah, so?"

"So the things in life you don't understand can't all be explained away by karma. How do you explain the fact that there are bad people who have everything life can offer?"

I thought for a moment. "Luck," I said. We both smiled and laughed.

"I'll be right back," I said. I walked around the corner to the bathroom to refresh my contact lenses. When I returned, I found her standing on the black leather couch by the window, wearing only her underwear and my Yale hat. She held an inappropriately full glass of red wine in her left hand.

"What are we drinking?" I asked.

She grinned after taking a long swig. "I pulled it from the back of your liquor cabinet. It's damn good."

I returned to the kitchen, eager to know if she'd uncorked the 2004 Mandolina Toccata Riserva. She had. "I've been holding onto that bottle for a while," I said. "Well, I'll never accuse you of being a cheap date."

"And I'll never accuse you of being less than a gentleman." She studied my face and smiled. "Unless you've got some pressing campaign business over there, I'd like it very much if you joined me on this fancy couch of yours."

"It's not all that fancy," I said.

"Good, then you won't mind if we break it."

"I'd probably mind a lot in the morning," I said. "Is that what you do, Parker? Go around breaking couches?"

"I've been known to break a couch now and then."

"So, what was that idea you wanted to run past me?"

"Well, I'm working on a piece on your guy," she said, peering down at me, "and I've got a couple of possible angles: that he's what we need to move forward, or that he'll divide us and take us backward. Which should I go with, Al?" She nodded at my glass. "You might wanna down that drink. I wouldn't want you to spill it all over this not-all-that-fancy couch of yours."

Dammit. I went to the bar and grabbed the bottle of scotch. I took a long swallow before returning to the couch, where she was now sitting. I watched with captivation as the drops of wine she'd accidentally spilled trailed down her chest toward her inner thighs before disappearing.

She was breathing heavily. "It's a little bright in here, no?"

"I don't think so," I said. "It's beautiful. Are you crazy?"

"As Ophelia," she replied, grabbing the back of my neck and pulling me toward her. "'There is a willow grows aslant a brook,'" she recited.

"Are you drowning?" I said.

"You too. I told you I'd ruin you."

I lifted her weightless body above my shoulders in one fluid motion and carried her up the stairs and onto the balcony. Under the cover of life-giving darkness, she breathed freely again. As I put my hands on her hips, she looked over her shoulder. "I wonder what the oh-so-perfect Bristol Davis would think about this?" A smirk crossed her face.

The thought of Bristol—her luminous eyes, the disappointment in her voice when I asked her to call Rob, my promise to take care of her heart—filled me with rage. Jessica's brown eyes, for a split second, flashed a deep, dark green.

"You're going to pay for that," I said quietly.

"I most certainly hope so."

CHAPTER SEVENTEEN

MONDAY, MAY 3, 2010

THE FOLLOWING MONDAY was a flurry of activity. When I wasn't on the phone putting out one of a thousand fires, I was sprinting between my office and Shane's as we strategized, debated, and finally settled on where to send Ron and Carmichael as they crisscrossed the state that Election Eve.

I called Jim Randolph at around four thirty. *Damn that Branford Darling.* For months, I'd possessed the power not only to take him out of contention in his primary battle but to also terminate his political career. And to add insult to injury, Darling was literally blowing Remini out of the water. When I called Jim that day, he said, as he had so many times before, that he'd had no word from Darling and he apologized profusely for his inability to broker the endorsement. More angry at myself for being bamboozled than with either of them for doing the bamboozling, I abruptly ended the call totally certain I wouldn't hear from Jim or Darling again. I never followed through with my threat to end Darling's career if he failed to endorse within twenty-four hours. I had no more chips to play.

At around six o'clock, I received a call from Chris Knight. "Thanks for taking this call, Al," he said. "I'm sure things must be crazy for you right now."

"Not a problem, Chris."

"I've got just one more question."

"Shoot."

"How do you feel about the fact that the major African-American PACs across the state waited until the final week of the primary to endorse Ron's campaign?"

How does a man feel after being stabbed in the back by his brother? Shackled as I was by Ron's political high road directive, I held my tongue. "Chris, we're just really ecstatic about receiving their endorsements. They had three eminently qualified candidates to choose from, and I'm sure it wasn't an easy decision to get to. Yes, it would've been nice to have these endorsements weeks ago, but we remain confident that Ron will win tomorrow and that these endorsements reflect the confidence Ron enjoys in the black community."

"That was pretty," Chris said. "Anything to say off the record?"

I exhaled loudly. "Chris, the behavior of the black PACs, flouting their long practice of endorsing at least a month before the primary election to help voters make thoughtful choices was irresponsible at best; at worst, it reflects the reality that none of them really wanted to endorse our campaign because they couldn't be sure we'd win. They just weren't willing to take a chance on us."

"Do you think their lack of confidence in your campaign was irrational in light of where Ron stood before last Tuesday night?"

"Chris, in September of 1952, President Eisenhower was struggling with the question of whether or not to keep Richard Nixon on the ticket as his vice president. You remember the scandal Nixon was dealing with, right?"

"The slush fund in California."

"Right. Anyway, as Eisenhower dragged his feet, Nixon offered him some friendly advice: 'There comes a time in matters like this when you've either got to shit or get off the pot.'"

Afterward, Shane, Bristol, and I took a call from Carmichael and Ron as they headed back east from a rally in Winston-Salem. Carmichael reported that all the members of the Commission appeared onstage with Ron at the rally—an occurrence for which Ron noted there was no precedent. Prior to that, Ron said, the most he'd ever seen were four or five ministers coming out publicly for a candidate. After joining the call, Roger informed us that he'd just gotten off of a conference call with our various operatives around the state heading up our GOTV effort. They'd confirmed that everything was in place for tomorrow, including transportation to and from the polls for pretty much everyone who'd expressed a need. With all the good news coming in, including the positive response we'd been getting from voters as a consequence of our seventy-two-hour TV and radio blitz, Shane acknowledged that cautious optimism wasn't entirely inappropriate.

I returned to my office at eight thirty to place a few more calls with unofficial operatives I'd been in close contact with over the previous several months to make sure they had everything they needed—and to get their reports. As nine o'clock rolled around, I decided to run across the hall to see if Bristol had already eaten. As I stood, a call came through from my mother.

"Hey, Alex, how are you?" she said. "I know you must be really busy tonight."

"I'm doing alright, considering," I said. "I haven't eaten all day. And I'm pretty tired."

"You *must* be really busy. I've never known you to miss a meal."

"Desperate times sometimes call for fasting."

"Well . . . I, ah . . . well, I don't know how to tell you this," she said, her voice starting to crack.

By that time in life I'd heard enough "I don't know how to tell yous" from my mother to know what was coming. I went immediately numb. "Who?" I asked.

"Grandpa . . . about twenty minutes ago," she said. "Massive heart attack."

The news hit me like a bag of bricks to the stomach, and as my abdominal muscles failed, I hunched over, nearly falling from my chair. My first thought was the conversation we'd shared about Bristol, his words just minutes before that meeting with Darling: *If you value your friendship with her, you'll either commit or let her go.* Then my promise to Bristol that night on Ninth Street: *I won't let you down.* And that talk with Billy on the way back from the airport in January: *I've just got to grow the hell up.*

My thoughts began to coalesce around my grandmother, my mother, and her three siblings. "How are you and Grandma?" I asked.

"I'm doing alright, I guess. It's just so sudden. I mean, he was old and had heart problems for years, but it's still so sudden. Tom is with Momma now. She's doing okay. I really feel badly for you. You've got such a big day tomorrow."

"Nothing's more important than family," I said. "I'm gonna hop in the car and head over to Rock City now."

She chuckled. "Momma said you'd do that. She really does know her grandson. She made me promise that I'd make sure you didn't do that. She said that Grandpa was very proud of your work on the campaign and would want you to finish the job. You stay put. Go on over to Rock City after things settle down tomorrow. I'm heading down first thing tomorrow morning."

"Are you sure?" I said. "I feel like I should be there."

"You know just as well as I do that your grandfather was all about finishing what you start. People are counting on you."

"But I just think—"

"Go win it for Grandpa."

"I love you, Mom."

"I love you too."

As the call ended, I pulled myself up from my chair. I stood and paced back and forth for a minute or so before the depth of the darkness outside my office window became an overwhelming distraction. At that point I stopped, looked, and listened as one painful memory conquered my conscience: that humid summer afternoon in the cleaners when I vowed to never come back. I felt my knees buckle as I fell to the ground. Lying on my back, I sobbed like a newborn taking its first breaths.

Some deaths are more devastating than others. Some change the way you think, and others change the way you live. As I struggled, for the first time in life, to compose myself after tragedy, still lying on the cold floor, I knew this death would change both. I'd always wondered, with intense guilt, how I'd feel when this family's linchpin passed on, leaving us in a dense, mountainous forest to fend for ourselves. I'd always assumed I wouldn't cry. I'd reasoned that while his death would cause excruciating pain, I'd successfully compartmentalize the loss into the "that's life" bucket and subsequently carry on relatively unchanged.

"Get up!" I shouted. But my knees remained incapable of executing my brain's commands. Then I saw him standing before me. *Go on now. Go finish the job. Don't waste time feeling sorry for me. There's work to be done.*

I decided I had to go to Bristol, at that very moment, to tell her what I'd done.

Instantly my knees regained function. I was able to stand. I walked briskly across the hall to her office. She was gone. I floated past the frenzied crush of volunteers crisscrossing the common area without hearing a sound. Once outside, I was nearly overwhelmed by the familiar, sweet scent of Southern evening air in the moments before rain. The street lamps above cast sharp, triangular rays into the pitch-black night. As I turned the corner leading to the parking lot, I noticed Bristol's car idling next to mine. Her driver's door was open, window down. I took a deep breath. For the first time since hanging up with my mother, I felt that everything would be okay. I approached the car, thoroughly thankful for her. Then she stepped out.

"Hey, you," I said.

"What's wrong? Have . . . have you been crying?"

"Oh no, it's . . . just my allergies acting up again."

"Oh. You should take some medicine. Do you have any with you?"

"Bristol, I ah . . . I don't know how to tell you this, but—"

Her face went blank. My stomach churned. *You can do this. You have to do this.*

"Al, I can't take any bad news right now. We've got too much work to do tonight. This will just have to—"

"I was with Jessica last Wednesday night."

She cast her eyes away. "What do you mean 'with Jessica'?"

"It was just supposed to be a nightcap. She asked me to meet for dinner last minute. Then she asked to come over for a nightcap, and I told her it wouldn't be a good idea, you know, because of you, but I agreed anyway, and then she mentioned a story. I just . . . I just . . . I failed you."

A single tear slid from the corner of her eye. Then she turned, sat back down in her car, and slammed the door shut. She looked straight ahead through the windshield. It felt like hours passed before she spoke. "You can tell Ron why I'm not coming back."

"Bristol, please don't."

She turned and looked up and into my eyes. "How could you?" she muttered. Her words sliced into my abdomen like a scalpel. "I guess I always knew," she said. "In the back of my mind, I knew I couldn't trust you. That you were still the same guy from law school."

I struggled to find words. In that moment, I realized that in the months since I'd asked her to join me on the campaign, she'd become my best friend.

She started the engine. "I'm done. I'm done, Al."

"Bristol, please!" I said, reaching for her hand. She slapped my arm away violently. "I can't make it through tonight alone. I just got terrible news."

She scoffed. "That's so like you. Poor Al, he's having a bad day!"

I felt the first few drops of rain. "But—"

"I don't want to hear it!" she screamed.

"Please, don't do this." My knees began malfunctioning again as buckets of rain poured down. There was no shelter for me, so I just stood there, alone.

"I hope she was worth it." Her voice cracked just as my mother's had a few moments earlier. As I studied Bristol's profile, I felt my lungs deflating with deathly swiftness. I brought my right hand to my chest as I gasped for oxygen. I staggered backwards while reaching for my knees, locking them in place just in time. Hunched over, I was startled by the sight of her phone crashing to the ground and disintegrating into a hundred thousand pieces in the puddles gathering at my feet. The sound of the crash registered with my brain several seconds later.

When I looked up, still hunched over, I found two inordinately narrow, devastated green eyes looking down at me. Time hovered, and as I watched her shake her head, I felt my head crash to the ground. Now flat on my back, my eyes met the orange moon above in the brief instant before my waterlogged eyes failed. I closed them tightly and saw Bristol and Al standing before each other on that beautiful August evening on Ninth Street. She rose to her toes and pressed her lips against his face. *You and I are going to win this thing.*

"We can't lose," I said, my insignificant voice lost amid the sound of a million raindrops colliding with the miles of pavement all around me.

Bristol rolled up the window and activated her car's high beams. At that precise moment, the warm sensation of us—and the nexus that had formed around us one magical August night that I'd faithfully believed would protect us from all worldly things lurking around us— extinguished. With some unexplainable vigor, I jumped to my feet, my head still throbbing, and commenced banging on her window. She looked ahead through the windshield as the window withdrew into the door. Time stood still again as she turned her face toward mine. Her tears were heavier now. I looked up at the sky again and found that the moon was no more. As I returned my eyes reluctantly to hers, I ached from the realization that I'd never see them again.

"I hope—sincerely hope—that one day you find someone you're willing to entrust with your heart," she said. "I hope she'll teach you how to love. Good-bye, Alexander."

As the window began to rise, I tried with what little strength remained in me to push it down. At the last possible moment I removed both hands from certain perdition. She put the car in gear, backed out of the lot, and peeled off and out of sight.

I stood alone in the dark as the walls of my life came crashing in. They stopped just short of crushing me but closed in tightly enough to exact an excruciating penance, close enough to make thinking about anything other than those walls impossible. The raw intensity of the agony I suffered in those moments shed light on a fact I'd never had occasion to appreciate physically before: the inescapable reality of my own mortality.

As I drove home that Election Eve, I didn't struggle to make sense of the confluence of pain in my life that night, nor did I question why God saw fit to burden me in this way. And in stark contrast to my usual tendency when confronted with adversity, I declined to utilize mind games to convince myself things weren't as bad as they seemed. I chose to experience all of it in its complete, unmitigated desolation.

I'd missed fifteen calls since leaving the office and entering my apartment that night. Without returning any of them, I turned my phone off and placed it on the kitchen counter. After pouring a scotch and lighting a cigar, I carried them both with me upstairs and onto the balcony. A gentle mist replaced the heavy rain that had endured for the entirety of the drive from Durham. Scotch never tasted as delightful as it did that night, and so I had four without consciously experiencing even a hint of inebriation.

A charcoal-gray Bimmer—the same model as Bristol's—passed by below. I hoped, for the tiniest of seconds, that it was her, and that she'd park, come up, and agree to forget the whole sordid mess.

That night, I came upon the inescapable lesson of my affair with Jessica Parker—and the mess into which my reckless actions over the course of the campaign had led me: man rejects growth at his own peril. I learned that a man cannot grow while hiding in the comfort of the familiar trappings of youth; that the ability to recognize, and then select, the path toward manhood while standing at the fork in the road is the only meaningful difference between men and grown boys; and that the quintessential element of manhood, therefore, is the ability to recognize life's irretrievable moments of opportunity and take the appropriate action within them.

That night, the end of one uncommon life cast a bright light onto the shameful particulars of my own. I'd often heard people talk about their "come to Jesus" moment—a crucible of intense emotional disruption that causes them to recognize the presence of a superhuman force only a fool would continue to ignore—a moment at which one realizes that the golden rule is golden for a reason. I don't know if Jesus came to me that night, but I did come to the end of an era. At last, I was forced to account for my failures.

I stood on that balcony until the birds welcomed the new day, thankful to have been given another, appreciative of having had Grandpa and Bristol in my life, and hopeful that their passing the prior day would give me the tools I needed to stop running.

That night, life forced me to come to terms with another lesson I'd previously learned but only occasionally taken to heart: Doing the right thing leads to positive outcomes. To be sure, it won't guarantee victory in every instance, but if you always do right, you never really lose. The explanation is simple: when you do the right thing, more often than not you end up in the company of others who habitually do the same.

Do the right thing.

One would be hard pressed to find a simpler phrase in the English language—or one fraught with more difficulty.

CHAPTER EIGHTEEN

ELECTION DAY
TUESDAY, MAY 4, 2010

I COULDN'T SLEEP past dawn, so I was first in line at my precinct. The smile that conquered my face as I gazed at Ron's name on the ballot must've been visible to everyone in Raleigh. When I got back home after swinging by the dry cleaners around the corner, I skipped coffee and passed out on the couch. After a short nap, I hopped in my car and made the rounds in Wake County, precinct by precinct. As I entered the walk-in closet later that afternoon to scan my tie rack, my stomach began churning. I was donning my best navy blue suit, just hours off the press. When I'd entered the dry cleaners earlier that morning to pick it up, the scent of perchloroethylene almost brought me to my knees.

After spending several minutes vacillating between a black necktie and a green bow tie, I settled on the latter. *We don't have a Scots-Irish candidate, but we could certainly use some of their luck.* Before heading to the office, I paused before the mirror over the bathroom sink. *You ready?* Then she appeared, her green eyes gazing at mine just as they had that night outside her apartment complex on Super Bowl Sunday. I could hear her voice: *If you want her, please, just tell me now.* I shook it off and downed a can of club soda before grabbing my suit jacket and jogging out the door.

I arrived at the office at six to meet with Shane, as we'd agreed the prior evening. Due to the overwhelming number of volunteers already packed into the common room, parking was particularly scarce. This problem was exacerbated by the presence of about a dozen news trucks from local and national news outlets in the lot next to our offices, where the Bristol and Al story had ended abruptly just a hair under twenty-four hours earlier.

This was it. All the road trips, all the late nights, all the phone calls, and all the maneuvering—it all came down to a single day. When I walked in, I found the common room buzzing with volunteers making last-minute calls to voters. Toward the back of the room, other volunteers were setting up tables, laying out freshly laundered white tablecloths, and unboxing bottles of champagne, wine, and beer. In no mood to socialize, I hurried past the volunteers, most of whom I knew by name, and back to Shane's office. Just before turning the corner into the hallway leading to the offices, I spotted our old friend Susan, who'd put on that incomparable hospitality suite performance in Asheville.

"Do my eyes deceive me," I started while stepping into Shane's office, "or did I just see Susan Ripple out there making calls for us?"

"No, that's Susan alright," Carmichael said, shaking my hand. "Word on the street is she left the party this morning."

"What?" I exclaimed.

"Apparently she and Preston had a full-on screaming match in front of party headquarters on Hillsborough Street this morning," he continued. "She took issue with the party's handling of our campaign."

"Wow!" I said. "Do we know specifics? I mean, there's a whole laundry list of things to choose from."

"She wouldn't say," Carmichael replied. "But I do know she slapped ol' Preston square on the face before walking off."

I grinned. "I guess they're not all rotten over there. I do wonder what our buddy Preston did to set her off, though."

"All I know is that today feels mighty different from all the others," Carmichael said.

"It does, doesn't it?" I said.

An almost eerie calm pervaded the four walls of Shane's office, like the motionless moments just before an August afternoon thunderstorm. Shane finally looked up from his laptop. "Mr. Carpenter, how are ya?"

"Stomach's churning," I said. "How you holdin' up?"

"I'll tell ya what, I'm feeling pretty good about everything," Shane said. "The turnout estimates I've been getting from our people at key precincts have been positive. And your reports from Wake County precincts throughout the day were all encouraging."

"Moderate to heavy black turnout in our key areas, low turnout in general statewide?" I asked.

"Exactly," Shane said. "If our base gets out today, we just might pull this thing off. Just wish we could've gotten on TV sooner."

"Where's Ron?" I asked.

"He's at the hotel suite with the family, resting I hope," Carmichael said. "Just dropped him off a few minutes ago."

"How's he doing?" I asked. "And what about Casey?"

"They seem reasonably calm," Carmichael said. "I think they've finally resigned themselves to the fact that it's out of their hands now."

"Wow, Casey too?" Shane said.

"Casey too," Carmichael said. "She's on her way to the hotel now. She hung up her cleats about half an hour ago."

"And Roger?" I asked.

"He's on the phone with operatives, making sure folks are getting to the precincts," Shane said. "Al, I've got one last assignment for you if you're up for it. I need you to have a look at the rules on runoffs and recounts. Carmichael's already printed them. Shouldn't take you too long to run through them. I just wanna make sure we're on top of things in case we need to be."

"You're thinkin' it'll be close enough for a recount?" I said.

"You don't?" Carmichael asked.

"Chris Knight and that damned Jessica Parker are still saying we can't pull it off," Shane said. "The thinking is that we've got the momentum but ran out of time."

"I guess it could be pretty tight," I said as Carmichael handed me a manila folder.

"Have a look," Shane said. "When you're done, let's meet back here and discuss."

"Aye aye," I said. I went to my office, closed the door, and digested the rules in about half an hour. I checked the state Board of Elections website for election returns even though I knew results wouldn't start coming in until after the polls closed at seven o'clock. I gathered the documentation and headed back to Shane's office, passing Carmichael on the way. As I entered, Shane shut his computer. I grabbed the wooden chair, one of the two solitary pieces of furniture in his office on that first walkthrough on February 4, and pulled it to the other side of his desk. Then I leaned back and parked my hands behind my head. "Fifteen minutes," I said.

"This is what it's all about," he said while removing his spectacles. "That feeling, the one in your gut right now, is what keeps me coming back to this racket again and again."

"It's crazy," I observed. "I haven't been here since I worked my hometown mayoral race back in high school. Guess I've been chasing that high ever since. Feels exactly the same."

"You clean up alright," Shane said. "Bow tie?"

"I'm channeling my inner Roger," I said while adjusting the green silk. "I guess you're too cool to throw a suit on for tonight's festivities?"

"I've got mine upstairs in the war room," Shane said. "So what's the skinny on the runoff rules?"

"It's pretty straightforward," I replied. "The top two vote getters go to a runoff if neither of them hits forty percent of the total votes cast. We knew that already."

"Simple enough," Shane said. "And recounts?"

"There's an automatic recount if a candidate's vote total comes within one half of one percent of the leading vote getter's total. As you know, before last Tuesday, I was projecting a turnout of less than five hundred thousand. I'm hoping that with the increased interest in this race over the last week, and with all the money we've raised, we'll be able to rouse an additional hundred thousand in the African-American and progressive communities. But that remains to be seen. Anyway, let's say the turnout is four hundred, and Jane gets one hundred seventy-five."

"That would put her over the magic forty percent number," Shane said.

"Right," I said. "At about forty-four. We'd have to get within 875 votes to force a recount."

"Okay," Shane said.

"There's one more thing," I said. "The recount isn't automatic—not literally, anyway. You have to request it."

"And how much time do you have to do that?"

"Five days."

"Thanks for looking into this."

"No problem," I said, rising from my chair.

"Wait a second, would ya?" he said. "Have a sit-down."

"What's up?"

"Have you heard anything more about the video footage?" he asked, almost at a whisper.

"Nothing more than what we've already discussed. Like I said, it's not going to air."

"So you think we're in the clear?"

"Correct," I replied. "But if it somehow gets out that I was negotiating a deal to suppress information that could've affected our chances . . . well, that's another story. The most important thing is that Ron's in the clear."

"Are you prepared to take one for the team if necessary after the primary?" he asked. "I mean, if any of the details of your dealings with Rob come out? Because I can't go near it. This is my livelihood."

"Your name won't come out of my mouth," I said. "It hasn't."

Shane lowered his head, rested his elbows on his knees, and tapped his fingertips together nervously. "Because I have no official knowledge of what you were doing with that reporter, and that's what I'll say if I'm ever questioned."

"Yeah, you knew nothing," I said. "That's what I'll say."

"This is a nasty business we're in, Carpenter," he said. "Watch yourself."

I smiled. "I'm a big boy, Shane. I can handle it. Besides, I did what I had to do to put us in a position to win."

"I want you to know how much I respect what you've done in this campaign. Before I came on back in February, this was your show. And I know I haven't always been the easiest to work with, but I've always had the best interests of the campaign in mind. If I've said or done anything that seemed like I was taking a shot at you, I want you to know that it was never personal. It's all been about winning. I know you're going to do great things, and I'm happy I had the chance to work with you."

I nodded and looked down for a moment. "We're professionals," I said. "We're not expected to get along all the time, but we are expected to put aside our differences and stay focused." I raised my head and looked him squarely in the eyes, not because the rules required it—though they did—but because I wanted to. "It's been a pleasure, Shane. Can't believe I'm actually saying that." I stood and extended my right hand.

"Godspeed, Carpenter," he said as we shook. "Your smarts have carried you a long way in this game. I trust you'll continue to defy the odds in whatever else you do."

"Thank you."

"So, did I live up to my name?"

I chuckled. "What, you mean the Redheaded Dread?"

Shane grinned from ear to ear. "That's the one."

"What do you think?"

"I sure hope so," he said. "Charismatic staffers win friends, but they don't win elections. I haven't made many friends doing this job, now for the fifth time, but I haven't lost a single election."

Around the corner our volunteers erupted in a round of applause and the familiar "Get Ron in!" chant.

"Either the other candidates just conceded the election to Ron or the polls just closed," I said.

"Well, that's that," Shane said. "I'm gonna change and head over to join Ron at the hotel. By the way, he told me not to leave headquarters without you."

"I'll be along in a bit," I said.

"Okay. It's room 541," Shane said before sprinting out the door.

The time was 7:02 p.m. when I returned to my office. I sat down at my desk, took a deep breath, and refreshed the Board of Elections website. The first numbers were in:

WOODALL: 4,430   BILLINGSWORTH: 2,756   JOHNSON: 1,987

I took another deep breath, leaned back in my chair, and exhaled. Then there was a knock at my door. "Come in," I yelled.

Carmichael poked his head into the room. "You alright?" he said. "You're being a little antisocial. People are asking about you."

"Not really in the mingling mood right now, Carmichael."

"You don't look so good, Carpenter," he said. "I mean, a whole heck of a lot worse than normal. What's the matter?"

"I'm fine," I said. "I'll be out in a minute."

"Any results yet?"

"Nothing statistically significant."

"Where are we?" he asked.

"Third."

"How's Remini doing against Darling?"

I clicked on the link for the Tenth District Democratic primary race. "She's actually up a few thousand," I replied.

"Good for her," he said. "Look, there's no point sitting in here all depressed. It's too early to know what's going to happen."

"I'll come out in a second."

"It's just a game, Carpenter," he said. "Nothing more, nothing less. Wise words from one of the craziest SOBs I ever met." He winked, and I chuckled softly as he closed the door behind him.

I turned my attention back to the computer screen and refreshed the results again:

WOODALL: 10,564   BILLINGSWORTH: 7,231   JOHNSON: 5,792

Jane was cleaning up in Wake County, a county where we thought we'd be competitive, especially in light of the WC-CSP endorsement, late though it was. Durham County, which we expected to take in a landslide, hadn't reported any numbers yet.

I traveled back in time to that walk home from Simmons's

apartment on November 4, 2008. I recalled the uneasy mixture of excitement and skepticism raging inside me, and my fixation with what would happen next. I also couldn't help but think about the mess I'd gotten myself into with Rob. If word got out that I'd tried to leverage the perception of white racism to my candidate's advantage, my political career would likely be over.

In that moment, alone in my office, I tried to medicate the anxiety by focusing on the prospect that Ron might still pull it out. No matter what happened to me in the days ahead, I might be able to bask—at least for a time—in the afterglow of a historic primary win. Then came another knock.

"Come in!" I said, now a little annoyed. She was the last person I expected, or wanted, to see. I felt immediately nauseous.

"Surprised?" Jessica asked as she strolled in. She closed the door behind her but remained by the threshold.

"Nothing surprises me anymore."

"Figured I'd come by and wish you and the boys good luck."

I snickered. "You're a piece of work, Parker."

She sauntered across the room, leaned across the desk and, before I could react, kissed my cheek. "What's wrong, darlin'? You look like you lost your best friend."

"I did—both of them."

She narrowed her eyes. "What do you mean?"

"I'm not going to discuss that with you."

She took a seat on the other side of my desk. "Well, I'm sorry to hear that."

"Now, if you don't mind, I'd like to be left alone."

"I'll leave—*after* you thank me."

"Thank *you*? For what?"

"You aren't that lucky, Al Carpenter."

"What are you talking about?"

"You know I've been dating Rob for several months now."

"I know that . . . so what?"

"Last Wednesday morning, he told me we were going to Paris to celebrate our six-month anniversary, and flying first class."

"What does that have to do with me?"

"Well, you know me. I had to get to the bottom of it. So I read his texts and e-mail. I wanted to know how he came up with that kind of cash. Turns out he planted that guy at the forum and cut a deal to pay him three grand. Rob figured that would be nothing compared to the amount he could get from your camp to keep the footage under wraps—or from Bill or Jane to make sure it got out." She paused to peer at me. "You okay, Carpenter? You're looking a little pale."

My heart pounded violently. "This is—"

"Unbelievable, right? Anyway, I texted Rob Wednesday night to tell him I knew about the whole plot. I knew about your meeting at Sandra's too. I watched from my car as you walked out. The next day, I made him destroy the footage and all the copies he made. As a journalist, it was kinda sad to watch. After that, I went to my bosses and told them the whole thing. They agreed, at my request, not to fire him. They also gave me that promotion."

I shook my head. "In exchange for your silence."

"Yes . . . and because of my superior talent." She began laughing uncontrollably.

"What's so funny?"

"I just have one question."

"What's that?"

"Where in the world were you gonna come up with fifteen thousand dollars? And Rob, he was dumb enough to believe you could get it. I swear, you boys are two of the most idiotic smart guys I ever did meet."

I pondered her words for a moment. *Isn't it possible he just threw out a ridiculous number but would've taken a lot less in the end?* "I could've gotten the money," I growled.

"Legally?"

"Well, probably not."

"That's what I thought."

"It's all a big game to you, isn't it, Jessica?" I said.

"A game you're in a position to win because of me. How about a thank you?"

I sighed heavily. "You're right. You saved my butt."

"You're welcome. By the way, how are things with you and the lovely Bristol Davis?"

"Things are fine."

She looked away. "Well, good," she stammered. "She's a good girl. I hope things work out."

"You do? I mean . . . so, is the trip to Paris still on?"

She cleared her throat while looking down at her lap. "I don't think we're gonna survive all this."

"Well, maybe it's for the best."

She fixed her eyes on mine. "Thank you, Al." She pulled her phone from her pants pocket and shot to her feet. "Look at the time! I've gotta get over to Raleigh. I'm due at Bill's party. Good luck!" Jessica scurried toward the door.

"Thanks," I said, rising up.

"You're welcome."

"Especially for putting me in front of a mirror."

She turned back suddenly after grabbing the doorknob. She snickered and gazed at me intently. "Al Carpenter, we all need a reminder from time to time. It's been a pleasure doing business with you."

She shut the door behind her, leaving me alone with my thoughts again—and Coltrane. At length, I closed my laptop, grabbed my suit jacket, and began the nine-block walk to the hotel.

*****

WHILE WALKING TO THE HOTEL, I received a text from J. C. Lockhart's old pal, Mary-Jane Fenway: *Good luck to you, Carmichael and Ron. You ran a great race!* Mary-Jane's status as an independent contractor had formally ended just over a month before that night, when she joined Jane's staff. The door to room 541 was slightly ajar, but I knocked anyway.

"Come in."

I immediately recognized that voice.

"Mrs. Johnson!" I said, hugging Ron's mother tightly as I entered. "How are you?"

"Al!" she said. "It's so good to see you. It's been so long. I haven't seen you in months."

"Well, I've been keeping busy," I said. I waved at Ron's sister, his two nieces, and a nephew watching cartoons in the living room as I walked past. The mood was almost disturbingly placid. Shane sat at a desk in the corner, his eyes glued to his computer screen.

I found Ron in the rear bedroom, reclining on one of the twin beds and watching SportsCenter. It was the first time in two months that I'd gone nearly twenty-four hours without seeing or speaking to him.

"How's it going?" I asked, pausing at the threshold.

"Come on in," he said. "Just back here catching up on the world of sports. You know, I haven't seen an entire game, basketball or football, since we started this thing. Just had some room service. First meal of the day. How was it out there?"

"Fun, actually," I said. "I spent the day canvassing Wake County precincts."

"Anything interesting happen?"

"Not really," I replied. "The volume was pretty abysmal at most precincts, but there was moderate to high turnout at almost every majority black precinct. If that's happening here in Durham, in Charlotte, down east, and in the Triad—well, who knows?"

"Yeah," he said distantly, returning his eyes to the television.

"Have you been following the returns?" I asked.

"Not really," he said. "I think Shane's been keeping tabs in the other room."

"Good enough," I said. "Well, I'll leave you to it."

"Ah, Al?"

"Yeah?"

"Any word from Branford?"

"Nothing," I replied.

"Hmm. Oh well. I guess we didn't really lose anything by trying, other than your time, which is pretty valuable. Thanks for your work on that. I know it must've been pretty damn frustrating trying to chase him down all these months."

"No worries," I said.

"I'd be lying if I said I wasn't curious about what went on there," Ron said. "Very strange stuff."

"Indeed."

"He gave us his word," he said, shaking his head. "Oh well. Everything will work out the way it's supposed to."

"For sure," I said before stepping back into the living room. I leaned in toward Shane. "Where are we?" I said.

"As of five minutes ago, Jane was just over eighty thousand, Ron was at fifty-five, and Bill was at forty-five."

A closer survey of the data on Shane's computer screen revealed that Durham County and four additional counties in which we'd long expected to perform well still hadn't reported any results. It was nine o'clock. Numerically, we were still in the race, but our fate would be sealed once those five counties reported.

As I studied the county-by-county returns, Shane wandered out of the living room and into the other bedroom, where I assumed Casey and the kids were resting. Roger called a few minutes later. I took the call on the balcony, where I'd retreated to grab some fresh air.

"Are you guys in the hotel suite?" he asked.

"Yessir."

"What's the mood?"

"Everyone's surprisingly sedate," I replied. "My guess is that the last few days of ripping and running killed what little energy everyone had left. Ron and Shane are like zombies in here."

"How about you?" he asked. "Keeping it together?"

"That which doesn't kill me . . ."

"I hear you, bruh," he said with a comforting chuckle. "I'm walking into the lobby now."

"See you in a bit."

Casey entered the suite as I slid open the balcony door. "Hey, Al!"

"Casey Johnson!" I said, trying my best to match her enthusiasm. "How are you?"

She smiled brilliantly. "Great! Just got here! I spent the day shooting from precinct to precinct in Orange County and Durham County. I had so many great conversations with folks who told me how happy they were that Ronny decided to run, how they'd been helping with the campaign, and how revved up they are about tonight."

"I really think we're in a great spot," I said. "I had a similar experience with voters in Wake County."

"Where's Ronny?" she asked.

"He's in the back bedroom," I said, pointing.

"Is he sleeping?"

"Not as of a few minutes ago."

"Let's go see," she said. She pushed the door open.

"Hey, honey!" he said, jumping up to wrap her in a bear hug. "How are you doing?"

Her eyebrows shot to the top of her forehead. "Good, good," she said after kissing him.

Shane and Roger entered the room together a few seconds later. I sat on the bed closest to the door and followed returns on my computer while Ron and Casey reclined on the other bed. Casey picked at a bowl of fruit on the room service cart next to the bed as Shane and Roger milled around the television.

"So, Al," Ron said, "where are we?"

"Two minutes ago, we were about twenty-five thousand behind Jane, but Durham County's numbers weren't in." I refreshed the website again. "And they're still not in."

"Well, look," Ron began, "I want you guys to know how proud I am of all of you. These last few days—weeks, really—have been a whirlwind of activity, and it's required your undivided attention and dedication. No matter what the outcome tonight, we can all rest well knowing we did our best, and that's all we could ever ask of ourselves."

After a few seconds of exchanging smiles and a few pats on the back, Roger began relating an interesting phone conversation he'd had earlier in the day with a political operative down east we'd hired a few weeks before. The hire was a last-ditch effort to close the gap between Ron and Jane among African-American voters in Pitt,

Martin, Beaufort, Bertie, and Washington Counties. The prior night, we'd learned from multiple sources that this guy had called Jane's representatives the week before in an attempt to get on her payroll for the last few days of the election and do for her precisely what he'd been hired to do for us. As Roger described the conversation, Casey sat next to me reviewing the latest election returns. "You know," she whispered, "we've come a long way. And we couldn't have done it without you."

As she spoke, good and bad campaign memories merged into one happy, nostalgic cloud. "I had a great time," I said. "It's something I'll take with me forever. I should be thanking you and Ron for taking a chance on a wet-behind-the-ears political novice from DC."

She leaned in closer. "By the way, Shane got a call from Bristol early this morning saying she wouldn't be around today. Is everything okay?"

"Um, yeah. I spoke to her. It's not as serious as it sounds, but there's some personal business she had to knock out today."

Casey stared searchingly into my eyes. "I see. Well, please let me know if I can do anything to help."

"Sure thing." As we talked, I clicked the refresh button repeatedly. At last, some eighty thousand votes came pouring in, including results from one hundred percent of precincts in Durham County.

Casey gazed unblinkingly at the screen. "Oh my God!" she shrieked.

"What happened?" Roger said.

"All precincts have reported," Casey said, her voice cracking slightly.

"From Durham?" Shane said.

"No," she said. "Statewide."

I refreshed one more time and looked at the results, then at the faces staring at Casey and me. All those months of work—it all came down to a few numbers on my computer screen.

Leaning against the wall, his arms folded and his eyes fixed on the window overlooking downtown Durham, Shane seemed totally collected. "What's the count?" he asked.

"Bill's out," I said.

"Good for starters," he said. "What's the count?"

"Woodall 260,171, and Johnson 258,921," I said. "With a total of 632,001 votes cast."

Shane removed his cell phone from his pocket and asked for the numbers again. The room was transfixed as he tapped at his phone screen. After a moment, he dropped the phone and raised his eyes to the ceiling. Ron gazed unblinkingly at Casey. "She's over forty," Shane exhaled. "Just barely."

"Those numbers seem really close," Casey said, having gathered herself. "We should look at the recount rules."

"We already have," I said. "We can call for a recount if our total number of votes falls within one half of one percent of Jane's total."

"Give me those numbers again," Shane said, bending to retrieve his phone.

"It's 260,171 and 258,921," I said.

After running the calculation with dispatch, a deep grin crept slowly across his face. "We're inside one half of one percent," he said. "Inside by fifty votes."

"Is the recount automatic?" Ron asked. The time for reclining had come and gone, apparently. He now sat on the side of the bed, his elbows resting on his thighs as he ran his hands over his head repeatedly.

"No," I said. "We have to make a formal written request."

"And how much, approximately, would a recount cost the state?" Ron asked.

"Several million dollars at least," Shane said.

"Dammit," Ron said, slowly pulling his right hand down over his face. "Well, that's that," he said conclusively.

Shane walked over to Ron, sat next to him, and turned to me. "We'll prepare the recount request first thing in the morning."

"No recount," Ron said.

"But . . . what . . . you can't be serious!" I stammered. "We've come too far to give up now! And who knows what would happen with a recount? Maybe her total dips below forty percent, and we're looking at a runoff. We'd beat her in a runoff! We've got all the momentum. We would've won outright if we had another week!" I turned to Shane. "How many votes did we lose by?" I said.

"Twelve hundred and fifty," Shane replied.

"Christ," Roger muttered. "Just over a thousand votes."

"We've got to do this, Ron," I said. "People are counting on you."

Ron looked at his feet. "We can't," he whispered. "I mean, we won't. I'm not going to call for a recount." He stood. "Please excuse us, everyone. I'd like a moment with Casey."

"Sure," Shane said, herding Roger and me toward the door. The temperature in the room—and my temper—hovered dangerously close to their respective boiling points. My eyes didn't leave Ron's until he was out of sight. It was my dying gasp. I hadn't felt so violently ill since I'd had the wind knocked out of me during a soccer game at age twelve.

Meanwhile, life continued uninterrupted in the living room. Ron's nieces and nephew sang and danced along with some Disney Channel program while their mother and grandmother tried their best to stay composed—I hadn't realized how thin the walls were. Upon entering the other bedroom, I found Ron's thirteen-year-old son and fourteen-year-old daughter sitting on the front edge of the king-sized bed watching the election coverage, totally dejected. I quietly shut the door as I walked back into the living room. The door to the other bedroom was still closed. Shane and Roger stood side by side before the sliding door.

"Can I have a word on the balcony please?" I said. Shane opened the door and we filed out after him. Reaching into my breast pocket, I removed three of the cigars Uncle Malcolm overnighted me Friday afternoon for this occasion and distributed them without a word. After lighting up, I tossed the matches to Shane.

"You gotta understand where he's coming from, Al," Roger said. "The longer this thing drags on, the more likely it is that the wrong folks will get a hold of it. It could turn very, very ugly with a quickness. And with what happened last week—I mean, the race thing is front and center. It could rip Democrats apart completely."

"And recounts are expensive," Shane said after releasing a lengthy stream of smoke from the corner of his pursed lips. "That's taxpayer money."

"This is politics," I shot back. "It's the last man standing. Why should we sacrifice all we've worked for? So everyone can get back to their lives and continue to pretend like race is no longer an issue? Again? No, that's precisely what we *can't* do. We have to attack that fallacy head on. If we don't push forward now, in two years all anyone's gonna remember about this primary is that a black guy got called a nigger, a bunch of black folks got mad, the liberal media establishment came running to his defense with a week left to go—and he still lost. How do you think that affects the next talented black guy or woman, or any person of color who decides to run? Maybe that person won't run because of this. And you know what that means? That Southern two-step grows stronger. We can't let that happen. This is bigger than this campaign. We can't just walk away."

Roger pushed off from the black steel railing, slowly wound back his right arm, and punched through the drywall separating our balcony from the one nextdoor as if it were wet cement.

"Roger!" Shane exploded. "What the—"

"Sorry about that," Roger said, looking at his feet.

"Shane," I said, "you've gotta get back in there and convince him."

"What do you want me to say?"

"Do you think Bill or Jane would think twice about calling for a recount?" I said. "You think Jack Monroe would advise Bill to stand down to avoid running up the taxpayers' tab for this primary?"

Shane sighed. "Look, hypotheticals don't matter right now. All that matters is the reality we're in and the public's perception of it."

"For the love of God, whatta ya think is gonna happen here, guys?" I exclaimed. "We call for a recount and people start rioting in the streets, an all-out race war that divides the party? And the whole thing gets blamed on Ron?"

"No, but you've gotta consider—" Roger started.

"Then what the hell are we talking about here?" I shouted. "Isn't this what we worked for? Why should we do something no other candidate would do?"

"If he wants a political career after this race is over," Roger said, "gracefully bowing out now buys him a lot of goodwill with Jane. A lot of her supporters are middle-aged and elderly white women, groups who consistently vote. Plus, Ron has something Jane needs right now: the attention and votes of lots of blacks. Ron could cut a deal with Jane—endorse her, and she agrees to endorse him when he runs next cycle if she loses this one. She doesn't have an ice cube's chance in hell of beating Rodney anyway."

"Goodwill in the next cycle?" I said incredulously. "There may not be a next cycle for Ron!"

Just then, Ron pushed back the sliding door and stepped onto the balcony. He offered a forced smile. "What, no cigar for the vanquished candidate?"

"Vanquished?" I said. "You're in the driver's seat."

He ignored me, immediately noticing the basketball-sized crater in the wall. "What happened here?"

I pointed at Roger's bloody right hand.

"You in pain?" Ron asked.

"I can't feel a thing right now," Roger replied.

Ron released a deep breath. "I just called Jane to congratulate her—and to concede the election," he said, avoiding our eyes. "Bill's going to address the media in a few minutes."

"Well," Shane said, looking at each of us in turn, "I guess it's about time we did the same. Let's load 'em up. I'll get Carmichael on the line."

Everyone walked back into the living room and toward the door—except me. Roger was the last to leave me on the balcony. "You need to be there when he delivers his speech," he said, now grimacing slightly.

"You oughtta get some ice on that thing," I said.

He looked me square in my eyes. "It's the right thing to do," he said, tossing his cigar over the railing.

Casey handed Roger a white towel as he stepped back into the suite and closed the sliding door shut. She met my eyes for a few seconds through the glass before abruptly walking away. I remained there alone, just as disappointed in them as I knew they must be in me.

As I stood there, I recalled that over the course of the campaign Ron had alternatively characterized this election as a battle for the soul of America and nothing more than a game. It was in those initial, raw moments of defeat that I first appreciated the harsh reality underlying that paradox—the battle was ours, but the game was his. In making the very personal decision to play the game, he'd taken on responsibility as a steward for the rest of us engaged in the battle, but it was his prerogative to step away at any time, as long as he did it responsibly. Reasonable minds could disagree about whether his decision to walk away in that moment was right, but what wasn't up for debate was whether or not he'd fought the good fight. Having done so, and having advanced the conversation on race across the nation, he'd earned the latitude to determine whether or not to exit and how to do it. And no matter how invested I'd become in his candidacy, it was still, at bottom, just a game.

As I turned toward the sliding door, my own conscience was supplanted by my mother's firm, comforting voice: *Go, Al. Watch his final speech. If you don't, you'll regret it for the rest of your days.*

*****

I HAILED AND HOPPED into a taxi downstairs. As the driver pulled up to the red light, I found myself behind the black Tahoe that had carried us safely to every corner of the state of North Carolina. After the short drive to campaign headquarters, I stood outside the main entrance waiting for Ron and his family to enter. I tried my best to smile.

Through the glass door and windows, I could see that headquarters was standing room only. The antennas from the news trucks parked among the many rows of sedans extended high into the darkness. As Ron and his entourage moved through the door that Carmichael held open for the last time, Candidate Johnson paused to shake my hand. With deafening roars radiating from inside, Ron yelled, "Enjoy this one, Carp—you deserve this as much as I do."

"This state is in great debt to you," I shouted in reply. "The game is over, but the battle endures."

He slapped my back with his left hand and said, "Let's go get it in, Carp."

I snickered. "I'd be remiss if I didn't tell you the whole country will see this," I said. Then I watched the Johnson clan as they walked out of the darkness and into the light to complete the impossible journey Ron had started almost a year before.

I waited until Ron, Casey, and the rest of the family had ascended the stage before entering the building. I stepped in, and having nowhere to go, remained right there next to the door. No longer a deputy campaign manager or senior advisor, I stood with a heavy heart among Ron's many supporters and watched as he ended the game.

"Ladies and gentlemen," Shane said, "Ron Johnson!"

After a minute-long ovation, Ron called on his fellow North Carolinians to continue the battle for America's soul. "You know, in 2008, a great energy swept across this country. Our nation witnessed a political reawakening as a man named Barack Obama captured our imaginations with a message that was as simple as it was grand: hope. For the first time in a long time, our politics reflected our hopes rather than our fears, our dreams rather than the tired old limitations of the past. Most important, we Americans were reminded of our power to effect real change with the ballot—and in dramatic fashion, we did just that.

"In early 2009, after the dust settled on that historic American moment, I, like many of you, began to give serious thought to what that moment meant. It quickly became clear to me that this great American moment would be defined largely by what we did next. That's the moment we find ourselves in now, the moment we've worked so hard over the course of this campaign to leverage to deliver to the people of this great state the change we voted for on November 4, 2008. Since that fateful night, we've had a choice: revert back to the same old divisive politics of the past or take this golden opportunity to write a distinctly new American story, one grounded in racial and socioeconomic progress, inclusion, and widening access to opportunity rather than continuing to pay lip service to those ideals. It's been a choice of whether to do rather than merely demonstrate, a question of whether or not we'll meet the challenge our state motto sets squarely before each of us: to be, rather than to seem.

"I got into this race, officially, last May, without the blessing of Washington and Raleigh insiders because, like you, I recognized that what we did next would have significant consequences, not just for us but for our most prized assets: our children. I wanted people to know that retreating now would be disastrous. I wanted to remind people that only decisive action in this moment could convert the hope of 2008 into real change in 2010 and beyond. That's why, from day one, we set out to make this campaign a vehicle for addressing real problems faced by real people.

"As I've traveled around the state, I've seen that North Carolinians are hurting. But I've also seen something else. From Asheville to Rock City and from Fayetteville to Elizabeth City, what I've seen is that we're down but not out. In city after city and in town after town, I've encountered that singular spirit of hope that makes North Carolinians so special, that tradition of resilience that carries us through the tough times and, having been so strenuously tested, makes us stronger.

"For months now, I've been asking you to join me in putting a stake in the ground for change. I've asked you to stand with me in sending a message to our state and nation that it's the people who empower their leaders, and that elected officials serve at the pleasure of the people, not the other way around.

"Your response has been nothing short of amazing. We started with nothing. We didn't get the backing of Washington insiders or the money that comes along with that backing. But make no mistake, we were *not* emptyhanded. You see, we were armed with a grand vision of what *could* be. We imagined a North Carolina where opportunity is not the exclusive possession of the privileged, a North Carolina where inclusion supplants exclusion, and where leaders actually fight for their constituents.

"Tonight, we just ran out of time. We didn't win this race, but we sent a clear message to Raleigh and Washington. Tonight, we the people made our voices heard! We made it clear that we won't be ignored in the political process. We've seen the smoke and mirrors that has clouded the political process for so long, and tonight we said, 'no more!' We've lived through the disastrous consequences of politics as usual, and tonight, we said, 'no more!' Tonight, through good ol' fashioned grassroots organizing, we sent a powerful message across this nation: in North Carolina, the people still decide elections. Tonight, we put a stake in the ground for change, and we won't retreat!"

At this the room erupted into thunderous applause. He shed no tears, but his eyes were soft in recognition of the moment.

"So what's next?" he continued once the applause died down. "We celebrate our successes in this race. This is a victory, and we can all be proud of the progress we set in motion over the last several months. When the pollsters and pundits said this couldn't be done, you kept making phone calls, you kept sending e-mails, you never stopped believing in the possibilities this campaign embodied, and you stood faithfully by my side. Tonight, I thank you for keeping the faith. It's because of you that I stand here, ready to keep working alongside each of you on behalf of the change you all worked so hard to make possible.

"I want to take this opportunity to congratulate Jane Woodall and Bill Billingsworth. We had great Democrats in this race. I've always said that the people win when there's a vigorous debate about the important challenges we face. We all pushed each other to be better, and I know that Jane, tonight's victor, is a better candidate because of it. But now it's time for Democrats to come together. We began this race with three goals in mind, and those goals remain unchanged tonight: sending Joseph Rodney back home to Winston-Salem, bringing popular accountability back to this US Senate seat, and, most important, finally delivering the change we made possible with our actions in 2008.

"Our work is far from over. We must renew our commitment to meeting the challenges that lie ahead in the summer months and down through to the November election. Make no mistake about this: Senator Rodney is going to fight. But we've gotta fight harder! And that means uniting behind our nominee, Jane Woodall, and helping her finish what we started in this campaign!"

Scanning the room, I observed that more than a few supporters were moved to tears. Though there were several moments during Ron's address when it appeared she might break, somehow Casey kept it together.

"In conclusion, let me say this: Don't forget what we did today. Hold this memory close to you and treasure it. Draw on this moment for inspiration in the tough months ahead. Let's stay fired up, let's remain focused, and by God, let's win this thing in November! Thank you, God bless you all, and may God bless the great state of North Carolina!"

Ron quickly descended into the gleeful crowd to exchange hugs and handshakes with volunteers. His smiles belied the heavy toll I knew the last hour had taken on him. Over the course of this campaign, his words and deeds left no doubt that he wanted this election more than anything—not for himself but for these people. And yet, having made his decision to concede, I couldn't help but think that there was a part of him that wanted to run away to some secluded place and be alone with his thoughts, whatever they were. Perhaps the palpable air of hope in that place buoyed his spirits long enough to get him around the room to do what the rules required of him: say thank you.

I turned to the elderly white man standing next to me. "Good night, be well," I said.

He raised his eyebrows. "You leaving already? The party's just gettin' started."

"I've had a long day. Time to hit the sack."

"Good night," he said. "Drive home safely."

"You too." And with that, I fled back to Raleigh. As I turned onto Highway 147 for what felt like the thousandth time, I received a call from Jack Monroe.

"Mr. Carpenter," he said.

"How are you, Jack?" It was the first time I'd asked that question of him with any genuine interest in his response.

"I've definitely been better. I figured I'd be able to get a hold of you. I told Bill there's no way Carpenter sticks around for all the boohooing."

"What can I say?" I said. "I've never been a big fan of funerals, but I stuck around for the eulogy."

"Your guy gave a great speech," he said. "I've gotta give credit where credit is due, Carpenter. You guys ran one hell of a race—and I'm talking about the one you ran before last Tuesday."

"Thanks, Jack. You know, I'd hoped we'd be on the same team."

"Primary's over, Carp," he said. "We're on the same team now."

"When Roger told me about the DSCC backing Bill and you joining his camp . . . I'm not gonna lie, that really screwed with me. I was already pretty jaded about politics, but that almost took me all the way out. Figured I couldn't trust anyone, that virtually no one's in it for the right reasons. That all anyone cares about is getting paid. I second-guessed everyone and everything. To be fair, it wasn't just you, but that was one of the last straws."

Jack laughed. "It was a business decision for me, for sure. I've got nothin' but love for Ron and Casey and all you guys, but I've got bills to pay, playa."

"I know," I replied. "It took a while to accept that, but I needed to go through the process of seeing it and figuring it out. It's a skill you've gotta have in this game—the ability to quickly ascertain why people are doing what they're doing."

"So you're saying I improved your ability to play this game?"

"That's right, Jack, I owe it all to you."

He laughed again. "The bill's in the mail."

"Congratulations, Jack," I said. "You did a great job in your own right. Hell, you convinced a lot of blacks that Bill actually cares about them. I'm not sure I believe he does, but I want to believe it. Bill's gonna be in this game for a long time. When he does win, I'd like to know he's in this for someone other than himself."

"I know he sometimes comes off as being a bit plastic, but that's only because he works so hard to convince people how much he cares. He's in it for the right reasons, man. I can assure you of that."

"That's good to know. Maybe now I can forgive you for that stunt you pulled at my apartment Tuesday night."

"What? Your apartment? Tuesday, you say? I don't recall that."

I chuckled. "Right."

"It was all business, Carp. Nothing else. All in the game."

"Nothing is *all* business Jack. What was it you said at my apartment? 'Business is nothing more than the furtherance of personal ends by other means.'"

"Who are you, Nixon? You recording conversations?"

"I'm not paranoid, Jack. I just had this nagging overabundance of optimism about people, which you thoroughly disabused me of—you and those black PACs."

"I can speak for myself but not for the PACs. I was just doing my job."

"And your job entailed screwing Ron with the MC-OCA and the DC-OSP?"

"What are you talking about?"

"Come off it, Jack. You think I really believe Ron's interview time *randomly* got changed to a time that made it impossible for him to appear in Charlotte and get back to Durham in time for his DC-OSP interview?"

"This is ridiculous, even for you."

"Jack, I know Bill was originally given the interview slot we ended up with. Once the MC-OCA announced its event, Bill's people went back to the DC-OSP and cut a deal."

"I think you're giving me a little too much credit, Carpenter," he said sharply.

"You still haven't denied cutting the deal, Jack. And you would've been the guy to cut that deal with Bill since you were still running things politically at DC-OSP. And, as fate would have it, a mere twenty-one days later, Bill hired you. But I suppose you think I'm letting an overly active imagination get the better of me, right?"

"I'm more than a little offended that you would even suggest something like this. What you're insinuating about me, not to mention the DC-OSP . . . well, it's pretty insulting."

"Don't worry, Jack. I understand you were just a player in a game. I've decided not to define you based on a few less than honorable moments. But that's just me. Maybe they paid you, maybe they—"

"No money crossed hands," he interrupted.

"Nothing's free in this world," I said. "The thing is, Jack, in a few weeks, I'm gone. Then you've got to deal with this mess. You've got to figure out if short-term political or financial gain here and there is worth it in the long run. At some point you'll be working for a black candidate, and you'll have to deal with the crap you've been perpetuating. This election shouldn't have been close. We both know that. If you and I and everyone else had done the right thing, the best candidate would've won."

"Al, I don't disagree, but you've got to face facts. You want people to do the right thing and vote for the guy who will help bring about change that's in their best interests over time. But how are they gonna eat in the short term?"

"It's precisely that kind of shortsighted thinking that's got things in the shape they're in now, Jack. You may not want to hear this, but you're in a unique position to change attitudes. It may not be in Bill or Jane's best interests, but it's in this state's best interests to stop using racism as a crutch to win elections."

He exhaled deeply. "You're right."

"It's good to hear from you, Jack."

"Really?"

"Yeah, really," I replied. "Don't get me wrong, though. You're a real SOB, and there've been many times when I wanted to slap you silly. But you're also my brother, so I want you to succeed. Let's just make sure we both keep our eyes fixed on that larger prize."

"That's mighty noble of you, Carpenter," he said. "How about a round of golf soon? Looks like we've both got some time on our hands now."

"What, you're not gonna convince Jane that she needs you on her payroll?"

"Of course I am," he said. "But that can wait a week."

"I'll give you a call in a few days, and we'll put something together," I said.

"For your sake, I hope your golf game is a lot less sloppy than your game with the ladies," he said. "You're a mess."

"I deserve that," I said. "But I'll just assume you meant that in the nicest, most brotherly way possible."

"Of course."

"Night, Jack."

"Wait, one more thing."

"What's that?"

He sighed. "You shouldn't be so hard on our people," he said.

"What do you mean?"

"I've listened to you complain about black folks not being all in for the cause, playing both sides, and using the system to fatten their pockets."

"I'm not saying that about all blacks," I said, "but yeah, that's something we both know goes on."

"True, but have you ever stopped to think about the complexities around all that? Maybe there's more to it than an inability on our part to see past a dollar in our pocket today."

"What are you getting at, Jack?"

"For the most part, our communities have been locked out of mainstream America economically," he continued. "So maybe more than a handful of us turn into quick-buck artists come election time every two years. But tell me, what other reasonably viable opportunities do we have? How many blacks have you seen running campaigns down here, Al? How many black-owned political consulting firms exist in this state, and how many actually get hired? Do you have any idea how many blacks in Durham County and Wilson County are living below the poverty line? I'm talking about folks who are so poor and have been that way for so long that they don't even waste time dreaming about something better for their kids. Just think about the intergenerational impact of something like that. Here's a statistic for you: Blacks make up twenty-two percent of this state's population. Do you know what percentage of businesses are black owned? Ten."

I was silent for several moments. "That's insane," I finally said.

"Carp, the reality is that our economic deprivation as a people, through centuries of structural discrimination, has undermined our ability to use politics as a means of changing our economic condition. I think that goes a long way in explaining your guy's loss tonight."

"I hadn't thought about it that way," I admitted.

"I don't mean to lecture you," he said. "But you need to understand the complexities around the choices people are making. Do you really think Keri Jameson, Raymond Brown, and all the others actually like having to play both sides? You think they take pride in that? You think they don't wish they could afford to cut Ron a max check and join him on the front lines?"

I thought for a moment. "Our economic deprivation has undermined our ability to use politics for change," I paraphrased.

"You know, it's funny how a person can know something and talk about it intelligently, even live it to an extent, and then forget it when it no longer serves their purposes."

"Here's some free advice, Carpenter: don't let your zeal to win cloud your understanding of the larger struggle."

"Point taken."

"While we were out here trying to win an election, there were thousands of others trying to navigate a system that tells them, on the one hand, 'you aren't working hard enough,' and then on the other, 'don't waste your time trying.'"

"It's not right," I said.

"You came down here and tried to make a difference," he said. "Some of the same people you were trying to help were too busy struggling to keep food on the table to draw what you see as an obvious connection between what they did in 2008 and what they've largely slept through in 2010. For me and you the connection is obvious, but then again, we're blessed to be in a position where we have time to think through, articulate, and really visualize how the politics of 2010 could literally make all the difference in the world for folks who just don't have time to worry about politics . . . even if they'd like to. All you can do—all we can do—is keep at it."

"So that's what we'll do."

"Congrats again, Al. Great effort."

"You too, Jack. You too."

CHAPTER
NINETEEN

WEDNESDAY, MAY 5, 2010

AFTER HAVING MY FIRST CUP of coffee that morning on the balcony, I returned to my bedroom and removed a duffle bag from my closet. While packing for the next week in Rock City, I received a text from Ron asking if I was available for lunch. He suggested our favorite lunch spot, the site of our first official working lunch back in August, undoubtedly figuring that this location would provide the incentive necessary to garner my acceptance. He figured correctly.

While driving to Mezcal, I considered the magnitude of what we almost did. The only thing more amazing than coming so close was what it took to get so close. It seemed the excitement Obama's 2008 candidacy generated was something decidedly unique to that moment, and perhaps more accurately, to him. It was a moment made possible by an impossibly rare combination of public anger with the past and the unparalleled opportunity to do something the human race might never forget. In the fall of 2008, the public watched closely as presidential candidates debated tough issues and formulated thoughtful policies to meet the difficult challenges the eventual winner would face. But the public's interest in the candidates and their politics was easily overshadowed by its infatuation with the opportunity to write a bold new history. What could be bigger than what we did in 2008? Nothing, apparently. And so, when the dust settled on that magnificent November night, Americans went back to the business of living their lives and paying their bills, wandering between heaven and earth in a waking sleep from which I feared they wouldn't soon be stirred. "A nigger can't win," I mumbled as I got out of the car.

I found Ron sitting on a bench just outside the entrance. It was an odd moment. For the first time since I'd seen him in Washington during Inauguration weekend, he wasn't "the candidate," and I wasn't his employee. He wore a tan blazer over a white button-down shirt, dark charcoal-gray slacks, and dark-brown leather loafers.

When I saw Citizen Johnson sitting there suitless, our loss hit me again like a slap in the face. As I stood there studying him, I recalled the dreams of victory I'd clung to so tightly during the campaign.

Ron looked at me, shielding his eyes from the sun. "Hey, man—how's it going?" he said, a lopsided grin on his face.

"Fine. Seems there may actually be life after this race," I replied.

"Yeah, unbelievably, the world just keeps spinning," he said. "They've got a table for us. Figured I'd wait for you to get here." I followed Ron inside and over to a booth—it was our usual table, though we never asked for it or referred to it as such.

Within seconds, the waitress was tableside. "Mr. Johnson, Mr. Carpenter, so great to see you again!" she said. "Can I start you out with drinks?"

"Abbbsolutely," I said. "I'll have a frozen margarita with salt, please."

"Make that two," Ron said.

When she left, I turned to Ron. "So, how are you enjoying being a regular person again?"

He laughed as he considered my question. "It's a little strange, to be honest. And a little bittersweet. On the one hand, it's nice because I woke up at ten o'clock this morning instead of the usual eight. On the other hand, I don't have Carmichael chauffeuring me around anymore."

"I hear that."

"I've also lost anonymity," he continued. "Never thought I'd miss that. Three total strangers came up and hugged me when I walked in here."

"I'm sure Casey and the kids will enjoy having you around more."

"Yeah, it'll be nice to pick the kids up from school sometimes and sit down to dinner most nights as a family. What about you? Malcolm called me today and told me about your grandfather. I'm so sorry. He was a great man."

"Thanks. It's ah . . . it's been difficult, but I've held it together okay."

"Why didn't you tell me?" he said.

"We had a job to do," I said. "I didn't want you or anyone else to be distracted from that."

"Let me know when you've got information about the arrangements. Casey and I will obviously be there."

"Will do."

"So, how are *you* adjusting to life after?"

"I don't know that I've really had time to adjust," I said. "I'm just so disappointed that we didn't get this done. We came so close, and it shouldn't have been close at all. So many people are so stuck in the past, so focused on doing things the old way. Then there are the others who talk about progress, but when it's time to put up, they're nowhere to be found."

"We did all we could do," he said. "I'm proud of the campaign we ran. We can't waste time dwelling on the negatives. We pushed things forward in ways we can't completely grasp so soon after the election. We inserted ourselves and our message into a conversation many folks didn't want us to take part in, and we did it with a voice that can't be ignored going forward. A few hundred more votes in a few key counties and the outcome changes."

"You know, there's still time to request a recount, and we can still—"

He held his hand up. "My mind is made up on that," he said.

I slammed my fist on the table, briefly disturbing the silverware and plates. More than a few patrons turned in our direction, including an interracial couple on the way to their table. As soon as they saw Ron, they walked over.

"Excuse us, Mr. Johnson, but we just had to stop and say congratulations on the campaign. And thanks so much for getting in the ring—you were inspiring."

The woman nodded in agreement. "Truly," she said. "We hope you'll run again."

"Thanks so much," Ron said. "That means a great deal."

I waited until the couple was out of earshot before resuming. "I just don't see how you can take this so casually."

"Look, Al, I'm just as disappointed as you are, even more so. But we've got to move on. We lost this one. But it's like you said last night—the battle endures. And there's still a lot of good I can do from outside the Senate."

"Have you considered running for the House of Representatives in 2012?" I asked.

"I don't know what I'm going to do," he said. "Right now, I'm just gonna enjoy this break—and this margarita—before I start practicing law again." He sat back in his chair. "Speaking of future races. . . when are you running for mayor?" The twinkle in his eye was unmistakable.

"I don't know . . . 2018, maybe. I'm not thinking about that right now."

Another waitress, this one a young black woman, returned with our drinks. She studied Ron's face carefully. "Hey, aren't you the guy who ran for Senate?" she said.

"Yes, I did run."

"Who'd you vote for?" I asked.

She looked down at her notepad. "I'm sorry I . . . I didn't, but I really liked your speech."

"Which one?" Ron asked.

"The one you gave last night," she said. "I wish I'd voted—for you."

"Yeah, me too," Ron said with a wry smile. "You and a couple hundred of your closest friends."

"Did you vote for Obama in 2008?" I asked.

"Of course," she replied.

"But you don't think this election cycle's important?"

She cocked her head to one side, considering the question. "I guess I just figured that with Obama in the White House, things would get better."

"How so?" I pressed.

"Through his agenda," she replied.

"His agenda?" I said incredulously. "Do you have any idea how the United States government—"

Ron leaned forward and interrupted me. "Thanks for taking time to speak with us," he said. "We're just going to have drinks today. Is that okay?"

"Of course," she said. She quickly vanished behind the kitchen doors.

"That's what's so frustrating about this whole thing!" I said. "Why even bother getting involved in politics?" I slumped against the booth. "You should just go back to private life. There's no point. Nothing's ever gonna change. One third actually gives a damn, another third is totally clueless, and the last third can't see past their own noses."

Ron stared at me for a while, then released a deep breath. "Let me tell you a story," he said. "About a year after I left my first big firm job to start my own practice with Bruce Aaron, we had a huge case come in the door. We'd only been up and running a few months at the time and had zero dollars in the bank. I was just a few years older than you, thirty-one years old. So into our office walks a black woman in her midfifties. Beverly Wood was her name. We both sit down, and she proceeds to tell me a story. About three weeks earlier, a busload of young kids—fifty-five black, two white, and one Hispanic—were traveling back to North Carolina from a Black History Month concert they'd participated in up in Philly. I'll never forget the name of that choir: the Martin Luther King Jr. All-Children's Choir." He took a swallow of his margarita. "On the way back, they stopped off to eat at a place called Robertson's."

"That huge all-you-can-eat buffet chain?"

"Right," he said. "So these fifty-eight children and their five adult chaperones walk in and ask to be seated. The manager, who happens to be standing at the front desk, says there're too many of them and suggests they go somewhere else. Ms. Wood—she was the choir director—informed me that the place was virtually empty and could easily have accommodated not only their busload but two more of the same size."

I let out a quick laugh. "This isn't gonna go so well for Robertson's, is it?"

Ron smiled. "So they go fifteen miles down I-95 to another Robertson's," he said. "They get there, unload the bus, walk to the door, and it's the same story: that manager won't let them in either. This one was a little more crowded, but still could've easily accommodated the group. So they pile back into the bus. Again, remember the name of this group: the Martin Luther King Jr. All-Children's Choir."

"Unbelievable!" I said.

"They get a few more miles down the road, and they see another Robertson's. 'What the hell?' they say. 'Let's try it again.' They pile out again, and the manager hits them with the same song and dance they'd heard twice now. This last one was even emptier than the first."

"Where were the restaurants?" I asked.

"Two in Virginia and one in North Carolina," he said. "So they get back to Raleigh and surprise, surprise, someone suggests that they—"

"File a federal suit," I said.

"That's right. So ol' Beverly Wood calls a lawyer friend, and that friend refers her to my law partner, Bruce. Now this is the kind of case lawyers have wet dreams about, and here it was, handed to us on a silver platter."

"My God," I said. "You got the case."

"Bruce and I call up the Robertson's general counsel, a good ol' boy by the name of G. Franklin Thickett, and we recount for him a slightly more colorful version of the story I just told you. Two days later, their outside counsel calls us and asks for an in-person meeting. They offered to come down to our offices in Raleigh, but Bruce and I figure we'll fly to New York as a gesture of goodwill."

"And because your offices were pretty crappy, I bet," I said.

"That too."

"Wait?" I said. "How could you afford the trip?"

"With the cash we knew we were about to make on this settlement, we not only bought first-class tickets, we brought our wives along, treated them to a six-hundred-dollar dinner, and caught a Broadway show."

I rolled my eyes. "Typical black folks," I said. "Spending money we don't actually have."

Ron laughed heartily. "We just figured we'd fake it until we made it. Anyway, we walk into this meeting at this Manhattan law firm—these offices were ridiculous, by the way—and it becomes immediately obvious that Robertson's has instructed them to just make this go away. They were already up to their necks in two other large pieces of racially charged litigation. From a PR standpoint, they couldn't afford to have three of these bad boys going at once. We knew that, and what's more, they knew that we knew. They had to settle. I mean, you tell me who in their right mind wants to go to trial against the Martin Luther King Jr. All-Children's Choir."

"Not me."

"Luckily they really didn't do their homework on us," Ron continued. "Bruce and I couldn't afford to front the choir the money to fight Robertson's in some drawn-out legal battle. Those New York boys could've litigated the law firm of Aaron & Johnson straight into bankruptcy. But Bruce and I had just come from big law firms; I guess they assumed we had some major cash stashed away. So these lawyers say, 'Look, you guys pick an arbitrator—anybody you want, short of Jackson or Sharpton—and we'll agree to be bound by that arbitrator's decision. No appeals, final and completely binding. And we'll sign an agreement in advance to that effect.'"

"Sounds air-tight," I said.

He nodded. "We agreed to that, and of course we picked the people we thought would be most sympathetic to our cause. But we also made sure they were respected members of the community, folks whose judgment no one would second-guess. There was more at stake than just money. There were kids involved, so it had to be squeaky clean."

"Abbbsolutely," I said.

"So Bruce and I compile a list. Number one on this list was one of my Harvard professors, and yours too, Larry Jackson—a noted African-American scholar, lawyer, and former judge with an unassailable record of fairness and high-flying intellect. Second was a well-known civil rights activist out of Raleigh, and third was a widely respected civil rights attorney from right here in Durham. There were two others whose names I forget, but you get the point. It was meant to be a slam dunk."

"All black?" I asked.

"What do *you* think?" he said, pursing his lips to hold back a smile. I laughed. "This thing was all sewn up, but we still wanted to make sure we did our homework regarding process. I mean, even Tiger Woods has squandered a few fifty-four hole leads. So we reached out to several influential civil rights folks from outside the state, and some constitutional law folks as well, just to make sure we weren't missing anything."

"And so that it would look like you were actually conducting a real search," I added.

He threw back his head and laughed. "They taught you well at HLS," he said. "'Sometimes winning in the law has nothing to do with the law itself.'"

"Professor Jackson," I said.

"You better believe it," Ron replied. "Anyway, we called up Rhonda Gaines, this big-time civil rights lawyer from out West, and left her a message letting her know we had this big matter and wanted her advice. She doesn't get back to us immediately, so I consult my Harvard Law School directory, which at that time listed each alum's home address and home number. I look up a young, up-and-coming constitutional law professor in Chicago named Barack Obama."

My mouth dropped. "Get outta here!"

Ron laughed almost uncontrollably. "If I'm lyin', I'm dyin'," he said.

"I'm gonna need another drink here!" I yelled to no one in particular.

"So we give this guy Barack Obama a call," Ron said, still laughing. "We don't get him on the phone immediately, but we leave him the same message we left Gaines."

"Unbelievable."

"Barack calls back about a week later," Ron continued. "He left a message apologizing for the delay and said he wanted to help however he could."

"This is ridiculous," I said.

"But by that time, Gaines had already gotten back to us, and in the flurry of events, we forgot to return Barack's call." Ron broke into a fit of laughter in which I immediately joined. This production drew the sustained attention of more than a few curious lunch-goers.

Once I'd calmed down, I said, "No wonder the White House didn't care so much for your candidacy!"

He grinned. "I doubt he remembers all that," he said. "But isn't it amazing how things happen? So anyway, turns out our first two choices for arbitrator can't do it for whatever reason, so we're left with the third guy on our list."

"The Durham civil rights attorney?"

"Right," he said. "And we're still superconfident about our prospects given that we've hand-selected the arbitrator. We have our initial meeting with the arbitrator and the Robertson's lawyers, and the arbitrator asks both sets of lawyers to get him position statements in two weeks. At the meeting, the parties agreed that there were three potentially valid explanations for what happened in those Robertson's restaurants, and that each of those explanations coincided with a dollar amount. Under one theory, Robertson's paid out a hundred million, under another, fifty million, and zero under the last."

"Wow."

"Bruce and I spent every waking moment of the next two weeks putting that position statement together. We went back through some of the classic briefs written in race discrimination cases. What we put together . . . I gotta tell you, it was pretty amazing stuff. Bruce is a great, great writer, and together, we knocked it out of the park. So the parties submitted their position statements, and we're thinking we're going to make some serious cash and that these kids are going to get enough money so that each of them has college and grad school paid for. The arbitrator says he'll rule in a week and send word by fax. Three weeks go by without a word from the guy. A full month later, we're still waiting. Bruce and I are nervous wrecks, but we don't dare call the arbitrator. One afternoon . . . I'll never forget, it was 1:45 p.m., and the fax machine started pulling paper. We'd gotten a special fax line solely for the purpose of receiving this decision, so I knew exactly what it was."

"I can't even imagine," I said.

"My stomach was a mess. Bruce was working from home that day. I picked up the phone and told him, 'The fax is coming in.' He was downtown and in the office in what felt like ten seconds."

Ron paused, gathered himself, and looked me squarely in my eyes. Then he leaned back and ran his hand over his head in that familiar way. "At the bottom of the page, in boldface type, were two characters: a dollar sign followed by a zero."

I sat back, stunned. "Wow."

Ron looked blankly into the distance, trying to fight off the same emotions that surely overtook him that day so many years ago. Then he began again. "Three scenarios, and he chose the one where these kids get nothing. The Martin Luther King Jr. All-Children's Choir."

"At the distinct risk of digging the dagger even deeper," I said, "may I ask how much you would've cleared had he gone with the hundred million theory?"

"Let's just say this: money wouldn't have been an issue in this campaign." He shook his head. "Mercilessly, the story doesn't end there. Somehow, we pick up the pieces of our lives and keep practicing law. About eight months later, Bruce and I are looking for new office space in downtown Raleigh. Ironically enough, that loss led to so much publicity that we were soon turning business away."

"Robertson's didn't negotiate for confidentiality?" I asked.

"Of course they did, but the fact that we were representing these kids wasn't a secret. And given that Robertson's ended up paying us nothing, there really wasn't anything to keep confidential. Let's just say that word got out."

"Got it."

"So anyway," he continued, "I walk into the lobby of the building to look at the office space and literally bump into the arbitrator. We go through the usual pleasantries, and then I bring it up. I said, 'Look, I just have to know what happened. How did you come to that conclusion?' He said, and I'll never forget it, 'You know, I've worked my entire life, and hell, I'm still working, old as I am.' Then he walked past me and out the front door."

"That's it?"

"That's all he said, but the story doesn't end there. As it turns out, during the time he was considering our arbitration, a certain conservative governor was looking to appoint someone to the court of appeals after the death of its most liberal member. Our friend was apparently interested in that seat."

"You don't mean—"

He shrugged. "I don't know," Ron said. "Since then, some people have suggested that he might've been trying to show the governor he wasn't as gung-ho on the civil rights thing as people thought."

"Let me guess—he didn't get the appointment, did he?"

Ron shook his head. "No, he didn't."

"And it only cost all those kids millions and millions of dollars," I said. "That's unreal."

"Oh, it's quite real, Al Carpenter," he said. "And that's life. I tell you this story because, yes, it's entertaining, but also to illustrate the importance of moving on and not dwelling on big losses, especially in cases where there's nothing you could've done differently to change the outcome. You get knocked down, but you find a way to come back. Sometimes, the setback is actually the setup for the comeback."

"I see."

"You can't allow yourself to get so jaded that you become incapacitated. You've lived long enough and spent enough time in politics to know how ugly things can get. But you can't do a lick of good if you get bogged down in the muck."

"I think you've made this point before," I said, staring into my now empty margarita glass. "Clearly, I needed reminding."

Our waitress reappeared. "Another round, gentlemen?"

"No, just the check," Ron said.

"I'm sorry about my little outburst earlier," I said.

"No worries," she said. "I can't imagine how you two must be feeling right now." She pulled a white slip of paper from her apron pocket. "I brought this on the off chance you might be done already. Whenever you're ready, gents."

"Thanks for understanding," I said as she walked away. Then I turned to Ron. "Appreciate the liquid lunch. And the pep talk."

"Oh, that's right, we were supposed to actually get lunch. Wanna grab something to go?"

"No worries. I'll grab something on the way back."

"Okay," he said, tossing a few bills on the table. "Shall we?"

"Let's do it," I said. With that, we rose from the booth and made our way toward the door. "When are you going back to work?"

"Two weeks," he replied as we came to the entrance.

"Good, so you get a little time off."

"Yep," he said. "What're you gonna do until you head up to New York to start practicing?"

"Shooting over to Rock City now to spend some time with the family. After the funeral, I think I'm gonna hop a plane to St. Maarten."

"A much-deserved and, I suspect, much-needed vacation."

As we walked into the blazing heat of that early May afternoon, I reached for a handshake, which he obliged. "I'll see you at the funeral," he said. "And just in case we don't get a chance to talk after the services, have a good time in St. Maarten." He winked. "But not too much fun. Don't bring anyone, or anything, back with you."

"What?" I said, smiling.

"I've seen it happen to the best of 'em," he said. "A friend of mine went down there twenty years ago to 'clear his head.' Three weeks later, he came back with a wife and ninety-nine other problems."

"Have you met me?" I said.

"I have," he said, "and my deep personal knowledge of your social proclivities with women sits at the forefront of my mind as I offer this advice."

"I'm turning all that around, Ron."

"Oh really? What happened?"

"Life."

He chuckled, then his face turned humorless. "Yeah, that happens to the best of 'em too. Thanks for everything, Al."

I nodded, and then we went our separate ways. I was just a few feet from my car when I heard a woman yell, "Mr. Johnson!"

I turned back toward the restaurant and saw our waitress running across the parking lot. Ron and I converged on her. "What is it?" he asked.

"Congressman Darling is about to hold a press conference," she said, out of breath. "Word is he's about to resign."

I looked at Ron. "Well I'll be a monkey's uncle," I said. We darted back inside Mezcal. The bar, virtually empty when we walked past it just moments before, was now three rows deep with people staring at the large plasma screen mounted on the wall. Onscreen, a fortysomething woman I assumed to be Darling's wife stood on one side of the podium. On the other side stood Julia Remini, her mouth set in a thin line. And then, flawlessly appointed as always, Congressman Branford Darling, Prince of the blue dog progressive Democrats, approached the podium.

"Good afternoon. I want to thank you all for gettin' over here on such short notice. Ordinarily, we would have given you at least a little more time, but things happened very quickly, and when the decision was made, I wanted to move ahead with all deliberate speed. I've called this presser for two reasons. The first, and by far the more important of the two, is to spend a bit of time addressin' an issue that came front and center over the course of the recently concluded Democratic US Senate primary battle. Second, for reasons I will set forth momentarily, I am concedin' yesterday's Tenth District Democratic primary election to the woman standin' to my left, Julia Remini. And, effective immediately, I am resignin' my seat in the United States House of Representatives."

A resounding gasp came from the throng mobbing the bar. Ron shot me a look of shock, and I'm sure my countenance expressed the same.

"Many of you—strike that, essentially all of you—don't know this, but Ron Johnson and I grew up together in Winston-Salem. We were best friends at a time and place in this nation's history, particularly here in North Carolina and in the rest of the South, when such friendships were, at best, frowned upon, and at worst, not at all tolerated. Even as young boys of five or six years old, we were keenly aware of our parents' unease regardin' our friendship. Nevertheless, we carried forward with it, and in the process, I'd like to think, we taught them a thing or two about the ridiculousness of selectin' one's friends and associates on the basis of a trait that has absolutely no bearin' on a person's character, talent, or intellect.

"Our friendship carried on into our teen years and continued at Duke University, where we both enrolled as freshmen in 1983. Durin' the second semester of our junior year, my friend Ron and I partnered up for a research project in a sociology seminar. The assignment required us to look back into our family trees to determine whether or not we might find some distant connection between our families. Our professor, a brilliant young African-American scholar by the name of Ms. Juanita Acheson, had spent the majority of her research focusin' on how closely related we all are despite our incessant attempts to highlight our differences. As it turns out, Ron and I discovered that several generations back, a slave owner in my family fathered a child with one of his slaves. This slave was part of a family that, in succeedin' generations, went on to give life to my friend—and cousin—Ron Johnson."

Darling looked down for a long moment, then raised his head. "I was, in a word, ashamed when we came across this information. And my shame led me to ask Professor Acheson to excuse Ron and me from presentin' our findings to the class. In hindsight, I wish she hadn't. As a consequence of her grantin' that request, I've been runnin' from the reality of my family history, and myself, ever since. When the project was over, and formal interaction with Ron was no longer required, I made the most regrettable and insidious mistake of my life: I ended my friendship with Ron Johnson. Not because he'd betrayed my trust, which he hadn't, and not because he'd ever wronged me—he hadn't. I did it because I couldn't bear to be friends with someone I knew was descended from a person members of my family once held as personal property.

"In the aftermath of last Tuesday's forum among the three major Democratic candidates for the US Senate, I watched along with the entire nation as not just African Americans, but Americans of all races, creeds, and socioeconomic backgrounds united together, stood tall, and rebuked the divisive and destructive sentiment uttered by an ignorant individual in the crowd that day. But unlike many Americans, I only watched. While so many of you fine citizens stepped up and took the action necessary to make sure those hateful words were brought into the bright light of day for public repudiation, I sat quietly by like the coward I am and did nothin'. And so once again, I gave in to my shame.

"Well that all ends today. I've come to realize from followin' the campaign of my friend Ron Johnson that this moment in our nation's history is far too important to ignore. The scourge of racism in America—and the ways in which people of all races buy into the destructive assumption that because things have been one way they cannot possibly be another—threaten to destroy this nation beyond repair or recollection.

"Several months ago, a young—and I might add, brave—staffer from Ron's campaign reached out to me askin' for a meetin'. I agreed, and at that meetin', he asked if I might consider endorsin' my old pal Ron Johnson. I knew such an endorsement would harm me politically. More specifically, I understood that endorsin' Ron might cause the more conservative Democrats in my district to stay home on Election Day, and if enough of them did, I knew Mrs. Remini here might just slip past me in the primary. Nevertheless, I agreed to endorse Ron because it was the right thing to do. Ron Johnson was and still is the best hope for North Carolina in the United States Senate. But, as you know, that endorsement never came. As I have time and time again, I gave in to my shame.

"Today, I hope you'll join me in beginnin' to make good on the worldwide declaration our founding fathers made more than two centuries ago: 'We hold these truths to be self-evident, that all men are created equal.' Today, I hope you'll join me in bringin' into the light, and then to an end, all the trickeries and deceits, all the backroom wheelin' and dealin' that, to be absolutely clear, whites and blacks alike have engaged in for the purposes of their own self-aggrandizement and pecuniary gain. You know what I'm talkin' about—that ol' 'vote for me, 'cause a black man can't win' foolishness. It stops today! And that ol' 'vote for me, 'cause a woman can't win' crap. That too stops today! Until we realize that tradin' on the tired divisions of the past, and the stereotypes and history of hatred attendin' those divisions, will only limit our progress as a country; until we realize that the advancement of some on the backs of others will only limit our progress as a country, no person and no nation is wrong for decidin' America doesn't deserve the respect of the rest of the world."

The members of the press gathered there with Darling began to applaud, as did the patrons standing with Ron and me at the bar. Many of them turned toward Ron as they clapped.

"It's not enough to support black candidates for office only when you and I stand to gain somethin' in the short term," Darling said. "It's not enough to support female candidates for that reason either. We have to do away with these divisions once and for all, because they are tearin' at the fabric of this nation!

"And so, in recognition of my role in the perpetuation of the politics of hatred toward racial minorities and women, and in particular for turning my back on my friend for all these years, today I announce, effective immediately, my resignation from the United States Congress. In addition, I call on every North Carolinian living in the Tenth District to vote for my new friend, the very talented and forward-thinking Mrs. Julia Remini, in November's general election. Let's send her to Washington this November and show the rest of the nation North Carolina means business when it talks about progress and inclusion."

"How about that?" I said. Ron just shook his head.

"In addition, let me say the followin': As a student at Duke, during the dedication of a library named after a man whose family, like mine, once owned slaves, I was quoted as saying, 'No one descended from folks who trafficked in human beings should have his or her name attached to anything meaningful, and that includes a library belonging to an institution whose students, faculty, and board adhere to the principles of equality and justice for all. Slave owners are among the most detestable animals this world has ever seen, and their progeny should be treated as such.'

"While I still agree with the spirit of those words, and the utter detestation for slavery that prompted them, I was wrong. To judge and then ostracize any American on the basis of the conduct, the limitations, the wealth, or any other attribute of his or her forbears is unfair and contrary to the spirit of inclusiveness to which our nation has long paid empty lip service and that we must finally begin to cultivate if America is to survive.

"Finally, I'd like to offer my sincere apologies to my family, to Ron, to Julia, and to my constituents, whose high trust I've betrayed. For those who would heap praise on me for what I've done today, for those who would call these actions courageous, I ask that you don't. They comprise nothin' more than the sad epitaph of a coward whose conscience finally overwhelmed his shame. I ask, instead, that you take part in the hard work that lies ahead in deliverin', once and for all, on the task this nation set for itself in its infancy, the idea that all the world now watches and waits for us to make good on at last: the equality of all persons before each other and the law. Thank you. May God bless you all, and may God continue to bless the great state of

North Carolina."

When I turned to Ron, I found our former waitress standing next to me instead. "Hey, were you that young staffer he was talking about?" she asked.

I considered lying, then thought better of it. "Yeah, that was me," I said without an ounce of pride.

"I'm sorry things turned out this way," she said. "But it looks like maybe some good came out of it."

"Maybe," I said. "Say, did you see where Mr. Johnson went?"

"Oh, he left a few minutes ago."

"Really? I'd better go catch him." I moved toward the exit, then turned around. "And again, I'm really sorry about earlier."

"Are you kidding?" she said. "Thank you. I'm twenty-three, and it wasn't until today that I was able to see who I am."

I snickered. "And who are you?"

She looked at her feet. "A part of the problem."

"Don't be too hard on yourself," I said. "We're all part of the problem until we're part of the solution. It's not how you start. It's how you finish."

"Thank you—I'm sorry, I never caught your name."

"Al. Al Carpenter."

"Good to meet you, Al Carpenter," she said. "Jenny Randall."

I pushed the door open. "Good luck out there, Jenny."

"Best of luck to you." Her sincere smile made me miss Bristol. Her eyes. Her scent. Her laughter. Our partnership.

*****

I CRUISED east on Interstate 40, leaving Durham and the politics of 2010 behind me—at least for a time. I was always annoyed by the speed limit on this stretch of the interstate. Sixty-five miles per hour was just too slow. My wish was that the general assembly would change it to seventy sometime soon. Those five miles per hour might make all the difference in the world for some folks. Maybe it would happen soon for North Carolinians, if they were lucky.

CHAPTER TWENTY

THE FUNERAL WAS DEVASTATING. It sapped what little physical and emotional stamina I had left in the aftermath of the campaign. My spirits were buoyed, however, by the company of so many aunts, uncles, and cousins, including Billy, and great-aunts and great-uncles who seemed to pop up most often over the years at occasions like this one. Ron and Casey were there too. Uncle Malcolm, Aunt Kelly, and their four children flew in from Atlanta the night before. Uncle Tom, who lived just a few miles west of Rock City in a small town called Momeyer, was by his mother's side within thirty minutes of his father's death.

As the sun beamed down brilliantly on our mourning clan, my grandfather's only surviving brother delivered the eulogy. With his typical rhetorical flair, he encouraged all those present to honor my grandfather by doing what he himself had done throughout his life. "If each of you," he said, "do right and work hard, you ought not have occasion to fear any man." Through the tears, I chuckled as I recalled our time together, especially when I was a young boy driving him stark crazy in that hotter-than-hell dry cleaners.

While speaking with friends and family at the repast after the funeral, two things became clear. First, I wasn't the only one my grandfather had incessantly encouraged to do right and work hard, and second, I wasn't the only one who felt they needed reminding that day.

I was able to steal some time with Casey. During those five minutes, Casey said that she and Ron had gone to dinner with Preston Roberts and his wife just two days before. Preston had phoned Ron the Thursday after the election and volunteered to make the drive across the state to Chapel Hill to buy dinner. Casey said no one so much as touched politics during that meal, and that I would've been particularly tickled by the gymnastics each of them employed to avoid that thorny topic. From what I gathered, Ron walked away from that dinner believing Preston had finally gotten over Ron's decision not to support his 2002 bid for Darling's seat.

"Maybe Preston's finally developed the capacity to behave like an adult," I said after taking a sip of sweet tea. "But I'm not convinced."

Casey smiled. "Me neither."

"Why does Ron think Preston's over the whole thing? Because he drove all the way to Chapel Hill?"

"No. Because Preston apologized."

I stayed in Rock City two more days before heading back to Raleigh on Tuesday—exactly a week after the election—to catch my flight to St. Maarten. Jim Randolph had called the day before the funeral and asked if I'd be willing to meet in person. I told him I'd rather not, but when he insisted that the meeting would be "well worth my time," I agreed to spare twenty minutes before my flight. We settled on a hotel bar just a hop, skip, and a jump from Raleigh-Durham International Airport.

Honestly, I took the meeting for one reason: curiosity. I was smart enough to know that there remained the outside possibility that Jim's insistence on meeting me at a time when I had nothing to offer him politically was evidence I stood to gain something. There is, of course, the school of thought that says my experience with the campaign— and what appeared, at least for the moment, my narrow escape from total public shame—gave me every incentive to run in the opposite direction. I should've been content to leave North Carolina as things stood. But I wasn't.

The nausea engulfing the pit of my stomach as I entered the hotel was almost identical to the feeling I'd experienced in the seconds immediately after Ron voiced his decision not to demand a recount. As I turned the corner, I spotted Jim tending to a martini that, due to the excessive volume of liquid brimming the cocktail glass, he sipped without the use of his hands. Though he looked significantly older in person than in his photograph on the NCSEP website (his thirty-seventh birthday was two weeks away), he was impossible to miss. His thick, red mane screamed Jack Kennedy, and as he rose from his chair to greet me, I struggled to recall the basis for the anger simmering inside me—until we shook hands. The disappointment I'd felt toward Ron in the campaign's final moments now took Jim as its target.

"Mr. Carpenter," he said as we finished shaking hands. "It's a pleasure to finally meet you in person. I'm not sure I believed all the rumors until now."

"Rumors?" I said.

"Your reputation with some of North Carolina's fairest women precedes you," he said. "And I thought I was good."

"If I were you," I began, "I'd take everything you've heard about me the way you'd smoke a fine cigar."

"How's that?"

"Enjoy it, but be careful not to inhale," I said. "I wish I'd known that before I smoked my first cigar in college . . . I probably wouldn't have spent two hours hugging a rancid dorm-room toilet that night."

"That's what college is for, right?" he said. "Practice makes perfect. You drinkin'?"

"I have a pretty good feeling that whatever it is you're about to feed me will go down a whole hell of a lot better with a scotch."

"You think I come bearing bad news?"

"It's been several months since you've had anything but that."

"Fair enough," he said while flagging the bartender. "Charlie, got anything in an Ardbeg back there? I believe my friend here is fond of it."

"Sure thing, Mr. Randolph," Charlie replied.

"Better make it a double," I said.

Charlie retrieved a lowball from below the dark oak counter, removed the Islay product from among the surprisingly respectable collection of spirits at his disposal, filled the glass nearly to the brim, and from his position some eight feet down the bar slid the glass so that it came to rest before me without wasting a single drop in transit. I imbibed the color, scent, and viscosity of the genial, peaty single malt before taking a first sip. "I think it's safe to start Jim," I said.

"Al, I asked to meet for two reasons. First off, I want to offer my sincere congratulations on a campaign well fought. We—I mean, you guys—damn near pulled it off. I want to thank you and Ron for all the hard work in pushing the NCSEP name out there on the trail. You just came a bit short is all. And for the life of me, I don't know how I'm gonna convince Jane to get behind the carbon bill."

"Good luck with that," I said. "Jane's not a drinker. You'll have to ply her with something else."

"I'll figure it out," he said. "But really, thank you."

"We had a deal. And a deal's a deal."

"Thank you, nevertheless," he said.

"You're welcome, though I'm not quite sure I know what to make of something like that coming from you."

"Speaking of not knowing what to make of something," Jim said, "how about Branford's presser? I can't believe it."

"Can't believe how he abandoned his best friend for all these years, or can't believe he didn't come clean about his relationship with your father?"

Jim cleared his throat. "That he resigned. Looks like this might be an important step in getting people to look past race and gender."

"Jim, with all due respect, I have a hard time believing you care at all about that kind of progress. Your interest in this election is carbon. You needed votes in Congress, period. And you made it very clear by first going after the least progressive candidates in our race that Ron's race was more important to you than his progressive politics."

"I'll level with you, Carpenter," he began with a tone of candor that, despite my disdain for him, successfully triggered a willingness to believe. "My father wasn't exactly a beacon of light for me on race. I remember him telling me when I was five years old that blacks were my inferiors, and that the only black folks I should address were those working in our house. It wasn't until after my twentieth birthday that I spent more than a few minutes in the presence of a black person who wasn't being paid to cook my meals, wash my clothes, or clean my room. I know you think I avoided Ron's candidacy because of some hang-up I have with race, but you're wrong. I kept trying to convince Jane and Bill to change their minds on the carbon bill because I know how the people in this state feel about race. I'm not a politician or a social engineer. I'm a clean tech guy, and yes, my objective in this primary, as it's been since I started NCSEP, was to do everything in my power to make our air cleaner, including making sure no one gets in the way of full implementation of the carbon bill. And I would've supported an armadillo for that Senate seat if that's what gave that bill the best shot. But I'm no racist.

"And I'll tell you something else: what Ron did in this race; the way he scratched and clawed at what were essentially insurmountable odds; the way he never wavered in his commitment to moving this state forward, even when virtually no one was listening—I gained a deep respect for him. At first, and I'll be honest about this, I saw a talented black man with no earthly chance of winning. Today I just see a man with great passion for progress. I guess I sort of thought the Obama thing was an anomaly, but I was wrong—Ron's the real deal."

"Well, it looks like we reached you," I said. "That's just about the best evidence of this campaign's success I've seen to date."

"Your campaign reached others too, and not just in the black community. There was a real groundswell of support for Ron toward the end."

"Right," I said. "It only took the N-word to get people to take the action they should've taken all along. What is it with Americans? Piss 'em off, and they take action. Give them some pie-in-the-sky, ambiguous sense of hope, and they take action. Give them a clear, point-by-point road map for getting the change they've requested, and they're not interested. I swear, we're like toddlers in a crib. We're big enough and smart enough to climb out of that prison, but if you put enough bells and whistles in there, we'll just play, forget where we are, and pass out."

"How do you really feel, Carpenter?" Jim exclaimed.

"It's just so frustrating."

"Most people will do nothing until it's no longer expedient. Necessity is the mother of all invention."

I sighed. "You said you requested this meeting for two reasons. I think we've beaten the first one dead. What's the second?"

"I haven't had a decent night's sleep since election night," he said.

"Tough break," I said.

"Despite my father's best efforts, and some of my own, it seems I developed a conscience somewhere along the way."

"Oh yeah?" I said. "Well congratu-freakin-lations. I hope you and your conscience are happy together."

"Come on, Carpenter," he said. "I'm trying to level with you."

"Who's stopping you?"

"There were folks in some very high places working against you and Ron."

"No shit, Jim. The whole state party apparatus was working against us. You gotta come better than that."

"It's a little more complicated than that," he said.

I took a long sip, returned the glass to the bar, and turned back to Jim. "Well, let's hear it."

"Last year, during the second week of September, I received a call from Branford," Jim began. "After catching up a bit—we hadn't spoken in nearly two months—he told me he'd been contacted by Preston Roberts regarding a call Preston received from a high-ranking DNC official. That official had asked Preston to do everything in his power to 'make things difficult' for Ron's campaign. Preston was also instructed that Congressman Darling, in light of his significant power and influence, should be consulted and involved in executing the plan." He paused there, waiting for my reaction.

"Go on," I said.

"Branford explained to me that the DNC had no doubt Ron

would lose. But they were extremely concerned, all the way up to the top brass, that Ron's candidacy, riding Obama's 2008 coattails, might garner just enough support among African Americans, young people, and progressives to fracture the party and make victory for a Democrat in November virtually impossible."

"Never heard that one before," I mumbled.

"And keep in mind that the DNC was already nervous about the prospect that *Citizens United* might come out the wrong way and result in conservative super PACs spending Democratic candidates for Congress nationwide into complete oblivion."

"Yup," I said.

"As the whole world can sort of deduce now, Branford was also interested in seeing Ron's candidacy fade away. If Ron really began to gain momentum, he feared reporters might start digging. And if that happened, it was only a matter of time before his dirty little secrets from college came out."

"Not to mention his little campaign finance problem," I said.

"Yes, maybe that too," he said. "I've worked with Darling in the past—politically, that is—as a go-between. I'd reach out to business folks he wanted to engage, set up meetings, and so forth and so on. The plan Preston and Branford settled on was to bring Ron down by going after you."

"Why me?"

"Ron is squeaky clean."

"And what do they have on me?"

"Nothing. But at the time, you were the most senior guy in the camp, so it made sense—find something embarrassing, bring you down, then take Ron out with an ad campaign questioning his judgment in hiring you. You know how it goes. It wouldn't much matter that Ron didn't know or wasn't involved in whatever we found. The hook would be that Ron lacks good judgment."

"Seems like you guys were grasping for straws."

"On my call with Branford, he mentioned that he'd met you in DC back in August, just after you finished sitting for the bar exam. He also mentioned a close friend of yours from HLS, Darden Leslie. You may not know this, but my brother, Sean, was in your graduating class."

"So Darling enlisted your help to dig up dirt on me?"

"Branford thought maybe Sean could provide some color on the extent of your friendship with Darden, and that something might turn up from that. Imagine Branford's delight when he learned that he'd hit the jackpot—best friends."

"Why would Sean help you? He hates NCSEP."

"But he loves him some Branford Darling."

I snorted. "You guys didn't find anything."

"No, other than that you and Darden were still close and spoke frequently. Sean also brought up the gig Darden snagged at the D triple-C."

"What then?"

"Branford suggested we keep digging, and said that if we couldn't find anything, he might be able to explore the possibility of wire taps."

"Jesus," I said. "So how many conversations have you illegally listened in on?"

"None," he replied. "You see, about a week before Vance-Aycock, the practical realities surrounding my business began to overshadow my loyalty to Branford."

"How's that?"

"While Preston and Branford were busy scheming on you and Ron, it was becoming clear that neither Jane nor Bill would ever support the carbon bill. I needed Ron to win. He was the only option left. From NCSEP's point of view, Jane or Bill winning in November would be no different from Rodney keeping his seat. Ron had been talking a lot about the importance of reducing our carbon footprint since he got in the race, and you'd already approached us multiple times about getting an endorsement."

"So you called Darden a week before Vance-Aycock and fed him the information about the illegal campaign contributions."

He nodded.

"And you assumed," I continued, "that once I got wind of that information, I'd use it to compel Darling to endorse Ron. And then, with some luck, Ron might win the seat."

"And get us one vote closer to keeping the American Clean Energy and Environmental Protection Act on the books."

"What made you so sure I'd take on the most powerful congressman in this state?"

"Isn't that what you did?"

"Well, sort of. But what made you so sure Darden would feed me that information?"

"What are the chances that your best friend, who happens to work at the D triple-C, doesn't tell you about a call directly related to the most popular congressman in Washington, and a congressman from North Carolina no less?"

"Low," I said.

"Another scotch?"

"No thanks," I said. "I wanna be sober for the rest of this story. So tell me this: What made you so certain Darling would endorse? That wouldn't have been popular with his base, and on top of that, he was actively working with Preston to take Ron out."

"I did struggle a bit with that," he said. "Then I put myself in Branford's shoes and asked myself, 'What's worse? Losing an election or going to jail?'"

"So why was Linda still playing hardball when I called the Monday morning after Vance?" I said. "Why didn't she immediately agree to my request for NCSEP's endorsement?"

"When you called our office I was just getting off a plane," he said. "I hadn't been able to speak with Linda just yet. I spoke with Branford early Monday morning, just before boarding a flight back to North Carolina. On that call, I explained that while I remained totally committed to carrying out his wishes related to Ron, the practical realities of my business made it necessary to endorse him."

"I don't get it," I said. "By endorsing Ron, you were working to bring about precisely the thing Darling, Preston, and the DNC were trying to prevent."

"Oh, I knew that, and so did Branford," he said. "But I framed the endorsement as part of NCSEP's larger program of backing progressive candidates for Senate nationwide. The way I put it to Branford was that it would look mighty suspicious for NCSEP to endorse so many other progressive Democratic Senate candidates around the nation while excluding the most progressive candidate right here in North Carolina."

"Well played," I said.

He winked. "I rather think so. I'll never forget Branford's last words as we ended that call: 'Fine. Go ahead and endorse him. Mercifully, your endorsement won't change the color of his skin.'"

"You do a pretty mean Branford Darling," I observed.

"I've spent a lot of time with that one," Jim opined while staring down regretfully into his cocktail.

"Well, it seems you aren't the only one who's acquired a conscience recently," I said. "But why are you coming to me with all this now? What are you getting? Who are you working for now? You think coming clean to me will score you some points with the man upstairs?"

"That wasn't my reasoning, but it sure doesn't hurt."

"Well, I'm happy for you and your conscience."

"My conscience requires that I disclose a few more things to you," he said.

"Oh, there's more?" I said. "Of course. Why wouldn't there be?"

"Preston and Branford had a top-secret meeting on Saturday afternoon at the Grove Park before that dinner," he said. "During that meeting, they penned the specifics of their plan to make things difficult for Ron."

My mind raced back to the afternoon of October 3, 2009—the same afternoon Darling made a point of breaking away from that horde of reporters to ask me to relay a message to his "old pal." Talk about hubris. "Did you ever see this document?" I asked.

"No, but I can tell you that the difficulty you had obtaining endorsements from the various black PACs and the rescheduling of Ron's DC-OSP interview came out of that meeting."

"So Jack Monroe did cut a deal! How much did he get?"

"Jack's not after money," he said. "It's influence he wants. And when Bill ramped things up with his campaign after the DSCC backed him—"

"There was a job waiting for him," I said. "And I assume Preston was in constant contact with Keri Jameson, Christian Tate, and others?"

"Almost daily, I'd hazard to guess."

"But you still haven't answered my question: What could you possibly gain by telling me all this? This can't all be about your newfound conscience."

"Well, I like you, Carpenter. Darling's out, so I have to start planning for the future. I think you have the stuff."

"I see."

"And who knows . . . Ron might run again. He's got nearly one hundred percent name recognition in the state now. He's a national figure. Then there's you. Candidates from all over the country will be knocking your door down to bring you on to consult."

"We lost an election that matters," I said. "It's just that you and the other so-called good guys are too busy swooning over Number Forty-Four to realize that the most important battle is the one being fought today. We can't afford to keep sending Democrats to general elections because they fit the mold of who's been electable in the past. That's not intelligent. Jim, this nation is engaged in a battle for progress that requires the changing of hearts and minds. You achieve that by doing something different. Barack Obama, as talented as he is, can't do it alone. The Constitution prohibits it. So tell me, what significant legislation can make it to Obama's desk with this broken Senate? And with the filibuster the Republicans are likely to get come November? And let me tell you, it's a not-so-minor miracle he got that carbon bill through at all."

"You did just about all you could," Jim said.

"No," I said. "I could've done more. After Darden told me about your call, we did some digging of our own. I knew about more than just the Lovejoy Library business. I knew it all . . . Ron and Branford's childhood friendship, the falling out in college, the great-great-great grandparents. I could've leveraged it all."

"So why didn't you?"

"On some level, I guess I didn't think it would be fair. His comments about descendants of slave owners at that rally—that's something *he* did. I had no qualms about using that as leverage, and I did. But the fact that his great-great-great grandfather owned slaves, and that Ron's folks were a part of that . . . well, that didn't happen on his watch."

"That's mighty noble of you, Carpenter," he said. "But why didn't you use the campaign finance stuff I fed Darden? That's something *he* did."

"I didn't know for sure. That was hearsay."

"Hearsay!" he exclaimed. "This ain't a court of law, Carpenter!"

"No, but we've got rules to follow nonetheless."

"Still, I say that's mighty noble of you."

"To hell with nobility, Jim," I said. "There's no nobility left in politics, at least not enough that it amounts to anything. I learned that from you. I learned that from so many people I naively thought would be with our campaign . . . people I thought were, in fact, supporting our campaign because they believe in the things Ron believes in. But now I know better. It's about whether you're on the inside or outside. That's it. That's all anyone cares about. The ideas and the policies, that's just stuff people talk about because they feel like they have to pretend to be about something. When the votes are counted, when the speechmaking is over, when all the cash has been spent to buy the votes, when all the deals are made and the music stops, those who find themselves on the inside split the bounty. That's what this game is all about."

"Good people can do good things in this game," he said. "You've just got to get a little dirty on the front end so folks know they can trust you."

I snickered. "Gotta love this country," I said. "In order to do good, you have to be dirty. Meanwhile, the actual good guys in this game, the ones who want to make a difference the right way, are squeezed out because they refuse to play by your rules. My goodness. And now you'll finish your martini and walk off into the sunset."

"That's not the view from where I'm sitting," he said. "The carbon bill is on life support now. We may not have the votes to save it in this next Congress. Rodney will likely win the general election. And progressive congressional candidates across the nation have lost, or are in serious danger of losing, their primary races."

"Let's just assume for the moment, God forbid, that the carbon bill dies, and let's also assume NCSEP is finished. So what? You'll still be filthy rich."

Jim took three deep, almost labored breaths. "What you don't understand, Mr. Carpenter, is that I'm not defined by my wealth. I genuinely care about the environment, and that's why I started this company in the first place."

"Yeah, but you have no qualms about using people to get what you want."

He raised his eyebrows. "And you do? For God's sake man, wake up! Is that not what you've been doing for the last nine months? Using everything and everyone you possibly could to your advantage? That's the game, Carpenter. You tried to use Branford. And in the ultimate irony, your campaign used racism to reach your political goals. And it almost worked!"

"Wait just one minute! Are you suggesting we planted that guy at the forum?"

"No, but didn't you leverage him to drive fundraising? The press conference, the ads, the—"

"I . . . I did what I had to do," I said.

"That's right!" he said. "You did what you had to do. And so the ends justify the means, right? You got a little dirty to accomplish something big for millions of people. Look, if what you and Ron really care about is progress and putting an end to divisions based on race and other artificial differences, then you won. Branford has made admissions that will change politics in this state forever. This state, this country will never be the same. Our actions sparked a real conversation about race. Before the past few weeks, when was the last time you saw white people go on television and acknowledge that blacks have legitimate gripes about systemic barriers to socioeconomic progress? When was the last time you saw black people acknowledge some of the fears whites have about affirmative action and other programs aimed at leveling the playing field? The ultimate solution to this nation's race problem is to be found not simply in judging the merits of the arguments on either side, but in a willingness to share and listen to each viewpoint with an open mind. That has been the single greatest obstacle to progress. In the next cycle, black and other minority candidates across the country will be positioned to do what Ron couldn't. That's a win. That's progress. You're a history guy, Carpenter. You know that virtuous outcomes often come from less than virtuous actions and actors."

I wanted desperately to counter him, but the words eluded me.

"Look, I get it," he continued. "You're still dealing with the loss. But be proud. You were resourceful. And you could've ruined Darling but you didn't, because, as you say, it wouldn't have been fair. Who knows? Maybe through your discretion, you've brought some respectability to the political process."

Respectability? I thought. In trying to blackmail Rob to suppress the fact that the forum bigot was a black man, I'd accomplished the very thing Uncle Tom had lambasted Jefferson for doing in the Declaration of Independence. I'd tried to engineer a massive demonstration project of my own, one that nearly succeeded in turning the tide of a statewide election. Even if the ends had justified the means, my actions put me on ground just as tenuous as that on which Jefferson and the Declaration of Independence stood. If I argued that my use of a racist stereotype was justified by my ultimate goal of progress, under the same logic, was the establishment of this nation as the world's preeminent economic superpower on the backs of black slaves not also justifiable?

"It's nothing to be ashamed of, Carpenter," Jim continued. "We Americans play to win. It's what defines us as Americans. There's plenty of time to clean up the messes we've made after we win. There's nothing wrong with that, as long as you do some good with the power you gain from winning."

I took a deep breath. "So, what's next for you?" I asked after polishing off the last of my scotch.

"Find Jane's vice, use it to change her mind on carbon, then fight like hell to get her elected in November."

"That won't be easy."

"The stuff that matters never is, right, Carpenter? What about you? You're something of a minor celebrity now. I have no doubt you'll leverage your newfound fame into a big payday. You should write a book. God knows you've got one hell of a story to tell." He inspected his watch intently. "I guess time does fly when you're having fun. I've actually got a meeting with Jane's people in a few minutes."

I snickered. "Let the plying begin," I said.

"Keep in touch, Carpenter. Onward and upward. You know, my father used to always tell me, 'While it's lonely at the top, never forget that it's even lonelier at the bottom.' In moments when you're grasping for motivation, remember that. I'm not proud of much of what my father did or said, but that's one thing I'll never forget."

"Take care, Jim, and good luck with your carbon bill."

"If you smarten up in the next few weeks and decide against practicing law, you should come work for me. Ever consider being a lobbyist? I think having you on my team would increase our chances of saving that legislation by a factor of ten."

"Who knows?" I said. "Maybe the Caribbean sun will totally burn out my brain, and I'll forget you were part of a scheme to destroy me before you weren't."

"Oh come now, Carpenter," he said while pulling a crisp fifty from his wallet and placing it under his glass. "Don't let a silly old grudge cloud your judgment. That was just part of the game. Now it's on to the next one. Whatta ya say?" At that, he extended his right hand to consummate something that felt like far more than an offer of employment.

"Thanks for the scotch," I said, declining to shake his hand.

He shrugged. "Well, thanks anyway for being such a good sport."

I shrugged. "What can I say? I've always been a stickler for rules."

CHAPTER TWENTY-ONE

THE NORTH CAROLINA I returned to around midday on Wednesday, June 30, was much warmer than the one I'd left on Tuesday, May 11. While cruising down that familiar stretch of Interstate 40 between the airport and Wade Avenue, the cabby brought me up to speed on several major news stories I'd missed during my time away. Jane had appointed Ron honorary chairman of her Senate campaign, my Lakers had defeated the Celtics in seven games for their second consecutive NBA title, and Branford Darling had been indicted on multiple counts under the federal campaign finance laws. One of the deals I'd made with myself during the flight to St. Maarten to justify the duration and expense of that vacation was that I'd totally cut myself off from the United States. So for the entirety of my Caribbean holiday, I avoided Americans and spent my days frolicking in the company of natives while keeping Ron's gender-specific St. Maarten admonitions near the forefront of my thoughts.

Immediately after setting foot inside my apartment, I checked in with my mother and grandmother. Then I dialed Darden and Simmons. Finally, I phoned Jennifer to float an idea I'd just proposed to Darden and Simmons—and to convince her to persuade Bristol to join the rest of us. Within the hour, Darden and Simmons had committed to spending the Fourth of July holiday in New York City. Jennifer politely declined and said Bristol had called me "crazy" for even suggesting the idea.

That weekend changed the game. At a 9:45 p.m. dinner on Friday, July 2—considered a late dinner in most American locales outside of Manhattan Island—Simmons proposed to Cassandra, his on-again, off-again girlfriend since December of our 3-L year. I suffered a minor heart attack as the words "Will you marry me?" registered in my brain. When dinner was over, Cassandra happily sent Simmons off into the night with his law school partners in crime. The three of us stumbled into Cedar Nightclub at around 1:30 a.m., and not five minutes into our first round at the bar, Darden informed us that in three weeks' time, he'd be flying to Vegas with Jennifer.

"For what?" Simmons asked.

"This may surprise you, Simmons," I said, "and perhaps even cause you to question your religion, but not everyone goes to Vegas for the hookers and free alcohol."

"For dinner with Vickie and Andreas," Darden said through a tight-lipped grin I'd never seen from him. "Vegas works best for their schedules." Darden generously granted me and Simmons a few moments to gather our respective jaws from the floor before offering the additional news that he was "pretty sure Jennifer's the one."

"I didn't know it had gotten that serious," Simmons said. "I mean you mentioned a few dates last fall in New York, but—"

"Neither did I," Darden interrupted. "It just sort of sneaked up on us."

"No . . . it just sort of sneaked up on *you*," I said while benignly slapping him twice on the cheek. "Well played, Jen baby. Kudos to her."

"Yeah, man," Simmons said. "She played it well . . . but it's not like she's a tough sell. She's supersmart *and* beautiful."

"So, when's your retirement party?" I said. "With the money you're about to come into—"

"My brotha," Simmons interrupted, "you're gonna be doing backstrokes in greenbacks in the pool at Daddy's Playhouse."

"Our boy D made it!" I exclaimed. "Darden Leslie . . . you've just won the Super Bowl! What are you going to do next?"

Darden snickered while shaking his head. "You're both idiots—you know that, right?"

"Don't get all sentimental on us now, Leslie," I said. "You may be getting married soon, but we're in the club tonight. There won't be too many more nights like these."

Simmons raised his glass. "Plan to win!"

"Negro, you're engaged," Darden said, rolling his eyes.

"Engaged but not married," Simmons distinguished. "Lead the way, *brotha Carpentah*."

"Who are you, Branford Darling?" I said.

"Many folks above the Mason-Dixon line are calling him a great man these days," Simmons said.

"Great man or great American?" Darden asked.

"What's the difference?" Simmons said as we descended the stairs. As we entered the bottom level of Cedar, I saw the familiar silhouette of DJ Ren behind the turntable. His mix of Top 40 and hip-hop classics never disappointed.

"Brotha . . . I'm going to blame that mental lapse on the alcohol," I said.

"'Preciate ya," Simmons replied as we approached the bar.

"By the way," I said, "congratulations again on your engagement, brotha. I had no idea you were going to change the game like *that* this weekend."

"Plan to win, right?" Simmons said, raising his glass. At that, we all touched glasses.

"Plan to win," Darden chimed in.

"Abbbsolutely," I said. "But what am I gonna do now that you two are getting married?"

Darden shook his head. "You can start by figuring out how to get Bristol to talk to you again."

"When was the last time you guys spoke?" Simmons asked.

I released a deep breath. "The night before the election."

Simmons let out a low whistle. "And she hasn't answered *any* of your calls?"

"Not a single one."

"Well, I hate to say this, but maybe that's the end for you guys," Darden said. "At least you came clean, though."

"Yeah, I don't know how you managed that," Simmons said.

"I had to."

Darden chuckled. "Easier said than done," he said. "Don't get me wrong, you really messed up, but I'm proud of how you handled it after the fact. Maybe there *is* hope for you."

"Cute guys, very cute," Simmons said. "Now can we get on with this night?" Simmons pushed off of the bar and into the Manhattanites reveling a few feet in front of us, leaving me alone with Darden.

"Brotha, when the dust has settled on this weekend, talk to Bristol."

"How?" I said. "She won't even answer my calls." *I have to let her go.*

"You're a pretty resourceful guy," Darden said. "I think you'll figure it out."

*****

AFTER SPENDING the next morning finalizing plans for Fourth of July weekend, I spent the afternoon catching up with Ron at Eagle Ridge Golf Club in Raleigh. On my way to the course, I received a call from Mary-Jane Fenway. She had several interesting pieces of gossip for me, many of which I discussed with Ron on the course that day. Two stood out: First, during my Caribbean sabbatical, Jack had maneuvered his way onto Jane's payroll as a senior political advisor. But far more salacious—and disappointing—was the news that Jack and Bristol had been dating since the beginning of June. What remained of the self-absorbed jerk in me assumed she was only dating him to hurt me. He'd been waiting for that breakup for quite some time, and everyone knew it.

Since Ron's car was in the shop, Casey had dropped Ron off at the golf course and I'd agreed to shuttle him home after the round. We discussed a variety of topics during the fifty-minute drive, including the public and media response to Darling's resignation and indictment, but we spent most of it on Bristol. I finally told him about the parking lot breakup on Election Eve.

"When Shane told me Bristol wasn't coming in on Election Day, I figured it had something to do with you," Ron said. "But I didn't want to bring it up that night, or at Mezcal the next day . . . I knew you weren't really in any condition to talk about that."

I sighed. "It's been tough."

"Man, that Jessica Parker doesn't take any prisoners."

"I don't blame Jessica," I said. "I shouldn't have let her come over in the first place."

"True. But you did the right thing in telling Bristol. That took guts."

"That's what I keep telling myself."

"And the episode in the parking lot happened right after you got the news about your grandfather?"

"Not even ten minutes later."

"I think I would've had a nervous breakdown at that point. I don't know how you held it together."

"I don't either," I admitted. "Maybe being an only child has something to do with it. You just learn to deal with things on your own. And my dad—"

"Yeah, that's certainly part of it," he interrupted. "But I'm pretty sure that's not all of it. You're a tough cookie, Carpenter."

"It's served me well, I suppose." I switched off the engine after pulling up next to his driveway.

"What's this?" he exclaimed. "You can't take me *all the way up* the driveway?"

"That was one of the perks of being the candidate. I tell you what, you run for office again, and I'll come back down here and drive you up to your door as often as you like."

"Regrettably, I'll have to pass," he said. "This time around I got your services for free. In a few weeks, your hourly rate will jump from zero to several hundred dollars. I can't afford you anymore."

"Can't say I didn't make the offer."

"When do you move?" he asked as we stood beside our respective car doors.

"End of the month," I said. "Going to shoot down to Atlanta and spend August with Uncle Malcolm and Aunt Kelly. We'll get a few rounds of golf in. Between shots, I'll fill him in on the specifics of his prodigal son's nine-month sociopolitical journey to Jesus."

"What I wouldn't give to be there to hear, and annotate, those recollections."

"Come down for a weekend," I said.

"Maybe I will," he said. "And let's try to sneak in a couple more lunches at Mezcal—and actually eat!"

"Sounds good."

"Have you spoken to Bristol?"

"No."

"I know you're probably enjoying your newly acquired bachelorhood, but maybe you should spend some time planning how you're gonna get her back."

"She's dating Jack now. I should just—"

"I've heard enough of your Cambridge chronicles, and spent enough time with her on this campaign, to know she's not one to let get away."

"It'll be a miracle if we're ever friends again."

"Al, I've seen the way she looks at you and how you look at her. That's not something that goes away overnight. The bottom line is you have to try. If it doesn't work, so be it. If you love her, then you'll be alright just knowing she's happy, even if it's with another man." Ron retrieved his golf bag from the trunk, dropped it onto the fragrant green lawn, and extended his right hand toward me. I accepted.

"Thanks for everything Al. You done good. And I'm proud of you, son."

"Thanks for teaching me how to play the game."

"You were a great student," he said. "Let's do it again sometime soon. And incidentally, it's not your game I'm proud of."

"No?" I said.

"It's the man you've become." He reached down for his

clubs, inserted his arms into the bag straps, and began walking unceremoniously toward the open garage.

"Have you spoken to Branford at all?" I asked.

Ron didn't bother turning around. "I called him right after the presser ended."

"What'd you say?"

"I thanked him," he said.

"And what did he say?"

"'You're welcome.'"

"That's it?"

"That's it and that's that."

I stood silent for a moment, wondering how two men with so much history and so much time wasted could spend so little time speaking in a moment like that. But then again, I suppose there wasn't much left to say. For the next several seconds, I was desperate to share the specifics of my conversation with Jim, and in particular the gross details of the Darling-Roberts plot. Then it went away. And it's a good thing it did, because I've since come to understand that sometimes people deserve to have their faith preserved. With a well-timed tale about a children's choir, a corporate conglomerate, and a couple of lucky lawyers, he'd explained why I had to keep playing the game, no matter how ugly it got from time to time. I owed him one.

"We'll get 'em next time," I shouted while opening the car door. Ron stopped abruptly before swiveling back toward me.

"We got 'em pretty good this time," he said. I pointed in his direction, and he pointed back. Then I eased into the driver's seat, put the key into the ignition, and briefly disengaged every muscle in my body. Obeying the posted speed limit of fifteen miles per hour for the first time, I pondered whether I might ever return to this sleepy, unassuming nook in Chapel Hill. And then, without looking back, I turned left and peeled off down Tobacco Road, with no destination in mind.

AUTHOR'S NOTE

THIS IS A WORK OF FICTION. This story is based, in part, on true events, but certain liberties have been taken with names, places, events, and dates, and the characters have been invented. Therefore, the characters portrayed herein bear absolutely no resemblance whatsoever to the persons who were actually involved in the true events on which this story is partially based, and any resemblance to actual persons, living or dead, is entirely coincidental.

But let me be clear: This novel was conceived and written with a purpose. It is meant to intrigue and agitate, to instill discomfort—and with any luck, those sensations will reawaken a dampened fire, restore lost imaginations, and galvanize again the action that in 2008 birthed one of the most incredible events, and opportunities, in our nation's history. I will only add the following to the words on the pages preceding this note: Objects at rest tend to stay at rest until acted upon by some outside force. The rest is up to you.

ACKNOWLEDGMENTS

IT TAKES A VILLAGE. These are words I didn't fully appreciate before embarking on this journey. I am thankful for everyone who contributed to this project, but I must acknowledge some by name. To Ken and Holly Lewis, thank you for your friendship, counsel, and optimism. There's still hope for real progress in North Carolina—and in America—because of doers like you.

I wish also to express deep gratitude to my inner circle of friends and family who shared a most precious asset—their time—in reading endless iterations of the manuscript and offering insightful suggestions, specialized expertise, and provocative ruminations during meals, summer afternoon check-ins, and various Hemingway breaks: in particular, Mom, Aunt G, Grandma, J. Goldberg, D. Stewart, K. Bryant, R. Jones, R. Westerfield, E. Kyles, and the Chester family. No good deed goes unpunished though, so I'll soon come knocking with the next manuscript. Get ready.

To my editor, Anitra Budd, thanks for bringing new tools to the construction site. Many thanks to my publishing consultant, Dara Beevas, for helping a brother connect the dots. And to my consigliere on virtually every aspect of this project, Dionna M. Dorsey, who shut the window each time I tried to toss the manuscript: it's happening. Thanks for believing. Grazie mille.

To my muse—*the* Queen—Erykah Abi Wright: we've never met in the physical sense, but your clever soul breathed new life into my own, and inspired my pen. On rainy autumn afternoons, through solitary winter nights, my thoughts sailed safely through the starry blue—and many storms too—on the wings of your words, voice, and energy. Thank you, especially, for November 21, 2000 and all seventy-one minutes and fifty seconds of the gift you gave the world that day. Nothing was the same. *Surely.*

To the District of Columbia, the city where it all began and the place I'll always call home: I love you dearly, I've been making plans for you, and I have your back. RIP to *our* brilliant mayor, Marion Shepilov Barry Jr., the man who never stopped fighting for those who needed him most. Your legacy is immortal.

Thank God for the election of Barack Obama. While I believe we could've done so much more together, I'm confident history will still accurately characterize his eight-year tenure as a worldwide watershed. Perhaps it suffices to note the following indisputable fact: in cities, large and small, all across the globe there are children who've only known an African-American White House occupant. #progress

And finally, to all those young dreamers out there struggling to find a voice amid the noise of purchased politicians, the burglarized privilege of the corporate political establishment, and the fog of demonstration project politics, I offer the following tried-and-true advice: pursue your passions fearlessly, be not discouraged by failure, and embrace the struggle—it is an essential element of the subsequent success.

D. Mitch
September 2016